EMILY HILDA YOUNG

(1880-1949) was born in Northumberland, the daughter of a ship-broker. She was educated at Gateshead High School and Penrhos College, Colwyn Bay, Wales. In 1902, after her marriage to a solicitor, J.A.H. Daniell, she went to live in Bristol, which was to become the setting of most of her novels. Her first, *A Corn of Wheat*, was published in 1910, followed by *Yonder* (1912), and *Moor Fires* (1916).

During the First World War Emily Young worked in a munitions factory, and as a groom in a local stables. However, after her husband's death at Ypres in 1917 she left Bristol for London, going to live with a married man, Ralph Henderson, Head Master of Alleyn's school in Dulwich. She continued to write. *The Misses Mallett*, published originally as *The Bridge Dividing*, appeared in 1922, preceding her most successful novel, *William* (1925). Then came *The Vicar's Daughter* (1928), *Miss Mole* (1930) – winning the James Tait Black Memorial Prize, *Jenny Wren* (1932), *The Curate's Wife* (1934) and *Celia* (1937). She lived with the Hendersons in South London until Ralph Henderson's retirement at the time of the Second World War when he and E.H. Young went, alone, to live in Bradford-on-Avon, Wiltshire. Here Emily Young wrote two children's books, *Caravan Island* (1940) and *River Holiday* (1942), and one further novel, *Chatterton Square*, published in 1947, two years before her death from lung cancer at the age of sixty-nine.

Virago publish *The Misses Mallett* and *Miss Mole*; *Jenny Wren* and *The Curate's Wife* will be published in 1985.

The Misses MALLETT
(The bridge dividing)

E.H. YOUNG

New Introduction by Sally Beauman

Published by VIRAGO PRESS Limited 1984
41 William IV Street, London WC2N 4DB

First published in Great Britain as *The Bridge Dividing* by Heinemann 1922

Virago edition offset from Jonathan Cape 1936 edition

British Library Cataloguing in Publication Data

Young, E.H.
    The Misses Mallett.
    I. Title
    823'.912 [F]   PR6047.0/
    ISBN 0-86068-441-5

Printed in Finland by Werner Söderström Oy,
a member of Finnprint

Contents

Introduction

In 1902, when she was twenty-two, Emily Young, the daughter of a Northumbrian ship-broker, married J.A.H. Daniell, a solicitor, and went to live with him in the district of Clifton, in Bristol. She remained there for the next sixteen years, leaving only after the death of her husband, who was killed at Ypres in 1917. She never returned; yet, of the seven major novels she wrote after the First World War, six are set in Bristol.

She rechristened it Radstowe (its original name was Bristowe), and, clearly, it was a place that permeated her imagination, for the city becomes a palpable force in her books, most noticeably in this, *The Misses Mallett*, her fourth novel, and the first in which her gifts as a novelist become really apparent.

Of course, for a novelist as skilled at social satire as Emily Young, Bristol in the early years of this century provided a rich background, as potentially rich as that given Jane Austen by the spas of eighteenth-century England. It was an ancient city, and a cultured one, attractive to writers and painters, with a celebrated theatre, a fine university, and several admired schools. It was also, because of its port, a rich city, with a prosperous and flourishing middle class whose fortunes had been made via the shipping, manufacturing and tobacco trades. It was not, therefore, a city in stasis (like nearby Bath, or Cheltenham) but a city constantly in flux, a city of social mobility, where the newly rich (like Mrs Spenser-Smith in a later novel, *Miss Mole*) juggled for position on the steps of the social ziggurat alongside those more traditional figures of the British upper-middle class, the lawyer, the man of the cloth, the landowner, the Army or Naval officer. For both the professional man and the social climber there was, and is, one area of Bristol in which it was most desirable to live: Clifton, a district of great beauty, placed with happy symbolism, at the top of the highest hill in a hilly city. Clifton, through which the characters in this book constantly walk, or ride, along routes so accurately described it would be possible to follow them still, is of central importance to this novel, and to several others Emily Young wrote later. It is worth while then, perhaps, to consider its social and natural geography, which has changed very little since the period in which she set her books.

Clifton, built around the apex of its large, flat-topped hill, is, very roughly, square in shape. Its houses surround one of the city's most famous features, the Downs, an area of open land – something like Hampstead Heath, but less wild, more open and more tamed, resembling the park of some great eighteenth-century estate. To the south are the eighteenth-century crescents and squares favoured by the older families and the professional classes, the setting for the Malletts' house in this novel. To the north and east are the very large, in some cases palatial, nineteenth-century houses built for the rich merchants of the city. To the west there are no houses: here the land falls away sharply down cliffs several hundred feet high, to the waters of the Avon gorge.

This gorge is spanned by the most famous landmark in Bristol, with which every schoolboy is familiar, Brunel's suspension bridge. The bridge connects the eighteenth-century area of Clifton with the district of Abbot's Leigh, and the erstwhile county of Somerset on the farther shore. To this day Leigh Woods is an area of spectacular natural beauty: there are large estates, thick woods, mysterious pools (like the Monk's Pool, which features in a key scene in this novel). The thickly-wooded areas extend to, cling to, the very edge of the gorge. It is still possible today to stand on the bridge Rose Mallett crosses at the beginning of this novel, and see on the one hand civilisation, a city; on the other, a forest of oak and pine. The deep gulf between the two, bridged by Brunel's extraordinary construction which seems suspended in air, is terrifyingly deep, notoriously attractive to suicides.

This topography, lovingly and brilliantly evoked by Emily

Young, is vital to an understanding of all her novels, but particularly *The Misses Mallett*, for it provides her with an image central to her work. As in the landscape, so in the lives of her characters: the expressive divide of the gorge and its bridge, between city and nature, the tamed and the wild, the safe and the unsafe, mirrors a spiritual divide in her creations. Her books, so delicate, so subtle, so full of nuance, are riven through their very centre; her characters themselves are hewn through with contradictory urges which they fight to bridge: on the one hand manners, propriety, all that is decorous and socially acceptable; on the other all the wilder instincts of the blood. Two opposites coexist in this novel: the tamed beauty of Clifton, and the untamed world across the bridge. They are, perhaps, as irreconcilable as the worlds of Thrushcross Grange and Wuthering Heights; the efforts of her characters make to reconcile them provided Emily Young with the motor for her narrative.

The Misses Mallett was reissued under that title in 1927, after the international success of her next, semi-autobiographical book, *William.* But it was, interestingly, originally published in 1922, under the odder but more telling title, *The Bridge Dividing*, a book whose very title was an anomaly. After all, a bridge does not divide – it joins, it links; but then the bridge she had in her mind's eye was a very unusual bridge, and the book was written at a time in her own life when, as it happened, she had good reason to believe that there were certain gulfs – social and spiritual – which even the most magical of constructs might never couple, or connect.

Emily Young, or E.H. Young, as she chose to be called when she wrote, was brought up in Northumberland, the third child of a large family of six daughters and one brother. Of the girls in the family only she and one other of her sisters – the actress Gladys Young – pursued careers. Her father, partner in the large firm of ship-brokers, Simpson, Spence and Young, was comfortably off. Emily received a good, middle-class, girl's education, first at Gateshead Grammar School, and then at Penrhos College in Wales. When she married Daniell she became less well-off; one of her nephews, Philip Sharp, remembered going to stay with her and her husband in Bristol and being earnestly told to note all the money spent on him by his kind, and childless, aunt and uncle, so that his own, better-off parents might find some way tactfully of reimbursing them.

Virtually nothing is known of her husband, or her marriage, though her family believed it to be happy. During it she wrote her three early novels (the first, *A Corn of Wheat*, was published in 1910, when she was thirty). She pursued her other interests, chiefly rock-climbing (she was a fearless and distinguished climber). She liked riding also, and – during the Great War – worked in stables, and in a munitions factory. In 1918, after her husband died, she left Bristol, and her life changed. It was at this point, the divide in her life, when she moved to London, that she began to write this novel.

She did not live alone; neither did she ever remarry. Rather, in circumstances quite extraordinary for the period, she lived with a married man, ostensibly in a separate flat, in the same house as his wife. The man, Ralph Henderson, was the Head Master of a public school, Alleyn's; the house in which they lived was in the school's gift, and administered by the school's board of governors. This set-up, which, if its true nature had become public knowledge would certainly have ended Henderson's academic career, was apparently totally amicable. Mrs Henderson was wife in name only, and she, her husband, and Mrs Daniell – as Emily Young was always called in private life – lived together there for some twenty years, until 1940, when Ralph Henderson retired from Alleyn's.

Henderson was the admired Head Master of a celebrated school, and an interesting man. He had taken a double first in mathematics at Oxford; he was an expert on butterflies; he published a learned work on the Old Testament, read Latin and Greek, was an accomplished horseman, and – like Emily Young – a distinguished amateur rock-climber. Emily Young's love for him was, quite clearly, the dominating influence of her life. Their association, never publicly acknowledged, endured until her death in August 1949 from lung cancer, and began, almost certainly, before the death of her husband.

Daniell and Henderson were friends; they were educated together at Bristol Grammar School, and it seems likely, though her family are now unsure on this point, that her husband first introduced her to the friend with whom she was to fall in love. Certainly their association went back at least as far as 1914, when Henderson and Emily went openly on holiday together to Holyhead, and her nephew Philip, to whom she was very close, joined them.

During their years together in London they lived at Sydenham Hill. Their life seems to have proceeded very calmly. Emily Young wrote in the mornings, and chose to write not at home, but ten minutes walk away, at 4 Hill Rise, Forest Hill, the home of her and Henderson's closest friends, the Gotchs, both teachers, and both also employed at Alleyn's. Each morning Miss Young took a coffee-break, and each morning Mrs Gotch joined her. The writer did not discuss her work – ever; it remained private, and she always retained a great antipathy to literary celebrity, in spite of the fact that her books sold well, and were critically a success (*Miss Mole*, her finest novel, won the James Tait Black Memorial Prize in 1931).

During the long school holidays Henderson, Emily Young and the Gotch family (though not Mrs Henderson) generally went away together, usually to the Peny-Gwryd hotel in North Wales. There they spent their time, the Gotchs' son, David Gotch, recalled, in a way absolutely conventional for persons of their interests and class. During the days they climbed; in the evenings they would play bridge, or work on the next term's timetable. There was no attempt at either subterfuge or explanation. Mr Henderson was on holiday with Mrs Daniell; they were friends; Mr and Mrs Gotch, who knew the true situation, were apparently chaperones. That was that. It was a wonderfully English solution; a potentially explosive situation was, for twenty years, defused by a combination of tact, reticence, and the ability to accommodate. During that time Emily Young, at regular two and three yearly intervals, produced the seven mature novels on which her reputation must stand.

After the Second World War, Ralph Henderson left Alleyn's and from 1940 onwards went into semi-retirement; he and Emily were both sixty. They went to live, alone together, in Bradford-on-Avon in Wiltshire, a place chosen because of its proximity to Calne, where their friend Mr Gotch was now Head Master of the Bentley School. Henderson held other, temporary, academic posts; Emily Young wrote one further novel, *Chatterton Square* (1947), and two childrens' books. She had begun a third, never completed, the year she died.

Ralph Henderson became her literary executor, and he left just one account of the woman he had loved for most of his life, but never married. Characteristically, he chose to write it – he termed it 'An Appreciation' – for his friend's school magazine, and the short piece was published in *The Bentleian* in 1950. It was a formal tribute, of the kind often published by one male friend about another: in it he spoke of her modesty, her charm, and her humour, her high standards and her self-deprecation – her English, her Clifton, virtues. Of the other side of her nature, the unconventional passionate side, which sparks in the heroines she created, and which must have been a force in their life together, he could not, and does not, speak.

The tribute is a touching one, but it leaves its subject shadowy, concealed behind a barrier of good taste; it is addressed to E.H. Young, but it conjures up Mrs Daniell. Emily Young would probably have preferred it so: there was something of the chameleon in her, as there is in many of her female characters who think much and express little, who take on the colour of their surroundings, sometimes as a protection, often simply because it amuses them to confuse. In her private life she was able to take advantage of her two names; they shielded the nature of her affair with Henderson, and they shielded her also from fame. When she was househunting with Mrs Gotch in Wiltshire, for instance, they visited one house where a copy of one of her novels was prominent on a table. 'Oh, do you like E.H. Young's books?' said Mrs Gotch. 'Very much,' replied the owner. 'Ah – well, Mrs Daniell here is their author . . .' She would never have made the admission herself; the duality of her name, of her life, of her nature, is dealt with openly only in her novels. There men and women wrestle with their secret selves; the battle is often funny, sometimes ludicrous, very truthful, and sometimes – as in the case of Rose Mallett – very close to tragedy, though the scales are never tipped quite that far.

The battle takes place against a background of quite ordinary events, the stuff of bourgeois life – family outings, and parties; the lives of the characters are measured out with coffee spoons. But behind that orderly exterior there are spectres: illness; death; poverty; disgrace; betrayal. They are passed over with deceptive lightness, often quickly, but the cross-hatching, the shading, is there, and it radically affects the tone of the novels. They are set, this novel is set, in Clifton, in the world of Mrs Daniell; but the yearnings her characters have for the other side, the wild side, is the world of E.H. Young. They battle; they attempt to form their bridges; the gulf remains, and there is the sense, for all the novel's deceptive quietude, that these characters are fighting for their lives.

The cast of *The Misses Mallett* is a small one, and almost entirely female: two ageing sisters, Caroline and Sophia, their younger, very beautiful, stepsister Rose, and later Henrietta, the child of their disreputable brother Reginald. They are backed up by a cast of other female characters, often glimpsed only briefly: Mrs Batty, the vulgar good-hearted wife of their family solicitor; their brother Reginald's wife, her landlady, their servants. They live in soft and feminine luxury in surroundings of the most exquisite taste, on the Clifton side of the bridge. They both reverence men, and take pleasure in their attentions, but comparatively few men enter their lives. The portrait of their father, a 'gloomy daub', the one ugly article in their house, is allowed to hang over the Sheraton sideboard; their brother's bedroom is maintained exactly as he left it, his repeated requests for money tolerated, though not his marriage out of his class. Men, the constant topic of their conversation, the subject of their thoughts and dreams and self-delusions, are also, mysteriously, excluded. 'We Malletts never marry!' Caroline cries gaily, between stories of old beaux and past conquests; she and her sister Sophia, who never speaks of the great lost love of her life, but preserves his memory in the mothballs of self delusion, share a bed. Their household has the air of an odd sybaritic nunnery; Rose, the central heroine of the book, grave, beautiful, chaste, a little capricious, has the air of a half-willing, half-reluctant novitiate. There is, really, only one man in the book (I discount the engaging, ugly, and eccentric Charles Batty, who, though important, smacks of authorial sleight-of-hand, and is never totally convincing). That man is Francis Sales, gentleman farmer, and he lives the other side of the bridge.

Sales is master of Sales Hall; he is tall, darkly handsome, and moody; he carries a considerable erotic charge. He has, in fact, many of the traditional appurtenances of the Brontë-esque romantic hero: descended out of Heathcliff and Rochester he is, at first sight, near cousin to the heroes of a present-day Mills and Boon. That resemblance, skilfully suggested by E.H. Young, is at once reined in by more realistic considerations. Sales is not master of some crumbling ill-omened house, but of a perfectly normal small estate with a flourishing dairy; his herds provide milk for Clifton and the Misses Mallett. Sales possesses an unruly sexual magnetism: he is also capable of petulance and masculine sulks; he is inarticulate, baffled by women, and – not an attribute of a romantic hero, this – kind. Rose Mallett, meeting him in the woods of his estate, and rejecting his proposal of marriage at the very beginning of the novel, does so precisely because he is insufficiently romantic: she dreams of playing some great role in the world; she foresees that she will be able to do so only 'through the agency of some man', and 'she must have that man colossal, for she was only twenty-three years old'.

In the brilliantly economical scene of their encounter, in which expectation is in constant counterpoint to actuality, Sales reveals himself as passionately in love, and therefore vulnerable; Rose leaves him: 'That was where he chiefly failed. The colossal gentleman of her imagination was a tyrant.'

Thus the scene is set for the rest of the novel, in which the dreams of women constantly buffet against the realities of men. With great skill, E.H. Young shows Francis Sales as he truly is, and as he is seen, transmuted, by the three women who fall in love with him. There is a rich vein of comedy here, in the gulf between women's fevered imaginations, and a man's quite simple and direct sexual needs, and E.H. Young subtly and compassionately mines it.

But she does not confine herself to the comedic vein as a less truthful writer, eager to score easy satiric points, might have done. She utilises satire, yes, and it is often very barbed indeed, but she also utilises other, more disparate elements – fairy-story and folk lore. (Rose is unawakened sexually, a sleeping beauty; Christabel, lying in her sickroom with her dog and her cat has an evil witch-like presence.) And she admits the possibility of passion; it gains in strength and conviction by its placing cheek-by-jowl with the illusory and the banal. Francis is an ordinary man writ clear, but he is not devoid of poetry. Spiritually as well as literally, he inhabits that strange region across the bridge, that other world, sometimes perceived as vernal, filled with the promise of regeneration; and at other times dark, magical and threatening, the terrain of gypsies and wild animals. It is here, perhaps, that the writer falters.

E.H. Young makes a stalwart attempt, in the scene set at Monk's Pool, to make Charles Batty, in every way the antithesis of the romantic hero, the one male character in the book capable of understanding the power of that place, and all it symbolises. It is arguable that the attempt flops; her material defeats her plan; something in the book is too big to be confined in such a convenient vessel. There, if anywhere, the novel fails: it is, interestingly, not a failure of imagination but of nerve.

The book has obvious felicities: strength of observation, moral irony, grace of style, though all those characteristics are more fully developed in the later *Miss Mole*, in which E.H. Young perfected an off-key eccentric mode of writing, and risked a much wider social canvas. Here there is still the sense of a writer trying to discover her own voice. The form has not yet stretched enough to accommodate the content; her odd solipsistic vision is at odds with a narrative convention that demands equal authenticity in a variety of viewpoints.

But the book's deficiencies are also its strength. Less assured, less disciplined than *Miss Mole*, this novel has a schizophrenic quality, as if two sides to its author's nature – Emily Young and Mrs Daniell as it were – fought to control material of such subversive vitality that it refused to submit. The result is a book that is imperfect, but resonant. It centres on a paradox: passion is real; it is also hyperbolic, fed by the inequalities of a deeply-flawed society, in which men, but not yet women, have discovered the power of self-definition. Here, the paradox is not resolved; the two worlds either side of the bridge coexist, and between them as between two magnetic poles is a force field of attraction and repulsion that cannot be broken.

It is a love story, which is unfashionable now. Its apparent simplicity and the limpidity of the style might make the male critic sniff and dismiss: a woman's book. But that is to miss the ambivalence that is at the heart of the writing, and which gives the novel its peculiar tensile strength. Emily Young's own life reverberated with paradox, of course. Perhaps that is why she writes about it so astutely, and in a way that, however much women's lives have changed in the interim, is perturbing still.

Sally Beauman, London 1983

Book I : *Rose*

ON the high land overlooking the distant channel and the hills beyond it, the spring day, set in azure, was laced with gold and green. Gorse bushes flaunted their colour, larch trees hung out their tassels and celandines starred the bright green grass in an air which seemed palpably blue. It made a mist among the trees and poured itself into the ground as though to dye the earth from which hyacinths would soon spring. Far away, the channel might have been a still, blue lake, the hills wore soft blue veils and, like a giant reservoir, the deeper blue of the sky promised unlimited supplies. There were sheep and lambs bleating in the fields, birds sang with a piercing sweetness, and no human being was in sight until, up on the broad grassy track which branched off from the main road and had the larch wood on one side and, on the other, rough descending fields, there appeared a woman on a horse. The bit jingled gaily, the leather creaked, the horse, smelling the turf, gave a snort of delight, but his rider restrained him lightly. On her right hand was the open country sloping slowly to the water; on her left was the stealthiness of the larch wood; over and about everything was the blue day. Straight ahead of her the track dipped to a lane, and beyond that the ground rose again in fields sprinkled with the drab and white of sheep and lambs and backed by the elm trees of Sales Hall. She could see the chimneys of the house and the rooks' nests in the elm tops and, as though the sight reminded her of something mildly amusing, the smoothness of her face was ruffled by a smile, the stillness of her pose by a quick glance about her, but if she looked for anyone she did not find him. There were small sounds from the larch wood, little creakings and rustlings, but there was no human footstep, and the only visible movements were made by

9

the breeze in the trees and in the grass, the flight of a bird and the distant gambolling of lambs.

She rode on down the steep, stony slope into the lane, and after hesitating for a moment she turned to the right where the lane was broadened by a border of rich grass and a hedge-topped bank. Here primroses lay snugly in their clumps of crinkled leaves and, wishing to feel the coolness of their slim, pale stalks between her fingers, Rose Mallett dismounted, slipped the reins over her arm and allowed her horse to feed while she stooped to the flowers. Then, in the full sunshine, with the soft breeze trying to loosen her hair, with the flowers in her bare hand, she straightened herself, consciously happy in the beauty of the day, in the freedom and strength of her body, in the smell of the earth and the sight of the country she had known and loved all her life. It was long since she had ridden here without encountering Francis Sales, who was bound up with her knowledge of the country, and who, quite evidently, wished to annex some of the love she lavished on it. This was a ridiculous desire which made her smile again, yet, while she was glad to be alone, she missed the attention of his presence. He had developed a capacity, which was like another sense, for finding her when she rode on his domains or in their neighbourhood, and she was surprised to feel a slight annoyance at his absence, an annoyance which, illogically, was increased by the sight of his black spaniel, the sure forerunner of his master, making his way through the hedge. A moment later the tall figure of Sales himself appeared above the budding twigs.

He greeted her in the somewhat sulky manner to which she was accustomed. He was a young man with a grievance, and he looked at her as though to-day it were personified in her.

She answered him cheerfully: 'What a wonderful day!'

'The day's all right,' he said.

Holding the primroses to her nose, she looked round. Catkins were swaying lightly on the willows, somewhere out of sight a tiny runnel of water gurgled, the horse ate noisily, the grass had a vividness of green like the concentrated thought of spring.

'I don't see how anything can be wrong this morning,' she said.

'Ah, you're lucky to think so,' he answered, gazing at her clear, pale profile.

'Well,' she turned to ask patiently, 'what is the matter with you?'

'I'm worried.'

'Has a cow died?' And ignoring his angry gesture, she went on: 'I don't think you take enough care of your property. Whenever I ride here I find you strolling about miserably, with a dog.'

'That's your fault.'

'I don't quite see why,' she said pleasantly; 'but no doubt you are right. But has a cow died?'

'Of course not. Why should it?'

'They do, I suppose?'

'It's the old man. He isn't well, and he's badgering me to go away, to Canada, and learn more about farming.'

'So you should.'

'Of course you'd say so.'

'Or do you think you can't?'

He missed, or ignored, her point. 'He's ill. I don't want to leave him'; and in a louder voice he added, almost shouted, 'I don't want to leave you!'

Her grey eyes were watching the swinging catkins, her hand, lifting the primroses, hid a smile. Again he had the benefit of her profile, the knot of her dark, thick hair and the shadowy line of her eyelashes, but she made no comment on his remark and after a moment of sombre staring he uttered the one word, 'Well?'

'Yes?'

'Well, I've told you.'

'Oh, I think you ought to go.'

'Then you don't love me?'

From under her raised eyebrows she looked at him steadily. 'No, I don't love you,' she said slowly. There was no need to consider her answer: she was sure of it. She was fond of him, but she could not romantically love some one who looked and behaved like a spoilt boy. She glanced from his handsome, frowning face in which the mouth was opening for protest to a scene perfectly set for a love affair. There was not so much as a sheep in sight: there was only the horse who, careless of these human beings, still ate eagerly, chopping the good grass with his teeth, and the spaniel who panted self-consciously and with a great affectation of exhaustion. The place was beautiful and the sunlight had some quality of enchantment. Faint, delicious smells were offered on the wind and withdrawn in caprice; the trees were all tipped with green and interlaced with blue air and blue sky; she wished she could say she loved him, and she repeated her denial half regretfully.

'Rose,' he pleaded, 'I've known you all my life!'

'Perhaps that's why. Perhaps I know you too well.'

'You don't. You don't know how – how I love you. And I should be different with you. I should be happy. I've never been happy yet.'

'You can't,' she said slowly, 'get happiness through a person if you can't get it through yourself.'

'Yes – if you are the person.'

She shook her head. 'I'm sorry. I can't help it.'

He reproached her. 'You've never thought about it.'

'Well, isn't that the same thing? And,' she added, 'you're so far away.'

'I can get through the hedge,' he said practically.

She smiled in the way that always puzzled, irritated and allured him. His words set him still farther off; he did not even understand her speech.

'Is it better now?' he asked, close to her.

'No, no better.' She looked at his face, so deeply tanned that his brown hair and moustache looked pale by contrast and his eyes extraordinarily blue. His appearance always pleased her. It was almost a part of the landscape, but the landscape was full of change, of mystery in spite of its familiarity, and she found him dull, monotonous, with a sort of stupidity which was not without attraction, but which would be wearying for a whole life. She had no desire to be his wife and the mistress of Sales Hall, its fields and woods and farms. The world was big,

12

the possibilities in life were infinite, and she felt she was fit, perhaps destined, to play a larger part than this he offered her, and if she could, as she foresaw, only play a greater one through the agency of some man, she must have that man colossal, for she was only twenty-three years old.

'No,' she said firmly, 'we are not suited to each other.'

'You are to me.' His angry helplessness seemed to darken the sunlight. 'You are to me. No one else. I've known you all my life. Rose, think about it!'

'I shall – but I shan't change. I don't believe you really love me, Francis, but you want some one you can growl at legitimately. I don't think you would find me satisfactory. Another woman might enjoy the privilege.'

He made a wild movement, startling to the horse. ' You don't understand me!'

'Well, then, that ought to settle it. And now I'm going.'

'Don't go,' he pleaded. 'And look here, you might have loosened your girths.'

'I might, but I didn't expect to be here so long. I didn't expect to be so pleasantly entertained.' She put out her hand for his shoulder, and, bending unwillingly, he received her foot.

'You needn't have said that,' he muttered, 'about being entertained.'

'You're so ungracious, Francis.'

'I can't help it when I care so much.'

From her high seat she looked at him with a sort of envy. 'It must be rather nice to feel anything deeply enough to make you rude.'

'You torture me,' he said.

She was hurt by the sight of his suffering, she wished she could give him what he wanted, she felt as though she were injuring a child, yet her youth resented his childishness: it claimed a passion capable of overwhelming her. She hardened a little. 'Good-bye,' she said, 'and if I were you, I should certainly go abroad.'

'I shall!' he threatened her.

'Good-bye, then,' she repeated amiably.

'Don't go,' he begged in a low voice. 'Rose, I don't believe

13

you know what you are doing, and you've always loved the country, you've always loved our place. You like our house. You told me once you envied us our rookery.'

'Yes, I love the rookery,' she said.

'And you'd have your own stables and as many horses as you wanted –'

'And milk from our own cows! And home-laid eggs!'

'Ah, you're laughing at me. You always do.'

'So you see,' she said, bending a little towards him, 'I shouldn't make a very good companion.'

'But I could put up with it from you!' he cried. 'I could put up with anything from you.'

She made a gesture. That was where he chiefly failed. The colossal gentleman of her imagination was a tyrant.

★

She rode home, up and along the track, on to the high road with its grass borders and across the shadows of the elm branches which striped the road with black. It was a long road accompanied on one side and for about two miles by a tall, smooth wall, unscalable, guarding the privacy of a local magnate's park. It was a pitiless wall, without a chink, without a roughness that could be seized by hands; it was higher than Rose Mallett as she sat on her big horse and, but for the open fields on the other side where lambs jumped and bleated, that road would have oppressed the spirit, for the wall was a solid witness to the pride and the power of material possession. Rose Mallett hated it, not on account of the pride and the power, but because it was ugly, monstrous, and so inhospitably smooth that not a moss would grow on it. More vaguely, she disliked it because it set so definite a limit to her path. She was always glad when she could turn the corner and, leaving the wall to prolong the side of the right angle it made at this point, she could take a side road, edging a wooded slope. That slope made one side of the gorge through which the river ran, and, looking down through the trees, she caught glimpses of water and a red scar of rock on the other cliff.

The sound of a steamer's paddles threshing the water came

to her clearly, and the crying of the gulls was so familiar that she hardly noticed it. And all the way she was thinking of Francis Sales, his absurdity, his good looks and his distress; but in the permanence of his distress, even in its sincerity, she did not much believe, for he had failed to touch anything but her pity, and that failure seemed an argument against the vehemence of his love. Yet she liked him, she had always liked him since, as a little girl, she had been taken by her stepsisters to a haymaking party at Sales Hall.

They had gone in a hired carriage, but one so smart and well-equipped that it might have been their own, and she remembered the smell of the leather seats warmed by the sun, the sound of the horse's hoofs and the sight of Caroline and Sophia, extremely gay in their summer muslins and shady hats, each holding a lace parasol to protect the complexion already delicately touched up with powder and rouge. She had been very proud of her stepsisters as she sat facing them and she had decided to wear just such muslin dresses, just such hats, when she grew up. Caroline was in pink with coral beads and a pink feather drooping on her dark hair; and Sophia, very fair, with a freckle here and there peeping, as though curious, through the powder, wore yellow with a big-bowed sash. She was always very slim, and the only fair Mallett in the family; but even in those days Caroline was inclined to stoutness. She carried it well, however, with a great dignity, fortified by reassurances from Sophia, and Rose's recollections of the conversations of these two was of their constant compliments to each other and the tireless discussion of clothes. These conversations still went on.

Fifteen years ago she had sat in that carriage in a white frock, with socks and ankle-strapped black shoes, her long hair flowing down her back, and she had heard then, as one highly privileged, the words she would hear again when she arrived home for tea. Under their tilted parasols they had made their little speeches. No one was more distinguished than Caroline; no girl of twenty had a prettier figure than Sophia's; how well the pink feather looked against Caroline's hair. Rose, listening intently, but not staring too hard lest her gaze should attract their attention to herself, had looked at the fields and at the high, smooth wall, and wondered whether she would rather reach Sales Hall and enjoy the party, or drive on for ever in this delightful company, but the carriage turned up the avenue of elms and Rose saw for the first time the house which Francis Sales now offered as an attraction. It was a big, square house with honest, square windows, and the drive, shadowed by the elms, ran through the fields where the haymaking was in progress. Only immediately in front of the house were there any flower-beds and there were no garden trees or shrubs. The effect was of great freedom and spaciousness, of unaffected homeliness; and even then the odd delightful mixture of hall and farm, the grandeur of the elm avenue set in the simplicity of fields, gave pleasure to Rose Mallett's beauty-loving eyes. Anything might happen in a garden that suddenly became a field, in a field that ended in a garden, and the house had the same capacity for surprise.

There was a matted hall sunk a foot below the threshold, and to Rose, accustomed to the delicate order of Nelson Lodge with its slim, shining, old furniture, its polished brass and gleaming silver, the comfortable carelessness of this place, with a man's cap on the hall table, a group of sticks and a pair of slippers in a corner, and an opened newspaper on a chair, seemed the very home of freedom. It was a masculine house in which Mrs. Sales, a gentle lady with a fichu of lace round her soft neck, looked strangely out of place, yet entirely happy in her strangeness.

On the day of the party Rose had only a glimpse of the interior. The three Miss Malletts, Caroline sweeping majestically ahead, were led into the hayfield where Mrs. Sales sat serenely in a wicker chair. It was evident at once that Mr. Sales, bluff and hearty, with gaitered legs, was fond of little girls. He realized that this one with the black hair and the solemn grey eyes would prefer eating strawberries from the beds to partaking of them with cream from a plate; he knew without being told that she would not care for gambolling with other children in the hay; he divined her desire to see the pigs and horses, and it was near the pigsties that she met Francis

16

Sales. He was tall for twelve years old and Rose respected him for his age and size; but she wondered why he was with the pigs instead of with his guests, to whom his father drove him off with a laugh.

'Says he can't bear parties,' Mr. Sales remarked genially to Rose. 'What do you think of that?'

'I like pigs, too,' Rose answered, to be surprised by his prolonged chuckle.

Mr. Sales, in the intervals of his familiar conversation with the pigs, wanted to know why Rose had not brought her father with her.

'Oh, he's too old,' Rose said, rather shocked. Her father had always seemed old to her, as indeed he was, for she was the child of his second marriage, and her young mother had died when she was born. Her stepsisters, devoted to the little girl, and perhaps not altogether sorry to be rid of a stepmother younger than themselves, had tried to make up for that loss, but they were much occupied with the social activities of Radstowe and they belonged to an otherwise inactive generation, so that if Rose had a grievance it was that they never played games with her, never ran, or played ball or bowled hoops as she saw the mothers of other children doing. For such sporting she had to rely upon her nurse who was of rather a solemn nature and liked little girls to behave demurely out of doors.

General Mallett saw to it that his youngest daughter early learnt to ride. Her memories of him were of a big man on a big horse, not talkative, somewhat stern and sad, becoming companionable only when they rode out together on the high Downs crowning the old city, and then he was hardly recognizable as the father who heard her prayers every night. These two duties of teaching her to ride and of hearing her pray, and his insistence on her going, as Caroline and Sophia had done, to a convent school in France, made up, as far as she could remember, the sum of his interest in her, and when she returned home from school for the last time, it was to attend his funeral.

She was hardly sorry, she was certainly not glad: she envied the spontaneous tears of her stepsisters, and she found the lugubriousness of the occasion much alleviated by the presence

17

of her stepbrother Reginald. She had hardly seen him since her childhood. Sophia always spoke of him as she might have spoken of the dead. Caroline sometimes referred to him in good round terms, sometimes with an indulgent laugh; and for Rose he had the charm of mystery, the fascination of the scapegrace. He was handsome, but good looks were a prerogative of the Malletts: he was married to a wife he had never introduced to his family and he had a little girl. What his profession was, Rose did not know. Perhaps his face was his fortune, as certainly his sisters had been his victims.

After the funeral he had several interviews with Caroline and Sophia, when Rose could hear the mannish voice of Caroline growing gruff with indignation and the high tones of Sophia rising to a squeak. He emerged from these encounters with an angry face and a weak mouth stubbornly set; but for Rose he had always a gay word or a pretty speech. She was a real Mallett, he told her; she was more his sister than the others, and she liked to hear him say so because he had a kind of grace and a caressing voice, yet the cool judgment which was never easily upset assured her that a man with his mouth must be in the wrong. He was, in fact, pursuing his old practice of extracting money from his sisters, and he only returned, presumably, to his wife and child, when James Batty, the family solicitor, had been called to the ladies' aid.

But they both cried when he went away.

'He is so lovable,' Sophia sobbed.

'My dear, he's a rake,' Caroline replied, carefully dabbing her cheeks. 'All the Malletts are rakes – yes, even the General. Oh, he took to religion in the end, I know, but that's what they do.' She chuckled. 'When there's nothing left! I'm afraid I shall take to it myself some day. I've sown my wild oats, too. Oh, no, I'm not going to tell Rose anything about them, Sophia. You needn't be afraid, but she'll hear of them sooner or later from anybody who remembers Caroline Mallett in her youth.'

Rose had received this confession gravely, but she had not needed the reassurance of Sophia: 'It isn't so, dear Rose – a flirt, yes, but never wicked, never! My dear, of course not!'

'Of course not,' Rose repeated. She had already realized that her stepsisters must be humoured.

*

Riding slowly, Rose recalled that haymaking party and her gradual friendship, as the years went by, with the unsociable young Sales, a friendship which had been tacitly recognized by them both when, meeting her soon after his mother's death, he had laid his arms and head on the low stone wall by which they were standing, and wept without restraint. It was a display she could not have given herself and it shocked her in a young man, but it left her in his debt. She felt she owed something to a person who had shown such confidence in her and though at the time she had been dumb and, as it seemed to her, far from helpful, she did not forget her liability. However, she could not remember it to the extent of marrying him; she had always shown him more kindness than she really felt and, in considering these things on her way home, she decided that she was still doing as much as he could expect.

She had by this time turned another corner and the high bridge, swung from one side of the gorge to the other, was before her. At the toll-house was the red-faced man who had not altered in the whiteness of a single hair since she had been taken across the bridge by her nurse and allowed to peep fearfully through the railings which had towered like a forest above her head. And the view from the bridge was still for her a fairy vision.

Seawards, the river, now full and hiding its muddy banks which, revealed, had their own opalescent beauty, went its way between the cliffs, clothed on one hand with trees, save for a big red and yellow gash where the stone was being quarried, and on the other with bare rock, topped by the Downs spreading far out of sight. Landwards the river was trapped into docks, spanned by low bridges and made into the glistening part of a patchwork of water, brick and iron. Red-roofed old houses, once the haunts of fashion, were clustered near the water but divided from it now by tram-lines, companion anachronisms to the steamers entering and leaving the docks, but

19

by the farther shore, one small strip of river was allowed to flow in its own way, and it skirted meadows rising to the horizon and carrying with them more of those noble elms in which the whole countryside was rich.

Her horse's hoofs sounding hollow on the bridge, Rose passed across, and at the other toll-house door she saw the thin, pale man, with spectacles on the end of his pointed nose, who had first touched his hat to her when she rode on a tiny pony by the side of her father on his big horse. That man was part of her life and she, presumably, was part of his. He had watched many Upper Radstowe children from the perambulator stage, and to him she remarked on the weather, as she had done to the red-faced man at the other end. It was a beautiful day; they were having a wonderful spring; it would soon be summer, she said, but on repetition these words sounded false and intensely dreary. It would soon be summer, but what did that mean to her? Festivities suited to the season would be resumed in Radstowe. There would be lawn tennis in the big gardens, and young men in flannels and girls in white would stroll about the roads and gay voices would be heard in the dusk. There would be garden-parties, and Mrs. Batty, the wife of the lawyer, would be lavish with tennis for the young, gossip for the middle-aged and unlimited strawberries and ices for all. Rose would be one of the guests at this as at all the parties and, for the first time, as though her refusal of Francis Sales had had some strange effect, as though that rejected future had created a distaste for the one fronting her, she was aghast at the prospect of perpetual chatter, tea and pretty dresses. She was surely meant for something better, harder, demanding greater powers. She had, by inheritance, good manners, a certain social gift, but she had here nothing to conquer with these weapons. What was she to do? The idea of qualifying for the business of earning her bread did not occur to her. No female Mallett had ever done such a thing, and not all the male ones. Marriage opened the only door, but not marriage with Francis Sales, not marriage with anyone she knew in Radstowe, and her stepsisters had no inclination to leave the home of their youth, the scene of their past successes, for her sake.

Rose sat very straight on her horse, not frowning, for she never frowned, but wearing rather a set expression, so that an acquaintance, passing unrecognized, made the usual reflection on the youngest Miss Mallett's pride, and the pity that one so young should sometimes look so old.

And Rose was wishing that the spring would last for ever, the spring with its promise of excitement and adventure which would not be fulfilled, though one was willingly deceived into believing that it would. Yet she had youth's happy faith in accident: something breathless and terrific would sweep her, as on the winds of storm, out of this peaceful, gracious life, this place where feudalism still survived, where men touched their hats to her as her due. And it was her due! She raised her head and gave her pale profile to the houses on one side, the trees and the open spaces of green on the other. And not because she was a Mallett though it was a name honoured in Radstowe, but because she was herself. Hats would always be touched to her, and it was the touchers who would feel themselves complimented in the act. She knew that, but the knowledge was not much to her; she wished she could offer homage for a change, and the colossal figure of her imagination loomed up again; a rough man, perhaps; yes, he might be rough if he he were also great; rough and the scandal of her stepsisters!

As she rode under the flowering trees to the stable where she kept her horse, she wondered whether she should tell her stepsisters of Francis Sales's proposal, but she knew she would not do so. She seldom told them anything they did not know already. They would think it a reasonable match; they might urge her acceptance; they were anxious for her to marry, but Caroline, at least, was proud of the inherent Mallett distaste for the marriage state. 'We're all flirts,' she would say for the thousandth time. 'We can't settle down, not one of us,' and holding up a thumb and forefinger and pinching them together, she would add, 'We like to hold men's hearts like that – and let them go!' It was great nonsense, Rose thought, but it had the necessary spice of truth. The Malletts were not easily pleased, and they were not good givers of anything except gold, the easiest thing to give. Rose wished she could give the difficult things – love, devotion, and self-sacrifice; but she could not, or perhaps she had no opportunity. She was fond of her stepsisters, but her most conscious affection was the one she felt for her horse.

She left him at the stable and, fastening up her riding-skirt, she walked slowly home. She had not far to go. A steep street, where narrow-fronted old houses informed the public that apartments were to be let within, brought her to the broad space of grass and trees called The Green, which she had just passed on her horse. Straight ahead of her was the wide street flanked by houses of which her home was one – a low white building hemmed in on each side by another and with a small walled garden in front of it; not a large house, but one full of character and of quiet self-assurance. Malletts had lived in it for several generations, long before the opposite houses were built, long before the road had, lower down, degenerated into a region of shops. These houses, all rechristened in a day of enthusiasm, Nelson Lodge, with Trafalgar House, taller, bigger, but not so white, on one side of it, and Hardy Cottage, somewhat smaller, on the other, had faced open meadows in General Mallett's boyhood. Round the corner, facing The Green, were a few contemporaries, and they all had a slight look of disdain for the later comers, yet no single house was flagrantly new. There was not a villa in sight and on The Green two old stone monuments, to long-dead and long-forgotten warriors, kept company with the old trees under which children were now playing, while nurses wheeled perambulators on the bisecting paths. The Green itself sloped upwards until it became a flat-topped hill, once a British or a Roman camp, and thence the river could be seen between its rocky cliffs and the woods Rose had lately skirted clothing the farther side in every shade of green.

She lingered for a moment to watch the children playing, the nursemaids slowly pushing, the elms opening their crumpled leaves like babies' hands. She had a momentary desire to stay, to wander round the hill and look with untired eyes at the familiar scene; but she passed on under the tyranny of tea. The Malletts were always in time for meals and the meals were exquisite, like the polish on the old brass door-knocker, like the furniture in the white panelled hall, like the beautiful old mahogany in the drawing-room, the old china, the glass bowls full of flowers.

Rose found Caroline and Sophia there on either side of a small wood fire, while, facing the fire and spread in a chair not too low and not too narrow for her bulk, sat Mrs. Batty, flushed, costumed for spring, her hat a flower garden.

'Just in time,' Caroline said. 'Touch the bell, please, Sophia.'

'Susan saw me,' Rose said, and the elderly parlourmaid entered at that moment with the teapot.

'Rose insists on having a latchkey,' Sophia explained. 'What would the General have said?'

'What, indeed!' Caroline echoed. 'Young rakes are always old prudes. Yes, the General was a rake, Sophia; you needn't look so modest. I think I understand men.'

'Yes, yes, Caroline, no one better, but we are told to honour our father and mother.'

'And I do honour him,' Caroline guffawed, 'honour him all the more.' She had a deep voice and a deep laugh: she ought, she always said, to have been a man, but there was nothing masculine about her appearance. Her dark hair, carefully tinted where greyness threatened, was piled in many puffs above a curly fringe: on the bodice of her flounced silk frock there hung a heavy golden chain and locket; ear-rings dangled from her large ears; there were rings on her fingers, and powder and a hint of rouge on her face.

She laughed again. 'Mrs. Batty knows I'm right.'

Mrs. Batty's tightly gloved hand made a movement. She was a little in awe of the Miss Malletts. With them she was always conscious of her inferior descent. No General had ever ornamented her family, and her marriage with James Batty had been a giddy elevation for her, but she was by no means humble. She had her place in local society: she had a fine house in that exclusive part of Radstowe called The Slope, and her husband was a member of the oldest firm of lawyers in the city.

'You are very naughty, Miss Caroline,' she said, knowing

23

that was the remark looked for. She gave a little nod of her flower-covered head. 'And we've just got to put up with them, whatever they are.'

'Yes, yes, poor dears,' Sophia murmured. 'They're different, they can't help it.'

'Nonsense,' Caroline retorted, 'they're just the same, there's nothing to choose between me and Reginald – nothing except discretion!'

'Oh, Caroline dear!' Sophia entreated.

'Discretion!' Caroline repeated firmly, and Mrs. Batty, bending forward stiffly because of her constricting clothes, and with a creak and rustle, ventured to ask in low tones, 'Have you any news of Mr. Mallett lately?' The three elder ladies murmured together; Rose, indifferent, concerned with her own thoughts, ate a creamy cake. This was one of the conversations she had heard before and there was no need for her to listen.

She was roused by the departure of Mrs. Batty.

'Poor thing,' Caroline remarked as the door closed. 'It's a pity she has no daughter with an eye for colour. The roses in her hat were pale in comparison with her face. Why doesn't she use a little powder, though I suppose that would turn her purple, and after all, she does very well considering what she is; but why, why did James Batty marry her? And he was one of our own friends! You remember the sensation at the time, Sophia?'

Sophia remembered very well. 'She was a pretty girl, Caroline, and good-natured. She has lost her looks, but she still has a kind heart.'

'Personally I would rather keep my looks,' said Caroline, touching her fringe before the mirror. 'And I never had a kind heart to cherish.'

Tenderly Sophia shook her head. 'It isn't true,' she whispered to Rose. 'The kindest in the world. It's just her way.'

Rose nodded understanding; then she stood up, tall and slim in her severe clothes, her high boots. The gilt clock on the mantelpiece said it was only five o'clock. There were five more hours before she could reasonably go to bed.

'Where did you ride to-day, dear?' Sophia asked.

24

'Over the bridge.' And to dissipate some of her boredom, she added, 'I met Francis Sales. He thinks of going abroad.'

There was an immediate confusion of little exclamations and a chatter. 'Going abroad? Why?'

'To learn farming.'

'Oh, dear,' Sophia sighed, 'and we thought – we hoped –'

'She must do as she likes,' Caroline said, and Rose smiled. 'The Malletts don't care for marrying. Look at us, free as the air and with plenty of amusing memories. In this world nobody gets more than that, and we have been saved much trouble. Don't marry, my dear Rose.'

'You're assuming a good deal,' Rose said.

'But Rose is not like us,' Sophia protested. 'We have each other, but we shall die before she does and leave her lonely. She ought to marry, Caroline; we ought to have more parties. We are not doing our duty.'

'Parties! No!' Rose said. 'We have enough of them. If you threaten me with more I shall go into a convent.'

Caroline laughed, and Sophia sighed again. 'That would be beautiful,' she said.

'Sophia, how dare you?'

Sophia persisted mildly: 'So romantic – a young girl giving up all for God'; and Caroline gave the ribald laugh on which she prided herself – a shocking sound. 'Rose Mallett,' Sophia went on, so lost in her vision that the jarring laughter was not heard, 'such a pretty name – a nun! She would never be forgotten: people would tell their children. Sister Rose!' She developed her idea. 'Saint Rose! It's as pretty as Saint Cecilia – prettier!'

'Sophia, you're in your dotage,' Caroline cried. 'A Mallett and a nun! Well, she could pray for the rest of us, I suppose.'

'But I would rather you were married, dear,' Sophia said serenely. 'And we have known the Sales all our lives. It would have been so suitable.'

'So dull!' Rose murmured.

'And we need praying for,' Caroline said. 'You'd be dull either way, Rose. Have your fling, as I did. I've never regretted it. I was the talk of Radstowe, wasn't I, Sophia? There was never

25

a ball where I was not looked for, and when I entered the ball-room' – she gave a display of how she did it – 'there was a rush of black coats and white shirts – a mob – I used just to wave them all away – like that. Oh, yes, Sophia, you were a belle, too –'

'But never as you were, Caroline.'

'You were admired for yourself, Sophia, but with me it was curiosity. They only wanted to hear what I should say next. I had a tongue like a lash! They were afraid of it.'

'Yes, yes,' Sophia said hastily, and she glanced at Rose, afraid of meeting scepticism in her clear young eyes; but though Rose was smiling it was not in mockery. She was thinking of her childhood when, like a happier Cinderella, she had seen her stepsisters, in satins and laces, with pendant fans and glittering jewels, excited, rustling, with little words of commendation for each other, setting out for the evening parties of which they never tired. They had always kissed her before they went, looking, she used to think, as beautiful as princesses.

'And men like what they fear,' Caroline added.

'Yes, dear,' Sophia said. A natural flush appeared round the delicate dabs of rouge. She hoped she might be forgiven for her tender deceits. Those young men in the white waistcoats had often laughed at Caroline rather than at her wit; she was, as Sophia had shrinkingly divined, as often as not their butt, and dear Caroline had never known it; she must never know it, never know it. She drew half her happiness from the past, as, so differently, Sophia did herself, and, drooping a little, her thoughts went farther back to the last year of her teens when a pale and penniless young man had been her secret suitor, had gone to America to make his fortune there – and died.

She had told no one; Caroline would have scorned him because he was shy and timid, and he had not had time to earn enough to keep her: he had not had time. She had a faded photograph of him pushed away at the back of a drawer of the walnut bureau in the bedroom she shared with Caroline, a pale young man wearing a collar too large for his thin neck, a young man with kind, honest eyes. It was a grief to her that she could

26

not wear that photograph in a locket near her heart, but Caroline would have found out. They had slept in the same bed since they were children, and nothing could be hidden from her except the love she still cherished in her heart. Some day she meant to burn that photograph lest unsympathetic hands should touch it when she died; but death still seemed far off, and sometimes, even while she was talking to Caroline, she would pretend to rummage in the drawer, and for a moment she would close her hand upon the photograph to tell him she had not forgotten. She loved her little romance, and the gaiety in which she had persisted, even on the day when she heard of his death and which at first had seemed a necessary but cruel disloyalty, had become in her mind the tenderest of concealments, as though she had wrapped her secret in beauty, laughter, music and shining garments.

'Oh, yes, dear Rose,' she said, lifting her head, 'you must be married.'

§ 2

The outward life of the Mallett household was elegant and ordered. Footsteps fell quietly on the carpeted stairs and passages; doors were quietly opened and closed. The cook and the parlourmaid were old and trusted servants; the house and kitchen maids were respectable young women fitting themselves for promotion, and their service was given with the thoroughness and deference to which the Malletts were accustomed. In the whole house there was hardly an object without beauty or tradition, the notable exception being the portrait of General Mallett which hung above the Sheraton sideboard in the dining-room, a gloomy daub, honoured for the General's sake.

From the white panelled hall, the staircase with its white banisters and smooth mahogany rail led to a square landing which branched off narrowly on two sides, and opening from the square were the bedroom occupied by Rose, the one shared by her stepsisters and the one which had been Reginald's. This room was never used, but it was kept, like everything else in that house, in a state of cleanliness and polish, ready for his arrival. He might come: if he needed money badly enough he would come, and in spite of the already considerable depletion of their capital, Caroline and Sophia lived in hope of hearing his impatient assault of the door-knocker, the brass head of a lion holding a heavy ring in his mouth. Rose, too, wished he would come, but that last interview with the lawyer Batty had been more successful than anyone but the lawyer himself had wished, and there was no knock, no letter, no news.

The usual life of parties, calls and concerts continued without any excitement but that felt by Caroline and Sophia in the getting of new clothes, the refurbishing of old ones, the hearing of the latest gossip, the reading of the latest novel. Sophia sometimes apologized for the paper-backed books lying about the drawing-room by saying that she and dear Caroline liked to keep up their French, but Caroline loudly proclaimed her taste for salacious literature. She had a reputation to keep up and she liked to shock her friends; but everything was forgiven to Miss Mallett, the more readily, perhaps, after Sophia's reassuring whisper, 'They are really charming books, quite beautiful, nothing anybody could disapprove of. Why, there is hardly an episode to make one shrink, though, of course, the French are different,' and the Radstowe ladies would nod over their tea and say, 'Of course, quite different!'

But Caroline, suspecting that murmured explanation, had been known to call out in her harsh voice, 'It's no good asking Sophia about them. She simply doesn't understand the best bits! She is *jeune fille* still, she always will be!' Sophia, blushing a little, would feel herself richly complimented, and the ladies laughed, Mrs. Batty uncertainly, having no acquaintance with the French language.

Rose read steadily through all the books in the house and gained a various knowledge which left her curiously untouched. She studied music, and liked it better than anything else because it roused emotions otherwise unobtainable, yet she did not care much for the emotional kind. Perhaps her intensest feeling was the desire to feel intensely, but being half ashamed of this desire she rarely dwelt on it; she pursued her way, calm and aloof and proud. She was beautiful and found pleasure in the contemplation of herself, and though she did not discuss her appearance as her stepsisters discussed theirs, she spent a good deal of time on it and much money on her plain but perfect clothes. All three had more money than they needed, but Rose was richer than the others, having inherited her mother's little fortune as well as her share of what the General had left. She was, as Caroline often told her with a hit at that gentleman's unnecessary impartiality, a very desirable match. 'But they're afraid of you, my dear; they were afraid of me, but I amused them, while you simply look as if they were not there. Of course, that's attractive in its way, and one must follow one's own line, but it takes a brave man to come up to the scratch.'

'Caroline, what an expression!'

'Well, I want a brave man,' Rose said, 'if I want one at all.'

Caroline turned on Sophia. 'What's language for except to express oneself? You're out of date, Sophia; you always were, and I've always been ahead of my time. Now, Rose,' – these personalities were dear to Caroline – 'Rose belongs to no time at all. That frightens them. They don't understand. You can't imagine a Radstowe young man making love to the Sphinx. They were more daring when I was young. Look at Reginald! Look at the General!'

'It was his profession,' Rose remarked.

'Yes, I suppose that's what he told himself when he married your mother, a mere girl, no older than myself, but he was afraid of her and adored her. I believe men always like their second wives best – they're flattered at succeeding in getting two. I know men. Our own mother was pious and made him go to church, but with your mother he looked as if he were in a temple all the time. Those big, stern men are always managed by their women; it's the thin men with weak legs who really go their own way.'

'Caroline,' Sophia sighed, 'I don't know how you think of such things. Is that an epigram?'

'I don't know,' Caroline said, 'but I shouldn't be surprised.'

Smiling in her mysterious way, Rose left the room, and Sophia, slightly pink with anxiety, murmured, 'Caroline, there's no one in Radstowe really fit for her. Don't you think we ought to go about, perhaps to London, or abroad?'

'I'm not going to budge,' Caroline said. 'I love my home and I don't believe in matchmaking, I don't believe in marriage. It wouldn't do her any good, but if you feel like that, why don't you exploit her yourself?'

'Oh – exploit! Certainly not! And you know I couldn't leave you.'

'Then don't talk nonsense,' Caroline said, and the life at Nelson Lodge went on as before.

Every day Rose rode out, sometimes early in the morning on the Downs when nobody was about and she had them to herself, but oftener across the bridge into the other county where the atmosphere and the look of things were immediately different, softer, more subtle yet more exhilarating. She went there now with no fear of meeting Francis Sales. He had gone to Canada without another word, and his absence made him interesting for the first time. If she had not been bored in a delicate way of her own which left no mark but an expression of impassivity she would not have thought of him at all; but the days went by and summer passed into autumn and autumn was threatened by winter, with so little change beyond the coming and going of flowers and leaves and birds, that her mind began to fix itself on a man who loved her to the point of disgust and departure; and to her love of the country round about Sales Hall was added a tender half-ironic sentiment.

Once or twice she rode up to the Hall itself and paid a visit to Mr. Sales who, crippled by rheumatism and half suffocated by asthma, was hardly recognizable as the man who had shown her the pigs long ago. In the little room called the study, where there was not a single book, or in the big clear drawing-room of pale chintzes and faded, gilt-framed water-colours, he entertained her with the ceremony due to a very beautiful and dignified young woman, producing the latest letter from his son and reading extracts from it. Sometimes there was a photograph of Francis on a horse, Francis with a dog, or Francis at a steam plough or other agricultural machine, but these she only pretended to examine. She had not the least desire to see how he looked, for in these last months she had made a picture of her own and she would not have it overlaid by any other. It

30

was a game of pretence; she knew she was wasting her time; she had her youth and strength and money and limitless opportunity for wide experience, but her very youth, and the feeling that it would last for ever, made her careless of it. There was plenty of time, she could afford to waste it, and gradually that occupation became a habit, almost an absorption. She warned herself that she must shake it off, but the effort would leave her very bare, it would rob her of the fairy cloak which made her inner self invisible, and she clung to it, secure in her ability to be rid of it if she chose.

Her intellect made no mistake about Francis Sales, but her imagination, finding occupation where it could, began to endow him with romance, and that scene among the primroses, the startlingly green grass, the pervading blue of the air, the horse so indifferent to the human drama, the dog trying to understand it, became the salient event of her life because it had awakened her capacity for dreaming.

She did not love him, she could never love him, but he had loved her, angrily, and, in retrospect, the absurd manner of his proposal had a charm. She would have given much to know whether his feeling for her persisted. From the letters read wheezily by Mr. Sales and sometimes handed to her to read for herself, she learnt so little that she was the freer to create a great deal and, riding home, she would break into astonished inward laughter. Rose Mallett playing a game of sentiment! And, crossing the bridge and passing through the streets where she was known to every second person, she had pleasure in the conviction that no one could have guessed what absurdity went on behind the pale, impassive face, what secret and unsuspected amusement she enjoyed; a little comedy of her own! The unsuitability of Francis Sales for the part of hero supplied most of the humour and saved her from loss of dignity. The thing was obviously absurd; she had never cared for dolls, but in her young womanhood she was finding amusement in the manipulation of a puppet.

The death of Mr. Sales in the cold March of the next year shocked her from her game. She was sorry he had gone, for she had always liked him, and he seemed to have taken with him the little girl who was fond of pigs, and while Caroline and Sophia mourned the loss of an old friend, Rose was faced with the certainty of his son's return. She would have to stop her ridiculous imaginings, she must pretend she had never had them for, when she saw him as flesh and blood, her game would be ruined and she would be shamed. The imminence of his arrival reminded her of his dullness, his handsome, sullen face and, more tenderly, of those tears which had put her so oddly in his debt. But she had no difficulty in casting away the false image she had made. She was, she found, glad to be rid of it; she liked to feel herself delivered of a weakness.

But she need not have been in such a hurry, for it was some months before the man who brought the milk from Sales Hall also brought the news that the master was returning. This information was handed to Caroline and Sophia with their early tea.

Sitting up in bed and looking grotesquely terrible, they discussed the event. Caroline, like Medusa, but with hair curlers instead of snakes sprouting from her head, and Sophia with her heavy plait hanging over her shoulder and defying with its luxuriance the yellowness of her skin, they sat side by side, propped up with pillows, inured to the sight of each other in undress.

'He has come back!' Sophia said ecstatically. 'Perhaps after all –'

'Oh, nonsense!' Caroline said as usual, 'she's meant for better things. My dear, she was born for a great affair. She ought to be the mistress of a king. Yes, something of that kind, with her looks, her phlegm.'

'But there are no kings in Radstowe,' Sophia said, 'and I don't think you ought to say such things.'

'It's my way. You ought to know that. And I can't control my tongue any more than Reginald can control his body.'

'Caroline!'

'And I don't want to. We're all wrapped up in cotton-wool nowadays. I ought to have lived in another century. I, too, would have adorned a court, and kept it lively! There's no wit left in the world, and there's no wickedness of the right kind. We might as well be Nonconformists at once.'

32

'Certainly not,' Sophia said firmly. 'Certainly not that.'

'But as you so cleverly remind me, there are no kings in Radstowe. There's not even,' she added with a mocking smile which made her face gay in a ghastly way, 'not even a foreign Count who would turn out an impostor. Rose would do very well there, too. An imitation foreign Count with a black moustache and no money! She would be magnificent and tragic. Imagine them at Monte Carlo, keeping it up! She would hate him, grandly; she would hate herself for being deceived; she would never lose her dignity. You can't picture Rose with a droop or a tear. They'd trail about the Continent and she would never come back.'

'But we don't want her to go away at all,' Sophia cried.

'And when she came to the point of being afraid of murdering him, she would leave him without any fuss and live alone and mysterious somewhere in the South of France, or Italy, or Spain. Yes, Spain. There must be real Counts there and she would get her love affair at last.'

'But she would still be married.'

'Of course!' Caroline, looking roguish, was terrible. 'That is necessary for a love affair, *ma chère.*'

'I would much rather she married Francis Sales and came to see us every week. Or any other nice young man in Radstowe. She would never marry beneath her.'

'On the contrary,' Caroline remarked, 'she's bound to marry beneath her – not in class, Sophia, not in class, though in Radstowe that's possible, too. Look at the Battys! But certainly in brains and manners.'

Sophia, clinging to her own idea, repeated plaintively, 'I would rather it were Francis Sales, and he must be lonely in that big house.'

It appeared, however, that he was not to be lonely, for Susan, entering with hot water, let fall in her discreet, impersonal way, another piece of gossip. 'John Gibbs says they think Mr. Francis must be bringing home a wife, Miss Caroline. He's having some of the rooms done up.'

'Ah!' said Caroline, and her plump elbow pressed Sophia's. 'Which rooms, I wonder?'

33

'I did not inquire, Miss Caroline.'

'Then kindly inquire this afternoon, and tell him the butter is deteriorating, but inquire first or you'll get nothing out of him.' She turned with malicious triumph to Sophia. 'So that dream's over!'

'We shall have to break it to her gently,' Sophia said; 'but it may not be true.'

In the dining-room over which the General's portrait tried, and failed, to preside, as he himself had done in life, and where he was conquered by an earlier and a later generation, by the shining eloquence of the old furniture and silver and the living flesh and blood of his children, Caroline gave Rose the news without, Sophia thought, a spark of delicacy.

'They say Francis Sales is bringing home a wife.'

'Really?' Rose said, taking toast.

'He has sent orders for part of the house to be done up.'

Rose raised her eyes. 'Ah, she's hurt,' Sophia thought, but Rose merely said, 'If he touches the drawing-room or the study I shall never forgive him'; and then, thoughtfully, she added, 'but he won't touch the drawing-room.'

'H'm, he'll do what his wife tells him, I imagine. No girl will appreciate Mrs. Sales's washy paintings.'

'Rose would,' Sophia sighed.

'Yes, I do,' Rose said cheerfully. She was too cheerful for Sophia's romantic little theory, but an acuter audience would have found her too cheerful for herself. She had overdone it by half a tone, but the exaggeration was too fine for any ears but her own. She was, as a matter of fact, in the grip of a violent anger. She was not the kind of woman to resent the new affections of a rejected lover, but she had, through her own folly, attached herself to Francis Sales, as, less unreasonably, his tears had once attached him to her, and the immaterial nature of the bond composed its strength. Consciously foolish as her thoughts had been, they became at that breakfast table, with the water bubbling in the spirit kettle and the faint crunch of Caroline eating toast, intensely real, and she was angry both with herself and with his unfaithfulness. She did not love him – how could she? – but he belonged to her; and now, if this piece of gossip

34

turned out to be true, she must share him with another. Jealousy, in its usual sense, she had none as yet, but she had forged a chain she was to find herself unable to break. It was her pride to consider herself a hard young person, without spirituality, without sentiment, yet all her personal relationships were to be of the fantastic kind she now experienced, all her obligations such as others would have ignored.

'We shall know more when John Gibbs brings the afternoon milk,' Caroline said.

Rose went upstairs and left her stepsisters to their repetitions. Her window looked out on the little walled front garden and the broad street. Tradesmen's carts went by without hurry, ladies walked out with their dogs, errand-boys loitered in the sun, and presently Caroline and Sophia went down the garden path, Caroline sailing majestically like a full-rigged ship, Sophia with her girlish, tripping gait. They put up their sunshades, and sailed out on what was, in effect, a foraging expedition. They were going to collect the news.

Outside the gate, they were hidden by the wall, but for a little while Rose could hear Caroline's loud voice. Without doubt she was talking of Francis Sales, unless she were asking Sophia if her hat, a large one with pink roses, really became her. Rose knew it all so well, and she closed her eyes for a moment in weariness. Suddenly she felt tired and old; the flame of her anger had died down, and for that moment she allowed herself to droop. She found little comfort in the fact that she alone knew of her folly, and calling it folly no longer justified it. She, too, had been rejected, more cruelly than had Francis Sales, for she had given him something of her spirit. And she had liked to imagine him far away, thinking of her and of her beauty; she had fancied him remembering the scene among the primroses and continuing to adore her in his sulky, inarticulate way. Well, he would think of her no more, but she was subtly bound to him, first by his need, and now, against all reason, by her thoughts. She had already learnt that time, which sometimes seems so swift and heartless, is also slow and kind. Her feelings would lose their intensity; she only had to wait, and she waited with that outward impassivity which did

35

not spoil her beauty; it suited the firm modelling of her features, the creamy whiteness of her skin, the clear grey eyes under the straight dark eyebrows, and the lips bent into the promise of a smile.

Caroline and Sophia waited differently, first for the afternoon milk and the information they wanted and, during the next weeks, for the rumours which slowly developed into acknowledged facts. The housekeeper at Sales Hall had heard from the young master: he was married and returning immediately with his wife. Caroline sniffed and hoped the woman was respectable; Sophia was charitably certain she would be a charming girl; and Rose, knowing she questioned one of the life occupations of her stepsisters, said coolly, 'Why speculate? We shall see her soon. We must go and call.'

'Of course,' Caroline said, and Sophia, with her fixed idea, which was right in the wrong way, said gently, 'If you're sure you want to go, dear.'

'Me?' asked Caroline.

'No, no, I was thinking of Rose.'

'Nonsense!' Caroline said, 'we're all going'; and Rose reassured Sophia with perfect truth, 'I have been longing to see her for weeks.'

§ 3

So it came about that the three sisters once more sat in a hired carriage and drove to Sales Hall. On the box was the son of the man who had driven them years ago, and though the carriage was a new one and the old horse had long been metamorphosed into food for the wild animals in the Radstowe Zoo, this expedition was in many ways a repetition of the other. Caroline and Sophia faced the horses and Rose sat opposite her stepsisters, but now she did not listen to their talk with ears stretched, not to miss a word, and she did not think her companions as beautiful as princesses. It was she who might have been a princess for another child, but she did not think of that. She looked with amusement and with misplaced pity at the other two. It was a September afternoon and they were very gaily dressed, and again Caroline had a feather drooping over her hair, while Sophia, more girlish, wore a wide hat with a blue bow, and both their parasols were tilted as before against the sun. It seemed to Rose that even the cut of their garments had not changed with time. The two had always the appearance of fashion plates of twenty years ago, but no doubt of their correctness ever entered their minds; and so they managed to preserve their elegance, as though their belief in themselves were strong enough to impose it on those who saw them. Without this faith, the severity of Rose's black dress, filmy enough for the season but daringly plain, must have rebuked them. The pearls in her ears and on her neck were her only ornaments; her little hat, wreathed with a cream feather, shaded her brow. She sat with the repose which was one of her gifts.

'I'm sure we all look very nice,' Caroline said suddenly, the very remark she had made when they went to the haymaking party, 'though you do look rather like a widow, Rose – a widow, getting over it very comfortably, as they do – as they do!'

'I'm glad I look so interesting,' Rose murmured.

'Oh, interesting, always. Yes.'

They were jogging along the road bordered by the high smooth wall, despairingly efficient, guarding treasures bought with gold; and the tall elm-trees looked over it as though they wanted to escape. The murmuring in their branches seemed to be of discontent, and the birds singing in them had a taunting note. The road mounted a little and the wall went with it, backed by the imprisoned trees. But at last, at the cross-roads, the wall turned and the road went on without it. There were open fields now on either hand, the property of Francis Sales, and another mile brought the carriage to the opening of the grassy track where Rose liked to think she had left her youth, but the road went round on the other side of the larch woods, and when these were passed Sales Hall came into sight.

'I always think,' Caroline said, 'it's a pity this beautiful avenue hasn't a better setting. Mere fields, and open to the road! It's undignified. It ought to have been a park.'

'With a high wall all round it,' Rose suggested.

'Exactly,' Caroline agreed. She was touching her fringe, giving little pats and pulls to her dress, preparatory to descent, and Sophia whispered, 'Just see, Caroline, that wisp of hair near my ear – so tiresome! I can never be sure of it.'

'Not a sign of it,' Caroline assured her. 'Now I wonder what we are going to find.'

They found the drawing-room empty and untouched. On the pale walls the water-colours were still hanging, the floral carpet still covered the floor, the faded chintzes had not been removed, and the light came clearly through the long windows with their pale primrose curtains. In the middle of the room was the circular settee to seat four persons, back to back, with a little woolwork stool set for each pair of feet. There were no flowers in the room, and they were not needed, for the room itself was like some pale, scentless and old-fashioned bloom.

The three Miss Malletts sat down: Caroline gay and aggressive as a parrot, and a parrot in a big gilded cage would not have been out of place; Sophia fitting naturally into the gentle scheme of things; Rose startlingly modern in her elegance.

'Well,' Caroline said, 'she's a long time. Changing her dress, I expect,' and she sniffed. But Mrs. Francis Sales entered in a pink cotton garment, her fair, curling hair a little untidy, for she had, she said, been in the old walled garden behind the house. There was, in fact, a rose hanging from her left hand. She was pretty, she seemed artless and defenceless, but her big blue eyes had a wary look, and in spite of that look spoiling an otherwise ingenuous countenance, Rose imagined herself noticeably old and mature. She thought it was no wonder that Francis was attracted, but at the same time she despised him for a failure in taste, as though, faced with the choice between a Heppelwhite chair and an affair of wicker and cretonne, he had chosen the inferior article, though she had to admit that, for a permanent seat, it might be more comfortable and certainly more yielding.

But as she watched Mrs. Sales presiding over the teacups, her scared eyes moving swiftly from the parlourmaid, entering with cakes, to Caroline, and from Caroline to Sophia, and then with added shyness to the woman nearest her own age, Rose found her opinion changing. Mrs. Francis Sales was timid, but she

38

was not weak; the fair fluffiness of her exterior was deceptive; and while Rose made this discovery and now and then dropped a quiet word into the chatter of the others, she was listening for Francis. He had been with his wife in the garden, but he was some time in following her, and Rose knew that Mrs. Sales was listening, too. She wondered whose ear first caught the sound of his feet on the matted passage; she felt an absurd inward tremor and, looking at Mrs. Sales, she saw that her pretty pink colour had deepened and her blue eyes were bright, like flowers. She was certainly charming in her simple frock, but her unsuitable shoes with very high heels and sparkling buckles hurt Rose's eye as much as the voice, also high and slightly grating, hurt her ear, and this voice sharpened nervously as it said, 'Oh, here is Francis coming.'

No, he was not the person of Rose's dreams, and she felt an immense relief: she had expected to be disappointed, but she was glad to find the old Francis, big, bronzed and handsome, smelling of the open air and tobacco and tweed, and no dangerous, disturbing, heroic figure.

For an instant he looked at Rose before he greeted the elder ladies, and then, as Rose let her hand touch his and pleasantly said, 'How are you?' she experienced a faint, almost physical shock. He was different after all, and now she did not know whether to be glad or sorry. Unchanged, she need not have given him another thought; subtly altered, she was bound to probe into the how and why. He sat beside her on the old-fashioned couch with a curled head, and his thirteen stone descending heavily on the springs sent up her light weight with a perceptible jerk.

'Clumsy boy!' Mrs. Sales exclaimed playfully.

Rose laughed. 'It's like the old see-saw. I was always in the air and you on the ground. Is it there still – near the pigsties?'

'Yes, still there.' But this threatened to become too exclusive a conversation, and Rose tried to do her share in more general topics.

Caroline, talking of the advantage of Radstowe, regretting the greater gaiety of the past, when Sophia and she were belles, was adding gratuitous advice on the management of husbands and some information on the ways of men. Mrs. Sales laughed and glanced now and then at Francis, but whether he responded Rose could not see, unless she turned her head. He ought certainly to have been smiling at so pretty a person, wrinkling his eyes in the way he had and straightening the mouth which was sullen in repose. Yet she was almost sure he was doing the minimum demanded of politeness, almost sure he was thinking of herself and was conscious of her nearness, just as she, for the first time, was physically conscious of his.

She rose, saying, 'May I look out of the window? I always liked this view of the garden.' And having gazed out and made the necessary remarks, she sat down, separated from him by the width of the room and with her back to the light, a strategical position she ought to have taken up before. But here she was at the disadvantage of facing him and a scrutiny of which she had not thought him capable. With his legs stretched out, his hands in his pockets, his eyes apparently half shut but unquestionably fixed on her, he was really behaving rather badly. She had never been stared at like this before and she told herself that under the shelter of his marriage he had grown daring, if not insolent; but at the same time she knew she was not telling herself the truth: he was simply in the position of a thirsty man who has at last found a stream. It appeared, then, that his wife did not sufficiently quench his thirst.

Rose carefully did not look his way, but she experienced an altogether new excitement, the very ancient one of desiring to taste forbidden fruit simply because it was forbidden; this particular fruit, as such, had no special charm; but she was born a Mallett and the half-sister of Reginald. She had, however, as he had not, a substantial basis of personal pride and a love of beauty which was at least as effectual as a moral principle and she had not Francis's excuse for his behaviour. She believed he did not know what he was doing; but she was entirely clear-sighted as to herself and she refused to encourage the silent intercourse which had established itself between them.

Caroline was in the midst of a piece of gossip, Sophia was interjecting exclamations of moderation and reproach, and Mrs. Sales was manifestly amused. Her chromatic giggle was

40

as punctual as Sophia's reproof, and Rose drew closer to the group made by the three, and said, 'I'm missing Caroline's story. Which one is it?' And now it was Francis who laughed.

'It's finished,' Caroline said. 'Don't tell your husband, at least till we have gone – and we ought to go at once.'

But the coachman was not on the box. He had been invited to take tea in the kitchen.

'We won't disturb him,' Sophia said. 'No, Caroline, let him have his tea. We ought to encourage teetotal drinking in his class. Perhaps Mrs. Sales will let us go round the garden. I am so fond of flowers.'

'Come and look at the pigsties,' Francis said to Rose, but, assuring him she had grown too old for pigs, she followed the rest.

The walled garden had a beautiful disorder. A grey kitten and a white puppy sat together on the grass, enjoying the sunshine and each other's company and pretending to be asleep; and though the kitten displayed no interest in the visitors, holding its personality of more importance than anything else, the puppy jumped up, barked, and rushed at each person in turn. Caroline, picking up her skirts and showing the famous Mallett ankle, said, 'Go away, dog!' in a severe tone, and the puppy rolled on the grass to show that he did not care and could not by any possibility be snubbed. Under an apple-tree on which the fruit was ripening were two cane chairs, a table, a newspaper and a work-basket.

'This is my favourite place,' Mrs. Sales said to Rose. 'I hate that drawing-room, and Francis won't have it touched. But I've got a boudoir that's lovely. He sent an order to the best shop and had it ready for a surprise, so if I'm not out of doors I sit there. Would you like to see it?'

'I should, very much,' Rose said.

'Then come quickly while the others are eating those plums off the wall.'

Rose looked back. 'I can't think what Sophia will do with the stone,' she murmured, smiling her faint smile.

Mrs. Sales was puzzled by this remark. 'Oh, she'll manage, won't she? You don't want to help her, do you?'

41

'No, I don't want to help her.'

'Come along, then.'

Rose saw the boudoir, a little room half-way up the stairs. 'It's Louis something,' said Mrs. Sales, 'but all the same, I think it's sweet, and pink's my favourite colour. Francis thought of that. I was wearing pink when I first met him.'

'I see,' Rose said. 'Was that long ago?'

'Only three months. I think we both fell in love at the same minute, and that's nice, isn't it? I know I'm going to be happy, but I do hope I shan't be dull. We're a big family at home. I'm English,' she added a little anxiously, 'but my father settled there.'

'I don't think you should be dull,' Rose said. 'Everybody in Radstowe will call on you, and there are lots of parties. And then there's hunting.'

'Yes,' said Mrs. Sales. Her eyes left Rose's face, to return a little wider, a little warier. 'Do you hunt too?'

'As often as I can. I only have one horse.'

'Francis says I am to have two.'

'And they will be good ones. He likes hunting and horses better than anything else, I suppose.'

'But he mustn't neglect the farm,' his wife said firmly, and she added slowly, 'I don't know that I need two horses, really. I haven't ridden much, and there's a lot to do in the house. I don't believe in people being out all day.'

'Well, you can't hunt all the year round, you know.'

Mrs. Sales let out a sigh so faint that most people would have missed it. 'It will be beginning soon, won't it?'

'It feels a long way off in weather like this,' Rose said. 'But they are getting into the carriage. I must go.'

Mrs. Sales lingered for an instant. 'I do hope we're going to be friends.' This was more than a statement, it was a request, and Rose shrank from it; but she said lightly, 'We shall be meeting often. You will see more of us than you will care for, I'm afraid. The Malletts are rather ubiquitous in Radstowe. It's fortunate for us, or Caroline would die of boredom, but I don't know how it appears to other people.'

She was going down the shallow stairs and the voice of Mrs.

Sales followed her sadly: 'He hasn't told me anything about any of his friends.'

'In three months? He hasn't had time, with you to think about!'

A laugh, pleased and self-conscious, reached her ears. 'No, but it's rather lonely in this old house. We're a big family at home – and so lively. There was always something going on. I wished we lived nearer Radstowe.'

'And I envy you here. It's peaceful.'

'Yes, it's that,' Mrs. Sales agreed.

'I'm a good deal older than you, you see,' Rose elaborated.

'That's just it,' said Mrs. Sales.

Rose laughed, and Francis, standing at the door, turned at the sound in time to catch the end of Rose's smile.

'What are you laughing at?'

'Mrs. Sales's candour.'

'Oh, was I rude?'

'No. Good-bye. I liked it.' Yet, as she settled herself in her place, she was not more than half pleased. She liked her superior age only because it marked a difference between her and the wife of Francis Sales.

'H'm!' Caroline said when the carriage had turned into the road and the figures in the doorway had disappeared. 'Pretty, but unformed.'

'They seem very happy,' Sophia said, 'but I do think she ought to have been wearing black. Her father-in-law has only been dead six months, and even Francis was not wearing a black tie.'

But if Caroline condemned men in general, she supported them in particular. 'Quite right, too. Men don't think of these things – and a black tie with those tweeds! Sophia, don't be silly and sentimental; but you always were, you always will be.'

'She might have had a white frock with a black ribbon,' Sophia persisted. 'Why, Rose looked more like our old friend's daughter-in-law.'

'But hardly like a bride,' Rose said. 'And you see, pink is her colour.'

'So it is, dear. One could see that. Pink and blue, just as

43

they were mine.' She corrected herself. '*Are* mine. Our complexions are very much alike; in fact, she reminded me a little of myself.'

'Nonsense, Sophia! If you had been like that I should have disowned you. However, she will do well enough for Sales Hall.'

Rose bent forward slightly. 'I like her,' she said distinctly. 'And she's lonely.'

'Well, my dear, she'll soon have half a dozen children to keep her lively.'

'Hush, Caroline! The man will hear you.'

Caroline addressed Rose. 'Sophia's modesty is indecent. I've done what I could for her.'

'Please listen to me,' Rose said. 'You are not to belittle Mrs. Sales to people, Caroline. You can be a powerful friend, if you choose, and if you sing her praises there will be a mighty chorus.'

'That's true,' Caroline said.

'Yes, that's true, dear Caroline,' Sophia echoed. 'And I think you're taking this very sweetly, Rose.'

'Sweetly? Why?'

Caroline pricked up her ears. 'What's this? I'm out of this. Oh, that old rubbish! She will have it you and Francis should have married. My dear Sophia, Rose could have married anybody if she'd wanted to. You'll admit that? Yes? Then can't you see' – she tapped Sophia's knee – 'then can't you see that Rose didn't want him? That's logic – and something you lack.'

'Yes, dear,' Sophia said with the meekness of the unconvinced. 'And of course it's wrong to think of it now that he's married to another.'

Caroline guffawed her loudest, and the astonished horse quickened his pace. The driver cast a look over his shoulder to see that all was well, for he had a sister who made strange noises in her fits; and Sophia, sitting in her drooping fashion, as though her head with its great knob of fair hair, in which the silver was just beginning to show, were too heavy for her body, had to listen to the old gibes which had never made and never would make any impression on her, though she would have felt

44

forlorn without them. She was the only puritanical Mallett in history, Caroline said. Oh, yes, the General had been great at family prayers, but he was trying to make up for lost time. It was difficult to believe that Sophia and Reginald were the same flesh and blood.

Sophia interrupted. She was fond of Reginald, but she had no desire to be like him, and Caroline knew he was a disgrace. They argued for some time, and Rose closed her eyes until the talk, never really acrimonious, drifted into reminiscences of their childhood and Reginald's.

It was strange that they should have chosen that day to speak so much of him, for when they reached home they found a letter addressed in an unfamiliar hand.

'What's this?' Caroline said.

It was a thin, cheap envelope bearing a London postmark, and Caroline drew out a flimsy sheet of paper.

'I must get my glasses,' she said. Her voice was agitated. 'No, no, I can manage without them. The writing is immense, but faint. It's from that woman.' She looked up, showing a face drawn and blotched with ugly colour. 'It's to say that Reginald is dead.'

Mrs. Reginald Mallett had written the letter on the day of her husband's funeral, and Caroline's tears for her brother were stemmed by her indignation with his wife. She had purposely made it impossible for his relatives to attend the ceremony.

'No,' Sophia said, 'the poor thing was distressed. We mustn't blame her.'

'And such a letter!' Caroline flicked it with a disdainful finger.

Rose picked up the sheet. 'I don't see what else she could have said. I think it's dignified – a plain statement. Why should you expect more? You have never taken any notice of her.'

'Certainly not! And Reginald never suggested it. Of course he was ashamed, poor boy. However, I am now going to write to her, asking if she is in need, and enclosing a cheque. I feel some responsibility for the child. She is half a Mallett, and the Malletts have always been loyal to the family.'

'Yes, dear, we'll send a cheque, and – shouldn't we? – a few kind words. She will value them.'

'She'll value the money more,' Caroline said grimly.

Here she was wrong, for the cheque was immediately returned. Mrs. Mallett and her daughter were able to support themselves without help.

'Then we need think no more about them,' Caroline said, concealing her annoyance, 'and I shall be able to afford a new dinner dress. Black sequins, I thought, Sophia – and we must give a dinner for the Sales.'

'Caroline, no, you forget. We mustn't entertain for a little while.'

'Upon my word, I did forget. But it's no use pretending. It really isn't quite like a death in the family, is it? Poor dear Reginald! I was very fond of him, but half our friends believe he has been dead for years. I shall wear black for three months, of course, but a little dinner to the Sales would not be out of place. We have a duty to the living as well as to the dead.'

Leaving her stepsisters to argue this point, Rose went upstairs and looked into Reginald's old room. She had known very little of him, but she was sorry he was dead, sorry there was no longer a chance of his presence in the house, of meeting him on the stairs, very late for breakfast and quite oblivious of the inconvenience he was causing, and on his lips some remark which no one else would have made.

His room had not been occupied for some time, but it seemed emptier than before; the mirror gave back a reflection of polished furniture and vacancy; the bed looked smooth and cold enough for a corpse. No personal possessions were strewn about, and the room itself felt chilly.

She was glad to enter her own, where beauty and luxury lived together. The carpet was soft to her feet, a small wood fire burned in the grate, for the evening promised to be cold, and the severe lines of the furniture were clean and exquisite against the white walls. A pale soft dressing-gown hung across a chair, a little handkerchief, as fine as lace, lay crumpled on a table, there was a discreet gleam of silver and tortoiseshell. This, at least, was the room of a living person. Yet, as she stood

46

before the cheval-glass, studying herself after the habit of the Malletts, she thought perhaps she was less truly living than Reginald in his grave. He left a memory of animation, of sin, of charm; he had injured other people all his life, but they regretted him and, presumably, he had had his pleasure out of their pain. And what was she, standing there? A negatively virtuous young woman, without enough desire of any kind to impel her to trample over feelings, creeds and codes. If she died that moment, it would be said of her that she was beautiful, and that was all. Reginald, with his greed, his heartlessness, his indifference to all that did not serve him, would not be forgotten: people would sigh and smile at the mention of his name, hate him and wish him back. She envied him; she wished she could feel in swift, passionate gusts as he had done, with the force and the forgetfulness of a passing wind. His life, flecked with disgrace, must also have been rich with temporary but memorable beauty. The exterior of her own was all beauty, of person and surroundings, but within there seemed to be only a cold waste.

She had been tempted the other afternoon, and she had resisted with what seemed to her a despicable ease: she had not really cared, and she felt that the necessity to struggle, even the collapse of her resistance, would have argued better for her than her self-possession. And for a moment she wished she had married Francis Sales. She would at least have had some definite work in the world; she could have kept him to his farming, as Mrs. Sales had set herself to do; she would have had a home to see to and daily interviews with the cook! She laughed at this decline in her ambition; she no longer expected the advent of the colossal figure of her young dreams; and she knew this was the hour when she ought to strike out a new way for herself, to leave this place which offered her nothing but ease and a continuous, foredoomed effort after enjoyment; but she also knew that she would not go. She had not the energy nor the desire. She would drift on, never submerged by any passion, keeping her head calmly above water, looking coldly at the interminable sea. This was her conviction, but she was not without a secret hope that she might at last be carried to some unknown

47

island, odorous, surprising and her own, where she would, for the first time, experience some kind of excess.

§ 4

The little dinner was duly given to the Sales. The Sales returned the compliment; and Mrs. Batty, not to be outdone, offered what could only adequately be described as a banquet in honour of the bride; there was a general revival of hospitality, and the Malletts were at every function. This was Caroline's reward for her instructed enthusiasm for Christabel Sales, and before long the black sequin dress gave way to a grey brocade and a purple satin, and the period of mourning was at an end. For Rose, these entertainments were only interesting because the Sales were there, and she hardly knew at what moment annoyance began to mingle definitely with her pity for the little lady with the wary eyes, or when the annoyance almost overcame the pity.

It might have been at a dinner-party when Christabel, seated at the right hand of a particularly facetious host, let out her high chromatic laughter incessantly, and the hostess, leaning towards Francis, told him with the tenderness of an elderly woman whose own romance lies far behind her, that it was a pleasure to see Mrs. Sales so happy. He murmured something in response and, as he looked up and met the gaze of Rose, she smiled at him and saw his eyes darken with feeling, or with thought.

After dinner he sought her out. She had known that would happen: she had been avoiding it for weeks, but it was useless to play at hide-and-seek with the inevitable, and she calmly watched him approach.

'Why did you laugh?' he asked at once, in his old, angry fashion. 'You were laughing at me.'

'No, I smiled.'

'Ah, you're not so free with your smiles that they have no meaning.'

'Perhaps not, but I don't know what the meaning was.'

'I believe you've been laughing at me ever since I came back.'

48

'Indeed, I haven't. Why should I?'

'God knows,' he answered with a shrug; ' I never do understand what people laugh at.'

'You're too self-conscious, Francis.'

'Only with you,' he said.

'Somebody is going to sing,' she warned him as a gaunt girl went towards the piano; and sinking on to a convenient and sheltered couch, they resigned themselves to listen – or to endure. From that corner Rose had a view of the long room, mediocre in its decoration, mediocre in its occupants. She could see her host standing before the fire, swinging his eye-glasses on a cord and gazing at the cornice as the song proceeded. She could see Christabel's neck and shoulders and the back of her fair head. Beside her a plump matron had her face suitably composed; three bored young men were leaning against a wall.

The music jangled, the voice shrieked a false emotion, and Rose's eyebrows rose with the voice. It was dull, it was dreary, it was a waste of time, yet what else, Rose questioned, could she do with time, of which there was so much? She could not find an answer, and there rose at that moment a chorus of thanks and a gentle clapping of hands. The gaunt girl had finished her song and, poking her chin, returned to her seat. The room buzzed with chatter; it seemed that only Francis and Rose were silent. She turned to look at him.

'This is awful,' he said.

'No worse than usual.'

'When do you think we shall have exhausted Radstowe hospitality? And the worst of it is we have to give dinners ourselves, and the same things happen every time.'

'I find it soporific,' said Rose.

'I'd rather be soporific in an arm-chair with a pipe.'

'This is one of the penalties of marriage,' Rose said lightly.

'Look here, I'm giving Christabel another jumping lesson to-morrow. I've put some hurdles up. Will you come? She's getting on very well. I'll take her hunting before long.'

'Does she like it?'

'Oh, rather! My word, it would have been a catastrophe if

49

she hadn't taken to it.' He paused, considering the terrible situation from which he had been saved. 'Can't imagine what I should have done. But she's never satisfied. She's beginning to jeer at the old brown horse. I've seen a grey mare that might do for her,' and he went on to enumerate the animal's points.

Rose said, 'Why don't you let her have her first season with the old horse? He knows his business. He'll take care of her.'

'She wouldn't approve of that. I tell you, she's ambitious. I'll go and fetch her and you'll hear for yourself.'

She watched him bending over his wife, and saw Christabel rise and slip a hand under his arm. The action was a little like that of a young woman taking a walk with her young man, but it betokened a confidence which roused a slight feeling of envy and sadness in Rose's heart.

'We have been talking about hunting,' she began at once.

'Oh, yes,' Christabel said. She looked warily from one to the other.

'I'm recommending you to stick to the old brown horse, but Francis says you laugh at him.'

'Would you ride him yourself?' Christabel asked.

'Not if I could get something better.'

'Well, then –' Christabel's tone was final.

But Rose persisted, saying, 'But, you see, this isn't my first season. Stick to the old horse for a little while.'

'No,' Christabel said firmly. 'If Francis thinks I can ride the mare, I should like to have her.'

Rose laughed, but she felt uneasy, and Francis said, 'I told you so. She has any amount of pluck. You come and watch.'

'No, I can't come to-morrow. I think I'll see her first in all her glory on the grey mare.'

'All the same,' Christabel added, 'if she's very expensive, I don't want her. Francis is extravagant over horses, and we have to be careful.'

'We'll economize somewhere else,' he said. 'The mare is yours.'

She suppressed a sigh. Rose was sure of it, and in after days she was to ask herself many times if she had been to blame in not interpreting that sigh to Francis. But she had to give Chris-

50

tabel, and Christabel especially, the loyalty of one woman to another. She would not wrench from her in a few words the pride Francis took in her, to which she sacrificed her fears. Rose had the astuteness of a jealousy she would not own, of a sense of possession she could not discard, and she had known, from the first moment, that Christabel was afraid of horses and dreaded the very name of hunting. And Rose divined, too, that if she herself had not been a horsewoman of some repute, Christabel would have been less ambitious; she would have been contented with the old brown horse; but Christabel, too, had an astuteness. No, she could not have interfered; yet when she first saw Christabel on the mare she was alarmed to the point of saying:

'Are you sure she's all right? You'd better keep beside her, Francis.'

The mare was fidgety and hot-headed. Christabel's hands were unsteady, her face was pale, her lips were tight; but she was gay, and Francis was proud to have her and her mount admired.

Rose looked round in despair. Could no one else see what was so plain to her? She was tempted to go home. She felt she could not bear the strain of watching that little figure perched on the grey beast that looked like a wraith, like a warning. But she did not go, and she learnt to be glad to have shared with Francis the horror of the moment when the mare, out of control and mad with excitement, tried a fence topping a bank, failed, and fell with Christabel beneath her.

On the ground there was a flurry of white and black, and then stillness, while over the fields the hounds and the foremost riders went like things seen in a dream, with the same callousness, the same speed.

Rose saw men dismount and run towards the queer, ugly muddle on the grass. She dismounted, too, and gave her horse to somebody to hold, but she did nothing. Other, more capable people were before her, and it struck her at that moment, while a bird in a bare hedge set up a short chirrup of surprise, how little used she was to action. She seemed to be standing alone in the big field: the rest was a picture with which she had nothing to do. There was a busy group near the fence, some

51

men came running with a door, and then the sound of a shot broke through her numbness. The mare had been put out of her pain; but what of Christabel?

She hurried forward; she heard some one say, 'Ah, here's Miss Mallett,' and she answered vaguely, 'Men are gentler.' But as they lifted Christabel, Rose held one of her hands. It felt lifeless; she looked small and broken; she made no sound.

'She's not conscious,' a man said, and at that she opened her eyes.

'My God, she's got some pluck!' Francis said. 'My God –'

She smiled at him, and he dropped behind with a gesture of despair.

'You were right,' he said to Rose, 'she wasn't equal to that brute.' He turned angrily. 'Why didn't you make me see?'

She made no answer then, or afterwards, to him, but over and over again, with the awful reiteration of the conscience-smitten, she set out her reasons for her silence. She might have told him that of these he was the chief. If he had looked at her less persistently on her visits to Sales Hall, if he had married another kind of woman, she would not have been afraid to speak, but she had tried not to extinguish what little flame of love still flickered in his heart for Christabel and she had succeeded in almost extinguishing her life, in reducing her to permanent helplessness.

This was Rose's first experience of how evil comes out of good. What would happen to that love, Rose did not know. For a time it burned more brightly, fanned by Christabel's heroism and Francis's remorse, but heroism can become monotonous to the spectator and poignant remorse cannot be endured for ever. Christabel's plight was pitiful, but Rose was sorrier for Francis. He had, as it were, engaged her compassion years ago, he had a prior claim, and as time went on, her pity for Christabel changed at moments to annoyance. It was cruel, but Rose had no fund of patience. She disliked illness as she did deformity, and though Christabel never complained of her constant pain, she developed the exactions of an invalid, and the suspicions. In those blue eyes, bluer, and more than ever wary, Rose saw the questions which were never asked.

In the bedroom which, with the boudoir, had been furnished and decorated by the best shop in Radstowe, for a surprise, Christabel lay on a couch near the window, with a nurse in attendance, the puppy and the kitten, both growing staid, for company. It tired her to use her hands, she had never cared for reading and she lay there with little for consolation but her pride in stoically bearing pain.

Often, and with many interruptions, she made Rose repeat the details of the accident.

'I was riding well, wasn't I?' she would ask. 'Francis was pleased with me. He said so. It wasn't my fault, was it? And then, when they were carrying me home did you hear what he said? Tell me what he said.'

And Rose told her: 'He said, "My God, she has got pluck!" Oh, Christabel, don't talk about it.'

'I like to,' she replied, but the day came when she insisted on this subject for the last time.

'Tell me what you thought when you saw me on the mare,' she said, and Rose, careless for once, answered immediately, 'I thought she wasn't fit for you to ride.'

'Ah,' Christabel said slowly, 'did you? Did you? But you didn't say anything. That was – queer.'

Rose said nothing. She was frozen dumb and there was no possible reply to such an implication; but she rose and drew on her gloves. She looked tall and straight in her habit, and formidable.

'Are you going? But you must have tea with Francis. He's expecting you.'

'I won't stay to-day,' Rose said. She was shaking with the anger she suppressed.

'But if you don't,' Christabel cried, 'he'll want to know why. He'll ask me!'

'I can't help that,' Rose said.

Tears came into Christabel's eyes. 'You might at least do that for me.'

'Very well. Because you ask me.'

'And you'll come again soon?'

The sternness of Rose's face was broken by an ironic smile. 'Of course! If you are sure you want me!'

53

She went downstairs and, as usual, Francis was waiting for her in the matted hall. He did not greet her with a word or a smile. He watched her descend the shallow flight, and together they went down the passage to the clear drawing-room, where the faded water-colours looked unreal and innocent and ignorant of tragedy.

'What's the matter?' he asked.

'Nothing.' She looked into the oval mirror which had so often reflected his mother's placid face. 'My hat's a little crooked,' she said.

He laughed without mirth. 'Never in its life. Has Christabel been worrying you?'

'Worrying me? Poor child –'

'Yes, it's damnable, but she does worry one – and you look odd.'

'I'm getting old,' she murmured, not seeking reassurance but stating a fact plain to her.

'You're exactly the same!' he said. 'Exactly the same!' He swept his face with his hands, and at that sight a new sensation seized her delicately, delightfully, as though a firm hand held her for an instant above the earth, high in the air, free from care, from restrictions, from the necessity for thought – but only for an instant. She was set down again, inwardly swaying, apparently unmoved, but conscious of the carpet under her feet, the chairs with twisted legs, the primrose curtains, the spring afternoon outside.

'Let us have tea,' she said. She handled the pretty flowered cups and under her astonished eyes the painted flowers were like a little garden, gay and sweet and gilded. She seemed to smell them and the hiss of the kettle was like a song. Then, as she handed him his cup and looked into his wretched face and remembered the bitter reality of things, she still could not lose all sense of sweetness.

'Don't say any more!' she said quickly. 'Don't say another word.'

'I won't, if you're sure you know everything. Do you?'

'Every single thing.'

'And you care?'

54

'Yes.' She drew a breath. 'I care – beyond speaking of it. Francis, not a word!'

It was extraordinary, it was inexplicable, but it was true and happily beyond the region of regrets, for if she had married him years ago she would never have loved him in this miraculous, sudden way, with this passion of tenderness, this desire to make him happy, this terrible conviction that she could not do it, this promise of suffering for herself. And the wonder of it was that he had no likeness to that absurd Francis of whom she had dreamed and whom she had not loved; no likeness, either, to the colossal tyrant. The man she loved was in some ways weak, he was petulant, he was a baby, but he needed her and, for a romantic and sentimental moment, she saw herself as his refuge, his strength. She could not, must not communicate those thoughts. She began to talk happily and serenely about ordinary things until she remembered that she had lingered past her usual hour and that upstairs Christabel must be listening for the sound of her horse's hoofs. She started up.

'Will you fetch Peter for me?'

'If you will tell me when you are coming again.'

'One day next week.'

He kissed her hand, and held it.

'Francis, don't. You mustn't spoil things.'

'I haven't said a word.'

'Silence is good,' she said.

§ 5

And she knew she could be silent for ever. Restraint and a love of danger lived together in her nature and these two qualities were fed by the position in which she found herself, nor would she have had the position changed. It supplied her with the emotion she had wanted. She had the privilege of feeling deeply and dangerously and yet of preserving her pride.

There was irony in the fact that Christabel, hinting at suspicions for which, in Rose's mind, there was at first no cause, had at last actually brought about what she feared, and if Rose had looked for justification, she might have found it there. But she did not look for it any more than Reginald would have done; she was like him there, but where she differed was in loyalty to an idea. She saw love as something noble and inspiring, worthy of sacrifice and, more concretely, she was determined not to increase the disaster which had befallen Christabel. Sooner or later, in normal conditions, her marriage must have been recognized as a failure, but in these abnormal ones it had to be sustained as a success, and it seemed to Rose that civilized beings could love, and live in the knowledge of their love, without injuring some one already cruelly unfortunate.

But, as the months went by, she found she had to reckon with two difficult people, or rather with two people, ordinary in themselves, cast by fate into a difficult situation. There was Christabel, with her countless idle hours in which to formulate theories, to lay traps, to realize that the devotion of Francis became less obvious; and there was Francis, breaking the spirit of their contract with his looks, and sometimes the letter, with his complaints and pleadings.

He could not go on like this for ever, he said. He saw her once a week for a few minutes, if he was lucky: how could she expect him to be satisfied with that? It was little enough, she owned, but more than it might have been. She could never make him admit, perhaps because he did not feel, how greatly they were blessed; but she saw herself as the guardian of a temple: she stood in the doorway forbidding him to enter less the place should be defiled, yet forbidding him in such a way that he should not love her less. Yet constantly saying 'No,' constantly shaking the head and smiling propitiatingly the while is not to appease; and those short hours of companionship in which they had once managed to be happy became times of strain, of disappointment, of barely kept control.

'I wish I could stop loving you,' he broke out one day, 'but I can't. You're the kind one doesn't forget. I thought I'd done it once, for a few months, but you came back – you came back.'

She smiled, seeming aloof and full of some wisdom unknown to him. She knew he could not do without her, still more she knew he must not do without her, and these certainties became the main fabric of her love. She had to keep him, less for her own sake than for that of her idea, but gradually the severe rules she had made became relaxed.

They were not to meet except on that one day a week demanded by Christabel, who also had to keep Francis happy and who would have welcomed the powers of darkness to relieve the monotony of her own life; but Rose could hardly take a ride without meeting Francis, also riding; or he would appear, on foot, out of a wood, out of a side road, and waylay her. He seemed to have an uncanny knowledge of her presence, and they would have a few minutes of conversation, or of a silence which was no longer beautiful, but terrible with effort, with possibilities and with dread.

She ought, she knew, to have kept to her own side of the bridge, to have ridden on the high Downs inviting to a rider, but she loved the farther country where the air was blue and soft, where little orchards broke oddly into great fields, where brooks ran across the lanes and pink-washed cottages were fronted by little gardens full of homely flowers and clothes drying on the bushes. There was a smell of fruit and wood fires and damp earth; there was a veil of magic over the whole landscape and, far off, the shining line of the channel seemed to be washing the feet of the blue hills. The country had the charm of home with the allurement of the unknown and, within sound of the steamers hooting in the river, almost within sight of the city lying, red-roofed and smoky with factories, round the docks and mounting in terraces to the heights of Upper Radstowe, there was an expectation of mystery, of secrets kept for countless centuries by the earth which was rich and fecund and alive. She could not deny herself the sight of this country. It had become dearer to her since her awakened feelings had brought with them the complexities of new thoughts. It soothed her though it solved nothing. It did not wish to solve anything. It lay before her with its fields, its woods, its patches of

57

heathy land, its bones of grey limestone showing where the flesh of the red earth had fallen away, its dips and hollows, its steep lanes, like the wide eye of a being too full of understanding to attempt elucidations; it would not explain; it knew but it would not impart the knowledge which must be gained through the experience of years, of storms, of sunshine, of calamity and joy.

And sometimes the presence of Francis with his personal claims and his complaints was an intrusion, almost an anachronism. He was of his own time, and the end of that was almost within sight, while the earth, immensely old, had a youth of its own, something which Francis would never have again. But perhaps, because he was essentially simple, he would have fitted in well enough if he had been less ready to voice his grievances and ruffle the calm which she so carefully preserved, which he called coldness and for which he reproached her often.

'I have no peace,' he grumbled.

'You would get it if you would accept things as they are. You have to, in the end, so why not now?'

She longed to give peace to him, but her tenderness was sane and she found a strange pleasure in the pain of knowing him to be irritable and childish. It made of her love a better thing, without the hope of any reward but the continuance of service.

'It's easier for you,' he said, and she answered, 'Is it?' in the way that angered him and yet held him, and she thought, without bitterness, that he had never suffered anything without physical or mental tears. 'Yes, you have peace at home, but I go back to misery.'

'It's her misery.'

'That doesn't make it any better,' he retorted justly.

'I know.' She touched his sleeve and, feeling his arm stiffen, removed her hand.

'And I feel a brute because I can't care enough. If it were you now –'

Almost imperceptibly Rose shook her head. She had no illusions, but she said, 'Then why not pretend it's me.

58

Tell her all you do. Ask her advice – you needn't take it.'

'And it's all a lie,' he growled.

She said serenely, 'It has to be, but there are good lies.'

She wished, with an intensity she rarely allowed herself, that he would be quiet and controlled. Though half her occupation would be gone, she would feel for him a respect which would rebound on her and make her admirable to herself, but she knew that life cannot be too lavish of its gifts or death would always have the victory. This was not what she had looked for, but it was good enough; she was necessary to him and always would be; she was sure of that, yet she constantly repeated it; moreover, she loved his bigness and his physical strength and the way the lines round his eyes wrinkled when he smiled; she knew how to make him smile and now and then they had happy interludes when they talked about crops and horses, profit and loss, the buying and selling of stock, and felt their friendship for each other like a mantle shared.

At the worst, she consoled herself, after a time of strain, it was like riding a restive horse. There was danger which she loved: there was need of skill and a light hand, of sympathy and tact, and she never regretted the superman who was to have ruled her with a fatiguing rod of iron. Here there was give and take; she had to let him have his head and pull him up at the right moment and reward docility with kindness: she even found a kind of pleasure, streaked with disgust, in dealing with Christabel's suspicions, half expressed, but present like shadowy people in her room.

Of these she never spoke to Francis, but she had a malicious affection for them; they had, as it were, done her a good turn, and though they hid like secret enemies in the corners, she recognized them as allies. And they looked so much worse than they were. She imagined them showing very ugly faces to Christabel, who could only judge them by their looks, and though it was cruel that she should be frightened by them, it was impossible to drive them away. Rose could only sit calmly in their presence and try to create an atmosphere of safety. She knew she ought to feel hypocritical in this attendance on her lover's wife, but it was not of her choosing. She did not like Christabel, she would have been glad never to see her again and, terrible as her situation was, it appealed to Rose less then it would have done if she had not herself come of people whose tradition was one of stoicism in trouble, of pride which refused to reveal its distress. Physically, Christabel had those qualities, but mentally she lacked them; it was chiefly to Rose that she betrayed herself, and at each farewell she exacted the promise of another visit soon. Was she fascinated by the sight of the woman Francis loved? And when had that love been discovered? And was she sure of it even now? She certainly had her sole excitement in her search for evidence.

In that bedroom, gaily decorated for a bride, she lay heroically bearing pain, lacking the devotion she should have had, finding her reward in the memory of her husband's appreciation of her courage, and her occupation, perhaps her pleasure, in a refinement of self-torture.

As soon as Rose entered the room she was aware of the scrutiny of those wary eyes, very wide open, as blue as flowers, and she knew that her own face was like a mask. The little dog wagged his tail, the cat made no sign, the nurse, after a cheerful greeting, went out of the room and Rose took her accustomed place beside the window. It had a view of the garden, the avenue of elms in which the rooks cawed continuously, the hedge separating the fields from the high-road where two-wheeled carts, laden with farm produce, jogged into Radstowe, driven by an old man or a stout woman, and returned some hours later with the day's shopping – kitchen utensils inadequately wrapped up and glistening in the sunshine, a flimsy parcel of drapery, a box of groceries. The old man smoked his pipe, the stout woman shook the reins on the pony's back; the pony, regardless, went at his own pace. Heavy farm carts creaked past, motor-cars whizzed by, the Sales Hall dairy cows were driven in for milking, and then for a whole half hour there might be nothing on the road. The country slept in the sunshine or patiently endured the rain.

For a member of a large and lively family this prospect,

seen from a permanent couch, was not exhilarating, but Christabel did not complain: she took advantage of every incident and made the most of it, but she never expressed a desire for more. She had, for so frail and shattered a body, an amazing capacity for endurance, as though she were upheld by some spiritual force. It might have been religion or love, or the desire to perpetuate Francis's admiration, but Rose believed, and hated herself for believing, that it was partly antagonism and a feverish curiosity. She had been cheated of her youth and strength, and here, with a beautiful, impassive face, was the woman who might have saved her, a woman with a body strongly slim in her dark habit, and firm white hands skilled in managing a horse. She had read the grey mare's mind, and now Christabel, delicately blue and pink and white, in a wrapper of silk and lace, her hands fidgeting each other as they had fidgeted the mare's mouth, thought she was reading the mind of Rose. She stared at her, fascinated but not afraid. There were things she must find out.

She asked one day, and it was nearly two years since the accident, 'Did they kill the mare?' And Rose, aware that Christabel had known all the time, answered, 'Yes, at once. Her leg was broken.'

'What a pity!'

Waiting for what would come next, Rose smiled and looked out of the window at the swaying elm tops.

'Such a useful animal!' Christabel said.

'Very dangerous,' Rose remarked, slipping deliberately into the trap.

'That's what I mean. But not quite dangerous enough. Poor Francis! He didn't know. He doesn't know now, does he? But of course not.'

Rose had a great horror of a debt and she owed something to Christabel, but now she felt she had paid it off, with interest. She breathed deeply, without a sound. Her tone was light.

'He knows all that is good for him.'

'You mean that is good for you.'

61

Rose stood up, pulled on her washleather gloves, sat down again. The hands on the silk coverlet were shaking.

'You are making yourself ill,' Rose said. She was tempted to take those poor fluttering hands into her own and steady them, but her flesh shrank from the contact. She was tempted, too, to tell Christabel the truth, but pride forbade her, and in a moment the impulse was gone, and with its departure came the belief that the truth would be annihilating. It would rob her of her glorious uncertainty, she would be destroyed by the knowledge that Rose had seen her fear, seen and tried to strengthen the slender hold she had on her husband's love. It was better to play the part of the wicked woman, the murderess, the stealer of hearts: and perhaps she was wicked; she had not thought of that before; the Malletts did not criticize their actions or analyse their minds and she had no intention of breaking their habits. She stood up again and said:

'Shall I call the nurse?'

'You're not going yet? You've only been here a few minutes.'

'Long enough,' Rose said cheerfully.

Tears came into Christabel's eyes. 'And Francis is out. If he doesn't see you he'll be angry, he'll ask me why.'

'You can tell him.'

'But,' the tone changed, 'perhaps you'll see him on your way home.'

'Yes, and then I can tell him instead.'

The tears overflowed, she was helplessly angry, she sobbed.

'Be quiet,' Rose said sternly. 'I shall tell him nothing. You know that. You are quite safe, whatever you choose to say to me. Perfectly safe.'

'I know. I can't help it. I lie here and think. What would you do in my place?'

'The same thing, I suppose,' Rose said.

'And you won't go?'

'Yes, I'm going. You can tell Francis I was obliged to get home early.'

'But you'll come again?'

'Oh, yes, I'll come again.'

'You don't want to.'

'No, I don't want to.'

'But you're always riding over here, aren't you?'

'Nearly every day.'

'Oh, then –' The words lingered meaningly until Rose reached the door and then Christabel said, 'I wish you'd ask your sisters to come and see me. They would tell me all the news.'

Rose went downstairs laughing at Christabel's capacity for mingling tragedy with the commonplace and sordid accusations with social desires, but though she laughed she was strangely tired and, stretching before her, she saw more weariness, more struggling, more effort without result.

She stood in the masculine, matted hall, with the usual worn pair of slippers in the corner, a stick lying across a chair, a collection of coats and hats on the pegs, and she felt she would be glad if she were never to see all this again, and for the first time she thought seriously of desertion. She wished she could go to some unfamiliar country where the people would all have new faces, where the language would be strange, the sights different, the smells unlike those which were wafted through the open door. She wanted a fresh body and a new world, but she knew that she would not get them, for leaving Francis would be like leaving a child. So she told herself, but at the back of her mind was the certainty that if she went he would soon attach himself to another's strength – or weakness: yes, to another's weakness, and she found she could not contemplate that event, less because she clung to him than because her pride could not tolerate a substitution which would be an admission of her likeness to other women. Yet in that very lack of toleration her pride was lowered, and if she was not clinging to him for her own sake, she was holding on to her place, her uniqueness, refusing the possibility that another woman could serve him, as she had served him with pain, with suffering. She was like a queen who does not love her throne supremely but will not abdicate, who would rather fail in her appointed place than see another succeed in it.

For a minute Rose Mallett sat down on the edge of the chair already occupied by the stick and she pressed both hands against her forehead, driving back her thoughts. Thinking was dangerous and a folly: it was a concession to circumstances, and she would concede nothing. She stood up, looked round for a mirror, remembered there was not one in the hall, and with little, meticulous touches to her hat, her hair and the white stock round her neck, she left the house.

She returned to a drawing-room occupied by Caroline and Sophia, yet strangely silent. There was not a sound but what came from the birds in the garden. Caroline's spectacles were on her nose and, though she was not reading the letter on her knee, she had forgotten to take them off, an ominous sign. Sophia's face was flushed with agitation, her head drooped more than usual, but she lifted it with a sigh of relief at Rose's entrance.

'We're in such trouble, dear,' she said.

'Trouble! Nonsense! No trouble at all! Look here, Rose, that woman has died now.' She shook the letter threateningly. 'Read this! Reginald's wife! I suppose she was his wife. I dare say he had dozens.'

'Caroline!' Sophia remonstrated.

Rose took the letter and read what Mrs. Reginald Mallett, believing herself about to die, had written in her big, sprawling hand. The letter was only to be posted after her death and she made no apology for asking the Malletts to see that her daughter had the chance of earning her living suitably. 'She is a good girl,' she wrote, 'but when I am gone her only friend will be the landlady of this house and there are young men about the place who are not the right kind. I am telling my dear girl that I wish her to accept any offer of help she gets from you, and she will do what I ask.'

'So, you see,' Caroline said as Rose looked up, 'we're not done with Reginald yet, and what I propose is that we send Susan for the girl to-morrow.'

64

'Yes, to-morrow,' Sophia echoed.

'Shall I go?' Rose asked. Sophia murmured gratitude, Caroline snorted doubt, and Rose added, 'No, I think not. She wouldn't like it. Susan would be better – but not to-morrow. You must write to the child – what's her name? Henrietta –'

'Yes, Henrietta, after our grandmother – the idea! I don't know how Reginald dared.'

'Is she a sacred character?' Rose asked dryly. 'Write to her, Caroline, and say Susan will come on the day that suits her best. You can't drag her away without warning. Let's treat her courteously, please.'

'Oh, Rose, dear, I think we are always courteous,' Sophia protested.

Caroline merely said, 'Bah!' and added, 'And what are we going to do with her when we get her? She'll giggle, she'll have a dreadful accent, Sophia will blush for her. I shan't. I never blush for anybody, even myself, but I shall be bored. That's worse, and if you think I'm going to edit my stories for her benefit, Sophia, you're mistaken. I never managed to do that, even for the General, and I'm too old to begin.' She removed her spectacles hastily. 'Too old for that, anyhow.'

Rose smiled. She thought that probably the child of Reginald Mallett, living from hand to mouth in boarding houses, the sharer of his sinking fortunes, the witness of his passions and despairs and infidelities, would find Caroline's stories innocent enough. Her hope was that Henrietta would not try to cap them, but the chances were that she would be a terrible young person, that she would find herself adrift in the respectability of Radstowe where she was unlikely to meet those young men, not of the right kind, to whom she was accustomed.

'She must have her father's room,' Sophia said. She was trying to conceal her excitement. 'We must put some flowers there. I think I'll just go upstairs and see if there's any little improvement we could make.'

They all went upstairs and stood in that room devoted

to the memory of the scapegrace, but they made no alterations, Sophia expressing the belief that Henrietta would prefer it as it was; and Caroline, as she wiped away two slow tears, saying that Reginald was a wretch and she could not see why they should put themselves to any trouble for his daughter.

Book II : *Henrietta*

AFTER luncheon Henrietta went to her room to unpack the brown tin trunk which contained all her possessions, and as she ascended the stairs with her hand on the polished mahogany rail, she heard Sophia saying, 'She's a true Mallett. She has the Mallett ankle. Did you notice it, Caroline?' And Caroline answered harshly, 'Yes, the Mallett ankle, but not the foot. Her foot is square, like a block of wood. What could you expect?' Then the drawing-room door was closed softly on this indiscretion.

Henrietta continued steadily up the stairs and across the landing to her father's room, and before the long mirror on the wall she halted to survey her reflected feet. Aunt Caroline had but exaggerated the truth; they were square, but they were small, and she controlled her trembling lips.

She pushed back from her forehead the black, curling hair. She was tired; the luncheon had been a strain, and the carelessly loud words of Caroline reminded her that she was undergoing an examination which, veiled by courtesy, would be severe. Already they were blaming her mother for her feet; and all three of them, the blunt Caroline, the tender Sophia, the mysteriously silent Rose, were on the watch for the maternal traits.

Well, she was not ashamed of them. Her mother had been good, brave, honest, loving, patient, and her father had been none of these things; but no doubt these aunts of hers put manners before morals, as he had done; and she remembered how, when she was quite a little girl, and the witness of one of the unpleasant domestic scenes which happened often in those days, before Reginald Mallett's wife had learnt forbearance, she had noticed her father's face twitch as though in pain. Glad of a diversion, she had asked him with eager sympathy,

'Is it toothache?' and he had answered acidly, 'No, child, only the mutilation of our language.' She remembered the words, and later she understood their meaning and the flushing of her mother's face, the compression of her lips, and she was indignant for her sake.

Yet she could feel for her father, in spite of the fact that whatever her accent or grammatical mistakes, her mother's conduct was always right and her father, with his charming air, a little blurred by what he called misfortune, his clear speech to which Henrietta loved to listen, was fundamentally unsound. He could not be trusted. That was understood between the mother and daughter: it was one of the facts on which their existence rested, it entered into all their calculations, it was the text of all her mother's little homilies. Henrietta must always pay her debts, she must tell the truth, she must do nothing of which she was ashamed, and so far Henrietta had succeeded in obeying these commands.

When Reginald Mallett died in the shabby boarding-house kept by Mrs. Banks, he left his family without a penny but with a feeling of extraordinary peace. They were destitute, but they were no longer overshadowed by the fear of disgrace, the misery of subterfuge, the bewildering oscillations between pity for the man who could not have what he wanted and shame for his ceaseless striving after pleasure, his shifts to get it, his reproaches and complaints.

In the gloomy back bedroom on the third story of the boarding-house he lay on a bed hung with dingy curtains, but in the dignity which was one of his inheritances. Under the dark, close-cut moustache, his lips seemed to smile faintly, perhaps in amusement at the folly of his life, perhaps in surprise at finding himself so still; the narrow beard of a foreign cut was slightly tilted towards the dirty ceiling, his beautiful hands were folded as though in a mockery of prayer. He was, as Mrs. Banks remarked when she was allowed to see him, a lovely corpse. But to Henrietta and her mother, standing on either side of the bed, guarding him now, as they had always tried to do, he had subtly become the husband and father he should have been.

68

'We must remember him like this,' Mrs. Mallett said, raising her soft blue eyes, and Henrietta saw that the small sharp lines which Reginald Mallett had helped to carve in her face seemed to have disappeared. It was extraordinary how placid her face became after his death, but as the days passed it was also noticeable that much of her vitality had gone too. She left herself in Henrietta's young hands and she, casting about for a way of earning her living, found good fortune in the terrible basement kitchen where Mrs. Banks moved mournfully and had her disconsolate being. The gas was always lighted in that cavernous kitchen, but it remained dark, mercifully leaving the dirt half unseen. A joint of mutton, cold and mangled, was discernible, however, when Henrietta descended to put her impecunious case before the landlady and, gazing at it, the girl saw also her opportunity. Mrs. Banks had no culinary imagination, but Henrietta found it rising in herself to an inspired degree and there and then she offered herself as cook in return for board and lodging for her mother and herself.

'I'm sure I'll be glad to keep you,' Mrs. Banks said: 'you give the place a tone, you do really, you and your dear Ma sitting in the drawing-room sewing of an evening; but it isn't only the cooking, though I do get to hate the sight of food. I get a regular grudge against it. But it's that butcher! Ready money or no meat's his motto, and how to make this mutton last –' She picked it up by the bone and cast it down again.

'Oh, I can manage butchers,' Henrietta said. 'Besides, we'll pay our way. You'll see. Leave the cooking to me.'

'I will, gladly,' Mrs. Banks said, wiping away a tear. 'Ever since Banks took it into his head to jump into the river, it seems like as if I hadn't any spirit, and that Jenkins turns up his ugly nose every time I put the mutton on the table – when he doesn't begin talking to it like an old friend. I can't bear Jenkins, but he does pay regular, and that's something. Well, I'll get on with the upstairs and leave you to it.'

And so Henrietta began the work which kept her amazingly happy, fed and sheltered her mother, who sat all day slowly making beautiful baby linen for one of the big shops, and cemented Henrietta's friendship with the lachrymose Mrs. Banks. To be faced with a mutton bone and a few vegetables, to have to wrest from these poor materials an appetizing meal, was like an exciting game, and she played it with zest and with success. She had the dubious pleasure of hearing Mr. Jenkins smack his lips and seeing him distend his nostrils with anticipation; the unalloyed one of watching the pale face of little Miss Stubb, the typist, grow delicately pink and less dangerously thin, under the stimulus of good food; the amusement of congratulating Mrs. Banks, in public, on her new cook, and seeing Mrs. Banks, at the head of the supper table, nod her head with important secrecy.

'I've made out,' she told Henrietta, 'that I've a daily girl, without a character, that's how I can afford her, in the basement, but I must say it's made that Jenkins mighty keen on fetching his own boots of a morning, but no lodgers below-stairs is my rule. You look out for Jenkins, my dear. He's no good. I know his sort.'

'Oh, I can manage Mr. Jenkins, too,' Henrietta said, and indeed she made a point of bringing him to the hardly manageable state for the amusement of proving her capacity. She despised him, but not for nothing was she Reginald Mallett's daughter; and Mr. Jenkins and the butcher and a gloomy old gentleman who emerged from his bedroom to eat, and locked himself up between meals, were the only men she knew. No doubt Mrs. Mallett, placidly sewing, was alive to the attentions and frustrations of Mr. Jenkins and had planned her letter to her sisters-in-law some time before she wrote it, but the idea of parting from her mother never occurred to Henrietta until Miss Stubb alarmed her.

'Your mother,' she said poetically, 'makes me think of snow melting before the sun. In fact, I can't look at her without thinking of snow and snowdrops and – and graves. Last spring I said to Mrs. Banks, "She won't see the leaves fall," I said, and Mrs. Banks agreed. She has been spared, but take care of her in these cold winds, Miss Henrietta, dear.'

'She has a cold, only a cold,' Henrietta said in a dead

70

voice, and she went upstairs. Her mother was in bed, and Henrietta looked down at the thin, pretty face. 'How ill are you?' she asked in a threatening manner. 'Tell me how ill you are.'

'I've only got a cold, Henry dear. I shall be up to-morrow.'

'Promise you won't be really ill.'

'Why should I be?'

'It's Miss Stubb – saying things.'

'Women chatter,' Mrs. Mallett said. 'If it's not scandal, it's an illness. You ought to know that.'

'They might leave you alone, anyway.'

'Yes, I wish they would,' Mrs. Mallett said faintly, and dropped back on her pillow.

Now, sitting in her father's room, with her mother only a few weeks dead, she reproached herself for her readiness to be deceived, for her preoccupation with her own affairs and the odious Mr. Jenkins, for the exuberance of life which hid from her the dwindling of her mother's, and the fact, now so plain, that when Reginald Mallett died his wife's capacity for struggling was at an end. She had suffered bitterly from the sight of his deterioration and from her failure to prevent it. In his sulky, torturing presence she had desired his absence, but this permanent absence was more than she could bear. And all Henrietta could do was to obey her mother's injunction to accept help from her aunts, but she had refused the offer of an escort to Radstowe and Nelson Lodge; she would have no highly respectable servant sniffing at the boarding-house – and she would have been bound to sniff in that permanently scented atmosphere – which was, after all, her home. She left with genuine regret, with tears.

'You mustn't cry, dearie,' Mrs. Banks said, holding Henrietta to the bosom of her greasy dress. 'It's a lucky thing for you.'

'Perhaps,' Henrietta said, 'but I'd rather be with you, and I can't bear to think of the cooking going to pieces. I'll send you some recipes for nice dishes.'

'Too many eggs,' Mrs. Banks said prophetically.

'I dare say, but you can manage if you think about it. And remember, if Miss Stubb has too much cold mutton, she'll lose her job, and then you'll lose her money. It will pay you to feed her. You haven't had a debt since I began to help you.'

'I know, I know; but I'll have them now, for certain. I've told you before that Banks took all my ideas with him when he dropped into the river,' Mrs. Banks said hopelessly, and on Henrietta's journey to Radstowe it was of Mrs. Banks that she chiefly thought. It seemed as though she were deserting a friend.

She was surprised by the smallness of Nelson Lodge as she walked up the garden path; she had pictured something more imposing than this low white building, walled off from the wide street; but within she discovered an inconsistent spaciousness. The hall was panelled in white wood, the drawing-room, sparsely but beautifully furnished, was white too, and she immediately felt, as indeed she looked, thoroughly out of harmony with her surroundings. She waited there, in her cheap black clothes, like some little servant seeking a situation; but her welcome, when it came, after a rustling of silken skirts on the stairs, assured her that she was acknowledged as a member of the family. Sophia took her tenderly to her heart and murmured, 'Oh, my dear, how like your father!' Caroline patted her cheek and said, 'Yes, yes, Reginald's daughter, so she is!' And a moment later, Rose entered, faintly smiling, extending a cool hand.

Henrietta's acutely feminine eye saw immediately that her Aunt Rose was supremely well-dressed, and all her past ideas of grandeur, of plumed hats and feather boas and ornamental walking shoes, left her for ever. She knew, too, that clothes like these were very costly, beyond her dreams, but she decided, in a moment, to rearrange and subdue the black trimming of her hat.

On the other hand, the appearance of the elder aunts almost shocked her. At the first glance they seemed bedizened and indecent in their mixture of rouge and more than middle age; but at the second and the third they became attractive, oddly distinguished. She felt sure of them, of their sympathy, of her ability to please them. It was Aunt

72

Rose who made her feel ill at ease, and it was Aunt Rose of whom she thought as she sat by her bedroom window and looked down at the back garden, bright with the flowers of spring.

Yet it was Aunt Caroline who had been unkind about her feet. They were like that, these grand people; they had beautiful manners but nothing superficial escaped them; they made no allowances, they went in for no deceptions, and though it was Caroline who had actually condemned the small, strong feet which now rested, slipperless, on the soft carpet, Henrietta was sure that Rose had seen them too. She had seen everything, though apparently she saw nothing, and Henrietta had to acknowledge her fear of Rose's criticism. It was formidable, for it would be unflinching in its standards.

'Well,' Henrietta thought, 'I can only be myself, and if I'm common – but I'm not really common – it's better than pretending; and of course I am rather upset by the house and the servants and all the forks and spoons. I hope there won't be anything funny to eat for dinner. I wish –' To her own amazement, she burst into a brief storm of tears. 'I wish I had stayed with Mrs. Banks.'

She had her place in the boarding-house, she was a power there, and she missed already her subtle, unrecognized belief in her superiority over Mrs. Banks and Miss Stubb and Mr. Jenkins and the rest. She was also honestly troubled about the welfare of the landlady, who was her only friend. It was strange to sit in her father's room and look at a portrait of him as a youth hanging on the wall, and remember that Mrs. Banks, who made him shudder, was her only friend.

She left her seat by the window to look more closely at that portrait, and after a brief examination she turned to the dressing-table to see in the mirror a feminine replica of the face on the wall. She had never noticed the likeness before. She had only to push back her hair and she saw her father. Where his nose was straight, hers was slightly tilted, but there was the same darkness of hair and eyes, the same modelling of the forehead, the same incipient petulance of the lips.

She was astonished, she was unreasonably pleased, and with the energy of her inspiration she swept back the curls of which her mother had been so proud, and pinned them into obscurity. The resemblance was extraordinary: even the low white collar of her blouse, fastened with a black bow, repeated the somewhat Byronic appearance of the young man; and as there came a knock at the door, she turned, a little shame-faced, but excited in the certainty of her success.

But it was only Susan, who gave no sign of astonishment at the change. She had come to see if she could help Miss Henrietta to unpack, but Henrietta had already laid away her meagre outfit in the walnut tallboy with the curved legs. Susan, however, would remove the trunk, and if Miss Henrietta would tell her what dress she wished to wear this evening, Susan would be able to lay out her things. The tin trunk clanked noisily though Susan lifted it with tactful care, and Henrietta blushed for it, but the aged portmanteau, bearing the initials *R.M.*, became in the discreet presence of Susan a priceless possession.

'It's full of books,' Henrietta said; 'I won't unpack them. I thought my aunts would let me keep them somewhere. They are my father's books.'

'There's an old bookcase belonging to Mr. Reginald in the box-room,' Susan said; 'I'll speak to Miss Caroline about it.'

'Did you know my father?' Henrietta asked at once.

'Yes, Miss Henrietta,' Susan said.

'Do you think I'm like him?'

'It's a striking likeness, Miss Henrietta,' and warming a little, Susan added, 'I was just saying so to Cook.'

'Did Cook know him, too?'

'Oh, yes, Miss Henrietta. Cook and I have been with the family for years. If you'll tell me which dress you wish to wear –'

'There's only one in the wardrobe,' Henrietta said serenely, for suddenly her shabbiness and poverty mattered no longer. She was stamped with the impress of Reginald Mallett, whom

74

she had despised yet of whom she was proud, and that impress was like a guarantee, a sort of passport. She had a great lightness of heart; she was glad she had left Mrs. Banks, glad she was in her father's home, and learning from Susan that the ladies rested in their own rooms after luncheon, she decided to go out and look on the scenes of her father's youth.

§ 2

This was not, she told herself, disloyalty to her mother, for had not that mother, whom she loved and painfully missed, sent her to this place? Her mother was generous and sweet; she would grudge no late-found allegiance to Reginald Mallett. Had she not said they must remember him at his best, and would she not be glad if Henrietta could find bits of that best in this old house, in the streets where he had walked, in the sights which had fed his eyes?

Henrietta started out, gently closing the front door behind her. The wide street was almost empty; a milkcart bearing the legend, 'Sales Hall Dairy,' was being drawn at an easy pace by a demure pony, his harness adorned with jingling bells. The milkman whistled and, as the cart stopped here and there, she missed the London milkman's harsh cry, and missed it pleasurably. This man was in no hurry, there was no impatience in his knock; the whole place seemed to be half asleep, except where children played on The Green under the old trees. This comparatively small space, mounting in the distance to a little hill backed by the sky, was more wonderful to Henrietta than Hyde Park when the flowers were at their best. There were no flowers here; she saw grass, two old stone monuments, tall trees, a miniature cliff of grey rock, and sky. On three sides of The Green there were old houses and there were seats on the grass, but houses and seats had the air of being mere accidents to which the rest had grown accustomed, and it seemed to Henrietta that here, in spite of bricks, she was in the country. The trees, the grass, the rocks and sky were in possession.

She followed one of the small paths round the hill and found herself in a place so wonderful, so unexpected, that she caught

75

back her breath and let it out again in low exclamations of delight. She was now on the other side of the hill and, though she did not know it, she was on the site of an ancient camp. The hill was flat-topped; there were still signs of the ramparts, but it was not on these she gazed. Far below her was the river, flowing sluggishly in a deep ravine, formed on her right hand and as far as she could see by high grey cliffs. These for the most part were bare and sheer, but they gave way now and then to a gentler slope with a rich burden of trees, while, on the other side of the river, it was the rocks that seemed to encroach on the trees, for the wall of the gorge, almost to the water's edge, was thick with woods. Here and there, on either cliff, a sudden red splash of rock showed like an unhealed wound, amid the healthier grey. And all around her there seemed to be limitless sky, huge fluffy clouds and gulls as white.

At the edge of the cliff where she stood, gorse bushes bloomed and, looking to the left, she saw the slender line of a bridge swung high across the abyss. Beyond it the cliffs lessened into banks, then into meadows studded with big elms and, on the city side, there were houses red and grey, as though the rocks had simply changed their shapes. The houses were clustered close to the water, they rose in terraces and trees mingled with their chimneys. Below there were intricate waterways, little bridges, warehouses and ships and, high up, the fairy bridge, delicate and poised, was like a barrier between that place of business and activity and this, where Henrietta stood with the trees, the cliffs, the swooping gulls. It was low tide and the river was bordered by banks of mud, grey too, yet opalescent. It almost reflected the startling white of the gulls' wings and, as she looked at it, she saw that its colour was made up of many; there was pink in it and blue and, as a big cloud passed over the sun, it became subtly purple; it was a palette of subdued and tender shades.

Henrietta heaved a sigh. This was too much. She could look at it but she could not see it all. Yet this marvellous place belonged to her, and she knew now whence had come the glamour in the stories her father had told her when she was a child. It had come from here, where an aged city had

76

tried to conquer the country and had failed, for the spirit of woods and open spaces, of water and trees and wind, survived among the very roofs. The conventions of the centuries, the convention of puritanism, of worldliness, of impiety, of materialism and of charity had all assailed and all fallen back before the strength of the apparently peaceful country in which the city stood. The air was soft with a peculiar, undermining softness; it carried with it a smell of flowers and fruit and earth, and if all the many miles on the farther side of the bridge should be ravished by men's hands, covered with buildings and strewn with the ugly luxuries they thought they needed, the spirit would remain in the tainted air and the imprisoned earth. It would whisper at night at the windows, it would smile invisibly under the sun, it would steal into men's minds and work its will upon them. And already Henrietta felt its power. She was in a new world, dull but magical, torpid yet alert.

She turned away and, walking down another little path threaded through the rocks, she stood at the entrance to the bridge and watched people on foot, people on bicycles, people in carts coming and going over it. She could not cross herself for she had not a penny in her pocket, but she stood there gazing and sometimes looking down at the road two hundred feet below. This made her slightly giddy and the people down there had too much the appearance of pigmies with legs growing from their necks, going about perfectly unimportant business with a great deal of fuss. It was pleasanter to see these country people in their carts, school-girls with plaits down their backs, rosy children in perambulators and an exceedingly handsome man on a fine black horse, a fair man, bronzed like a soldier, riding as though he had done it all his life.

She looked at him with admiration for his looks and envy for his possessions, for that horse, that somewhat sulky ease. And it was quite possible that he was an acquaintance of her aunts! She laughed away her awed astonishment. Why, her own father had been such as he, though she had never seen him on a horse. She had, after all, to adjust her views a little, to remember that she was a Mallett, a member of an honoured Radstowe family, the granddaughter of a General, the daughter of a gentleman, though a scamp. She was ashamed of the something approaching reverence with which she had looked at the man on the horse, but she was also ashamed of her shame; in fact, to be ashamed at all was, she felt, a degradation, and she cast the feeling from her.

Here was not only a new world but a new life, a new starting point; she must be equal to the place, the opportunity and the occasion; she was, she told herself, equal to them all.

In this self-confident mood she returned to Nelson Lodge and found Caroline, in a different frock, seated behind the tea-table and in the act of putting the tea into the pot.

'Just in time,' she remarked, and added with intense interest, 'You have brushed back your hair. Excellent! Look, Sophia, what an improvement! And more like Reginald than ever. Take off your hat, child, and let us see. My dear, I was going to tell you, when I knew you better, that those curls made you look like an organ-grinder. Don't hush me, Sophia; I always say what I think.'

Henrietta was hurt; this, though Caroline did not know it, was a rebuff to the mother who loved the curls; but the daughter would not betray her sensibility, and as Rose was not present she dared to say, 'An organ-grinder with square feet.'

'Oh, you heard that, did you? Sophia said you would. Well, you must be careful about your shoes. Men always look at a woman's feet.' She displayed her own, elegantly arched, in lustrous stockings and very high-heeled slippers. 'Sophia and I – Sophia's are nearly, but not quite as good as mine – are they Sophia? – Sophia and I have always been particular about our feet. I remember a ball, when I was a girl, where one of my partners – he ended by marrying a ridiculously fat woman with feet like cannon balls – insisted on calling me Cinderella because he said nobody else could have worn my shoes. Delightful creature! Do you remember, Sophia?'

Sophia remembered very well. He had called her Cinderella, too, for the same reason, but as Caroline had been the first to report the remark, Sophia had never cared to spoil her pleasure in it. And now Caroline did not wait for a reply, Rose entering at that moment, and her attention having to be called to the change in Henrietta's method of doing her hair. Henrietta stiffened at once, but Rose threw, as it were, a smile in her direction, and said, 'Yes, charming,' and helped herself to cake.

'And now,' said Caroline, settling herself for the most interesting subject in the world, 'your clothes, Henrietta.'

'I haven't any,' Henrietta said at once; 'but I think they'll do until I go away. I thought I should like to be a nurse, Aunt Caroline.'

'Nurse! Nonsense! What kind? Babies? Rubbish! You're going to stay here if you like us well enough, and we've made a little plan' – she nodded vigorously – 'a little plan for you.'

'We ought to say at once,' Sophia interrupted with painful honesty, 'that it was Rose's idea.'

'Rose? Was it? I don't know. Anyhow, we're all agreed. You are to have a sum of money, child; yes, for your father's sake, and perhaps for your own too, a sum of money to bring you in a little income for your clothes and pleasures, so that you shall be independent like the rest of us. Yes, it's settled. I've written to our lawyer, James Batty. Did your father ever mention James Batty? But, of course, he wouldn't. He married a fat woman, too, but a good soul, with a high colour, poor thing. Don't say a word, child. You must be independent. Nursing! Bah! And if we don't take care we shall have you marrying for a home.'

'This is your home,' Sophia said gently.

'No sentiment, Sophia, please. You're making the child cry. The Malletts don't marry, Henrietta. Look at us, as happy as the day is long, with all the fun and none of the trouble. We've been terrible flirts, Sophia and I. Rose is different, but at least she hasn't married. The three Miss Malletts of Nelson Lodge! Now there are four of us, and you must keep up our reputation.'

Overwhelmed by this generosity, by this kindness, Henrietta

did not know what to say. She murmured something about her mother's wish that she should earn her living, but Caroline scouted the idea, and Sophia, putting her white hand on one of Henrietta's, assured her that her dear mother would be glad for her child to have the comforts of a home.

'I'm not used to them,' Henrietta said. 'I've always taken care of people. I shan't know what to do.'

They would find plenty for her to do; there were many gaieties in Radstowe and she would be welcomed everywhere. 'And now about your clothes,' Caroline repeated. 'You are wearing black, of course. Well, black can be very pretty, very French. Look at Rose. She rarely wears anything else, but when Sophia and I were about your age, she used to wear blue and I wore pink, or the other way round.'

'You do so still,' Rose remarked.

'A pink muslin,' Caroline went on in a sort of ecstasy, 'a Leghorn hat wreathed with pink roses – when was I wearing that, Sophia?'

'Last summer,' Rose said dryly.

'So I was,' Caroline agreed in a matter-of-fact voice. 'Now, Henrietta. Get a piece of paper and a pencil, Sophia, and we'll make a list.'

The discussion went on endlessly, long after Henrietta herself had tired of it. It was lengthened by the insertion of anecdotes of Caroline's and Sophia's youth, and hardly a colour or a material was mentioned which did not recall an incident which Henrietta found more interesting than her own sartorial affairs.

Rose had disappeared, and the dressing-bell was rung before the subject languished. It would never be exhausted, for Caroline, and even Sophia, less vivid than her sister in all but her affections, grew pink and bright-eyed in considering Henrietta's points. And all the time Henrietta had her own opinions, her own plans. She intended as far as possible to preserve her likeness to her father, which was, as it were, her stock-in-trade. She pictured herself, youthfully slim, gravely petulant, her round neck rising from a Byronic collar fastened with a broad, loose bow, and she fancied the society of Radstowe exclaiming with one voice, 'That must be Reginald Mallett's daughter!'

She was to learn, however, that in Radstowe the memories of Reginald Mallett were somewhat dim, and where they were clear they were neglected. It was generally assumed that his daughter would not care to have him mentioned, while praises of her aunts were constant and enthusiastic and people were kind to Henrietta, she discovered, for their sakes.

The stout and highly-coloured Mrs. Batty was an early caller. She arrived, rather wheezy, compressed by her tailor into an expensive gown, a basket of spring flowers on her head. She and Henrietta took to each other, as Mrs. Batty said, at once. Here was a motherly person, and Henrietta knew that if she could have Mrs. Batty to herself she would be able to talk more freely than she had done since her arrival in Radstowe. There would be no criticism from her, but unlimited good nature, a readiness to listen and to confide and a love for the details of operations and illnesses in which she had a kinship with Mrs. Banks. Indeed, though Mrs. Batty was fat where Mrs. Banks was thin, cheerful where she was gloomy, and in possession of a flourishing husband where Mrs. Banks irritably mourned the loss of a suicide, they had characteristics in common and the chief of these was the way in which they took to Henrietta.

'You must come to tea on Sunday,' Mrs. Batty said. 'We are always at home on Sunday afternoons after four o'clock. I have two big boys,' she sighed, 'and all their friends are welcome then.' She lowered her voice. 'We don't allow tennis – the neighbours, you know, and James has clients looking out of every window – but there's no harm, as the boys say, in knocking the billiard balls about. I must say the click carries a good way, so I tell the parlourmaid to shut the windows. And music – my boy Charles,' she sighed again, 'is mad on music. I like a tune myself, but he never plays any. You'll hear for yourself if you come on Sunday. Now you will come, won't you, Miss Henrietta?'

'Yes, she'll come,' Caroline said. 'Do her good to meet young people. We're getting old in this house, Mrs. Batty,' and she guffawed in anticipation of the usual denial, but for once Mrs. Batty failed. Her thoughts were at home, at Prospect House, that commodious family mansion situate in its own grounds, and in one of the most favourable positions in Upper Radstowe. So the advertisement had read before Mr. Batty bought the property, and it was all true.

'John,' Mrs. Batty went on, 'is more for sport, though he's in the sugar business, with an uncle. Not my brother – Mr. Batty's.' She was anxious to give her husband all the credit. 'They are both good boys,' she added, 'but Charles – well, you'll see on Sunday. You promise to come.'

Henrietta promised, and with Mrs. Batty's departure Caroline spoke her mind. She was convinced that the lawyer and his wife were determined to secure Henrietta as a daughter-in-law.

'He knows all our affairs, my dear, and James Batty never misses a chance of improving his position. Good as it is, it would be all the better for an alliance with our family, but I shall disown you at once if you marry one of those hobble-dehoys. The Batty's, indeed! Why, Mrs. Batty herself –'

'Caroline, don't!' Sophia pleaded. 'And I'm sure the young men are very nice young men, and if Henrietta should fall in love –'

'She won't get any of my money!' Caroline said.

'But Henrietta won't be in a hurry,' Sophia announced; and so, over her head, the two discussed her possible marriage as they had discussed her clothes, but with less interest and at less length and, as before, Henrietta had her own ideas. A rich man, a handsome one, a gay life; no more basement kitchens, no more mutton bones! Already the influence of Nelson Lodge was making itself felt.

§ 3

It was at dinner that the charm of the house was most apparent to Henrietta. Even on these spring evenings the curtains were drawn and the candles lighted, for Caroline said she could not dine comfortably in daylight. The pale flames were repeated in the mahogany of the table; the tall candlesticks, the silver appointments, were reflected also in a blur, like a grey mist; the furniture against the walls became merged into the shadows and Susan, hovering there, was no more than an attentive spirit.

There was little talking at this meal, for Caroline and Sophia loved good food and it was very good. Occasionally Caroline murmured, 'Too much pepper,' or 'One more pinch of salt and this would have been perfect,' and bending over her plate, the diamonds in her ears sparkled to her movements, the rings on her fingers glittered; and opposite to her Sophia drooped, her pale hair looking almost white, the big sapphire cross on her breast gleaming richly, her resigned attitude oddly at variance with the busy handling of her knife and fork.

The gold frame round General Mallett's portrait dimly shone, the flowers on the table seemed to give out their beauty and their scent with conscious desire to please, to add their offerings, and for Henrietta the grotesqueness of the elder aunts, their gay attire, their rouge and wrinkles, gave a touch of fantasy to what would otherwise have been too orderly and too respectable a scene.

In this room of beautiful inherited things, where tradition had built strong walls about the Malletts, the sight of Caroline was like a gate leading into the wide, uncertain world and the sight of Rose, all cream and black, was like a secret portal leading to a winding stair. At this hour, romance was in the house, beckoning Henrietta to follow through that gate or down that stair, but chiefly hovering about the figure of Rose who sat so straight and kept so silent, her white hands moving slowly, the pearls glistening on her neck, her face a pale oval against the darkness. She was never more mysterious or more remote; with her even the common acts of eating and drinking seemed, to Henrietta, to be made poetical; she was different from everybody else, but the girl felt vaguely that the wildness of which Caroline made a boast and which never developed into more than that, the wildness which had ruined her father's life, lay numbed and checked somewhere behind the amazing stillness and control of Rose. And she was like a woman who had suffered a great sorrow or who kept a profound secret.

It was at this hour, when Henrietta was half awed, half soothed, yet very much alive, feeling that tremendous excitements lay in wait for her just outside, when she was wrapped in beauty, fed by delicate food, sensitive to the slim old silver under her hands, that she sometimes felt herself actually carried back to the boarding-house, and she saw the grimy tablecloth, the flaring gas jets, the tired worn faces, the dusty hair of Mrs. Banks and the rubber collar of Mr. Jenkins, and she heard little Miss Stubb uttering platitudes in her attempt to raise the mental atmosphere. There was a great clatter of knives and forks, a confusion of voices and, in a pause, the sound of the exclusive old gentleman masticating his food.

Then Henrietta would close her eyes and, after an instant, she would open them on this candle-lighted room, the lovely figure of Aunt Rose, the silks and laces and ornaments of Aunt Caroline and Aunt Sophia; and between the courses one of these two would repeat the gossip of a caller or criticize the cut of her dress.

No, the conversation was not much better than that of the boarding-house, but the accents were different. Caroline would throw out a French phrase, and Henrietta, loving the present, wondering how she had borne the past, could yet feel fiercely that life was not fair. She herself was not fair: she was giving her allegiance to the outside of things and finding in them more pleasure than in heroism, endurance and compassion, and she said to herself, 'Yes, I'm just like my father. I see too much with my eyes.' A little fear, which had its own delight, took hold of her. How far would that likeness carry her? What dangerous qualities had he passed on to her with his looks?

She sat there, vividly conscious of herself, and sometimes she saw the whole room as a picture and she was part of it; sometimes she saw only those three whose lives, she felt, were practically over, for even Aunt Rose was comparatively old. She pitied them because their romance was past, while hers waited for her outside; she wondered at their happiness, their interest in their appearance, their pleasure in parties; but she felt most sorry for Aunt Rose, midway between what should have been the resignation of her stepsisters and the glowing anticipation of her niece. Yet Aunt Rose hardly invited sympathy of any kind and the smile always lurking near her lips gave Henrietta a feeling of discomfort, a suspicion that Aunt Rose was not only ironically aware of what Henrietta wished to conceal, but endowed with a fund of wisdom and a supply of worldly knowledge.

She continued to feel uncertain about Aunt Rose. She was always charming to Henrietta, but it was impossible to be quite at ease with a being who seemed to make an art of being delicately reserved; and because Henrietta liked to establish relationships in which she was sure of herself and her power to please, she was conscious of a faint feeling of antagonism towards this person who made her doubt herself.

Aunt Caroline and Aunt Sophia were evidently delighted with their niece's presence in the house. They liked the sound of her laughter and her gay voice and though Sophia once gently reproached her for her habit of whistling, which was not that of a young lady, Caroline scoffed at her old-fashioned sister.

'Let the girl whistle, if she wants to,' she said. 'It's better than having a canary in a cage.'

'But don't do it too much, Henrietta, dear,' Sophia compromised. 'You mustn't get wrinkles round your mouth.'

'No.' This was a consideration which appealed to Caroline. 'No, child, you mustn't do that.'

They admitted her to a familiarity which they would not have allowed her, and which she never attempted, to exceed, but she was Reginald's daughter, she was a member of the family, and her offence in being also the daughter of her mother was forgotten. Caroline and Sophia were deeply interested in Henrietta. Henrietta was grateful and affectionate. The three were naturally congenial, and the happiness and sympathy of the trio accentuated the pleasant aloofness of Rose. Aunt Rose did not care for her, Henrietta told herself; there was something odd about Aunt Rose, yet she remembered that it was Aunt Rose who had thought of giving her the money.

Three thousand pounds! It was a fortune, and on that Sunday when Henrietta was to pay her first visit to Mrs. Batty, Aunt Caroline, turning the girl about to see that nothing was amiss, said warningly, 'You are walking into the lion's den, Henrietta. Don't let one of those young cubs gobble you up. I know James Batty, an attractive man, but he loves money, and he knows our affairs. He married his own wife because she was a butcher's daughter.'

'A wholesale butcher,' Sophia murmured in extenuation, 'and I am sure he loved her.'

'And butchers,' Caroline went on, 'always amass money. It positively inclines one to vegetarianism, though I'm sure nuts are bad for the complexion.'

'I don't intend to be eaten yet,' Henrietta said gaily. She was very much excited and she hardly heeded Sophia's whisper at the door:

'It's not true, dear – the kindest people in the world, but Caroline has such a sense of humour.'

Henrietta found that the Batty lions were luxuriously housed. The bright yellow gravel crunched under her feet as she walked up the drive; the porch was bright with flowering plants arranged in tiers; a parlourmaid opened the door as though she conferred a privilege and, as Henrietta passed through the hall, she had glimpses of a statue holding a large fern and another bearing a lamp aloft.

She was impressed by this magnificence; she wished she could pause to examine this decently draped and useful statuary but she was ushered into a large drawing-room, somewhat over-heated, scented with hot-house flowers, softly carpeted, much-becushioned, and she immediately found herself in the embrace of Mrs. Batty, who smelt of eau-de-cologne. Mrs. Batty felt soft, too, and if she were a lioness there were no signs of claws or fangs; and her husband, a tall, spare man with grey hair and a clean-shaven face, bowed over Henrietta's hand in a courtly manner, hardly to be expected of the best-trained of wild beasts.

But for these two the room seemed to be empty, until Mrs. Batty said 'Charles!' in a tone of timid authority and Henrietta discovered that a fair young man, already showing a tendency to baldness, was sitting at the piano, apparently studying a sheet of music. This, then, was one of the cubs, and Henrietta, feeling herself marvellously at ease in this house, awaited his approach with some amusement and a little irritation at his obvious lack of interest. Aunt Caroline need have no fear. He was a plain young man with pale, vague eyes, and he did not know whether to offer one of his nervous hands at the end of over-long arms, or to make shift with an awkward bow. She settled the matter for him, feeling very much a woman of the world.

'Now, where's John?' Mrs. Batty asked, and Charles answered, 'Ratting, in the stable.'

Mrs. Batty clucked with vexation. 'It's the first Sunday for weeks that I haven't had the room full of people. Now you won't want to come again. Very dull for a young girl, I'm sure.'

'Well, well, you can have a chat with Miss Henrietta,' Mr. Batty said, 'and afterwards perhaps she would like to see my flowers.' He disappeared with extraordinary skill, with the strange effect of not having left the room, yet Mrs. Batty sighed. Charles had wandered back to the piano, and his mother, after compressing her lips and whispering, 'It's a mania,' drew Henrietta into the depths of a settee.

'Will he play to us?' she asked.

'No, no,' Mrs. Batty answered hastily. 'He's so particular. Why, if I asked you to have another cup of tea, he'd shut the piano, and that makes things very uncomfortable indeed. You can imagine. And John has this new dog – really I don't think it's right on a Sunday. It's all dogs and cricket with him. Well, cricket's better than football, for really, on a Saturday in the winter I never know whether I shall see him dead or alive. I do wish I'd had a girl.' She took

87

Henrietta's hand. 'And you, poor dear child, without a mother – what was it she died of, my dear? Ah, you'll miss her, you'll miss her! My own dear mother died the day after I was married, and I said to Mr. Batty, "This can bode no good." We had to come straight back from Bournemouth, where we'd gone for our honeymoon, and by the time I was out of black my trousseau was out of fashion. I must say Mr. Batty was very good about it. It was her heart, what with excitement and all that. She was a stout woman. All my side runs to stoutness, but Mr. Batty's family are like hop-poles. Well, I believe it's healthier, and I must say the boys take after him. Now I fancy you're rather like Miss Rose.'

'They say I am just like my father.'

Mrs. Batty said 'Ah!' with meaning, and Henrietta tried to sit straighter on the seductive settee. She could not allow Mrs. Batty to utter insinuating ejaculations and, raising her voice, she said:

'Mr. Batty, do play something.'

Charles Batty gazed at her over the shining surface of the grand piano and looked remarkably like an owl, an owl that had lost its feathers.

'Something? What?'

'Charles!' exclaimed Mrs. Batty.

'Oh, I don't know,' Henrietta murmured. She could think of nothing but a pictorial piece of music her mother had sometimes played on the lodging-house piano, with the growling of thunder-storms, the twittering of birds after rain and a suggestion of church bells, but she was determined not to betray herself.

'Whatever you like.'

He broke into a popular waltz, playing it derisively, yet with passion, so that Mrs. Batty's ponderous head began to sway and Henrietta's feet to tap. He played as though his heart were in the dance, and to Henrietta there came delightful visions, thrilling sensations, unaccountable yearnings. It was like the music she had heard at the theatre, but more beautiful. Her eyes widened, but she kept them lowered, her mouth softened and she caught her lip.

'Now I call that lovely,' Mrs. Batty said, with the last chord. His look questioned Henrietta and she, cautious, simply smiled at him, with a tilt of the lips, a little raising of the eyebrows, meant to assure him that she felt as he did.

'If you'd play a pretty tune like that now and then, people would be glad to listen,' Mrs. Batty went on. 'I'm sure I quite enjoyed it.'

Henrietta's suspicions were confirmed by these eulogies: she knew already that what Mrs. Batty appreciated, her son would despise, and she kept her little smile, saying tactfully, 'It certainly made one want to dance.'

'Can you sing?' he asked.

'Oh, a little.' She became timid. 'I'm going to learn.' With those vague eyes staring at her, she felt the need of justification. 'Aunt Caroline says every girl ought to sing. She and Aunt Sophia used to sing duets.'

'Good heavens!' The exclamation came from the depths of Charles Batty's being. 'They don't do it now, do they?'

Henrietta's pretty laughter rang out. 'No, not now.' But though she laughed there came to her a rather charming picture of her aunts in full skirts and bustles, their white shoulders bare, with sashes round their waists and a sheet of music shared, their mouths open, their eyes cast upwards.

'Every girl ought to sing,' Charles quoted, and suddenly darted at Henrietta the word, 'Why?'

'Oh, well –' It was ridiculous to be discomposed by this young man, to whom, she was sure, she was naturally superior; but sitting behind that piano as though it were a pulpit, he had an air of authority and she was anxious to propitiate him. 'Well –' Henrietta repeated, hanging on the word.

'For your own glorification, that's all,' Charles told her. 'That's all.' He caught his head in his hands. 'It drives me mad.'

'Charles!' Mrs. Batty said again. That word seemed to be the whole extent of her intercourse with him.

'Mad! Music – divine! And people get up and squeak. How they dare! A violation of the temple!'

'Oh, dear me!' Mrs. Batty groaned.

89

'You play the piano yourself,' Henrietta said.

'Because I can. I'd show you if you cared about it.'

'I think I would rather go and see Mr. Batty's flowers.'

'Yes, dear, do. Charles, take her to your father.' Mrs. Batty was very hot; it would be a relief to her to heave and sigh alone.

Charles rose and advanced, stooping a little, carrying his arms as though they did not belong to him and, in the hall, beside one of the gleaming statues, he paused.

'I've offended you,' he said miserably. 'I make mistakes – somehow. Nobody explains. I shall do it again.'

'You were rather rude,' Henrietta said. 'Why should you assume that I squeak?'

'Sure to,' Charles said hopelessly, 'or gurgle. Look here, I'll teach you myself, if you like.'

'I won't be bullied.'

'Then you'll never learn anything. Women are funny,' he said; 'but then everybody is. Do you know, I haven't a single friend in the world?'

'Why not?'

He shook his head. 'I don't know. I don't get on.'

'If it comes to that, I haven't a friend of my own age, either. And you have a brother.'

'Ratting!' Charles said eloquently. 'You'll hear the noise.' He handed her over to his father's care.

She was more than satisfied with her afternoon. She did not see John Batty but she heard the noise; she was aware that Mr. Batty considered her a delightful young person; she had sufficiently admired his flowers and he presented her with a bunch of orchids. For Mrs. Batty she felt an amused affection; she was interested in the unfortunate Charles. She felt her life widening pleasantly and, as she crunched again down the gravel drive, the orchids in her hand, she felt a disinclination to go home. She wanted to walk under the great trees which, spread with brilliant green, made a long avenue on the other side of the road; to wander beyond them, where a belt of grass led to a wild shrubbery overlooking the gorge at its lowest point.

Here there were unexpected little paths running out to promontories of the cliff and, at a sudden turn, she would find herself in what looked almost like danger. Below her the rock was at an angle to harbour hawthorn trees all in bud, blazing gorse bushes, bracken stiffly uncurling itself and many kinds of grasses, but there were nearly two hundred feet between her and the river, now at flood, and she felt that this was something of an adventure. She followed each little path in turn, half fearfully, for she was used to a policeman at every corner; but she met no tramp, saw no suspicious-looking character and, finding a seat under a hawthorn tree at a little distance from the cliff's edge, she sat down and put the orchids beside her.

It was part of the strange change in her fortune that she should actually be handling such rare flowers. She had seen them in florists' windows insolently putting out their tongues at people like herself who rudely stared, and now she was touching them and they looked quite polite, and she thought, with the bitterness which, bred of her experiences, constantly rose up in the midst of pleasures, 'It's because they know I have three thousand pounds and six pairs of silk stockings.'

Then she noticed that one of the flowers was missing, a little one of a fairy pink and shape, and almost immediately she heard footsteps on the grass and saw a man approaching with the orchid in his hand. She recognized the man she had seen riding the black horse on the day she arrived in Radstowe and her heart fluttered. This was romance, this, she had time to think excitedly, must be preordained. But when he handed her the flower with a polite, 'I think you dropped this,' she wished he had chosen to keep the trophy. If she had had the happiness of seeing him conceal it!

She said nervously, 'Oh, yes, thank you very much. I'd just missed it,' and as he turned away she had at least the minor joy of seeing a look of arrested interest in his eyes.

She sat there holding the frail and almost sacred branch. She supposed she was in love; there was no other explanation of her feelings; and what a marvellous sequence of

91

events! If Mr. Batty had not given her the orchids this romantic episode could not have happened. And she was glad that the eyes of the stranger had not rested on her that first day when she was wearing her shabby, her atrociously cut clothes. Fate had been kind in allowing him to see her thus, in a black dress with a broad white collar, a carefully careless bow, silk stockings covering her matchless ankles and – she glanced down – shoes that did their best to conceal the squareness of her feet.

She recognized her own absurdity, but she liked it: she had leisure in which to be absurd, she had nothing else to do, and romance, which had seemed to be waiting for her outside Nelson Lodge, had now met her in the open! She was not going to pass it by. This was, she knew, no more than a precious secret, a little game she could play all by herself, but it had suddenly coloured vividly a life which was already opening wider; and she would have been astonished and perhaps disgusted, to learn that Aunt Rose had once occupied herself with similar dreamings. But she was spared that knowledge and she was tempted to wait in her place on the chance that the stranger would return, but, deciding that it was hardly what a Mallett would do, she rose reluctantly, carrying the pink orchid in one hand, the less favoured ones in the other.

The evening was exquisite: she saw a pale-blue sky fretted with green leaves, striped with tree trunks astonishingly black; she heard steamers threshing through the water and giving out warning whistles, sounds to stir the heart with the thoughts of voyage, of danger, and of unknown lands; and as she walked up the long avenue of elms she found that all the people strolling out after tea for an evening walk had happy, pleasant faces.

She met fathers and mothers in loitering advance of children, shy lovers with no words for each other, an old lady in a bath chair propelled by a man as old, young men in check caps, with flowers in their coats, earnest people carrying prayer-books and umbrellas, girls with linked arms and shrill laughter; and she envied none of them: not the children, finding interest in everything they saw; not the parents, proud in possession; not the old lady whose work was done, not the young men and women eyeing each other and letting out their enticing laughter; she envied no one in the world. She had found an occupation, and that night, sitting at the dinner-table, she was conscious of the difference in herself and of a new kinship with these women, the two who could look back on adventures, rosy and poetic, the one who seemed shrouded in some delicate mystery. It was as though she, too, had been initiated; she was surer of herself, even in the presence of Aunt Rose, with her beauty like that of a white flower, the faint irony of her smile.

§ 4

A few days later Rose said, 'I want to take you to see a friend of mine, a Mrs. Sales.'

'Do the milkcarts belong to them?' Henrietta asked at once.

'Yes.' Rose was amused. 'Mrs. Sales is an invalid and she would like to see you. Shall we go on Saturday?' She added as she left the room, 'Mrs. Sales was hurt in a hunting accident, but you need not avoid the subject. She likes to talk about it.'

'What a good thing,' Henrietta said, practically.

Aunt Rose was dressed for walking and Henrietta was afraid of being asked to go with her, but Aunt Rose made no such suggestion. Since Sunday Henrietta had been exploring Radstowe and its suburbs with an enthusiasm surprising to the elder aunts, who did not care for exercise; but Henrietta was as much inspired by the hope of seeing that man again as by interest in the old streets, the unexpected alleys, the flights of worn steps leading from Upper to Lower Radstowe, the slums, cheek by jowl with the garden of some old house, the big houses deteriorated into tenements. All these had their own charm and the added one of having been familiar to her father, but she never forgot to watch for the hero on the horse, the restorer of her orchid. If she met him, should she bow to him, or pretend not to see him? She had practised various expressions before the glass, and had almost decided to look up as he passed and flash a glance of puzzled recognition from her eyes. She thought she could do it satisfactorily and to-day she meant to cross the bridge for the first time. He had been riding over the bridge that afternoon and what had happened once might happen again. Moreover, she had a feeling that across the water there was something waiting for her. Certainly behind the trees clothing the gorge there was the real country, with cows and sheep and horses in the meadows, with the possibility of rabbits in the lanes, and she had never yet seen a rabbit running wild. There were innumerable possibilities on that farther side.

She crossed the bridge, stood to look up and down the river, to watch the gulls, white against the green, to consider the ant-like hurrying of the people on the road below and the clustered houses on the city side, a medley of shapes and colours, rising in terraces, the whole like some immense castle guarding the entrance to the town. And as before, carriages and carts went and came over, schoolgirls on bicycles, babies in perambulators, but this time there was no man on a horse. She knew that this mattered very little; her stimulated excitement was hardly more than salt and pepper to a dish already appetizing enough, and now and then as she went along the road on a level with the tree-tops in the gorge and had glimpses of water and of rock, she had to remind herself of her preoccupation.

She passed big houses with their flowery gardens and then, suddenly timorous, she decided not to go too far afield. She might get lost, she might meet nasty people or horned beasts. A little path on her right hand had an inviting look; it might lead her down through the trees to the water's edge. It was all strewn and richly brown with last autumn's leaves and on a tree a few yards ahead she saw a brilliant object – tiny, long-tailed, extraordinarily swift. It was out of sight before she had time to tell herself that this was a squirrel; and again she had a consciousness of development. She had

94

seen a squirrel in its native haunts! This was wonderful, and she approached the tree. The squirrel had vanished, but these woods, within sound of a city, yet harbouring squirrels, seemed to have become one of her possessions. She was enriched, she was a different person, and she, whose familiar fauna had been stray cats and the black beetles in Mrs. Banks' kitchen, was actually in touch with nature. She now felt equal to meeting unattended cows, but the woods offered enough excitement for to-day.

She found that her path did not immediately descend. It led her levelly to an almost circular green space; then it became enclosed again and soft to the feet with grass; and just ahead of her, blocking her way, she saw two figures, those of a woman and a man. Their backs were towards her, but there was no mistaking Aunt Rose's back. It was straight without being stiff, her dress fell with a unique perfection and the little hat and grey floating veil were hers alone.

For an instant Henrietta stood still, and the man, turning to look at his companion, showed the profile of her stranger. At the same moment he touched Aunt Rose's hand and before Henrietta swerved and sped back whence she had come, she saw that hand removed gently, as though reluctantly, and the head, mistily veiled, shaken slowly.

Her first desire was for flight and, safely on the road again, she found her heart beating to suffocation; she was filled with an indignation that almost brought her to tears; it was as though Aunt Rose had deliberately robbed her of treasure – Aunt Rose, who was almost middle-aged! For a moment she despised that fair, handsome man whose image had filled her mind for what seemed a long, long time; then she felt pity for him who had no eyes for youth, yet she remembered his look of arrested interest.

But steadying her thoughts and enjoying her dramatic bitterness, she laughed. He had merely surprised her likeness to Aunt Rose and that was all. Her dream was over. She had known it was a dream, but the awakening was cruel; it was also intensely exciting. She did not regret it; she had at least discovered something about Aunt Rose. She had a

95

lover. That look of his, that pleading movement of his hand, were unmistakable; he was a lover, and perhaps she, Henrietta Mallett, alone knew the truth. She had suspected a secret, now she knew it; and she had a sense of power, she had a weapon. She imagined herself standing over Aunt Rose, armed with knowledge, no longer afraid; she was involved in a romantic, perhaps a shameful, situation. Aunt Rose was meeting a lover clandestinely in the woods while Aunt Caroline and Aunt Sophia sat innocently at home, marvelling at Rose's indifference to men, yet rejoicing in her spinsterhood; and Henrietta felt that Rose had wronged her stepsisters almost as much as she had wronged her niece. She was deceitful; that, in plain terms, accounted for what had seemed a mysterious and conquered sorrow. It was Henrietta who was to suffer, through the shattering of a dream.

She went home, walking quickly, but feeling that she groped in a fog, broken here and there by lurid lights, the lights of knowledge and determination. She was younger than Aunt Rose, she was as pretty, and she was the daughter of Reginald Mallett who, though she did not know it, had always wanted the things desired by other people. She could continue to love her stranger and at the back of her mind was the unacknowledged conviction that Aunt Rose's choice must be well worth loving. And again how strangely events seemed to serve her: first the dropping of an orchid and now the leaping of a squirrel! She felt herself in the hands of higher powers.

She had a feverish longing to see Rose again, to see her plainly for the first time and dressing for dinner was like preparing for a great event. Yet when dinner-time came everything was surprisingly the same. The deceived Caroline and Sophia ate with the usual appetite, Susan hovered with the same quiet attention, and Rose showed no sign of a recent interview with a lover. Across the candlelight she looked at Henrietta kindly and Henrietta remembered the three thousand pounds. She did not want to remember them. They constituted an obligation towards this woman who did not sufficiently appreciate her, who met that man secretly, in a wood, who was beautiful with a far-off kind of beauty, like that of the stars. And while these angry thoughts passed through Henrietta's mind, Rose's tender expression had developed into a smile, and she asked, 'Did you have a nice walk?'

Henrietta gulped. She looked steadily at Rose, and on her lips certain words began to form themselves, but she did not utter them, and instead of saying as she intended, 'Yes, I went across the bridge and into those woods on the other side,' she merely said, 'Yes, yes, thank you,' and smiled back. It had been impossible not to smile and she was angry with Aunt Rose for making her a hypocrite. Perhaps she had smiled like that in the wood and she did not look so very old. Even the flames of the candles, throwing her face into strong relief as she leaned forward, did not reveal any lines.

'Don't walk too much, child,' Caroline said. 'It enlarges the feet. Girls nowadays can wear their brothers' shoes and men don't like that. Have I ever told you' – Caroline was given to repetition of her stories – 'how one of my partners, ridiculous creature, insisted on calling me Cinderella for a whole evening? Do you remember, Sophia?'

'Yes, dear,' Sophia said, and she determined that some day, when she was alone with Henrietta, she would tell her that she, too, had been called Cinderella that night. It was hard, but, since she loved her sister, not so very hard, to ignore her own little triumphs, yet she would like Henrietta to know of them. 'Dear child,' she murmured vaguely.

'We have our shoes made for us,' Caroline went on. 'It's necessary.' She snorted scorn for a large-footed generation.

Rose laughed. She said, 'Walk as much as you like, Henrietta. Health is better than tiny feet.'

Henrietta had no response for this remark. For the first time she felt out of sympathy with her surroundings, and her resentment against Rose spread to her other aunts. They were foolish in their talk of men and little feet; they knew, for all their worldliness, nothing about life. They had never known what it was to be insufficiently fed or clothed; they

97

had never battled with black beetles and mutton bones, their white hands had never been soiled by greasy water and potato skins and she felt a bitterness against them all.

'Nonsense, Rose; what do you know about it?' Caroline asked. 'You're a nun, that's what you are.'

'Ah, lovely!' Sophia sighed, but Henrietta, thinking of that man in the wood, raised her dark eyebrows sceptically.

'Lovely! Rubbish! A nun, and the first in the family. All our women,' Caroline turned to Henrietta, 'have broken hearts. They can't help it. It's in the blood. You'll do it yourself. All except Rose. And our men –' she guffawed; 'yes, even the General – but if I tell you about our men Sophia will be shocked.'

'The men!' Henrietta straightened herself and looked round the table. Her dark eyes shone, and the anger she was powerless to display against Aunt Rose, the remembrance of her own and her mother's struggles, found an outlet. 'You can't tell me anything I don't know. I don't think it is funny. Haven't I suffered through one of them? My father, he wasn't anything to boast about.'

'Henrietta,' Sophia said gently, and Caroline uttered a stern, 'What are you saying?'

'I don't care,' Henrietta said. 'Perhaps you're proud of all the harm he did, but my mother and I had to bear it. He was weak and selfish; we nearly starved, but he didn't. Oh, no, he didn't!' With her hands clasped tightly on her knee she bent over the table and her head was lowered with the effect of some small animal prepared for a spring. 'Do you know,' she said, 'he wore silk shirts? Silk shirts! and I had only one set of underclothing in the world! I had to wash them overnight. That was my father – a Mallett! Were they all like that?'

There was silence until Caroline, peeling an apple with trembling fingers, said severely, 'I don't think we need continue this conversation.' Her indignation was beyond mere words; she was outraged; her brother had been insulted by this child who owed his sisters gratitude; the family had been held up to scorn, and Henrietta, aware of what she had done and of her obligations, was overwhelmed with regret, with confusion, with the sense that, after all, it was she who really loved and understood her father.

'We will excuse you, Henrietta, if you have finished your dessert,' Caroline said. She had a great dignity.

This was a dismissal and Henrietta stood up. She could not take back her words, for they were true: she did not know how to apologize for their manner; she felt she would have to leave the house to-morrow and she had a sudden pride in Aunt Caroline and in her own name. But there was nothing she could do.

Most unexpectedly, Rose intervened. 'You must forgive Henrietta's bitterness,' she said quietly. 'It is natural.'

'But her own father!' Sophia remonstrated tearfully, and added tenderly, 'Ah, poor child!'

Henrietta dropped into her chair. She wept without concealment. 'It isn't that I didn't love him,' she sobbed.

'Ah, yes, you loved him,' Sophia said. 'So did we.' She dabbed her face with her lace handkerchief. 'It is Rose who knows nothing about him,' she said, with something approaching anger. 'Nothing!'

'Perhaps that is why I understand,' Rose said.

'No, no, you don't!' Henrietta cried. She could not admit that. She would not allow Aunt Rose to make such a claim. She looked from Caroline to Sophia. 'It's we who know,' she said. Yes, it was they three who were banded together in love for Reginald Mallett, in their sympathy for each other, in the greater nearness of their relationship to the person in dispute. She looked up, and she saw through her tears a slight quiver pass over the face of Rose and she knew she had hurt her and she was glad of it. 'You must forgive me,' she said to Caroline.

'Well, well; he was a wretch – a great wretch – a great dear. Let us say no more about it.'

It was Rose, now, who was in disgrace, and it was Henrietta, Caroline and Sophia who passed an evening of excessive amiability in the drawing-room.

Henrietta felt heroically that she had thrown down her

glove and it was annoying, the next morning, to find Rose would not pick it up. She remained charming; she was inimitably calm: she seemed to have forgotten her offence of the night before and Henrietta delighted in the thought that, though Rose did not know it, she and Henrietta were rivals in love, and she told herself that her own time would come.

She had only to wait. She was a great believer in her own luck, and had not Aunt Caroline assured her that all the Mallett women were born to break hearts – all but Aunt Rose? Some day she was bound to meet that man again and, looking in the glass after the Mallett manner, she was pleased with what she saw there. She was her father's daughter. Her father had never denied himself anything he wanted, and since her outbreak against him she felt closer to him; she was prepared to condone his sins, even to emulate them and find in him her excuse. She looked at the portrait on the wall, she kissed her hand to it. Somehow he seemed to be helping her.

But with all her carefully nurtured enmity, she could not deny her admiration for Aunt Rose. She was proud to sit beside her in the carriage which took them to Sales Hall, and on that occasion Rose talked more than usual, telling Henrietta little stories of the people living in the houses they passed and little anecdotes of her own childhood connected with the fields and lanes.

Henrietta sighed suddenly. 'It must be nice,' she said, 'to be part of a place. You can't be part of London, in lodging-houses, with no friends. I should love to have had a tree for a friend, all my life. It sounds silly, but it would make me feel different.' She was angry with herself for saying this to Aunt Rose, but again she could not help it. She saw too much with her eyes and Aunt Rose pleased them and she assured herself that though these softened her heart and loosened her tongue, she could resume her reserve at her leisure. 'There was a tree, a cherry, in one of the gardens once, but we didn't stay there long. We had to go.' She added quickly, 'It was too expensive for us. I suppose they charged for the tree, but I did long to see it blossom; and this spring,' she waved a hand, 'I've seen hundreds – I've seen a squirrel –' She stopped.

'Dear little things,' Rose said. They were jogging alongside the high, bare wall she hated, and the big trees, casting their high, wide branches far above and beyond it, seemed to be stretching out to the sea and the hills.

'Have you seen one lately?' Henrietta asked.

'What? A squirrel? No, not lately. They're shy. One doesn't see them often.'

'Oh, then I was lucky,' Henrietta said. 'I saw one in those woods we've just passed, the other day.' She looked at her Aunt Rose's creamy cheek. There was no flush on it, her profile was serene, the dark lashes did not stir.

'Soon,' Rose said, 'you will see hills and the channel.'

'And when shall we come to Mrs. Sales' house? Is she an old lady?'

'I don't think you would call her very old. She is younger than I am.'

'Oh, that's not old,' Henrietta said kindly. 'Has she any children?'

'No, there's a cat and a dog – especially a cat.'

'And a husband, I suppose?'

'Yes, a husband. Do you like cats, Henrietta?'

'They catch mice,' Henrietta said informatively.

'I don't think this one has ever caught a mouse, but it lies in wait – for something. Cats are horrible; they listen.' And she added, as though to herself, 'They frighten me.'

'I'm more afraid of dogs,' Henrietta said.

'Oh, but you mustn't be.'

'Well,' Henrietta dared, 'you're afraid of cats.'

'I know, but dogs, they seem to be part of one's inheritance – dogs and horses.'

'All the horses I've known,' Henrietta said with her odd bitterness, 'have been in cabs, and even then I never knew them well.'

'Francis Sales must show you his,' Rose said. 'There are the hills. Now we turn to the left, but down that track and across the fields is the short cut to Sales Hall. One can ride that way.'

'I should like to see the dairy,' Henrietta remarked, 'or do they pretend they haven't one?'

Rose smiled. 'No, they're very proud of it. It's a model dairy. I've no doubt Francis will be glad to show you that, too. And here we are.'

The masculine hall, with its smell of tobacco, leather and tweed, the low winding staircase covered with matting, its walls adorned with sporting prints, was a strange introduction to the room in which Henrietta found herself. She had an impression of richness and colour; the carpet was very soft, the hangings were of silk, a fire burned in the grate though the day was warm and before the fire lay the cat. The dog was on the window-sill looking out at the glorious world, full of smells and rabbits which he loved and which he denied himself for the greater part of each day because he loved his mistress more, but he jumped down to greet Rose with a great wagging of his tail.

She stooped to him, saying, 'Here is Henrietta, Christabel. Henrietta, this is Mrs. Sales.'

The woman on the couch looked to Henrietta like a doll animated by some diabolically clever mechanism, she was so pink and blue and fair. She was, in fact, a child's idea of feminine beauty and Henrietta felt a rush of sorrow that she should have to lie there, day after day, watching the seasons come and go. It was marvellous that she had courage enough to smile, and she said at once, 'Rose Mallett is always trying to give me pleasure,' and her tone, her glance at Rose, startled Henrietta as much as if the little thin hand outside the coverlet had suddenly produced a glittering toy which had its uses as a dagger. She, too, looked at Rose, but Rose was talking to the dog and it was then that Henrietta became really aware of the cat. It was certainly listening; it had stretched out its fore-paws and revealed shining, nail-like claws, and those polished instruments seemed to match the words which still floated on the warm air of the room.

'And now she has brought you,' Christabel went on.

'It was kind of you to come. Do sit here beside me. Tell me what you think of Rose. Tell me what you think,' she laughed, 'of your aunt. She's beautiful, isn't she?'

'Yes, very,' Henrietta said, and she spoke coldly, because she, too, was a Mallett, and she suspected this praise uttered in Rose's hearing and still with that sharpness as of knives. She had never been in a room in which she felt less at ease: perhaps she had been prejudiced by Aunt Rose's words about the cat, but that seemed absurd and she was confused by her vague feelings of anger and pity and suspicion.

However, she did her best to be a pleasant guest. She had somehow to break the tenseness in the room and she called on her reserve of anecdote. She told the story of Mr. Jenkins trying to fetch his boots and catch a glimpse of Mrs. Banks's daily help who could cook but had no character; she described the stickiness of his collar; and because she was always readily responsive to her surroundings, she found it natural to be humorous in a somewhat spiteful way; and at a casual mention of the Battys, she became amusing at the expense of Charles and felt a slight regret when she had roused Christabel's laughter. It seemed unkind; he had confided in her; she had betrayed him; and Rose completed her discomfiture by saying, 'Ah, don't laugh at poor Charles. He feels too much.'

Christabel nodded her head. 'Your aunt is very sympathetic. She understands men.' She added quickly, 'Have you met my husband?'

'No,' Henrietta said, 'I've only seen your carts.'

The two women laughed and it was strange to hear them united in that mirth. Henrietta looked puzzled. 'Well,' she explained, 'it was one of the first things I noticed. It stuck in my head.' Naturally the impressions of that day had been unusually vivid and she saw with painful clearness the figure of the man on the horse, as enduring as though it had been executed in bronze yet animated by ardent life.

'Well,' Christabel said, 'you are to have tea with the owner of the carts. Rose has tea with him every time she comes. It's part of the ceremony.' She sighed wearily; the cat moved

103

an ear; the nurse entered as a signal that the visitors must depart. 'You'll come again, won't you?' Christabel asked, holding Henrietta's hand and, as Rose said a few words to the nurse, she whispered, 'Come alone'; and surprisingly, from the hearthrug, there was a loud purring from the cat.

It was like release to be in the matted corridor again and it was in silence that Rose led the way downstairs. Henrietta followed slowly, looking at the pictures of hounds in full cry, top-hatted ladies taking fences airily, red-coated gentlemen immersed in brooks, but at the turn of the stairs she stood stock-still. She had the physical sensation of her heart leaving its place and lodging in her throat. Her stranger was standing in the hall; he was looking at Aunt Rose, and she knew now what expression he was wearing in the wood; he was looking at her half-angrily and as though he were suffering from hunger. She could not see her aunt's face, but when Henrietta stood beside her, Rose turned, saying, 'Henrietta, let me introduce Mr. Sales.'

He said, 'How do you do?' and then she saw again that look of interest with which she seemed to have been familiar for so long. 'I think I have seen you before,' he said.

'It was you who picked up my orchid.'

'Of course.' He looked from her to Rose. 'I couldn't think who you reminded me of, but now I know.'

'I don't think we are very much alike,' Henrietta said.

Rose laughed. 'Oh, don't say that. I have been glad to think we are.'

'You might be sisters,' said Francis Sales.

This little scene, being played so easily and lightly by this man and woman, had a nightmare quality for Henrietta. It had the confusion, the exaggerated horror of an evil dream, without the far-away consciousness of its unreality. Here she was, in the presence of the man she loved and it was wicked to love him. She had longed to meet him and now she wished she might have kept his memory only, the figure on the horse, the man with the pink orchid in his hand. She had suspected her Aunt Rose of a secret love affair, she had now discovered her guilty of sin. The evidence was slight, but Henrietta's conviction was tremendous. She was horrified, but she was also elated. This was drama, this was life. She was herself a romantic figure; she was robbed of her happiness, her youth was blighted; the woman upstairs was wronged and Henrietta understood why there were knives on her tongue: she understood the watchfulness of the cat.

Yet, as they sat in the cool drawing-room with its pale flowery chintz, its primrose curtains, the faded water-colours on the walls and Aunt Rose pouring tea into the flowered cups, she might, if she had wished, have been persuaded that she was wrong. Perhaps she had mistaken that angry, starving look in the man's eyes; it had gone; nothing could have been more ordinary than his expression and his conversation. But she knew she was not wrong and she sat there, on the alert, losing not a glance, not a tone. Her limbs were trembling, she could not eat and she was astonished that Aunt Rose could nibble biscuits with such nonchalance, that Francis Sales could eat plum cake.

He was, without doubt, the most attractive man she had ever seen; his long brown fingers fascinated her. And again she wondered at the odd sequence of events. She had seen his name on the carts, she had seen him on the horse, he had picked up her pink orchid, she had been led by Fate and a squirrel into the wood and now she found him here. It was like a play and it would be still more like a play if she snatched him from Aunt Rose. In that idea there was the prompting of her father, but her mother's part in her was a reminder that she must not snatch him for herself. No, only out of danger; men were helpless, they were like babies in the hands of women, and hands could differ; they could hurt or soothe, and she imagined her own performing the latter task. She saw it as her mission, and on the way home she told herself that her silence was not that of anger but of dedication.

§ 5

She thought Aunt Rose looked at her rather curiously, though there was no expression so definite in that glance.

105

Her aunts did not ask questions, they never interfered, and if Henrietta chose to be silent it was her own affair. She was, as a matter of fact, swimming in a warm bath of emotion and she experienced the usual chill when she descended from the carriage and felt the pavement under her feet. She had dedicated herself to a high purpose, but for the moment it was impossible to get on with the noble work. The mere business of life had to be proceeded with, and though the situation was absorbing it receded now and then until, looking at her Aunt Rose, she was reminded of it with a shock.

She looked often at her aunt, finding her more than ever fascinating. She tried to see her with the eyes of Francis Sales, she tried to imagine how Rose's clear grey eyes, so dark sometimes that they seemed black, answered the appeal of his, yet, as the days passed, Henrietta found it difficult to remember her resignation and her wrongs in this new life of luxury and pleasure.

She woke each morning to the thought of gaiety and to the realization of comfort and the blessed absence of anxiety. Her occupation was the getting of enjoyment and she took it all eagerly yet without greed, and as she was enriched she became generous with her own offerings of laughter, sympathy and affection. She liked and looked for the brightening of Caroline and Sophia at her approach, she became pleasantly aware of her own ability to charm and she rejoiced in an exterior world no longer limited to streets. Each morning she went to her window and looked over and beyond the roofs, so beautiful and varied in themselves, to the trees screening the open country across the river and if the sight reminded her to sigh for her own sorrows and to think bitterly of Aunt Rose, she had not time to linger on her emotions. Summer was gay in Upper Radstowe. There were tea-parties and picnics, she paid calls with her aunts and learnt to play lawn tennis with her contemporaries. Her friendship with the Battys ripened.

She was always sure of her welcome at Prospect House, and though she often assured herself that she could love no one but Francis Sales, that was no reason why others should not love her. From that point of view John Batty was a failure. He took her to a cricket match, but finding that she did not know the alphabet of the game, and was more interested in the spectators than in the players, he gave her up. He admired her appearance, but it did not make amends for ignorance of such a grossness; and, equally displeased with him, she returned home alone while he watched out the match.

The next day when she paid her usual Sunday visit, she ignored him pointedly and mentally crossed him off her list. Charles, ugly and odd, was infinitely more responsive, though he greeted her on this occasion with reproach.

'You went to a cricket match yesterday with John.'

'It was very boring and I got a headache. I shall never go again.'

'He said he wouldn't take you.'

Henrietta smiled subtly, implying a good deal.

'I shouldn't have thought,' Charles went on mournfully, 'of suggesting such a thing.'

'My aunts were rather shocked. I went on the top of a tramcar with him.'

'But if you can go out with him, why shouldn't you go out with me?'

'But where?' Henrietta questioned practically.

'Well, to a concert.'

'When?'

'When there is one. I don't know. They won't have one in this God-forsaken place until the autumn.'

'That's a long time ahead.'

He spread his hands. 'You see, I never have any luck. I just want you to promise.'

'Oh, I'll promise,' Henrietta said.

'It will be the first time I've been anywhere with a girl,' he said. 'I don't get on.'

'Have you wanted to?'

He sighed. 'Yes, but not much.' Her laughter, which was so pretty, startled him: it also delighted him with its music, and his sad eyes grew wider and more vague. He had an inspiration. 'I'll take you home now.'

'I'm not going home. I've promised to go to Sales Hall.'

'Sales Hall – oh, yes, he's the man who talks at concerts – when he goes. I know him. Have you ever wanted to murder anyone? I've wanted to murder him. I might some day. You'd better warn him.'

Was this another strand in the web of her drama, she wondered. Was Aunt Rose involved in this too? She breathed quickly. 'Why, what has he done to you?'

He ground his teeth, looking terrible but ineffectual. 'Stolen beauty. That's what his sort does. He kills lovely things that fly and run, for sport, and he steals beauty, spoils it.'

'Who?' she whispered.

'That man Sales.'

'No, no. Who has he stolen and spoilt?'

'Heavenly music – and my happiness. I lost a bar – a whole bar, I tell you. I'll never forgive him. I can't get it back.'

'If that's all –' Henrietta gestured.

'And there are others,' Charles went on. 'I never forget them. I meet them in the streets and they look horrible – like beetles.'

'I believe you're mad,' Henrietta said earnestly. 'It's not sense.'

'What is sense?' Henrietta could not tell him. She looked at him, a little afraid, but excited by this proximity to danger. And I thought you would understand.'

'Of course I do.' She could not bear to let go of anything which might do her credit. 'I do. But you exaggerate. And Mr. Sales –' She hesitated, and in doing so she remembered to be angry with Charles Batty for maligning him. 'How can you judge Mr. Sales?' she asked with scorn. 'He is a man.'

'And what am I?' Charles demanded.

'You're – queer,' she said.

'Yes' – his face twisted curiously – 'I suppose if I shot things and chased them, you'd like me better. But I can't – not even for that, but perhaps, some day –' He seemed to lose himself in the vagueness of his thoughts.

She finished his sentence gaily, for after all, it was absurd to quarrel with him. 'Some day we'll go to a concert.'

He recovered himself. 'More than that,' he said. He nodded his head with unexpected vigour. 'You'll see.'

She gazed at him. It was wonderful to think of all the things that might happen to a person who was only twenty-one, but she hastily corrected her thoughts. What could happen to her? In a few short days events had rushed together and exhausted themselves at their source! There was nothing left. She said good-bye to Charles and thought him foolish not to offer to accompany her. She said, 'It's a very long way to Sales Hall,' and he answered, 'Oh, you'll meet that man somewhere, potting at rabbits.'

'Do you think so? I hope he won't shoot me.' And she saw herself stretched on the ground, wounded, dying, with just enough force to utter words he could never forget – words that would change his whole life. She was willing to sacrifice herself and she said good-bye to Charles again, and sorrowfully, as though she were already dead. She tried to plan her dying words, but as she could not hit on satisfactory ones, she contented herself with deciding that whether she were wounded or not, she would try to introduce the subject of Aunt Rose; and as she went she looked out hopefully for a tall figure with a gun under its arm.

She met it, but without a gun, on the track where, on one side, the trees stood in fresh green, like banners, and on the other the meadows sloped roughly to the distant water. He had been watching for her, he said, and suddenly over her assurance there swept a wave of embarrassment, of shyness. She was alone with him and he was not like Charles Batty. He looked down at her with amusement in his blue, thick-lashed eyes, and it was difficult to believe that here was the hero, or the villain, of the piece. She felt the sensation she had known when he handed her the orchid, and she blushed absurdly when he actually said, as though he read her thoughts, 'No orchids to-day?'

'No.' She laughed up at him. 'That was a special treat.

I didn't see Mr. Batty this afternoon, and he couldn't afford to give them away every Sunday.'

'Do you go there every Sunday?'

'Yes; they're very kind.'

'They would be.'

This reminded her a little of Mr. Jenkins, though she cast the idea from her quickly. Mr. Jenkins was not worthy of sharing a moment's thought with Francis Sales; his collar was made of rubber, his accent was grotesque; but the influence of the boarding-house was still on her when she asked very innocently, 'Why?'

'Oh, I needn't tell you that.'

It was Mr. Jenkins again, but in a voice that was soft, almost caressing. Did Mr. Sales talk like this to Aunt Rose? She could not believe it and she was both flattered and distressed. She must assert her dignity and she had no way of doing it but by an expression of firmness, a slight tightening of lips that wanted to twitch into a smile.

'Mr. Charles Batty,' the voice went on, 'seems to have missed his opportunities, but I have always suspected him of idiocy.'

'I don't know what you mean,' she said untruthfully, and then, loyally, she protested. 'But he's not an idiot. He's very clever, too clever, not like other people.'

'Well, there are different names for that sort of thing,' he said easily, and she was aware of an immense distance between her and him – he seemed to have put her from him with a light push – and at the same time she was oppressively conscious of his nearness. She felt angry, and she burst out, 'I won't have you speaking like that about Charles.'

'Certainly not, if he's a friend of yours.'

'And I won't have you laughing at me.'

He stopped in his long stride. 'Don't you laugh yourself at the things that please you very much?'

'Oh, don't!' she begged. He was too much for her: she was helpless, as though she had been drugged to a point when she could move and think, but only through a mist, and she felt that his ease, approaching impudence, was as indecent as Aunt Rose's calm. It was both irritating and pleasing to know that she could have shattered both with the word she was incapable of saying, but her nearest approach to that was an inquiry after the health of Mrs. Sales. He replied that she was looking forward to Henrietta's visit. She had very few pleasures and was always glad to see people.

'Aunt Rose' – here was an opportunity – 'comes, doesn't she, every week?'

He said he believed so.

'Did you know her when she was a little girl?'

He gave a discouraging affirmative.

'What was she like?'

'I don't know.' He had, indeed, forgotten.

'Well, you must remember her when she was young.'

'Young?'

Henrietta nodded bravely though he seemed to smoulder. 'As young as I am.'

'She was exactly the same as she is now. No, not quite.'

'Nicer?'

'Nicer? What a word! Nice!' He looked all round him and made a flourish with his stick. He could not express himself, yet he seemed unable to be silent. 'Do you call the sky nice?'

'Yes, very, when it's blue.'

He gave, to her great satisfaction, the kind of laugh she had expected. 'Let us talk about something a little smaller than the sky,' he said. He looked down at her, and she was relieved to see the anger fading from his face; but she was glad to have learnt something of what he felt for Aunt Rose. To him she was like the sky whence came the rain and the sunshine, where the stars shone and the moon, and she wondered to what he would have compared herself. 'You said we might be sisters.'

He looked again. She wore a broad white hat in honour of the season, her black dress was dotted with white; from one capable white hand she swung her gloves; she tilted her chin, a trick she had inherited from her father, in a sort of challenge.

'You like the idea?' he asked.

'I don't believe it. I'm really the image of my father. Did you know him?'

'No. Heard of him, of course.'

'It's him I'm like,' Henrietta repeated firmly.

'Then the story of his good looks must be true.'

Mixed with her pleasure, she had a return of disappointment. Here was Mr. Jenkins once more, and while it was sad to discover his re-incarnation in her ideal, it was thrilling to resume the kind of fencing she thought she had resigned. She forgot her virtuous resolves, and the remainder of the walk was enlivened by the hope of a thrust which she would have to parry, but none came. Francis Sales seemed to have exhausted his efforts, and at the door he said with a sort of sulkiness, 'I think you had better go up alone. You must let me see you home.'

This was not her first solitary visit to Christabel Sales, and she half dreaded, half enjoyed meeting the glances of those wide blue eyes, which were searching behind their innocence and hearing remarks which, though dropped carelessly, always gave her the impression of being tipped with steel. She was bewildered, troubled by her sense that she and Christabel were allies and yet antagonists, and her jealousy of her Aunt Rose fought with her unwilling loyalty to one of her own blood. There were moments when she acquiesced in the suggestions offered in the form of admiration, and others when she stiffened with distaste, with a realization that she herself was liable to attack, with horror for the beautiful luxurious room, the crippled woman, the listening cat. Henrietta sometimes saw herself as a mouse, in mortal danger of a feline spring, and then pity for Christabel would overcome this weariness; she would talk to her with what skill she had for entertainment, and she emerged exhausted, as though from a fight.

This evening she was amazed to be received without any greeting, but a question: 'Has Rose Mallett told you why I am here?' Christabel was lying very low on her couch. Her lips hardly moved; these might have been the last words she would ever utter.

'Yes, a hunting accident. And you told me about it yourself.'

There was a silence, and then the voice, its sharpness dulled, said slowly, 'Yes, I told you what I remembered and what I heard afterwards. A hunting accident! It sounds so simple. That's what they call it. Names are useful. We couldn't get on without them. I get such queer ideas, lying here, with nothing to do. Before I was married I never thought at all. I was too happy.' She seemed to be lost in memory of that time. Henrietta sat very still; she breathed carefully as though a brusqueness would be fatal, and the voice began again. 'They call you Henrietta. It's only a name, but it doesn't describe you; nobody knows what it means except you, but it's convenient. It's the same with my hunting accident. Do you see?'

Henrietta said nothing. She had that familiar feeling of being in the dark, and now the evening shadows augmented it. She was conscious of the cat behind her, on the hearthrug.

'Do you see?' Christabel persisted.

'Things have to be called something,' Henrietta said.

'That's just what I have been telling you. And so Rose Mallett calls it a hunting accident.' A high-pitched and thin laugh came from the pillows. 'She was terribly distressed about it. And she actually told me she had suspected that mare from the first. She told me! It's funny – don't you think so?'

'No,' Henrietta said stoutly, 'not funny at all.' She spoke in a very firm and reasonable voice, as though only her common sense could combat what seemed like insanity in the other. 'I think it's very sad.'

'For me? Oh, yes, but I wasn't thinking of that. I was thinking of your charming aunt, the most beautiful woman in Radstowe. That's what I have heard her called. Yet why hasn't she married? Can't she find anybody' – the voice was gentle – 'to love her? She suspected that mare but she warned nobody. Funny –'

Henrietta had a physical inward trembling. She felt a dreadful rage against the woman on the couch, a sickening

113

disgust, such as she would have felt at looking down a dark, deep well and seeing slime and blind ugliness at the bottom. She felt as though her ears were dirty; she tried to move, but she sat perfectly still and, dreading what would come next, she listened, fascinated.

'Perhaps she is in love with somebody. Does she get many letters, Henrietta? She is very reserved, she doesn't tell me much; but, of course, I'm interested in her.' She laughed again. 'I am very anxious for her happiness. It would comfort me to know anything you can tell me.'

Henrietta managed to stand up. 'I know nothing,' she said in a slightly broken voice. 'I don't want to know anything.'

Christabel interrupted smoothly. 'Perhaps you are wise or you couldn't stay happily in that house. They're all like witches, those women. They frighten me. You must be very brave, Henrietta.'

'I'm very grateful,' Henrietta said; 'and I shan't come here again, no, never. I don't know what you have been trying to tell me, but I don't believe it. It's no good crying. I shall never come back. They're not witches.' She had a vision of them at the dinner table, Rose like a white flower, Caroline and Sophia jewelled, gaily dressed, a little absurd, oddly distinguished. 'Witches! They are my father's sisters, and I love them.'

'Ah, but you don't know Rose,' Christabel sobbed. 'And don't say you will never come again. And don't tell Francis. He would be angry.'

'How could I tell him?' Henrietta asked indignantly. 'No, no, I don't want to see either of you again. I shall go away – go away –' She left the room to the sound of a horrible, faint weeping.

She meant what she had said. She thought she would go away from Radstowe and forget Christabel Sales, forget Francis Sales, whom she would no longer pretend to love; forget those insinuations that Aunt Rose was guilty of a crime. This place and these people were abhorrent to her, she felt she had been poisoned and she rushed down the long avenue where, overhead, the rooks were calling, as though she

114

could only be saved by the clean night air beyond the house. She was shocked; she believed that Christabel was mad; the thought of that warm room where the cat listened, made her gasp, and her horror extended to Francis Sales himself. The place felt wicked, but the clear road stretching before her, the pale evening sky and the sound of her own feet tapping the road restored her.

She was glad to be alone and, avoiding the short cut, she enjoyed the sanity of the highway used by ordinary men and women in the decent pursuit of their lives. But now the road was empty and though at another time she would have been afraid of the lonely country, to-night she had a sense of escape from greater perils than any lurking here. And before long it all seemed like a dream, but it was a dream that might recur if she ran the risk.

No, she would never go there again, she would never envy Aunt Rose a lover from that house, she would never believe that the worst of Christabel's implications were true. They were the fabrications of a suspicious woman, and though her jealousy might be justified, it seemed to Henrietta that she deserved her fate. She was hateful, she was poisonous, and Henrietta felt a sudden tenderness for Aunt Rose and Francis Sales. They could not help themselves, for they were unfortunate, she longed to show them sympathy and she saw herself taking them by the hand and saying gently, 'Confide in me. I understand.' She imagined Aunt Rose melting at that touch and those words into tears, perhaps of repentance, certainly of gratitude, but at this point Henrietta's fancies were interrupted by the sound of footsteps behind her. She quickened her pace, then began to run, and the steps followed, gaining on her. She could not outrun them and she stopped, turning to see who came.

'Miss Mallett!' It was the voice of Francis Sales. She sank down on a heap of stones, panting and laughing. He sat beside her. 'What's the matter?'

'I don't know. I hate to hear anybody coming behind me. It might have been a tramp. I'm very much afraid of tramps.'

'I said I would see you home.'

'Yes, I forgot. Let us go on.'

'You didn't stay long.'

'I don't think Mrs. Sales is very well.'

'She isn't. She gets hysterical and that affects her heart. I thought you would do her good.' He seemed to blame Henrietta. 'And I thought a walk with you would do me good, too. I have a pretty dull life.'

'Aren't you interested in your cows and things?'

'A man can't live on cows.'

'But you have other things and you live in the country. People can't have everything. I don't suppose you'd change with anybody really, if you could. People are like that. They grumble, but they like being themselves. Suppose you were a young man in a shop, measuring cloth or selling bacon. You'd find that much duller, I should think.'

He laughed a little. 'Where did you learn this wisdom?'

'I've had experience,' she said staidly. 'Yes, you'd find it duller.'

'Perhaps you're right. But then, you might come to buy the bacon. I should look forward to that.'

In the darkness, these playful words frightened her a little; they hurt her sense of what was fitting from him to her and at the same time they pleased her with their hint of danger.

'Would you?' she asked slowly.

He paused, saying, 'May I light a pipe?' and by the flame of the match he examined her face quite openly for a moment. 'You know I would,' he said.

She met his look, her eyes wavered and neither spoke for a long time. She was oppressed by his nearness, the smell of his tobacco, her own inexplicable delight. From the trees by the roadside birds gave out happy chirrups, country people in their Sunday clothes and creaking boots passed or overtook the silent pair; a man on a horse rode out from a gate and cantered with very little noise on the rough grass edging the road. Henrietta watched him until he disappeared and then it seemed as if he had never been there at all. A sheep in a field uttered a sad cry and every sight and

116

sound seemed a little unreal, like things happening on a stage.

And gradually Henrietta's excitement left her. The world seemed a sad and lonely place; she remembered that she herself was lonely; there was no one now to whom she was the first, and she had a longing for her mother. She wished that instead of returning to Nelson Lodge with its cleanliness and richness and comfort, she might turn the key of the boarding-house door and find herself in the narrow passage with the smell of cooking and the gas turned low; she wished she could run up the stairs and rush into the drawing-room and find her mother sitting there, sewing by the fire, and see her look up and hear her say, 'Well, Henry dear, what have you been doing?' After all, that old life was better than this new one. The troubles of her mother, her own young struggles for food and warmth, the woes of Mrs. Banks, had in them something nobler than she could find in the distresses of Christabel and Aunt Rose and Francis Sales, something redeeming them from the sordidness in which they were set. She checked a sob.

'It's a long way,' she sighed.

'Are you tired?' His voice was gentle.

'Yes, dreadfully.'

'Then let us sit down again.'

'No, I must go on. I must get back.'

'If you would talk to me, you wouldn't notice the distance.'

'I don't want to talk. I'm thinking. When we get to the bridge you can go back, can't you? There will be lights and I shall be quite safe.'

'Very well, but I wish you'd tell me what's the matter.'

'I'm very unhappy,' Henrietta said with a sob.

'What on earth for? Look here,' – he touched her arm – 'did Christabel say anything?'

'I don't know why it is.'

'Are you going to cry?'

'It's no good crying.'

He held the arm now quite firmly and they faced each other. 'You'd better tell me the whole story.'

Her lips quivered. She wished he would loosen his grip and hoped he would go on holding her for ever. It was a moment of mingled ecstasy and sadness. 'Oh,' she almost wailed, 'can't I be unhappy if I want to?'

He gave a short laugh, saying, 'Poor little girl,' and stooping, kissed her on the mouth. She endured that kiss willingly for a moment and then, very lightly, struck him in the face.

§ 6

Afterwards there was some satisfaction in thinking that she had done the dramatic thing – what the pure-minded heroine always did to the villain; but at the time the action was spontaneous and unconsidered. Henrietta was not really avenging an insult: she was simply expressing her annoyance at her pleasure in it. Being, when she chose, a clear-sighted young woman, she realized this, but she also knew that Francis Sales would find the obvious meaning in the blow. For herself, she sanely determined to blot that episode from her mind: it was maddening to think of it as an insult and dangerous to remember its delight, and she was able calmly to tell her aunts that Mr. Sales had seen her home.

'Then why didn't he come in?' Caroline asked with a grunt. 'Leaving you on the doorstep like a housemaid!'

'He only came as far as the bridge.'

'My dear child! What was he thinking of? Men are not what they were, or is it the women who are different? They haven't the charm! They haven't the old charm! My difficulty was always to get rid of the creatures. I'm disappointed in you, Henrietta.'

'But he's married,' Henrietta said gravely. 'I only needed him on the dark roads and I should think he wanted to go back to Mrs. Sales.'

'It would be the first time, then,' Caroline said.

'Why, isn't he fond of her?'

'Don't ask dangerous questions, child – and would you be fond of her yourself?'

'She's very pretty.'

'Now, Caroline, don't,' Sophia begged.

Caroline chuckled. 'Don't what?'

'Say what you were going to say.'

Caroline chuckled again. 'I can't help it. My tongue won't be tied. I'm like all the Malletts –'

'But not before the child.'

'You're a prude, Sophia, and if Henrietta imagines that a man like Francis Sales, any man worth his salt – besides, Henrietta has knocked about the world. She is no more innocent than she looks.'

'She doesn't mean half she says,' Sophia whispered.

'And neither is Francis Sales,' Caroline persisted. 'Ridiculous! Dark roads, indeed! I don't think I care for your wandering about at night, Henrietta.'

'I won't do it again,' Henrietta said meekly.

'Sophia and I –' Caroline began one of her reminiscences, to which neither Sophia nor Henrietta listened. To the one, they were familiar in their exaggeration, and the other had her own thoughts, which were bewilderingly confused.

She had meant to stand between Francis Sales and Aunt Rose; later she had wished to help them, now she did not know whether she wanted to help or hinder. The thing was too much for her, but she wondered if Aunt Rose had ever experienced such a kiss. Meeting her a few minutes later on the stairs, with her slim hand on the polished rail, a beautiful satin-shod foot gleaming below the lace of her dress, she seemed a being too ethereal for a salute so earthly, and because she looked so lovely, because Christabel had been unjust, Henrietta forgot to feel unfriendly.

Rose said unexpectedly, 'Oh, Henrietta, I am glad you have come back. You seem to have been away for a long time.'

'I went to the Battys' to tea and then to Sales Hall. I promised Mrs. Sales. Do you mind?'

'Of course not; but I missed you.'

'Oh! Oh! I never thought of that.'

'I always miss you,' Rose said gravely. 'You have made a great difference to us all.'

Henrietta's mouth opened with astonishment. 'I had no idea. And I do nothing but enjoy myself.'

Rose laughed. 'That's what we want you to do. You must be as happy as you can.'

This, from Aunt Rose, was the most wonderful thing that had happened yet. Henrietta was overcome by astonishment and gratitude. 'I had no idea. I never dreamt of your liking me. I thought you just put up with me.'

'You haven't given me much chance,' Rose said in a low voice, 'of doing anything else.'

It was true: Henrietta could not flourish when she thought herself unappreciated, but now she expanded like a flower blossoming in a night.

'Oh, if we could be friends! There's nobody to talk to except Charles Batty, and I hated, I simply hated being at Sales Hall to-night.' She tightened her lips and opened them to say, 'I shan't go there again. I said so. She is a terrible woman.'

'She has a great deal to bear.'

'Yes, and she counts on your remembering that,' Henrietta said acutely.

'What was the matter to-night?'

'Hints,' Henrietta whispered. 'Hints,' and she added nervously, 'about you.'

Rose made a slight movement. 'Don't tell me.'

'And the cat. I ran away. She was crying, but I didn't care. I ran all down the avenue on to the road. Mr. Sales had said he would take me home, but I didn't wait. It was much better under the sky. Then I heard footsteps, and it was Mr. Sales running after me.' She paused. Two stairs above her, Aunt Rose stood, listening with attention. She was, as usual, all black and white; her neck, rising from the black lace, looked like a bowl of cream laid out of doors to cool in the night.

'He kissed me,' Henrietta said abruptly.

Rose did not move, and before she spoke Henrietta had time to wonder what had prompted her to that confession. She had not thought about it, the words had simply issued of themselves.

'Kissed you?'

'Yes,' Henrietta said, and suddenly she wanted to make it easier for Aunt Rose. 'I think he was sorry for me. I told him I was unhappy, but I couldn't tell him why, I couldn't say it was his wife. I think he meant it kindly.'

'I am sure he did,' Rose said with admirable self-possession. 'You look very young in that big hat, you are very young, and perhaps he guessed what you had been through. Don't think about it any more.'

'No.' Henrietta seemed to have no control over her tongue. 'But then, you see, I hit him.'

Rose managed a laugh. 'Oh, Henrietta, how primitive!'

'Yes,' Henrietta agreed, but she knew she had betrayed Francis Sales. She knew and Rose knew that she would not have struck him if the kiss had been paternal. 'I suppose it was vulgar,' she murmured sadly, yet not without some skill.

Rose descended the two stairs without a word and went to the bottom of the flight, but there she paused, saying, 'Take off your things and let us have some music.'

Henrietta was learning to sing, and in defiance of Charles Batty's prophecy, she neither squeaked nor gurgled. She piped with a pretty simplicity and with an enjoyment which made her forget herself. Yet she looked charming, standing in the candle-light beside the shining grand piano on which Aunt Rose accompanied her, and to-night she felt they were united in more than the music: they were friends, they were fellow-sufferers, and long after Henrietta had tired of singing, Rose went on playing, mournfully, as it seemed to Henrietta, consoling herself with sweet sounds. Sophia sat before her embroidery frame, slowly pushing her needle in and out; Caroline read a novel with avidity and an occasional pause for chuckles, and when Rose at length dropped her hands on her knees and remained motionless, staring at the keys, Henrietta startled her aunts by saying firmly, 'I am just going to enjoy life.'

Rose raised her head and her enigmatic smile widened a little. Caroline exclaimed, 'Good gracious! Why not?' Sophia said gently, 'That is what we wish.'

Henrietta stiffened herself for questions which did not come. Nobody expressed a desire to know what had caused this solemn declaration: Caroline went on reading, Sophia embroidering: Rose retired to bed.

Henrietta was not daunted by this indifference. She persisted in her determination; she cast off all thoughts of ministering like an angel, or revenging like a demon; she enjoyed the gaieties with which the youth of Radstowe amused itself during the summer months; she accompanied her aunts to garden parties, ate ices, had her fortune told in tents, flirted mildly and endured Charles Batty's peculiar half-apprehensive tyranny.

Nothing went amiss with Charles but what he seemed to blame her for it, and while she resented this strange form of attention, she had a compensating conviction that he was really paying tribute and she knew that the absence of his complaints would have left a blank. Fixing her with his pale eyes, he described the bitterness of life in his father's office, his mismanagement of clients, his father's sneers, his mother's sighs; his sufferings in not being allowed to go to Germany and study music.

'If I were a man,' Henrietta said, voicing a pathetic faith in masculine ability to break bonds, 'I would do what I liked. I'd go to Germany and starve and be happy. A man can do and get anything he really wants.'

'Ah, I shall remember that,' he said. 'But I can't go to Germany now,' he added darkly, and when she asked him for a reason, he groaned. 'Even you – even you don't understand me.'

In this respect she understood him perfectly well, but she did not wish to clear the mysterious gloom, not devoid of excitement, in which they moved together; and they parted for the summer holidays, miserably on his part, cheerfully on hers. She was going to Scotland with Aunt Rose and the prospect was so delightful that she did not trouble to inquire about his movements.

She was surprised and almost disappointed that he did not reproach her for this thoughtlessness when, on her return, she went to call on Mrs. Batty and hear about her annual holiday at Bournemouth. Mrs. Batty had suffered very much from the heat, Mr. Batty had suffered from dyspepsia, and they were glad to be at home again, though it was to find that John, without a hint to his parents, had engaged himself to a girl with tastes like his own.

'But it's bull-dogs with her, instead of terriers,' Mrs. Batty sighed. 'She brings them here and they slobber on the carpets – dirty things. And golf. But she's a nice girl, and they go out before breakfast with the dogs and have a game – but I did hope he would look elsewhere, dear.' She gazed sentimentally at Henrietta. 'I don't feel she will ever be a daughter to me. Of course, I kissed her and all that when I heard the news, but now she just comes in and says, "Hullo, Mrs. Batty! Where's John?" And that's all. I do like affection. She'll kiss the bull-dogs, though,' Mrs. Batty added grimly; 'but whether she ever kisses John, I can't say. And as for Charles, he never looks at a girl, so I'm as badly off as ever. Worse, for Charles, really Charles hasn't a word to throw at me. He comes down to breakfast and you'd think the bacon had upset him, and it's the best I can get. And his father sits reading the paper and lifting his eyebrows over the edge at Charles. He's very cool, Mr. Batty is. Half the time, John comes in late for breakfast, after his game, you know, and then he's in too much of a hurry to talk. They might all be dumb. With Charles it's all that piano business. I tell him I wish he'd go to Germany and be done with it, though I never think musicians are respectable, with all that hair. Anyhow, Charles is getting bald, and he says he's too old to start afresh. And then he glares at his father. It's all very unpleasant. Still, he's a good boy really. They're both good boys. I've a lot to be thankful for; and, my dear,' – her voice sank, and she laid a plump hand on Henrietta's – 'Mr. Batty says we may give a ball after Christmas. Everybody in Radstowe. We shall take the Assembly Rooms. The date isn't fixed, and now and then, if he isn't feeling well, Mr. Batty says he can't afford it. But that's nonsense, we shall have it; but don't say a word. I've told nobody else, but somehow, Henrietta, I always want to tell you everything, as if you were my daughter.' Mrs. Batty sighed heavily. 'If only Charles were different!'

However, Charles surprised his mother that evening by walking to the gate with Henrietta. Arrived there, he announced firmly that he would take her home.

'I'm going for a walk,' Henrietta said.

'Oh, a walk. Well, all right. Where shall we go? I know, I will take you where you've never been before.'

It was October and already the lamps were lighted in the streets; they studded the bridge like fairy lanterns for a fairy path to that world of woods and stealthy lanes and open country where the wind rustled the gorse bushes on the other side. Below, at the water's edge, more lamps stood like sentinels, here and there, straight and lonely, fulfilling their task, and as Charles and Henrietta watched, the terraces of Radstowe became illuminated by an unseen hand. Over everything there was a suggestion of enchantment: lovers, strolling by, were romantic in their silence; a faint hoot from some steamer was like a laugh.

'It will be dark over there, won't it?' Henrietta asked.

'Frightfully. We'll cut across the fields.'

'Not to Sales Hall?'

'Sales Hall? What for? To see that miserable fellow? We're not going near Sales Hall.'

She breathed a word.

'What did you say?' he asked.

'Cows,' she breathed again.

'Perhaps.'

'But in the winter,' she said hopefully, 'I should think they shut them up at night, poor things.'

'Not cold enough yet for that.'

'I'm afraid of them, you know.'

'Domestic animals,' he said calmly.

'Horns,' she whispered.

They said no more. Their path edged those woods which in their turn edged the gorge; but here and there the trees spread themselves more freely and, through the darkness,

Henrietta had glimpses of furtive little paths, of dips and hollows. A small pool, thick with early fallen leaves, had hardly a foot of gleaming surface with which to gaze like an unwinking eye at the emerging stars. But this skirting of the wood came to an end and there stretched before their feet, which made the only sound in the quiet night, a broad white road where the arched gateway of a distant house looked like the fragment of a temple.

'I like this,' Henrietta said; 'I feel safe.'

'Not for long,' Charles replied sternly. He opened a gate and through a little coppice they reached a fence. 'You'll have to climb it.' The broad fields on the other side were as dark as water and as still. It was surprising, when she jumped down, to find she did not sink, to find that she and Charles could walk steadily on this blackness, cut here and there by the deeper blackness of a hedge. There were no cows, but sheep stumbled up and bleated at their approach, and for some time the tinkling of the bell-wether's bell accompanied them like music.

'There's a stile here,' Charles said, and from this they plunged into another wood where birds fluttered and twittered and, in the undergrowth, there were small stealthy sounds.

'I wouldn't come here alone,' Henrietta said, 'for all the world.'

Charles said nothing. Mrs. Batty was right: it was like walking with a dumb man. They left the wood and walked downhill beside a ploughed field, and in the shelter of a high wall. An open lane brought them to a gate, the gate opened on a rough road through yet another wood of larch and spruce and fir. The road was deeply rutted and they walked in single file until Charles turned, saying, 'This is what I've brought you to see. This is "The Monks' Pool." '

A large pond, almost round and strewn with dead leaves about its edge, lay sombrely on their right hand, without a movement, without a gleam. It was like a pall covering something secret, something which must never be revealed, and opposite, where the ground rose steeply, tall firs stood up, guardians of the unknown. Faint quackings came from some unseen ducks among the willows and water gurgled at the invisible outlet of the pond; there were little stirrings and sighings among the trees. The protruding roots of an oak offered a seat to Henrietta, and behind her Charles leaned against the trunk.

It was comfortable to have him there, to be able to look at this dark beauty without fear, and as she sat there she heard an ever-increasing number of little sounds; they were caused by she knew not what: small creatures moving among the pine needles, night birds on the watch for prey, water rats, the flop of fish, the fall of some leaf over-ripe on the tree, her own slow breathing, the muffled ticking of her heart; and into this orchestra of tiny instruments there came slowly, and as if it grew out of all these, another sound.

It was the voice of Charles, and it was so much a part of this rare experience, it seemed so right a complement, that at first she did not listen to the sense of what he said. The words had no clearer meaning than had the other voices of the night; the whole thing was wonderful – the tall, im-mobile trees, the small, secret sounds, the black lake like an immense, mysterious pall, the steady booming of the voice, had the effect of magic.

This was essential beauty revealed to her ears and eyes, but gradually the words formed themselves into sentences and were carried to her brain. She understood that Charles was talking of himself, of her, with an eloquence born of long-considered thoughts. He was telling her how she ap-peared to him as a being of light and sweetness and necessity; he was telling her how he loved her; he was asking for nothing, but he was saying amazing things in language worthy of his thoughts of her.

That muffled ticking of her heart went on like distant drum beats, the symphony of tiny instruments did not pause, the dominant sound of Charles's voice continued, and now, as she listened, she heard nothing but his voice. He was not pathetic, he did not plead, he did not claim: he spoke of very old and lasting things, and it was like hearing some one read a tale. She did not stir. She forgot that this

126

was Charles: it was a simple heart become articulate. And then suddenly the voice stopped and the orchestra, as though in relief, in triumph, seemed to play more loudly. A water rat dived again, a duck quacked sleepily and a branch of a tree creaked mournfully under a lost puff of wind.

Henrietta turned her head and saw Charles Batty standing motionless against the tree. His hat was tilted a little to one side and his eyes were staring straight before him. Even the darkness was not entirely kind to him, but that did not matter. She wondered if he knew what he had been saying: she could not remember it all, but it would come back. As they went home over the dark fields, she would remember it. It seemed to have everything and yet nothing to do with her: it was like poetry that, without embarrassment, profoundly moves the hearer, and his very voice had developed the dignity of his theme.

He did not speak again. In complete silence they retraced their steps and at the gate of Nelson Lodge he left her. In the little high-walled garden she stood still. This had been a wonderful experience. She felt uplifted, better than herself, yet she could not resist speculating on her probable feelings if another than Charles Batty, if, for instance, Francis Sales, had poured that rhapsody into the night.

Book III : *Rose and Henrietta*

EARLY one October afternoon, Rose Mallett rode to Sales Hall. She went through a world of brown and gold and blue, but she was hardly conscious of beauty, and the air, which was soft, yet keen, and exciting to her horse, had no inspiriting effect on her. She felt old, incased in a sort of mental weariness which was like armour against emotion. She knew that the spirit of the country, at once gentle and wild, furtive and bold, was trying to reach her in every scent and sound: in the smell of earth, of fruit, of burning wood; in the noise of her horse's feet as he cantered on the grassy side of the road, in the fall of a leaf, the call of a bird or a human voice become significant in distance; but she remained unmoved.

This was, she thought, like being dead yet conscious of all that happened, but the dead have the excuse of death and she had none; she was merely tired of her mode of life. It seemed to her that in her thirty-one years the sum of her achievement was looking beautiful and being loved by Francis Sales: she put it in that way, but immediately corrected herself unwillingly. Her attitude towards him had not been passive; she had loved him. She had owed him love and she had paid her debt; she had paid enough, yet if to-day he asked for more, she would give it. Her pride hoped for that demand; her weariness shrank from it.

And he had kissed Henrietta. The sharpness of that thought, on which from the first moment on the stairs she had refused to dwell, steeling her mind against it with a determination which perhaps accounted for her fatigue, was like a physical pain running through her whole body, so that the horse, feeling an unaccustomed jerk on his mouth, became alarmed and restive. She steadied him and herself. A kiss was nothing – yet she had always denied it to Francis Sales. She could not blame him, for she saw how her own fastidiousness had endangered his. He needed material evidence of love. She ought, she supposed, to have sacrificed her scruples for his sake; mentally she had already done it, and the physical refusal was perhaps no more than pride which salved her conscience and might ruin his, but it existed firmly like a fortress. She could not surrender it. Her love was not great enough for that; or was it, she asked herself, too great? She could not comfort herself with that illusion, and there came creeping the thought that for some one else, some one too strong to need such a capitulation, she would have given it gladly, but against Francis, who was intrinsically weak, she had held out.

Life seemed to mock at her; it offered the wrong opportunities, it strewed her path with chances of which no human being could judge the value until the choice had been made; it was like walking over ground pitted with hidden holes, it needed luck as well as skill to avoid a fall. But, like other people, she had to pursue her road: the thing was to hide her bruises, even from herself, and shake off the dust.

She had by this time reached the track which was connected with so much of her life, and she drew rein in astonishment. They were felling the trees. Already a space had been cleared and men and horses were busy removing the fallen trunks; piles of branches, still bravely green, lay here and there, and the pine needles of the past were now overlaid by chippings from the parent trees. What had been a still place of shadows, of muffled sounds, of solemn aisles, the scene of a secret life not revealed to men, was now half devastated, trampled, and loud with human noises. It had its own beauty of colour and activity, there was even a new splendour in the unencumbered ground, but Rose had a sense of loss and sacrilege. Something had gone. It struck her that here she was reminded of herself. Something had gone. The larch trees which had flamed in green for her each spring were dead and she had this strange dead feeling in her heart.

She saw the figure of Francis Sales detach itself from a little group and advance towards her. She knew what he would say. He would tell her, in that sulky way of his, how many weeks had passed since he had seen her and, to avoid hearing that remark, she at once waved a hand towards the clearing and said, 'Why have you done this?'

He shrugged his shoulders. 'To get money.'

'But they were my trees.'

'You never wrote,' he muttered.

She made a gesture, quickly controlled. Long ago when, in the first exultation of their love and their sense of richness, they had marked out the limits of their intercourse, so that they might keep some sort of faith with Christabel and preserve what was precious to themselves, it had been decided that they were not to meet by appointment, they were not to speak of love, no letters were to be exchanged, and though time had bent the first and second rules, the last had been kept with rigour. It was understood, but periodically she had to submit to Francis Sales's complaint, 'You never wrote.'

'So you cut down the trees,' she said half playfully.

'Why didn't you write?'

'Oh, Francis, you know quite well.'

He was looking at the ground; he had not once looked at her since her greeting. 'You go off on a holiday, enjoying yourself, while I – who did you go with?'

'With Henrietta,' Rose said softly.

'Oh, that girl.'

'Yes, that girl. But here I am. I have come back.' She seemed to invite him to be glad. 'And,' she went on calmly, feeling that it did not matter what she said, 'what a queer world to come back to. I miss the trees. They stood for my childhood and my youth; yes, they stood for it, so straight – I must go on. Christabel is expecting me.'

'She didn't tell me.'

'No?' Rose questioned without surprise. 'I suppose I shall see you at tea?' she said.

He nodded and she touched her horse. Something had happened to him as well as to her and a mass of pain lodged itself in her breast. He was different, and as though he had suspected the weary quality of her love he had met her with the same kind, or perhaps with none at all. A little while ago she was half longing for release from this endless necessity of controlling herself and him; from the shifts, the refusals and the reproaches which had gradually become the chief part of their intercourse; and now he had dared to seem indifferent, though he had not forgotten to reproach! She could almost feel the healthy pallor of her face change to a sickly white; her anger chilled and then stiffened her into a rigidity of body and mind and when she dismounted she slid down heavily, like a figure made of wood.

The man who took her horse looked at her curiously. Miss Mallett always had a pleasant word for him and, conscious of his stare, she forced a smile. She had not ridden for weeks, she told him; she was tired. He was amused at that. She had been born in the saddle; he remembered her as a little girl on a Shetland pony and he did not believe she could ever tire. 'Must be something wrong somewhere,' he said, examining girth and pommels.

'It's old age coming on,' Rose said gravely.

He thought that a great joke. He was twice her age already and considered himself in his prime. He led the horse away and Rose went into the house.

How extraordinarily limited her life had been! It had passed almost entirely in this house and Nelson Lodge and on the road between the two. Of all her experiences the only ones that mattered had been suffered here, and they had all been of one kind. Even Henrietta's fewer years had been more varied. She had known poverty and been compelled to the practical application of her wits, she had baffled Mr. Jenkins, she had been kissed by Francis Sales.

Rose stood for a moment in the hall and looked for the mirror which was not there. She did not wish to give Christabel Sales the satisfaction of seeing her look distraught, but a peep in the glass of one of the sporting prints reassured her. Her appearance almost made her doubt the reality of the feelings which consisted of a great heat in the head and a deadly cold weight

132

near her heart and which forced these triumphant words from her lips – 'At least Henrietta has never felt like this.'

She entered Christabel's room calmly, smiling and prepared for news, but at the first sight of the invalid, lying very low in her bed and barely turning her head at the sound of the opening door, she thought that perhaps Christabel's weakness had at last overcome her enmity.

'I'm very ill,' she said faintly.

'I'm sorry.'

'Oh, don't say that. You may as well tell the truth – to me.'

'Then I must say again that I am sorry.'

'I wonder why.'

To that Rose made no answer, and before Christabel spoke again she had time to notice that the cat had gone. She breathed more easily. The cat had gone, the trees were going and Francis was going too. Suddenly she felt she did not care. The idea of an empty world was pleasant, but if Francis were really going, the cat might as well have stayed.

'Tell me what you did in Scotland,' Christabel said.

'I showed Henrietta all the sights.'

'Oh, Henrietta – she's a horrid girl. She has stopped coming to see me.'

'You made yourself so unpleasant.'

'Did she tell you that? Do you think she told Francis?'

'I know she didn't.'

'But I can't make out why she should tell you.'

'Henrietta and I are great friends.'

'How did you manage that?'

'I don't know,' Rose said slowly. 'What has happened to the cat?'

'It's gone. It went out and never came back.'

'How queer.'

'Some one must have killed it.'

'I don't think so,' Rose said thoughtfully. 'I think it decided to go. I'm sure it did.'

'What do you mean? What do you mean?' Christabel cried. 'Had you something to do with that, too?'

'Not that I know of.' Rose laughed. She was tired of considering every word before she uttered it.

'With that too!' Christabel repeated a little wildly, and then in a firm voice she said, 'You've got to tell me.'

'But I don't know. You must make all inquiries of the cat. It was a wise animal. It knew the time had come.'

'I think you're mad,' Christabel said.

'Animals are very strange,' Rose went on easily, 'and rats leave sinking ships.'

A cry of terror came from Christabel. 'You mean I'm going to die!'

'No, no!' Rose became sane and reassuring. 'I never thought of that. It might have known it was going to die itself and an animal likes to die decently alone. It had been getting unhealthily fat.'

Christabel kept an exhausted silence, and Rose regretting her cruelty, aware of its futility, said gently, 'Shall I get you a kitten?'

'No, no kitten. They jump about. The old cat was so quiet. And I miss him.' A tear rolled down either cheek. 'It has been so lonely. Everybody was away.'

'Well, we've all come back now,' Rose said.

'Yes, but that Henrietta – she's deserted me.'

'It was your own fault, Christabel. You horrified her.'

'It should have been you who did that.'

'Things don't always have the effect we hope for. You said too much.'

'Ah, but not half what I could have said.'

'Too much for Henrietta, anyhow. I don't think she will come again.'

Christabel smiled oddly and Rose knew that now she was to hear some news. 'You can tell her,' Christabel said, 'that I shan't say anything to upset her. I shall say nothing about you – as she loves you so much. Does she love you? I dare say. You make people love you – for a little while.' Her voice lingered on those words. 'Yes, for a little while, but you don't keep love, Rose Mallett. No, you don't. I'm sorry for you now. Tell Henrietta she needn't be afraid, because I'm sorry for you. Yes, you and I are in the same boat, in the same deserted boat.

If there were any rats they would run away. You said so yourself.'

'I said the cat had gone.'

'Then you knew?'

Rose shook her head. It was her turn to smile. She was prepared for anything Christabel might say, she was even anxious to hear it, but when Christabel spoke in a mysteriously gleeful manner, she had difficulty in repressing a shudder. It was not, she told herself, that she suffered from the knowledge now imparted by Christabel with detail and with proofs, but her malice, her salacious curiosity were more than Rose could bear. She felt that the whole affair, which at first, so long ago, had possessed a noble sadness, a secret beauty, the quality of a precious substance enclosed in a common vial, was indecent and unclean.

'So you see,' Christabel said, 'you haven't kept him; you won't keep Henrietta.'

Rose said nothing. She was thinking of what she might have done and she was glad she had not done it.

'You don't seem to mind,' Christabel said. 'Why don't you ask me why I'm so sure?' She laughed. 'I ought to know how to find things out by this time, and I know Francis, yes, better than you do. When I had my accident – it wasn't worth it, was it? – I said to myself, "Now he won't be faithful to me." When I knew I should have to lie here, I told myself that. And now you –' Her voice almost failed her. 'I suppose you haven't been kind enough to him.'

'I think it's time I went,' Rose said.

'And you'll never come back?'

'Yes, if you want me.'

'I can say what I like to you.'

'You can, indeed,' Rose murmured.

'And tell Henrietta to come too.'

'No, I can't ask Henrietta.'

'I promise to be like a maiden aunt. Ah, but she has three already – she knows what they are. That won't attract her. I'll be like an invalid in a Sunday School story-book.'

'I'll tell her of your promise,' Rose said.

There remained the task of having tea with Francis Sales and breaking the bonds of which he had tired. She made it easy for him. That was necessary for her dignity, but beyond the desire for as much seemliness as could be saved from the general ugliness of their mistake, she had no feeling; yet she thought it would be good to be in the open air, on horseback, free. If there had been anything still owing, she had paid her debt with generosity. She gave him the chance he wanted but did not know how to take, and she had to allow him to appear aggrieved. She was cruel: she was tired of him; she was, he sneered, too good for him. The words went on for some time, and if some of them were new, their manner was wearisomely familiar. She was amazed at her own endurance, now and in the past, and at last she said, 'No, no, Francis. Say no more. This is too much fuss. Perhaps we have both changed.'

'It was you who began it.'

'Was it? How can one tell?'

'You began it,' he persisted. 'There was a time when you went white, like paper, when we met, and your eyes went black. Now I might be a sheep in a field.'

She was standing up, ready to go. 'One gets used to things,' she said.

'I have never been used to you,' he muttered, and she knew that, telling this truth, he also explained a good deal. 'I never should be. You're like nobody else – nobody.'

'But it is too much strain,' she murmured slowly.

'Yes – well, it is you who have said it. I had made up my mind – I'm not ungrateful – I never intended to say a word.'

She smiled. This was the first remark which had really touched her. She found it so offensive that a smile was the only weapon with which to meet it. 'I know that.'

'But mind,' he almost shouted, 'there's nobody like you.'

'Yes, yes, I know that too.' She turned to him with a silencing sternness. 'I tell you I know everything.'

§ 2

The old groom who held her horse nodded with satisfaction when he helped her into the saddle. She had not lost her spring and he tightened her girths in a leisurely manner and arranged her skirt with the care due to a fine rider and a lady who understood a horse, yet one who was always ready to ask an old man's advice. He had a great admiration for Miss Mallett and, conscious of it and rather pathetically glad of it, she lingered for the pleasure of talking to some one who seemed simple and untroubled. He had spent all his life on the Sales estate, and she wondered whether, though, like herself, of a limited outward experience, he also had known the passions of love and disgust and shame. He was sixty-five, he told her, but as strong as ever, and she envied him: to be sixty-five with the turmoil of life behind him, yet to be strong enough to enjoy the peace before him, was a good finale to existence. She was only thirty-one, but she was strong too, and she felt as though she had come through a storm, battered and exhausted but whole and ready for the calm which already hovered over her. She said, 'The young are always sorry for the old, but that is one of the many mistakes they make. I think it must be the best time of all.'

'If you have them that cares for you,' he answered.

That was where her own happiness would break down. There were her stepsisters, who would probably die before herself; there was Henrietta, who would form ties of her own; and there was no one else. If she had had less faith in Francis Sales's love and, at the same time, had been capable of pandering to it, she might have had his devotion for her old age, the devotion of a somewhat querulous and dull old man. Now she had not even that to hope for, and she was glad. She had always wanted the best of everything, and always, except in the one fatal instance, refused what fell below her standard. She had not realized until now that Francis Sales had always been below it. She had at least tried to wrap their love in beauty, but that sort of beauty was not enough for him. It was her scruples, he said, which had been his undoing, and there was truth in that, but she had to remember that when originally she had disappointed him, he had found comfort quickly in Christabel; when Christabel failed him he had returned to her; and now he had found consolation, if only of a temporary kind, in some one else. When would he seek yet another victim of his affection and his griefs? He was, she thought scornfully, a man who needed women, yet she knew that if he had pleaded with her to-day, saying that in spite of everything he needed her, she would have listened.

She admitted her responsibility, it would always be present to her, for she had that kind of conscientiousness, and having once helped him, she must always hold herself ready to do it again. The chain binding them was not altogether broken, but she no longer felt its weight. She had a lightness of spirit unknown for years; the anger, the jealous rage and the disgust had vanished with a completeness which made her doubt their short existence, and she began to make plans for a new life. There was no reason now why she should not wander all over the world, yet, on the very doorstep of Nelson Lodge, she found a reason in the person of Henrietta – flushed and gay and just returned from a tea party. She had enjoyed herself immensely, but her head ached a little. It had been all she could do to understand the brilliant conversation. There had been present a budding poet and a woman painter and she had never heard people talk like that before.

'I didn't speak at all, except to Charles,' she said.

'Oh, Charles was there?'

'Yes. I thought it safer not to talk but I looked as bright as I could, and of course I asked for cakes and things. They all ate a lot. I was glad of that. But most of them still looked hungry at the end. And Charles has taken tickets for me for the concerts, next to him, in a special corner where you can sometimes hear the music through the whispering of the audience. That's what he says!'

'But, Henrietta, I have taken tickets for you too.'

'Thank you, but perhaps they will take them back.'

'Henrietta, you really can't sit in a corner with Charles when I'm in another part of the hall.'

'Can't I? Well, Charles will be very angry, but he'll have to put up with it. If you explained to him, Aunt Rose, he'd understand. And I'd really rather sit with you. I shall be able to look at people and if I crackle my programme you won't

138

glare. Of course, I shall try not to. Will you explain to him? And I did promise to go to a concert with him some day.'

'Then you must. I'll tell him that, too. Are you afraid of him, Henrietta?'

'He shouts,' Henrietta said, 'and I'm sorry for him. And I do like him very much. I feel inclined to do things just to please him.'

'Don't let that carry you too far.'

'That's what I'm afraid of. Not him, exactly, but me.'

'I didn't suspect you of such tenderness. I shall have to look after you.'

'I wish you would.'

'And if you are feeling very kind some day, perhaps you will go and see Christabel Sales. She has promised to behave herself.'

Henrietta's expression tightened. 'I don't want to go. It's a dreadful place.'

'I know,' Rose said, and she added encouragingly, 'but the cat has gone.'

They were standing together in the hall and against the white panelled walls, the figure of Rose, in the austere riding-habit, one gauntletted hand holding her crop, the other resting lightly on her hip, had an heroic aspect, like a statue in dark marble; but her eyes did not offer the blank gaze, the calm effrontery of stone: they looked at Henrietta with something like appeal against this obsession of the cat.

'Oh, I'm glad the cat's gone,' Henrietta murmured. 'What happened to it?'

Rose shook her head. 'It disappeared.'

They stared at each other until Henrietta said, 'But all the same, I don't want to go.' And then, because Rose would not help her out, she was obliged to say, 'It's Mr. Sales.' Her voice dropped. 'I haven't seen him since I hit him.'

Rose turned to go upstairs. 'I shouldn't think too much of that.'

'You don't think it matters?'

'No.'

Henrietta looked after her and followed her for a step. 'You think I may go?' Her voice was dull under her effort to control

139

it. She felt that the stately figure moving up the stairs was deliberately leaving her to face a danger, sanctioning her desire to meet it. She felt her fate was in the answer made by Rose.

'I think you can take care of yourself perfectly well, Henrietta,' and like a sigh, another sentence floated from the landing where Rose stood, out of sight: 'You are not like me.'

This was a mysterious and astonishing remark. Henrietta did not understand it and in her excited realization that the door so carefully locked by her own hand had been opened by Aunt Rose, she did not try to understand it. Aunt Rose had said she was able to take care of herself, and it was true, but honesty and a weak clinging to safety urged her to answer, 'But you see, you see I don't want to do it!'

These words were not uttered. She stood, looking up towards the empty landing with a hand pressed against her heart. It was beating fast. The spirit of Reginald Mallett, subdued in his daughter for some months, seemed to be fluttering in her breast and it was Aunt Rose who had waked it up. It was not Henrietta's fault, she was not responsible; and suddenly, the ordinary happiness she had been enjoying was transferred into an irrational joy. She went singing up the stairs, and Rose, sitting in her room in a state of limpness she would never have allowed anybody to see, heard a sound as innocent as if a bird had waked to a sunny dawn.

Henrietta sang, but now and then she paused and became grave when the spirit of that mother who lived in her memory more and more dimly, as though she had died when Henrietta was a child, overcame the spirit of her father. Her mission was to be one of kindness to Christabel Sales, and if – the song burst out again – if adventure came in her way, could she refuse it? She would refuse nothing – the song ceased – short of sin. She looked at herself and saw a solemn feminine edition of the portrait hanging behind her on the wall. She was like her father, but she took pride in her greater conscientiousness; her vocabulary was larger than his by at least one word.

A few days later she set out on that road and past those trees which had been the safe witnesses of so much of Rose Mallett's life, but their safeness lay in their constant muteness, and they had no message for Henrietta. Walking quickly, she rehearsed her coming meeting with Francis Sales, but when she actually met him on the green track, on the very spot where Rose had pulled up her horse in amazement at the scene of transformation, Henrietta, like Rose, had no formal greeting for him.

She said, 'The trees! What are you doing with them?'

'Turning them into gold.'

'But they were beautiful.'

'So are lots of things they will buy.' She moved a little under his look, but when he said, 'I'm hard up,' she became interested.

'Really? I thought you were frightfully rich. You ought to be with all these belongings.' She looked round at the fields dotted with sheep and cattle, the distant chimneys of Sales Hall, the fallen trees and the team of horses dragging logs under the guidance of workmen in their shirt sleeves. 'I know all about being poor,' she said, 'but I don't suppose we mean the same thing by the word. I've been so poor –' She stopped. 'But there's a lot of excitement about it. I used to hope I should find a shilling in my purse that I'd forgotten. A shilling! You can do a lot with a shilling. At least I can.'

'I wish you'd tell me how.'

'Pretend you haven't got it. That's the beginning. You haven't got it, so you can't have what you want.'

'I never have what I want.'

'Then you mustn't want anything.'

'Oh, yes, that's so easy.'

'Well' – she descended to details with an air of kindness – 'what do you want? Let's work it out. We'd better sit on the wall. After all, it's rather lovely without the trees. It's so clear and the air's so blue, as if it's trying to make up. Now tell me what you want.'

'Something money can't buy.'

'Then you needn't have cut down the trees.'

'I shouldn't have if I'd thought you'd care.'

She said softly but sharply, 'I don't believe that for a moment. Why don't you tell the truth?'

'Do you want to hear it?'

'I'm not sure.'

'Then I'll wait while you make up your mind.'

Sitting on the wall, his feet rested easily on the ground while hers swung free, and while he seemed to loll in complete indifference, she was conscious of a tenseness she could not prevent. She hated her enjoyment of his manner, which was impudent, but it had the spice of danger that she liked and it was in defiance of the one and encouragement of the other that she said, 'I'm sure you would never talk to Aunt Rose like that.'

'I should never give your Aunt Rose my confidence,' he said severely.

It was impossible not to feel a warmth of satisfaction, and she asked shortly, 'Why not?'

'She wouldn't understand. You're human. I'm devilish lonely. Well, you know my circumstances.' A shadow which seemed to affect the brightness of the autumn day, even deadening the clear shouting of the men and the jingling of the chains attached to the horses, passed over Francis Sales's face. 'One wants a friend.'

A cry of genuine bewilderment came from Henrietta. 'But I thought you were so fond of Aunt Rose!'

From sulky contemplation of his brown boots and leggings, he looked at her. His eyes, of a light yet dense blue, were widely opened. 'What makes you think that? Did she tell you?'

Henrietta's lip curled derisively. 'No, it was you, when you looked at her. And now you have told me again.' She had a moment of thoughtful contempt for the blundering of men. There was Charles, who always seemed to wander in a mist, and now this Francis Sales, who revealed what he wished to hide. He was mentally inferior to Mr. Jenkins, who had a quickness of wit, a vulgar sharpness of tongue which kept the mind on the alert; but physically she had shrunk from Mr. Jenkins's proximity, while that of Francis Sales, in his well-cut tweeds and his shining boots, who seemed as clean as the air surrounding him, had an attraction actually enhanced by his heaviness of spirit. He was like a child possessed, consciously or unconsciously, of a weapon, and her sense of her own superiority was corrected by fear of his strength and of the subtle weakness in her own blood.

142

She heard a murmur. 'She has treated me very badly. I've known her all my life. Well –'

Henrietta, with a gentleness he appreciated and a cleverness he missed, said commiseratingly, 'She wouldn't let you take her hand in the wood.'

'What on earth are you talking about? Look here, Henrietta, what do you mean?' There had been so many occasions of the kind that it was impossible to know to which one she referred, and, looking back, his past seemed to be blocked with frustrations and petty torments. 'What do you mean?' he repeated.

'Never mind.'

'This is some gossip,' he muttered.

'Yes, among the squirrels and the rabbits. Woods are full of eyes and ears.'

'Well,' he said, 'the eyes and ears will have to find another home. There will soon be no wood left.'

So he had tried to take Aunt Rose's hand in this wood too! She laughed with the pretty trill which made her laughter a new thing every time.

'I don't see the joke,' he grumbled.

She turned to him. 'I don't think you've laughed very much in your life. You're always being sorry for yourself.'

'I have been very unfortunate,' he replied.

'There you are again! Why don't you tell yourself you're lucky not to squint or turn in your toes? You'd be much more miserable then – much. But thinking yourself unfortunate, when you're not, is a pleasant occupation.'

'How do you know?'

'I know a lot,' Henrietta said. 'But I never thought myself unfortunate, so I wasn't.'

'Very noble,' Sales said sourly.

'No. I told you it was exciting to be poor. You're not poor enough. A new dress,' she went on, clasping her hands; 'first of all, I had to save up – in pennies.' She turned accusingly. 'You don't believe it.'

'It must have taken a long time.'

'It did, but not so long as you would think, because it cost so little in the end. I saved up, and then I looked in the shop windows, and then I talked about it for days, and then I bought the stuff. Mother cut out the dress, and then I made it.'

'And the result was charming.'

'I thought so then. Now I know it wasn't, but at the time I was happy.'

'Well,' he said, 'that's very interesting, but it doesn't help me.'

'But I could help you if you told me your troubles. I should know how.'

'Telling my troubles would be a help.'

'Here I am, then.'

'What's the good?' he said. 'You'll desert me, too.'

'Not if you're good.'

'Oh, if that's the stipulation –' He stood up. His tone, which might have been provocative, was simply bored. She knew she had been dull, and her lip trembled with mortification.

'Why, of course!' she cried gaily, when she had mastered that weakness. 'Aunt Caroline warned me against you this very afternoon. She said – but, never mind. I'm not going to repeat her remarks. And anyhow, Aunt Sophia said they were not true. Aunt Rose,' Henrietta said thoughtfully, 'was not there. I don't suppose either of them is right. And now I'm going to see Mrs. Sales.'

He ran after her. 'Henrietta, I shouldn't tell her you've seen me.'

She frowned. 'I don't like that.'

'It's for her sake.'

Henrietta turned away without a word, but she pondered, as she went, on the dangerous likeness between right and wrong and the horrible facility with which they could be, with which they had to be, interchanged. One became bewildered, one became lost; she felt herself being forced into a false position: she might not be able to get out. Aunt Rose had sent her, Francis Sales was conspiring with her – she made her father's gesture of helplessness, it was not her fault. But she made up her mind she would never allow Francis Sales to find her dull again, for that was unfair to herself.

Rose Mallett, who had always accepted conditions and not criticized them, found herself in those days forced to a puzzled consideration of life. It seemed an unnecessary invention on the part of a creator, a freak which, on contemplation, he must surely regret. She was not tired of her own existence, but she wondered what it was for and what, possessing it, she could do with it. Her one attempt at usefulness had been foiled, and though she had never consciously wanted anything to do, she felt the need now that she was deprived of it. She passed her days in the order and elegance of Nelson Lodge, in a monotonous satisfaction of the eye, listening to the familiar chatter of Caroline and Sophia, dressing herself with tireless care and refusing to regret her past. Nevertheless, it had been wasted, and the only occupation of her present was her anxiety for Francis Sales. She could not rid herself of that claim, begun so long ago. She had to accept the inactive responsibility which in another would have resolved itself into earnest prayer but which in her was a stoical endurance of possibilities.

What was he doing? What would he do? She knew he could not stand alone, she knew she must continue to hold herself ready for his service, but a prisoner fastened to a chain does not find much solace in counting the links, and that was all she had to do. It seemed to her that she moved, rather like a ghost, up and down the stairs, about the landing, in the delicate silence of her bedroom; that she sat ghost-like at the dining-table and heard the strangely aimless talk of human beings. She supposed there were countless women like herself, unoccupied and lonely, yet her pride resented the idea. There was only one Rose Mallett; there was no one else with just her past, with the same mental pictures and her peculiar isolation, and if she had been a vainer woman she would have added that no other woman offered the same kind of beauty to a world in need of it. Her obvious consolation was in the presence of Henrietta, though she had little companionship to give her aunt, and no suspicion that Rose, almost unawares, began to transfer her interests to the girl, to set her mind on Henrietta's happiness. She would take her abroad and let her see the world.

Caroline sniffed at the suggestion, Sophia sighed.

'The world's the same everywhere,' Caroline said. 'If you know one man you know them all.'

'But if you know a great many, you will know one all the better. However,' she smiled in the way of which her step-sisters were afraid, 'I wasn't thinking of men.'

'That's where you're so unnatural.'

'I was thinking of places – cities and mountains and plains.'

'You'll get the plague or be run away with by brigands.'

'I think Henrietta and I would rather like the brigands. We must avoid the plague.'

'Smallpox,' Caroline went on, 'and your complexions ruined.'

'I wish you would stay at home,' Sophia said. 'Caroline and I are getting old.'

'Nonsense, Sophia! I'd go myself for twopence. But I'd better wait here and get the ransom money ready, and then James Batty and I can start out together with a bag of it.' She laughed loudly at the prospect of setting forth with the respectable James. 'And it wouldn't be the first elopement I'd planned either. When I was eighteen I set my mind on getting out of my bedroom window with a bundle – no, of course I never told you, Sophia. You would have run in hysterics to the General. But there was never one among them all who was worth the inconvenience, so I gave it up. I always had more sense than sentiment.' She sighed with regret for the legions of disappointed and fictitious lovers waiting under windows, with which her mind was peopled. 'Not one,' she repeated.

No one took any notice. Sophia, drooping her heavy head, was thinking of brigands in a far country and of Caroline and herself left in Nelson Lodge without Rose and without Henrietta. If they really went away she determined to tell Henrietta the story of her lover, lest she should die and the tale be unrecorded. She wanted somebody to know; she would tell Henrietta on the eve of her departure, among the bags and boxes. He had gone to America and died there, and that continent was both sacred to her and abhorrent.

'Don't go to America,' she murmured.

'Why not?' Caroline demanded. 'Just the place they ought to go to. Lots of millionaires.'

Rose reassured Sophia. 'And it is only an idea. I haven't said a word to Henrietta.'

Henrietta showed no enthusiasm for the suggestion. She liked Radstowe. And there was the Battys' ball. It would be a pity to miss that. She must certainly not miss that, said Caroline and Sophia. And what was she going to wear? They had better go upstairs at once, to the elder ladies' room, and see what could be done with Caroline's pink satin. She had only worn it once, years ago. Nobody would remember it, and trimmed with some of her mother's lace, the big flounce and the fichu, it would be a different thing. Sophia could wear her apricot.

'Come along, Henrietta. Come along, Rose. We must really get this settled.'

They went upstairs, Caroline moving with heavy dignity, but keeping up her head as she had been taught in her youth. Nothing was more unbecoming than ducking the head and sticking out the back. Sophia went slowly, holding to the balustrade, so very slowly that Henrietta did not attempt to start. She said softly to Rose, 'How slowly she goes. I've never noticed it before.'

'She always goes upstairs like that,' Rose said. 'It is not natural to her to hurry.'

Henrietta followed and found Sophia panting a little on the landing. She laid hold of her niece's arm. 'A little out of breath,' she whispered. 'Don't say anything, dear child, to Caroline. She doesn't like to be reminded of our age.'

They went into the bedroom and Rose, drifting into her own room, heard the opening of the great wardrobe doors. She would be called in presently for her advice, but there would be a lot of talk and many reminiscences before she was needed. She stood by the fire, which, giving the only light to the room, threw golden patches on the white dressing-gown lying across a chair, and made the buckles on her shoes sparkle like diamonds.

She was wondering why Henrietta's eyes had darkened as though with fear at the idea of going away. She had been very quick in veiling them, and her voice, too, had been quick, a little tremulous. There was more than the Battys' ball in her desire to stay in Radstowe. Was it Charles whom she was loth to leave? Afterwards, perhaps in the spring, she had said it would be nice to go. It was kind of Aunt Rose, and Aunt Rose, gazing down at the fire, controlled her longing to escape from this place too full of memories. She would not leave Henrietta who had to be cared for, perhaps protected; she would not persuade her who had to be happy, but she felt a sinking of the heart which was almost physical. She rested both hands on the mantelshelf and on them her weight. She felt as though she could not go on like this for ever. She, who apparently had no ties, was never free; she had the duties without the joys, and for these few minutes, before a knock came at the door, she allowed herself the relief of melancholy. She was incapable of tears, but she wished she could cry bitterly and for a long time.

The knock was Henrietta's. She entered a little timidly. Aunt Rose was not free with invitations to her room and to Henrietta it was a beautiful and mysterious place. She had a childlike pleasure in the silver and glass on the dressing-table, in glimpses of exquisite garments and slippers worn to the shape of Aunt Rose's slim foot, and Aunt Rose herself was like some fairy princess growing old and no less lovely in captivity, but to-night, that dark straight figure splashed by the firelight reminded her of words uttered by Christabel. She had said that all Henrietta's aunts were witches, and for the first time the girl agreed. In the other room, brilliantly lighted, Caroline and Sophia were bending somewhat greedily over a mass of silks and satins and laces, their cheeks flushed round the dabs of rouge, their fingers active yet inept, fumbling in what might have been a brew for the working of spells; and here, straight as a tree, Aunt Rose looked into the fire as though she could see the future in its red heart, but her voice, very clear, had a reassuring quality. It was not, Henrietta thought, a witch's voice. Witches mumbled and screeched, and Aunt Rose spoke like water falling from a height.

148

'Come in, Henrietta. Is the consultation over?'

'It has hardly begun. What a lot of clothes they have, and boxes of lace, boxes! I think you will have to decide for them. And Aunt Caroline snubs Aunt Sophia, all the time.'

'Did they send you to fetch me?'

'Yes, but we needn't go back yet, need we? Aunt Caroline wants to wear her emeralds, but she says they will look vulgar with pink satin. There's some lovely grey stuff like a cobweb. She says it was in her mother's trousseau and I think she ought to wear that, but she says she is going to keep it until she's old!'

'Then she'll never wear it. She will never make such an admission.'

'And she won't let Aunt Sophia have it because she says it would make her look like a dusty broom. And it would, you know! She's really very funny sometimes.'

'Very funny. We're queer people, Henrietta.'

'Are we? And I'm more theirs than yours.'

'As far as blood goes, yes.' She spoke very quietly, but she felt a great desire to assert, for once, her own claims, instead of accepting those of others. She wanted to tell Henrietta that in return for the secret care, the growing affection she was giving, she demanded confidence and love; but she had never asked for anything in her life. She had taken coolly much she could easily have done without, admiration and respect and the material advantages to which she had been born, but she had asked for nothing. Cruelly conscious of all that lay in the gift of Henrietta, who sat in a low chair, her chin on the joined fingers of her hands, Rose continued to look at the fire.

'You mean I'm really more like you?' Henrietta said. 'Am I? I'm like my father,' and she added softly, 'terribly.'

'Why terribly?'

Henrietta moved her feet. 'Oh, I don't know.'

'I wish you'd tell me.'

'He was queer. You said we all were, and I'm a Mallett, too, that's all. Don't you think we ought to go and see about the dresses now? Aunt Rose, they're bothering me to wear white, the only thing for a young girl, but I want to wear yellow. Don't you think I might?'

149

Rose, who had felt herself on the brink of confidences, as though she peered over a cliff, and watched the mists clear to show the secret valley underneath, now saw the clouds thicken hopelessly, and retreated from her position with an effort.

'Yellow? Yes, certainly. You will look like a marigold. Henrietta –' She did not know what she was going to say, but she wanted to detain the girl for a little longer, she hoped for another chance of drawing nearer. 'Henrietta, wait a minute.' She moved to her dressing-table, smiling at what she was about to do. It seemed as though she were going to bribe the girl to love her, but she was only yielding to the pathetic human desire to give something tangible since the intangible was ignored. 'When I was twenty-one,' she said, 'your father gave me a present.'

'Only when you were twenty-one?'

'Well,' Rose excused him, 'we didn't know each other very well. He was a great deal from home, but he remembered my twenty-first birthday and he gave me this necklace. I think it's beautiful, but I never wear it now, and I think you may like to have it. Here it is, in its own box and with the card he wrote – "A jewel for a rose." '

Holding it in her cupped hands, Henrietta murmured with delight: 'May I have it really? How lovely! And may I have the card, too? He did say nice things. Are you sure you can spare the card? I expect he admired you very much. He liked beautiful women. My mother was pretty, too; but I don't believe he ever gave her anything except a wedding-ring, and he had to give her that.'

'Oh, Henrietta – well, his daughter shall have all he gave me.'

'If you're sure you don't want it. What are the stones?'

'Topaz and diamonds; but so small that you can wear them.'

'Topaz and diamonds! Oh!' And Henrietta, clasping it round her neck and surveying herself by the candles Rose had lighted, said earnestly, 'Oh, I do hope he paid for it!' This was the first thought of Reginald Mallett's daughter.

Rose was horrified into laughter, which seemed hysterically continuous to Henrietta, and through it Rose cried tenderly, 'Oh, you poor child! You poor child!'

150

Henrietta did not laugh. She said gravely, 'All the same, I'm glad I had him for a father. Nobody but he would have chosen a thing like this. He had such taste.' She looked at her aunt. 'I do hope I have some taste, too.'

'I hope you have,' Rose said with equal gravity. She laughed no longer. 'There are many kinds, and though he knew how to choose an ornament, he made mistakes in other ways.'

Henrietta unclasped the necklace and laid it down. She looked, indeed, remarkably like her father. Her eyes flashed above her angry mouth. 'You mean my mother!'

'No, Henrietta. How could I? I did not know your mother, and from the little you have told us I believe she was too good for him.'

'How can I tell you more,' Henrietta protested, 'when I know what you would be thinking? You would be thinking she was common. Aunt Caroline does. She does! I don't know how she dare! No, I won't have the necklace.'

'You must believe what I say, Henrietta. Your mother was not the only woman in your father's life, and I was referring to the others.'

'You need not speak of them to me,' Henrietta said with dignity.

'I won't do so again. That, perhaps, is where my own taste failed.' She decided to put out no more feelers for Henrietta's thoughts. It was what she would have resented bitterly herself, and it did no good. She was not clever at this unpractised art, and she told herself that if her own affection could not tell her what she wished to know, the information would be useless. Moreover, she had Henrietta's word for it that she was terribly like her father.

'So put on the necklace again. It suits you better than it does me, so well that we can pretend he really chose it for you.'

'Yes,' Henrietta said, fingering it again, 'if you promise you never think anything horrid about my mother.'

'The worst I have ever thought of her,' Rose said lightly, 'is envying her for her daughter.'

She saw Henrietta's mouth open inelegantly. 'Me? Oh, but you're not old enough.'

151

'I feel very old sometimes.'

'I thought you were when I first saw you,' Henrietta said, looking in the glass and swaying her body to make the diamonds glitter, 'but now I know you never will be, because it's only ugly people who get old. When your hair is white you'll be like a queen. Now you're a princess, though Mrs. Sales says you're a witch. Oh, I didn't mean to tell you that. It was a long time ago. She is never disagreeable now. I'm going to see her again to-morrow.'

'I wish you would go in the morning, Henrietta. The afternoons get dark so soon and the road is lonely.'

'She doesn't like visitors in the morning,' Henrietta said. 'I love this necklace. Could I wear it to the dance?'

'It depends on the dress. If you are really to look like a marigold you must wear no ornaments. If you had yellow tulle –' And Rose took pencil and paper and made a rough design, talking with enthusiasm meanwhile, for like all the Malletts, she loved clothes.

The next day Caroline had to stay in bed. She had been feverish all night and Sophia appeared in Rose's bedroom early in the morning, her great plait of hair swinging free, her face yellow with anxiety and sleeplessness and lack of powder, to inform her stepsister that dear Caroline was very ill: they must have the doctor directly after breakfast. Sophia was afraid Caroline was going to die. She had groaned in the night when she thought Sophia was asleep. 'I deceived her,' Sophia said. 'I hope it wasn't wrong, but I knew she would be easier if she thought I slept. Now she says there is nothing the matter with her and she wants to get up, but that's her courage.'

Caroline was not allowed to rise and after breakfast and an hour with Sophia behind the locked door she announced her readiness to see the doctor, who diagnosed nothing more serious than a chill. She was very much disgusted with his order to stay in bed. She had not had a day in bed for years; she believed people were only ill when they wanted to be and, as she did not wish to be, she was not ill. She had no resource but to be unpleasant to Sophia, to the silently devoted Susan and to Rose who had intended to go to Sales Hall with Henrietta. She was not able to do that, but later in the afternoon she set out to meet her so that she might have company for part of the dark way home.

Afterwards, she could never make up her mind whether she was glad or sorry she had gone. She had expected to meet Henrietta within a mile or two of the bridge, and the further she went without a sight of the small figure walking towards her, the more necessary it became to proceed, but she felt a deadly sickness of this road. She loved each individual tree, each bush and field and the view from every point, but the whole thing she hated. It was the personification of mistake, disappointment and slow disillusion, but now it was all shrouded in darkness and she seemed to be walking on nothing, through nothing and towards nothing. She herself was nothing and she thought of nothing, though now and then a little wave of anxiety washed over her. Where was Henrietta?

She became genuinely alarmed when, in the hollow between the track and the rising fields, she saw a fire and discovered by its light a caravan, a cart, a huddle of dark figures, a tethered pony, and heard the barking of dogs. There were gipsies camping in the sheltered dip. If Henrietta had walked into their midst, she might have been robbed, she would certainly have been frightened; and Rose stood still, listening intently.

The cleared space, where the wood had been, stretched away to a line of trees edging the main road and above it there was a greenish colour in the sky. There was not a sound but what came from the encampment. Down there the fire glowed like some enormous and mysterious jewel and before it figures which had become poetical and endowed with some haggard kind of beauty passed and vanished. They might have been employed in the rites of some weird worship and the movements which were in reality connected with the cooking of some snared bird or rabbit seemed to have a processional quality. The fire was replenished, the stew was stirred, there was a faint clatter of tin plates and a sharp cracking of twigs: a figure passed before the fire with extraordinary gestures and slid into the night: another figure appeared and followed its predecessor: smoke rose and a savoury smell floated on the air.

153

Suddenly a child wailed and Rose had the ghastly impression that it was the child who was in the pot.

Cautiously she stepped into the clearing; the dogs barked again and she ran swiftly, as silently as possible, leaping over the small hummocks of heath, dodging the brushwood and finding a certain pleasure in her own speed and in her fear that the dogs would soon be snapping at her heels. If she did not find Henrietta on the road, she would go on to Sales Hall. Very high up, clouds floated as though patrolling the sky; they found in her fleeting figure something which must be watched.

She was breathless and strangely happy when she reached the road. She was pleased at her capacity for running and her dull trouble seemed to have lifted, to have risen from her mind and gone off to join the clouds. She laughed a little and dropped down on a stone, and above the hurried beating of her heart she heard fainter, more despairing, the cry of the gipsy child. 'It isn't cooked yet,' she thought. There was a deeper silence, and she imagined a horrible dipping into the pot, a loud and ravenous eating.

For a few minutes she forgot her quest, conscious of a happy loss of personality in this solitary place, feeling herself merged into the night, looking up at the patrolling clouds which, having lost her, had moved on. She sat in the darkness until she heard, very far off, the beat of a horse's hoofs, the rumble of wheels. She remembered then that she had to find Henrietta. The road towards Sales Hall was nowhere blurred by a figure, there was no sound of footsteps, and the noise of the approaching horse and cart was distantly symbolic of human activity and home-faring; it made her think of lights and food.

She looked back, and not many yards away two figures stepped from the sheltering trees by the roadside. On the whiteness of the road they were clear and unmistakable. Their arms were outstretched and their hands were joined and, as she looked, the two forms became one, separated and parted. The feet of Henrietta went tapping down the road and for a moment Francis stood and watched her. Then he turned. He struck a match, and Rose saw his face and hands illuminated like a paper lantern. The match made a short, brilliant journey in the air and fell extinguished. He had lighted his pipe and was advancing towards her. She, too, advanced and stopped a few feet from him and at once she said calmly, 'Was that Henrietta? I came to find her.'

He stammered something; she was afraid he was going to lie, yet at the same time she knew that to hear him lie would give her pleasure; it would be like the final shattering and trampling of her love: but he did not lie.

'Yes, Henrietta,' he said sullenly. 'There are gipsies in the hollow. I shall turn them out to-morrow.'

'Let them stay there,' she said, she knew not why.

'They're all thieves,' he muttered.

Neither spoke. It was like a dream to be standing there with him and hearing Henrietta's footsteps tapping into silence. Then Rose asked in genuine bewilderment, 'Why did you let her go home alone? Why did you leave her here?'

'She wouldn't have me. She's safe now'; and raising his voice, he almost cried, 'You shouldn't let her come here!' It was a cry for help, he was appealing to her again, he was the victim of his habit. She smiled and wondered if her pale face was as clear to him as his was to her.

'No, I should not,' she said slowly. 'I should not. One does nothing all one's life but make mistakes.' Her chief feeling at that moment was one of self-disgust. She moved away without another word, going slowly so that she should not overtake Henrietta.

§ 4

Henrietta was going very fast, impelled by the fury of her thoughts, and she forgot to be afraid of the lonely country, for she felt herself still wrapped in the dangerous safety of that man's embrace, and the darkness through which she went was still the palpitating darkness which had fallen over her at his touch. The thing had been bound to happen. She had been watching its approach and pretending it was not there, and now it had arrived and she was giddy with excitement, inspired with a sense of triumph, tremulous with apprehension.

Her thoughts were not of her lover as an individual, but of

155

the situation as a whole. Here she was, Henrietta Mallett, from Mrs. Banks's boarding-house, the chief figure in a drama and an unrepentant sinner. She could not help it: she loved him; he needed her. Since that day when she had offered him friendship and help, he had been depending on her more and more, a big man like a neglected baby. She had strenuously fixed her mind on the babyish side of him, but all the time her senses had been attracted by the man, and now, by the mere physical experience of the force of his arms, she could never see him as a child again. She clung to the idea of helping him, to the thought of his misfortunes, for that was imperative, but she was now conscious of her fewer years, her infinitely smaller bodily strength, the limitations of her sex.

And suddenly, as she moved swiftly, hardly feeling the ground under her feet, she began to cry, with emotion, with fear and joy. What was going to happen to her? She loved him. She could still feel the violence of his clasp, the roughness of his coat on her cheeks, the iron of his hands, so distinctly that it seemed to have happened only a moment ago, yet she was nearly home. She could see the lights of the bridge as though swung on a cord across the gulf, and she dried her eyes. She was exhausted and hungry and when she had passed over the river she made her way to a shop where chocolates could be bought. She knew their comforting and sustaining properties. It was unromantic, but hunger asserts itself in spite of love.

It was getting late and the shop was empty but for one assistant and a tall young man. This was Charles Batty, taking a great deal of trouble over his purchase, for spread before him on the counter was an assortment of large chocolate boxes adorned with bows of ribbon and pictures of lovers leaning over stiles and red-lipped maidens caressing dogs.

'I don't like these pictures,' Henrietta heard him mutter bashfully.

'Here's one with roses. Roses are always suitable.'

'No,' he said, 'I want a big white box with crimson ribbon.'

Henrietta stepped up to his side. 'I'll help you choose,' she said.

He started, stared, forgot to take off his hat. He gazed at her with the absorption of some connoisseur looking at the perfect thing he has dreamed of: he looked without greed and with a sort of ecstasy which left his face expressionless and embarrassed Henrietta in the presence of the arch girl behind the counter.

Charles waked up. 'I want a white one,' he repeated, 'with crimson ribbon. No pictures.' The assistant went away and he turned to Henrietta. 'It's for you,' he said.

'Charles, don't speak so loud.'

'I don't care. But I suppose you're ashamed of me. Yes, of course, that's it.'

'Don't be silly,' Henrietta said, 'and do be quick, because I want some chocolates myself.'

With the large box, white and crimson-ribboned and wrapped in paper, under his arm, he waited until she was served, and then they walked together down the street, made brilliant with the lights of many little shops.

'This is for you,' he said, 'but I'll carry it.'

'But this isn't the way home.'

'No.' They turned back into the dimmer road bordering The Green.

'I suppose you wouldn't walk round the hill?'

'I don't mind.' She felt as she might have done in the company of some large, protective dog. He was there, saving her from the fear of molestation, but there was no need to speak to him, it was almost impossible to think consecutively of him, yet she did remind herself that a very long time ago, when she was young, he had said wonderful things to her. She had forgotten that fact in the stir of these last days.

'I got these chocolates for you,' he said again. 'I thought perhaps that was the kind of thing I ought to do. I don't know, and you can't ask people because they'd laugh. Why didn't you come to tea on Sunday?'

'I can't come every Sunday.'

'Of course you can. Considering I'm engaged to you, it's only proper.'

'I don't know what you mean.'

'Yes,' he said, 'you may not be engaged to me, but I'm engaged to you. That's what I've decided.'

She laughed. 'You'll find it rather dull, I'm afraid.'

'No,' he said. 'I can do things for you.' She was struck by that simple statement, spoilt by his next words: 'Like these chocolates.'

He was very insistent about the chocolates and proud of his idea. She thanked him. 'But I don't want you to give me things.'

'You can't stop me. I'm doing it all the time.'

They had reached the highest point of the hill and they halted at the railing on the cliff's edge. Below them, the blackness of earth gave way to the blackness of air and the shining blackness of water, and slowly the opposing cliff cleared itself from a formless mass into the hardly seen shapes of rock and tree. Here was beauty, here was something permanent in the midst of change, and it seemed as though the hand of peace were laid on Henrietta. For a moment the episode on the other side of the water and the problem it involved took their tiny places in the universe instead of the large ones in her life and, strangely enough, it was Charles Batty who loomed up big, as though he had some odd fellowship with immensity and beauty.

'What do you give me?' she asked. 'I don't want it, you know, but tell me.'

'I told you that night when you listened and took it all. I don't think I can say it again.'

'No, but you're not to misunderstand me, and you mustn't go on giving and getting nothing back.'

'That's just what I can do. Not many people could, but I can. Perhaps it's the only way I can be great, like an artist giving his work to a world that doesn't care.'

The quick sense she had to serve her instead of knowledge and to make her unconsciously subtle, detected his danger in the words and some lack of homage to herself. 'Ah, you're pretending, and you're enjoying it,' she said. 'It's consoling you for not being able to do anything else.'

'Who said I couldn't do anything else?'

158

'Well, you nearly did, and I don't suppose you can. If you could, you wouldn't bother about me.'

He was silent and though she did not look at him she was very keenly aware of his tall figure wrapped in an overcoat reaching almost to his heels and with the big parcel under his left arm. He was always slightly absurd and now, when he struck the top bar of the railing with his left hand and uttered a mournful, 'Yes, it's true!' the tragedy in his tone could not repress her smile. Yet if he had been less funny he might have been less truly tragic.

'So, you see, I'm only a kind of makeshift,' she remarked.

'No,' he said, 'but I may have been mistaken in myself. I'm not mistaken about you. Never!' he cried, striking the rail again.

They were alone on the hill, but suddenly, with a clatter of wings, a bird left his nest in the rocks and swept out of sight, leaving a memory of swiftness and life, of an intenser blackness in the gulf. Far below them, to the left, there were lights, stationary and moving, and sometimes the clang of a tramcar bell reached them with its harsh music: the slim line of the bridge, with here and there a dimly burning light, was like a spangled thread. The sound of footsteps and voices came to them from the road behind the hill.

'But after all,' Charles said more clearly, 'it doesn't matter about being acclaimed. It's just like making music for deaf people: the music's there; the music's there. And so it doesn't matter very much whether you love me. It's one's weakness that wants that, one's loneliness. I can love you just the same, perhaps better; it's the audience that spoils things. I should think it does!'

'So you're quite happy.'

'Not quite,' he answered, 'but I have something to do, something I can do, too. Music – no, I'm not good enough. I'm no more than an amateur, but in this I can be supreme.'

'You can't be sure of that,' she said acutely. 'If you wrote a poem you might think it was perfect, but you wouldn't absolutely know till you'd tried it on other people. So you can't be sure about love.'

'You mightn't be,' he said with a touch of scorn. 'You may depend on other people, but I don't.'

She made a small sound of scorn. 'No, you'll never know whether you're doing this wonderful work of yours well or not because,' she said, cruelly exultant, 'it won't be tested.'

'Ah, but it might be. You've got to do things as though they will be.'

'I suppose so,' she said indifferently. 'And now I must go back.'

He turned obediently and thrust the parcel at her.

'But aren't you going to take me home?' she asked.

'No, I don't think I need do that. I shall stay here.'

'Then I won't have your chocolates. I didn't want them, anyhow, but now I won't take them.'

'I don't understand you,' he said miserably.

'Doesn't the painter understand his paints or the musician his instruments? No, you'll have to begin at the beginning, Charles Batty, and work very hard before you're a success.'

She ran from him fleetly, hardly knowing why she was so angry, but it seemed to her that he had no right to be content without her love; she felt he must be emasculate, and the guilty passion of Francis Sales was, by contrast, splendid. But for that passion, Charles Batty might have persuaded her she was incapable of rousing men's desire and not to rouse it was not to be a woman. Accordingly, she valued Francis and despised the other, yet when she had reached home and run upstairs and was standing in the dim room where the firelight cast big, uncertain shadows, like vague threats, on walls and ceiling, she suffered a reaction.

The scene on the road became sinister: she remembered the strange silence of the trees and the clangorous barking of the dogs, the hoarse voices from the encampment in the hollow. It had been very dark there and an extraordinary blackness had buried her when she was in that man's arms. It had been dark, too, on the hill, but with a feeling of space and height and freedom. If Charles had been a little different – but then, he did not really want her; he was making a study of his sorrow, he was gazing at it, turning it round and over, growing familiar with all its aspects. He was an artist frustrated of any power but this of feeling and to have given him herself would simply have been to rob him of what he found more precious. But she and Francis Sales were kin; she understood him: he was not better than herself, perhaps he was not so good and he, too, was unhappy, but he did not love her for those qualities of which Charles Batty had talked by the Monks' Pool, he wove no poetry about her: he loved her because she was pretty; because her mouth was red and her eyes bright and her body young: he loved her because, being her father's daughter, her youth answered his desire with enough shame to season appetite, but not to spoil it. And she thought of Christabel as of some sick doll.

Dinner was a strange meal that night. Caroline's chair was empty, and the sighs of Sophia were like gentle zephyrs in the room. Henrietta's silence might have been interpreted as anxiety about her aunt and Susan informed the cook, truly enough, that Miss Henrietta had a feeling heart.

It was only Rose who could have explained the nature of the feeling. She was fascinated by the sight of Henrietta, her rival, her fellow dupe. Rose looked at her without envy or malice or covetousness, but with an extraordinary interest, trying to find what likeness to herself and what differences had attracted Francis Sales.

There was the dark hair, curly where hers was straight, dark eyes instead of grey ones, the same warm pallor of the skin, in Henrietta's case slightly overlaid with pink; but the mouth, ah! it must be the mouth and what it meant that made the alluring difference. Henrietta's mouth was soft, red and mutinous; in her father it had been a blemish, half hidden by the foreign cut of moustache and beard, but in Henrietta it was a beauty and a warning. Rose had never properly studied that mouth before and under the fixity of her gaze Henrietta's eyelids fluttered upwards. There were shadows under her eyes and it seemed to Rose that she had changed a little. She must have changed. Rose had never been in the arms of Francis Sales; she shuddered now at the thought, but she knew that she, too, would have been different after that experience.

161

She looked at Henrietta with the sadness of her desire to help her, the fear of her inability to do it; and Henrietta looked back with a hint of defiance, the symbol of her attitude to the cruel world in which fond lovers were despised and love had a hard road. Rose restrained an impulse to lean across the table and say quietly, 'I saw you to-night with Francis Sales and I am sorry for you. He told me I should not let you meet him. He said that himself, so you see he does not want you,' and she wondered how much that cry of his had been uttered in despair of his passion and how much in weariness of Henrietta and himself.

Rose leaned back in her chair and immediately straightened. She was intolerably tired but she refused to droop. It seemed as though she were never to be free from secrecy: after her release there had been a short time of dreary peace and now she had Henrietta's fight to wage in secret, her burden to carry without a word. And this was worse, more difficult, for she had less power with which to meet more danger. Between the candle lights she sent a smile to Henrietta, but the girl's mouth was petulantly set and it was a relief when Sophia quavered out, 'She won't be able to go to the Battys' ball! She will be heart-broken.'

Rose and Henrietta were momentarily united in their common amazement at the genuineness of this sorrow and to both there was something comic in the picture of the elderly Caroline, suffering from a chill and bemoaning the loss of an evening's pleasure. Henrietta cast a look of scornful surprise at her Aunt Sophia. Was the Battys' ball a matter for a broken heart? Rose said consolingly, 'It isn't till after Christmas. Perhaps she will be well enough.'

'And Christmas,' Sophia wailed. 'Henrietta's first Christmas here! With Caroline upstairs!'

'I don't like Christmas,' Henrietta said. 'It makes me miserable.'

'But you will like the ball,' Rose said. 'Why, if it hadn't been for the ball we might have been in Algiers now.'

'With Caroline ill! I should have sent for you.'

'Shall we start, Henrietta, in a few weeks' time?' She ignored

Henrietta's vague murmur. 'Oh, not until Caroline is quite well, Sophia. We could go to the south of France, Henrietta. Yes, I think we had better arrange that.' Rose felt a slightly malicious pleasure in this proposal which became a serious one as she spoke. 'You must learn to speak French, and it is a long time since I have been abroad. It will be a kindness to me. I don't care to go alone. We have no engagements after the middle of January, so shall we settle to go then?' There was authority in her tone. 'We shall avoid brigands, Sophia, but I think we ought to go. It is not fair that Henrietta's experiences should be confined to Radstowe.'

'Quite right, dear.' Sophia was unwillingly but nobly truthful. 'We have a duty to her father, but say nothing to Caroline until she is stronger.'

Henrietta was silent but she had a hot rage in her heart. She felt herself in a trap and she looked with sudden hatred and suspicion at her Aunt Rose. It was impossible to defy that calm authority. She would have to go, in merest gratitude she must consent; she would be carried off, but she looked round wildly for some means of escape.

The prospect of that exile spoilt a Christmas which otherwise would not have been a miserable one, for the Malletts made it a charming festival with inspired ideas for gifts and a delightful party on Christmas Day, when Caroline was allowed to appear. She refused to say that she was better; she had never been ill; it was a mere fad of the doctor and her sisters; she supposed they were tired of her and wanted a little peace. However, she continued to absorb large quantities of strengthening food, beef tea, meat jelly and heady tonic, for she loved food, and she was determined to go to the ball.

This was on New Year's Eve, and all that day, from the moment when Susan drew the curtains and brought the early tea, there was an atmosphere of excitement in Nelson Lodge and Henrietta permitted herself to enjoy it. Francis Sales was to be at the ball. She forgot the threatened exile, she ignored Charles Batty's tiresome insistence that she must dance with him twice as many times as with anybody else, because he was engaged to her.

'I don't believe you can dance a bit,' she cried.

'I can get round,' he said. 'It's the noise of the band that upsets me – jingle, jingle, bang, bang! But we can sit out when we can't bear it any longer.'

'That would be very amusing,' Henrietta said.

Susan, drawing Henrietta's curtains, remarked that it was a nice day for the ball and then, looking severely at Henrietta and arranging a wrap round her shoulders, she said, 'I suppose Miss Caroline is going.'

'Oh, I hope so,' Henrietta said. 'She's not worse, is she?'

'Not that I know of, Miss Henrietta, but I'm afraid it will be the death of her.' She seemed to think it would be Henrietta's fault and, in the kitchen, she told Cook that, but for Miss Henrietta, the Battys, who were close-fisted people – you had only to look at Mr. Batty's mouth – would not be giving a ball at all, but they had their eyes on Miss Henrietta for that half-witted son of theirs. She was sure of it. And Miss Caroline was not fit to go, it would be the death of her. Cook was optimistic. It would do Miss Caroline good; she was always the better for a little fun.

The elder ladies breakfasted in bed to save themselves all unnecessary fatigue, and throughout the day they moved behind half-lowered blinds. Henrietta was warned not to walk out. There was a cold wind, her face would be roughened; and when she insisted on air and exercise she was advised to wear a thick veil. Both ladies offered her a shawl-like covering for the face, but Henrietta shook her head.

'Feel,' she said, lifting a hand of each to either cheek.

'Like a flower,' Sophia said.

'The wind doesn't hurt flowers. It won't hurt me.'

Fires were lighted in the bedroom earlier than usual. Caroline and Sophia again retired to their room, leaving orders that they were not to be disturbed until four o'clock, and a solemn hush fell on the house.

While the ladies were having tea, Susan was busy in their bedroom laying out their gowns and Henrietta, chancing to pass the open door, peeped in. The bed was spread with the rose-pink and apricot dresses of their choice, with petticoats of

164

corresponding hues, with silken stockings and long gloves and fans; and on the mound made by the pillows two pairs of very high-heeled slippers pointed their narrow toes. It might have been the room of two young girls and, before she fluttered down to tea, Henrietta took another glance at the mass of yellow tulle on her own bed. She wished Mrs. Banks and Miss Stubb could see her in that dress. Mrs. Banks would cry and Miss Stubb would grow poetical. She would have to write and tell them all about it.

At eight o'clock the four Miss Malletts assembled in the drawing-room. Caroline was magnificent. Old lace veiled the shimmering satin of her gown and made it possible to wear the family emeralds: these, heavily set, were on her neck and in her ears; a pair of bracelets adorned her arms. Seen from behind, she might have been the stout and prosperous mother of a family in her prime and only when she turned and displayed the pink patches on yellow skin, was her age discernible. She was magnificent, and terrible, and Henrietta had a moment of recoil before she gasped, 'Oh, Aunt Caroline, how lovely!'

Sophia advanced more modestly for inspection. 'She looks about twenty-one!' Caroline exclaimed. 'What a figure! Like a girl's!'

'You're prejudiced, dear Caroline. I never had your air. You're wonderful.'

'We're all wonderful!' Henrietta cried.

They had all managed to express themselves: Caroline in the superb attempt at overcoming her age, and Sophia in the softness of her apparel; Rose, in filmy black and pearls round her firm throat, gently proud and distant; and Henrietta was like some delicately gaudy insect, dancing hither and thither, approaching and withdrawing.

'Yes, we're all wonderful,' Henrietta said again. 'Don't you think we ought to start? It's a pity for other people not to see us!'

With Susan's help they began the business of packing themselves into the cab. Caroline lifted her skirts and showed remarkably thin legs, but she stood on the doorstep to quarrel with Sophia about the taking of a shawl. She ought to have a lace one round her shoulders, Sophia said, for the Assembly Rooms were always cold and it was a frosty night.

'Sophia, you're an idiot,' Caroline said. 'Do you think I'm going to sit in a ball-room in a shawl? Why not take a hot-water bottle and a muff?'

'At least we must have the smelling salts. Susan, fetch the salts. Miss Caroline might need them.'

Miss Caroline said she would rather die than display such weakness and she stepped into the cab which groaned under her weight. Another fainter groan accompanied Sophia's entrance and Rose and Henrietta, tapping their satin shoes on the pavement, heard sounds of bickering. Sophia had forgotten her handkerchief and Susan fled once more into the house.

The cabman growled his disapproval from the box. 'I've another party to fetch,' he said. 'And how many of you's going?'

'Only four,' Henrietta said sweetly, 'and we shan't be a minute.'

'I've been waiting ten already,' said the man.

The handkerchief was handed into the darkness of the cab and Rose and Henrietta followed. 'Mind my toes,' Caroline said. 'Susan, tell that disagreeable fellow to drive on.'

They had not far to go, but the man did not hurry his horse. Other cabs passed them on the road, motor-cars whizzed by.

'We shall be dreadfully late,' Henrietta sighed.

'I am always late for balls,' Caroline said calmly.

Rose, leaning back in her corner, could see Henrietta's profile against the window-pane. Her lips were parted, she leaned forward eagerly. 'We shall miss a dance,' she murmured.

Caroline coughed. 'Oh, dear,' Sophia moaned. 'Caroline, you should be in bed.'

'You're a silly old woman,' Caroline retorted.

'But you'll promise not to sit in a draught; Henrietta, see that your Aunt Caroline doesn't sit in a draught.' But Henrietta was letting down the window, for the cab had drawn up before the portals of the Assembly Rooms.

In the cloak-room, Rose and Henrietta slipped off their wraps, glanced in the mirror, and were ready, but there were anxious little whisperings and consultations on the part of the elder ladies and Henrietta cast a despairing glance at Rose. Would they never be ready? But at last Caroline uttered a majestic 'Now' and led the way like a plump duck swimming across a pond with a fleet of smaller ducks behind her.

No expense and no trouble had been spared to justify the expectations of Radstowe. The antechamber was luxuriously carpeted, arm-chaired, cushioned, palmed and screened, and the hired flunkey at the ballroom door had a presence and a voice fitted for the occasion.

'Miss Mallett!' he bawled. 'Miss Sophia Mallett! Miss Rose Mallett! Miss Henrietta Mallett!'

The moment had come. Henrietta lifted her head, settled her shoulders and prepared to meet the eyes of Francis Sales. The Malletts had arrived between the first and second dances and the guests sitting round the walls had an uninterrupted view of the stately entrance. Mrs. Batty, in diamonds and purple satin, greeted the late-comers with enthusiasm and James Batty escorted Caroline and Sophia to arm-chairs that had all the appearance of thrones. Mrs. Batty patted Henrietta on the shoulder.

'Pretty dear,' she said. 'Here you are at last. There are a lot of boys with their programmes half empty till you come, and my Charles, too. Not that he's much for dancing. I've told him he must look after the ugly ones. We're going to have a quadrille for your aunts' sake!' And then, whispering, she asked, 'What do you think of it? I said if we had it at all, we'd have it good.'

'It's gorgeous!' Henrietta said, and off the stage she had never seen a grander spectacle. The platform at the end of the room was banked with flowers and behind them uniformed and much-moustached musicians played with ardour, with rapture, their eyes closing sentimentally in the choicest passages. Baskets of flowers hung from the chandeliers, the floor was polished to the slipperiness of ice and Mrs. Batty, on her hospitable journeys to and fro, was in constant danger of a fall.

The society of Radstowe, all in new garments, appeared to Henrietta of a dazzling brilliance, but she stood easily, holding her head high, as though she were well used to this kind of glory. Looking round, she saw Francis Sales leaning against a wall, talking to his partner and smiling with unnecessary amiability. A flame of jealousy flickered hotly through her body. How could he smile like that? Why did he not come to her? And then, in the pride of her secret love, she remembered that he dare not show his eagerness. They belonged to each other, they were alone in their love, and all these people, talking, laughing, fluttering fans, thinking themselves of immense importance, had no real existence. He and she alone of all that company existed with a fierceness that changed the sensuous dance-music into the cry of essential passion.

Young men approached her and wrote their initials on her programme which was already marked with little crosses against the numbers she had promised to Francis Sales. Charles Batty, rather hot, anxious and glowering, arrived too late. His angry disgust, his sense of desertion, were beyond words. He stared at her. 'And my flowers,' he demanded.

'Charles, don't shout.'

'Where are my flowers? I sent some – roses and lilies and maidenhair. Where are they?'

'I haven't seen them.'

'Ah, I suppose you didn't like them, but the girl in the shop told me they would be all right. How should I know?'

'I haven't seen them,' she repeated. Over his shoulder she saw the figure of Francis Sales coming towards her.

'I ordered them yesterday,' Charles continued loudly. 'I'll kill that girl. I'll go at once.'

'The shop will be shut,' Henrietta reminded him. 'Oh, do be quiet, Charles.' She turned with a smile for Francis.

'She hasn't a dance left,' Charles said.

'Mr. Sales took the precaution of booking them in advance,' Henrietta said lightly, and with a miserable gesture Charles went off, muttering, 'I hadn't thought of that. Why didn't some one tell me?'

That ball was to be known in Nelson Lodge as the one that killed Miss Caroline, but Miss Caroline had her full share of pleasure out of it. It was the custom in Radstowe to make much of Caroline and Sophia: they were respected and playfully loved and it was not only the middle-aged gentlemen who asked them to dance, and John and Charles Batty were not the only young ones who had the honour of leading them into the middle of the room, taking a few turns in a waltz and returning, in good order, to the throne-like arm-chairs. Francis Sales had their names on his programme, but with him they used the privilege of old friends and preferred to talk.

'You can keep your dancing for Rose and Henrietta,' Caroline said.

'He comes too late for me,' Rose said pleasantly. He gave her something remarkably like one of his old looks and she answered it with a grave one. There was gnawing trouble at her heart. She had watched his meeting with Henrietta. It had been wordless; everything was understood. She had also seen the unhappiness of Charles Batty, and, on an inspiration, she said to him, 'Charles, you must take pity on an old maid. I have all these dances to give away.'

For him this dance was to be remembered as the beginning of his friendship with Rose Mallett; but at the moment he was merely annoyed at being prevented from watching Henrietta's dark head appearing and disappearing among the other dancers like that of a bather in a rough sea. He said, 'Oh, thank you very much. Are you sure there's nobody else? But I suppose there can't be'; and holding her at arm's length, he ambled round her, treading occasionally on her toes. He apologized: he was no good at dancing: he hoped he had not hurt her slippers, or her feet.

She paused and looked down at them. 'You mustn't do that to Henrietta. Her slippers are yellow and you would spoil them.'

'She isn't giving me a single dance!' he burst out. 'I asked her to, but I never thought I ought to get a promise. Nobody told me. Nobody tells me anything.'

An icily angry gentleman remonstrated with him for standing in the fairway and Rose suggested that they should sit down.

'You see, I'm no good. I can't dance. I can't please her.'

'Charles, you're still in the way. Let us go somewhere quiet and then you can tell me all about it.'

He took her to a small room leading from the big one. 'I'll shut the door,' he said, 'and then we shan't hear that hideous din.'

'It is a very good band.'

'It's profane,' Charles said wearily. 'Music – they call it music!' He was off at a great pace and she did not try to hold him in. She lay back in the big chair and seemed to study the toes on which Charles Batty had trampled. His voice rolled on like the sound of water, companionable and unanswerable. Suddenly his tone changed. 'Henrietta is very unkind to me.'

'Is there any reason why she shouldn't be?'

'I do everything I can think of. I've told her all about myself.'

'She would rather hear about herself.'

'I've done that, too. Perhaps I haven't done it enough. I've given her chocolates and flowers. What else ought I to do?'

Her voice, very calm and clear after his spluttering, said, 'Not too much.'

'Oh!' This was a new idea. 'Oh! I never thought of that. Why –'

She interrupted his usual cry. 'Women are naturally cruel.'

'Are they? I didn't know that either.' He swallowed the information visibly. She could almost see the process of digestion. 'Oh!' he said again.

'They don't mean to be. They are simply untouched by a love they don't return.' She added thoughtfully: 'And inclined to despise the lover.'

'That's it,' he mourned. 'She despises me.' And in a louder voice he demanded, not of Rose Mallett, but of the mysterious world in which he gropingly existed, 'Why should she?'

'She shouldn't, but perhaps you yourself are making a mistake.'

170

She heard indistinctly the word, 'Impossible.'

'You can't be sure.'

'I'm quite certain about that – about nothing else.' His big hands moved. 'I cling to that.'

'Then you must be ready to serve her. Charles, if I ever needed you –'

'I'd do anything for you because you're her aunt. And besides,' he said simply, 'you're rather like her in the face.'

'Thank you, but it's her you may have to serve – and not me. I want her to be happy. I don't know where her happiness is, but I know where it is not. Some day I may tell you.' She looked at him. He might be useful as an ally; she was sure he could be trusted. 'Promise you will do anything I ask for her sake.'

He turned the head which had been sunk on his crumpled shirt. 'Is anything the matter?' he asked, concerned, and more alert than she had ever seen him.

She said, 'Hush!' for the door behind was opening and it let in a murmur of voices and a rush of cold, fresh air. Rose shivered and, looking round, she saw Henrietta and Francis Sales. Her cloak was half on and half off her shoulders, her colour was very high and her eyes were not so dazzled by the light that she did not immediately recognize her aunt. It was Francis Sales who hesitated and Rose said quickly, 'Oh, please shut the door.'

He obeyed and stood by Henrietta's side, a pleasing figure, looking taller and more finely made in his black clothes.

'Have you been on the terrace?'

'Yes, it's a glorious night.'

'You'll get cold,' Charles said severely. She had been out there with the man who murdered music and who, therefore, was a scoundrel, and Charles's objection was based on that fact and not on Francis Sales's married state. He had not the pleasure of feeling a pious indignation that a man with an invalid wife walked on the terrace with Henrietta. He would have said, 'Why not?' and he would have found an excuse for any man in the beauty, the wonder, the enchantment of that girl, though he could not forgive Henrietta for her friendship with the slaughterer of music and of birds.

171

He glared and repeated, 'You'll be ill.'

Henrietta pretended not to hear him, and Rose said thoughtfully and slowly, 'Oh, no, Charles, people don't get cold when they are happy.'

'I suppose not.' He felt in a vague way that he and Rose, sitting there, for he had forgotten to stand up, were united against the other two who stood, very clear, against the gold-embossed wall of the room, and that those two were conscious of the antagonism. They also were united and he felt an increase of his dull pain at the sight of their comeliness, the suspicion of their likeness to each other. 'I suppose not,' Charles said, and after that no one spoke, as though it were impossible to find a light word, and unnecessary.

Each one was aware of conflict, of something fierce and silent going on, but it was Rose who understood the situation best and Charles who understood it least. His feelings were torturing but simple. He wanted Henrietta and he could not get her: he did not please her, and that Sales, that Philistine, that handsome, well-made, sulky-looking beggar knew how to do it.

But Rose was conscious of the working of four minds: there was her own, sore with the past and troubled by a present in which her lover concealed his discomfiture under the easy sullenness of his pose. He, too, had the past shared with her to haunt him, but he had also a present bright with Henrietta's allurements yet darkly streaked with prohibitions, struggles and surrenders, and Rose saw that the worst tragedy was his and hers. It must not be Henrietta's. In their youth she and Francis had misunderstood, and in their maturity they had failed, each other; it was the fault of neither and Henrietta must not be the victim of their folly. Looking at the big fan of black feathers spread on her knee, Rose smiled a little, with a maternal tenderness. Henrietta was her father's daughter, wilful and lovable, but she was also the daughter of that mother who had been good and loving. Henrietta had her father's passion for excitement but, being a woman, she had the greater need of being loved, and Rose raised her eyes and looked at Charles with an ironical appreciation of his worthiness, of his comicality. She saw him with Henrietta's eyes, and her white shoulders lifted and dropped in resignation. Then she looked at Henrietta and smiled frankly. 'Another dance has begun,' she said. 'Somebody must be looking for you.'

'No,' Henrietta said, 'it's with Mr. Sales,' and turning to him with the effect of ignoring Rose, she said in a clear voice which became slightly harsh as she saw him gazing at her aunt oddly, almost as though he were astonished by a new sight, 'Shall we go back to the terrace or shall we dance?'

'You'll get cold,' Charles said again angrily.

'Let us dance,' Sales said.

The door to the ball-room closed behind them and Charles let out a groan. 'You see!' he said.

Rose hoped he did not see too much and she was reassured when he added, 'She takes no notice of me.'

'Poor Charles, but you know you treat her a little like a child. You shouldn't talk of catching cold. You're too material.'

She was surprised to hear him say with a sort of humble pride, 'Only before other people. She's heard me different.' Then, dropping into the despair of his own thoughts, and with the rage of one feeling himself sinking hopelessly, he cried out, 'It's like pouring water through a sieve.'

The voice of Rose, very calm and wise, said gently, 'Continue to pour.'

'It's all very fine,' he muttered.

'Continue to pour. It may be all you can do, but it is worth while.'

'I told her I would do that, one night, on the hill. She said she didn't want it.'

'She doesn't know,' Rose said in the same voice, comforting in its quietness. She stood up. 'We had better go back now, and remember, you promise to do for her anything I ask of you.'

'Of course,' he said, 'but I shall do it wrong.'

She laid her hand on his arm. 'It must be done rightly. It must. It will. Now take me back.'

He resigned her unwillingly, for he felt that she was his

strength, to the partner who claimed her, but as she prepared to dance, Charles returned hurriedly and, ignoring the affronted gentleman who had already clasped her, he said anxiously, 'This service – what is it? Is there something wrong?'

She looked deeply into his eyes. 'There must not be.'

And now, for him in the sea of dancers, there were two dark heads bobbing among the waves.

The hours sped by; the lavish supper was consumed; dresses and flowers lost their freshness; the musicians lost their energetic ardour; the man at the piano was seen to yawn cavernously above the keys. The guests began to depart, leaving an exhausted but happy Mrs. Batty. She had been complimented by Miss Mallett on the perfection of her arrangements, on the brilliance of the assembly, on the music and even on the refreshments, and Mrs. Batty had blessed her own perseverance against Mr. Batty's obstinacy in the matter of the supper. He had wanted light refreshments and she had insisted on a knife-and-fork affair, and Miss Caroline had actually remarked on the wisdom of a solid meal. She had no patience with snacks. Mrs. Batty intended to lull Mr. Batty to slumber with that quotation.

In the cab, as the Malletts jolted home in the care of the same surly driver, Caroline complaisantly spoke of her congratulations. She would not have said so much to anybody else, but she knew Mrs. Batty would be pleased.

'So she was, dear,' Sophia said, but her more delicate social sense was troubled. 'Though I do think one ought to treat everybody as one would treat the greatest lady in the land. I think we ought to have taken for granted that everything would be correct.'

'Rubbish! You must treat people as they want to be treated. She was panting for praise, and she got it, and anyhow it's too late to argue.'

They had stayed to the end so that Henrietta's pleasure should not be curtailed, and now she was leaning back, very white and still.

'I believe the child's asleep,' Sophia whispered.

'No, I'm not. I'm wide awake.'

174

'Did you enjoy it, dear?'

'Very much,' said Henrietta.

'I kept my eye on you, child,' Caroline said.

Henrietta made an effort. 'I kept my eye on you, Aunt Caroline. I saw you flirting with Mr. Batty.'

'Impudence! Sophia, do you hear her? I only danced with him twice, though I admit he hovered round my chair. They always did. I can't help it. We're all like that. You should have seen your father at a ball! There was no one like him. Such an air! Ah, here we are. I suppose this disagreeable cabman must be tipped.'

'I'll see to that,' Rose said. It was the first time she had spoken. 'Be quick, Caroline. Don't stand in the cold.'

'The dancing has done me good,' Caroline said, and she lingered on the pavement to look at the stars, holding her skirts high in the happy knowledge of her unrivalled legs and feet. 'No, Sophia, I am not cold, or tired; but yes, I'll take a little soup.'

They sat round the roaring fire prepared for them and drank the soup out of fine old cups. Caroline chattered; she was gay; she believed she had been a great success; young men had paid court to her; she had rapped at least one of them with her fan; a grey-haired man had talked to her of her lively past. But Sophia had much ado to prevent her heavy head from nodding. Henrietta was silent, very busy with her thoughts and careful to avoid the eyes of Rose.

'I think,' Caroline said, 'we ought to give a little dance. We could have this carpet up. Just a little dance –'

'But Henrietta and I,' Rose said distinctly, 'are going away.'

'Oh, nonsense! You must put it off. We ought to give a dance for the child. Now, how many couples? Ten, at least. Sophia, you're asleep.'

'No, dear. A party. I heard. But if you're ready now, I think I'll go to bed.'

'Go along. I'll follow.'

'Oh, no, Caroline, we always go together.'

'Well, well, I'll come, but I could stay here and talk for hours. I could always sit you out and dance you out, couldn't I?'

'Yes, dear. You're wonderful. Such spirit!'

They kissed Rose; they both kissed Henrietta on each cheek.

'A little dance,' Caroline repeated, and patted Henrietta's arm. 'Good child,' she murmured.

Henrietta went upstairs behind them, slowly, not to over-take Sophia. She did not want to be left down there with Aunt Rose. She wanted solitude, and she knew now what people meant when they talked of being in a dream. Under her hand the slim mahogany rail felt like the cold, firm hand of Francis Sales when, after their last dance together, he had led her on to the terrace again. They were alone there, for the wind was very cold, but for Henrietta it was part of the exquisite mantle in which she was wrapped. She was wrapped in the glamour of the night and the stars and the excitement of the dance, yet suddenly, looking down at the dark river, she was chilled. She said, and her voice seemed to be carried off by the wind, 'Aunt Rose is going to take me away.'

He bent down to her. 'What did you say?'

She put her lips close to his ear. 'Aunt Rose is going to take me away.'

He dropped her hand. 'She can't do that.'

'But she will. I shall have to go,' and he said gloomily, 'I knew you would leave me, too.' She felt helpless and lonely: her happiness had gone; the wind had risen. She said loudly, 'It's not my fault. What can I do? I shall come back.'

He stood quite still and did not look at her. 'You don't think of me.'

'I think of nothing else. How can I tell her I can't leave you? She has been good to me.'

'She was once good to me, too. That won't last long.'

'Ah, that's not true!' she cried.

'Go, then, if she's more to you than I am. I'm used to that.'

She moved away from him. Why did he not help her? He was a man; he loved her, but he was cruel. Ah, the thought warmed her, it was his love that made him cruel: he needed her; he was lonely. Under her cloak, she clasped her gloved hands in a helplessness which must be conquered. What shall I do? she asked the stars. Across the river the cliff was sombre;

176

it seemed to listen and to disapprove. The stars were kinder: they twinkled, they laughed, they understood, and the lights on the bridge glowed steadily with reassurance. She turned back to Francis Sales. 'You must trust me,' she said firmly.

He put his hands heavily on her shoulders. 'I won't let you go.'

A murmur, inarticulate and delighted, escaped her lips. This was what she wanted. Very small and willing to be commanded, she leaned against him. 'What will you do with me?' she whispered, secure in his strength. She laughed. 'You will have to take me away yourself!'

'You wouldn't come,' he said with unexpected seriousness.

So close to him that the wind could not steal the words, she answered, 'I would do anything for one I loved.'

The memory of her own voice, its tenderness and seduction, startled her in the solitude of her room. She had not known she could speak like that. She dropped her face into her hands, and in the rapture of her own daring and in the recollection of the excitement which had frozen them into a stillness through which the beating of their hearts sounded like a faint tap of drums, there came the doubt of her sincerity.

Had she really meant what she said? Yet she could have said nothing else. The words had left her lips involuntarily, her voice, as though of itself, had taken on that tender tone. She could not have failed in that dramatic moment, but now she was half afraid of her undertaking. Well, her hands dropped to her sides, she had given her word; she had promised herself in an heroic surrender and her very doubts seemed to sanctify the act.

For a long time she sat by the fire, half undressed, her immature thin arms hanging loosely, her sombre eyes staring at the fire. She wished this night might go on for ever, this time of ecstasy between a promise and its fulfilment. She had seen disillusionment in another and did not laugh at its possibility for herself; it would come to her, she thought, as it had come to her mother, who had hoped her daughter would find happiness in love; and Henrietta wondered if that gentle spirit was aware of what was happening.

177

The thought troubled her a little, and from her mother, who had been a neglected wife, it was no more than a step to that other, lying on her back, tortured and lonely. If Christabel Sales had a daughter, what would be her fierce young thoughts about this thief, sitting by the fire in a joy which was half misery? Yet she was no thief: she was only picking up what would otherwise be wasted. It seemed to her that life was hardly more than a perpetual and painful choice. Some one had to be hurt, and why should it not be Christabel? Or was she hurt enough already? And again, what good would she get from Henrietta's sacrifice? No one would gain except Henrietta herself, she could see that plainly, and she was prepared to suffer; she was anxious to suffer and be justified.

The coals in the grate began to fade, the room was cold and she was tired. Slowly she continued her undressing, throwing down her dainty garments with the indifference of her fatigue. She feared her thoughts would stand between her and sleep, but, when she lay down, warmth gradually stole over her and soothed her into forgetfulness. She slept, but she waked to unusual sounds in the house: a door opened, there were footsteps on the landing and then a voice, shrill and frightened. She jumped out of bed. Sophia was on the landing; Rose was just opening her door; Susan, decently covered by a puritanical dressing-gown, had been roused by the noise. Caroline was in pain, Sophia said. She was breathing with great difficulty. 'I told her she ought to take a shawl,' Sophia sobbed.

Fires had to be lighted, water boiled and flannels warmed, and the voice of Caroline was heard in gasping expostulation. Henrietta dressed quickly. 'I'm going for the doctor,' she told Rose, who was already putting on her coat, and Henrietta noticed that she still wore her evening gown. She had not been to bed, and for a moment Henrietta forgot her Aunt Caroline and stared at her Aunt Rose.

'I am going,' Rose said quietly.

'Oh, hadn't you better stay here? Aunt Sophia is in such a fuss.'

'We'll go together,' Rose said. 'I can't let you go alone.'

Henrietta laughed a little. This care was so unnecessary for one who had given herself to a future full of peril.

They went out in the cold darkness of the morning, walking very fast and now and then breaking into a run, and with them there walked a shadowy third person, keeping them apart. It was strange to be yoked together by Caroline's danger and securely separated by this shadow. They did not speak, they had nothing to say, yet both thought, What difference is this going to make? But on their way back, when the doctor had been roused and they had his promise to come quickly, Henrietta's fear burst the bonds of her reserve. 'You don't think she is going to die, do you?'

Rose put her arm through Henrietta's. 'Oh, Henrietta, I hope not. No, no, I'm not going to believe that,' and, temporarily united, the third person left behind though following closely, they returned to the lighted house. As they stood in the hall they could hear the rasping sound of Caroline's breathing.

§ 6

John Gibbs, of Sales Hall, milkman and news carrier, shook his head over the cans that morning. Mrs. Sales was very bad. The master had fetched the doctor in the early morning. He had set out in the same car that brought him from the dance. Cook and Susan looked at each other with a compression of lips and a nodding of heads, implying that misfortune never came singly, but they did not tell John Gibbs of the illness in their own house. They had imbibed something of the Mallett reserve and they did not wish the family affairs to be blabbed at every house in Radstowe. But when the man had gone, Susan reminded Cook of her early disapproval of that ball. It would kill Miss Caroline, it would kill Mrs. Sales.

'She wasn't there, poor thing,' Cook said.

'But he was, gallivanting. I dare say it upset her.'

Susan was right. Christabel Sales had fretted herself into one of her heart attacks; but the Malletts did not know this until later. At present they were concerned with Caroline, about whom the doctor was reassuring. She was very ill, but she had herself remarked that if they were expecting her to die they would be disappointed, and that was the spirit to help recovery.

179

A nurse was installed in the sick-room, Sophia fluttered a little less and Rose and Henrietta ignored their emotion of the early morning; they also avoided each other. They were both occupied with the same problem, though Henrietta's thoughts had taken definite shape; above her dreaming, her practical mind was dealing with concrete details, and Rose was merely speculating on the future, and the more she speculated, the surer she became of the necessity to interfere. Her plan of carrying Henrietta to other lands was frustrated for the present by Caroline's illness and she dared not allow things to drift. There was a smouldering defiance in Henrietta's manner: she was absorbed yet wary; she seemed to have a grudge against the aunt who had missed nothing at the dance, who had seen her exits and entrances with Francis Sales and interrupted their farewell glance, the wave of Henrietta's gloved hand towards the tall figure standing in the porch of the Assembly Rooms to see her depart.

There was a certain humour about the situation, and for Rose an impeding feeling of hypocrisy. Here she was, determined to put obstacles on the primrose path where she herself once had dallied. It looked like the envy of age for youth, it looked like inclining to virtue because the opposite was no longer possible for her, like tardy loyalty to Christabel; but she must not be hampered by appearances.

Her chief fear was of hardening Henrietta's temper, and she came to the conclusion that she must appeal to Francis Sales himself. It was an unpleasant task and, she dimly felt, she hardly knew why, a dangerous one; and meeting Henrietta that day at meals or in the hushed quiet of the passages, she felt herself a traitor to the girl. After all, what right had she to interfere? She had no right, and her double excuse was her knowledge of Francis Sales' character and her certainty that Henrietta was chiefly moved by her dramatic instinct. And again Rose wished that the hair of Charles Batty's head were thicker and that he could supply the counter-attraction needed; but she might at least be able to use him; there was no one else.

That night, after an evening spent in soothing Sophia's fears which had been roused by the unnatural gentleness of Caroline, and treating Henrietta to all the friendliness she would receive, Rose went out to post a letter to Francis Sales. She had asked him, with an irony she had no doubt he would miss, to meet her in the hollow where the gipsies had encamped and where so many of their interviews had taken place. It was within a few yards of that bank of primroses where he had asked her to marry him.

Caroline was better the next morning and it was easy for Rose to escape. She chose to ride. It was one of those mild January days which already promise the return of spring. Birds chirped in the leafless trees, the earth was damp and seemed to stir with the efforts of innumerable roots to produce a richer life, yet the leaves of autumn were still lying on the ground. How she loved this country, this blue air, this smell of fruit present even before the blossom was on the trees, the sight of wood smoke curling from the cottage chimneys, the very ruts in the road! A little while ago she had told herself she was sickened by it: it was the symbol of failure and young, tender, ruined hopes, but the love of it lay deeply in her heart; all this, the failure and the ruin, were of her life and it could be no more cast off than could the hands which had refused the kissing and clasping of Francis Sales.

This was her own country: the strange, unbridled, stealthy wildness of it was in her blood; it was in Henrietta through her father, it was in Francis, too, and due to it was this tragic muddle in which they found themselves. She had a faint, despairing feeling that she could not fight against it, that her mission would only be another failure, yet she counted on Francis's easy tenderness of heart. The very weakness which persuaded him to an action could turn him from it, and it was to his tenderness she must appeal.

She reached the track and, raised high on her horse, she could see the fields with the rough grass and gorse bushes sloping to the channel; the pale strip of water like silver melted in the heart of the hills and falling slowly to the sea; the blue hills themselves like gates keeping a fair country. The place where the wood had been was like a brown and purple rug,

181

but before long the pattern would be complicated by creeping green. Where the trees had murmured and whispered or stood silent, listening, there was now no sound, no secrecy; the place lay candidly under the wide sky, but, from a field out of sight, a sheep bleated disconsolately, with a sound of infinite, uncomprehending woe, and a steamer in the river sent out a distant hoot of answering derision.

The gipsies had departed; the ashes of their fire made a black patch on the ground and a few rags fluttered in the wind. There was no human being in sight and she rode down the slope to wait in the hollow. She was beginning to wonder if Francis had received her letter when, with a dreary sense of watching a familiar scene reacted, she saw him in the lane with Henrietta by his side. Here was an unexpected difficulty, and she could do nothing but ride towards them, raising her whip in greeting.

She said at once to Francis, 'Did you get my letter?' She saw Henrietta's face flush angrily, but she knew that the time had come for her to speak. 'I asked you to meet me here.'

He was staring at her and his mouth moved mechanically. 'No, I didn't get it by the first post. Perhaps it's there now.' With his eyes still fixed on her, he moved back a step.

'No.' Rose smiled. 'Don't go and get it. Fortunately you are here. I want to talk to you, Henrietta, please –' Her voice was gentle, she leaned forward in the saddle with a charming gesture of request, but Henrietta shook her head. She was antagonized by that charm which was holding Francis's eyes. A loosened curl had fallen over her forehead, giving to the severity of her dress, copied from that portrait of her father, a dishevelling touch, as though a young lady were suddenly discovered to be a gipsy in an evil frame of mind.

'If it's anything to do with me, I'm going to stay,' she said. 'If it hasn't, I'll go.' She looked at Francis and added, between her teeth, 'But it must have.' Those words and that look claimed him for her own.

Rose lifted her chin and looked over the two heads, the uncovered one of Francis Sales and Henrietta's, with her hat a little askew, and, absurdly, Rose remembered that the child had washed her hair the night before: that was why the hat was crooked and the curl loose, making the scene undignified and funny above the pain of it. Rose spoke in a voice heightened by a tone. 'It concerns you both,' she said.

'Ah, then, you needn't say it, need she, Francis?'

'Francis,' she repeated the name with a grave humour, 'this is not fair to Henrietta.'

'I know that,' he muttered, and Rose saw Henrietta shoot at him a thin look of scorn.

Henrietta said, 'But I don't care about that, and anyhow, we're not going to do it any more. We're tired of these meetings' – she faced him – 'aren't we? We had just made up our minds to have no more of them.'

'I'm glad of that,' said Rose, and she fancied that the hurried beating of her heart must be plain through the thick stuff of her coat.

Henrietta laughed, showing little teeth, and Rose thought, 'Her teeth are too small. They spoil her.'

'No, you need not spy on us any more,' Henrietta said.

Francis made a movement of distaste. He said, as though the words cost him much labour, 'Henrietta, don't.'

But there seemed to be no limit to what Rose could bear. She stooped forward suddenly and put her cheek against the horse's neck in an impulsive need to express affection, perhaps to get it.

'You think I don't understand,' she said quietly, 'but I do, too well.' She paused, and in her overpowering sense of helplessness, of distrust, she found herself making, without a quiver, the confession of her own foolishness.

'I don't know whether Francis has told you that he and I were once in love with one another. At least that is what we called it.' Very pale, appearing to have grown thinner in that moment, she looked at the horse's ears and spoke as though she and Henrietta were alone. 'Until quite lately. Then he realized, we both realized, our mistake. But it seems that Francis must have somebody to – to meet, to kiss. Between me and you there has been some one else.' With a wave of her hand, she put aside that thought. 'We used to meet here often. This place must be full of memories for him. For me, the whole countryside is scattered with little broken bits of love. It breaks so easily, or it may be only the counterfeit that breaks. Anyhow, it broke, it chipped. I thought you ought to know that.' She touched her horse with her heel and turned down the lane. She went slowly, sitting very straight, but she had the constant expectation of being shot in the back. She had to remind herself that Henrietta had no weapon but her eyes.

It was those eyes Francis Sales chiefly remembered when he had parted from Henrietta and turned homewards. There had been scorn in them, anger, grief, jealousy and expectation. If she had not been so small, if they had not been raised to his, if he could have looked levelly into them as he did into the clear grey eyes of Rose, things might have been different. But she was little and she had clung to him, looking up. She had told him she could never see her Aunt Rose again. How could she? Was he sure he did not love Rose still? Was he sure? He ought to be, for it was he who had made Henrietta love him. He had liked that tribute too much to contradict it, but Rose Mallett was right: whoever had been the promoter of this business, it was not fair to Henrietta, and the thought of Rose, so white and straight, was like wind after a sultry day. She was like a church, he thought; a dim church with tall pillars losing themselves in the loftiness of the roof; yes, that was what was the matter with her: she was cold, but there was no one like her, you could not forget her even in the warmth of Henrietta's presence. One way and another, these Malletts tortured him.

He walked home, trying to find some way out of this maze of promises to Henrietta and of self-reproach, and his mental wanderings were interrupted by an unwelcome request from the nurse that he should go at once to Mrs. Sales. She seemed, the woman warned him, to be very much excited: would he please be careful? She must not have another heart attack.

As he entered the room, it seemed to him that he had been treading on egg-shells all his life, but a sudden pity swept him at the sight of his wife, very weak from the pain of the night

184

before last, yet intensely, almost viciously alive. He wished he had not gone to the Battys' ball; it had upset her and done him no good. If it had not been for that walk on the terrace –

He shut the door gently and stood by her. 'Are you in pain?' he asked. He felt remorsefully that he did not know how to treat her; he had not love enough, yet with all his heart he wanted to be kind.

'You haven't kissed me to-day,' she said. 'No, don't do it. You don't want to, do you?'

'Yes, I do,' he said, and as he bent over her he was touched by the contented sigh she gave. If he could begin over again, he told himself, with the virtue of the man who has committed himself fatally, things would be different. If he hadn't brought Henrietta to such a pass, they should be different now.

'I've never stopped being fond of you, Christabel.'

She laughed and disconcerted him. 'Or of your horses, or your dogs,' she said. 'No one could expect you to care much for a useless log like me. No one could have expected you not to go to that dance.' Tears filled her eyes. 'But I was lonely. And I imagined you there –'

'I wish I hadn't gone,' he said truthfully.

She seemed to consider that remark, but presently she asked, 'Have you lost something?'

He had lost a great deal, for Rose despised him; that had been plain in the face which once had been so soft for him.

'I asked you,' Christabel said, 'if you had lost something.'

'Yes – no, nothing.'

She let out a small piercing shriek. 'You're lying, lying! But why should I care? You've done that for years. And Rose has been so kind, hasn't she, coming to see me every week? Take your letter, Francis. Yes, I've read it! I don't care. I'm helpless. Take it!' From its hiding-place under the coverlet she drew the letter and threw it at him. It fluttered feebly to the ground. She had made a tremendous effort, trying to fling it in his face, and it had fallen as mildly as a snowflake. She began to sob. This was the climax of her suffering, that it should fall like that.

He picked it up and read it. It was no good trying to

185

explain, for one explanation would only necessitate another. He was deeply in the mire, they were both, they were all in it, and he did not know how to get anybody out, but he had to stop that sobbing somehow. His pity for Christabel swelled into his biggest feeling. He crumpled the letter angrily and, at the sound, she held her breathing for a moment. Of course, she should have crumpled the letter and then she might have hit him with it.

'I wish to God I'd never seen her,' she heard him say with despairing anger. And then, more gently, 'Don't cry, Christabel. I can't bear to hear you. The letter's nothing. I shall never meet her again. I must take more care of you.' He took her hand and stroked it. He would never meet Rose again, but he had an appointment with Henrietta.

'You promise? But no, it doesn't matter if you love her.'

'I don't love her.'

'But you did.'

He passed his free hand across his forehead. No, he would not keep that appointment with Henrietta, or he would only keep it to tell her it was impossible. He could not go with this wailing in his ears and he knew that piteous sound was his salvation. It gave him the strength to appear weak. 'Don't cry. It's all right, Christabel. Look, I'll burn the confounded letter and I swear it's the only one I've ever had from her.' It was to Rose, he admitted miserably, that he owed the possibility of telling that truth.

Her weeping became quieter. 'Tell her,' she articulated, 'I never want to see her again.'

'But,' he said petulantly, 'haven't I just told you I never want to meet her?'

'Then write – write – I don't mind Henrietta.'

'No!' he almost shouted, 'not Henrietta either!'

She turned to him a face ravaged with tears and misery. 'Why not Henrietta?' she whispered.

'I hate the lot of them,' he muttered. 'They're all witches.'

She laughed joyously. 'That's what I've said myself!' She gave him both her thin, hot hands to hold. 'But it's worth while, all this, if you are going to be good to me.'

He kissed her then as the sinner kisses the saint who has wrought a miracle of salvation for him. 'We've had bad luck,' he murmured. 'You've had the worst of it.' He stroked her cheek. 'Poor little thing.'

§ 7

Once out of sight of the two standing in the lane, Rose rode home quickly. She felt she had a great deal to do, but she did not know what it was. Her head was hot with the turmoil of her thoughts. There was no order in them; the past was mixed with the present, the done with the undone: she was assailed by the awful conviction that right was prolific in producing wrong. If she had not preserved her own physical integrity, these two, who were almost like her children – yes, that was how she felt towards them – would not have been tempted to such folly. For it was folly: they did not love each other, and she remembered, with a sickening pang, the expression with which Francis had looked at her. She told herself he loved her still; he had never loved anybody else and she had only pity and protection and a deep-rooted fondness to give him in return. She cared more passionately for Henrietta, who was now the victim of the superficial chastity on which Rose had insisted.

If she had known that Henrietta was to suffer, she would have subdued her niceness, for if Francis had been in physical possession of her body, she would have had no difficulty in possessing his mind. Holding nothing back, she could also have held him securely. She did not want him, but Henrietta would have been saved. But then Rose had not known: how could she? And Henrietta might be saved yet, she must be saved. The obvious method was to lay siege to the facile heart of Francis, but there was no time for that. Rose was not deceived by Henrietta's enigmatic words. They were tired of meeting stealthily, she had said. What did that mean? Her head grew hotter. She had to force herself into calm, and the old man at the toll-house on the bridge received her usual greeting as she passed, but, as she went slowly to

187

the stables, there was added to her anxiety the thrilling knowledge that at last, and for the first time, she was going to take definite action. Her whole life had been a long and dull preparation for this day. She began to take a pleasure in her excitement: she had something to do; she was delivered from the monotony of thought.

On her way from the stables she met Charles Batty going home for his midday meal, and she stopped him. 'Charles!' she said. She presented to his appreciative eyes a very elegant figure in the habit looped up to show her high slim boots, with her thick plait of hair under the hard hat, her complexion defying the whiteness of her stock; while to her he appeared with something of the aspect of an angel in a long top coat and a hat at the back of his head. 'Charles,' she said again, tapping her boot with her whip, 'I'm in trouble. Would you mind walking home by the hill? I want you to help me, but I can't tell you how. Not yet.'

He walked beside her without speaking and they came to the place where he had stood with Henrietta and she had flouted him; whither she had wandered on her first day in Radstowe, that high point overlooking the gorge, the rocks, the trees, the river; that scene of which not Charles, nor Rose, nor Henrietta could ever tire.

'Not, yet,' she repeated. 'Will you meet me this afternoon?'

'Look here,' he remonstrated, 'if Henrietta found out –'

She had not time to smile. 'It's for her sake.'

'I'll do anything,' he said.

'Then will you meet me this afternoon at five o'clock? Not here. I may not be able to get so far. Where can we meet?'

'Well, there's the post-office. Can't mistake that.'

'No, no, I may have something important, very important, Charles, to say to you. At five o'clock, will you be on The Green? There's a seat by the old monument. It won't take a minute to get there. Are you listening? On The Green at five o'clock. Come towards me as soon as you see me and at once we'll walk together towards the avenue. Wait till six, and if I don't come, will you still hold yourself in readiness

188

at home? Don't forget. Don't be absent-minded and forget what you are there for, and even if there's a barrel-organ playing dreadful tunes, you'll wait there? For Henrietta.'

'I don't understand this about Henrietta.'

'That doesn't matter, not in the least. Now what are your instructions?'

He repeated them.

'Very well. I trust you.'

They separated and she went home, a little amused by her melodramatic conduct, but much comforted by the fact that Charles, though ignorant of his part, was with her in this conspiracy. She was met by reproaches from Sophia.

'Oh, Rose, riding on such a day! And Henrietta out, too! Suppose we'd wanted something from the chemist!'

'But you didn't, did you? And there are four servants in the house. How is Caroline now?'

'Very quiet. Oh, Rose, she's very ill. She lets me do anything I like. She hasn't a fault to find with me.'

'Let Henrietta sit with her this afternoon while Nurse is out.'

'No, no, Rose, I must do what I can for her.'

'I should like Henrietta to feel she is needed.'

'I don't think Caroline would be pleased. I'll see what she says.'

Caroline was distressingly indifferent but, as Henrietta went to her room on her return and sent a message that she had a headache and did not want any food, she was left undisturbed. Sophia became still more agitated. What was the matter with the child? It would be terrible if she were ill, too. Would Rose go and take her temperature? No, Rose was sure Henrietta would not care for that. She had better be left to sleep. If only she could be put to sleep for a few days!

Now that she was in the house and locked into her room, Rose was alarmed. She was afraid she had done wrong in making that confession; she had played what seemed to be her strongest card but she had played it in the wrong way, at the wrong moment. She had surely roused the girl's antagonism and rivalry, and there came to Rose's memory many little scenes in which Reginald Mallett, crossed in his desires,

189

or irritated by reproaches, had suddenly stopped his storming, set his stubborn mouth and left the house, only to return when need drove him home.

But if Henrietta went, and Rose had no doubt of her intention, she would not come back. She had the unbending pride of her mother's class, and Rose's fear was changed into a sense of approaching desolation. The house would be unbearable without Henrietta. Rose stood on the landing listening to the small sounds from Caroline's room and the unbroken silence from Henrietta's. If that room became empty, the house would be empty too. There would be no swift footsteps up and down the stairs, no bursts of singing, no laughter: she must not go; she could not be spared. For a moment Rose forgot Francis Sales's share in the adventure: she could only think of her own impending loneliness.

She went quickly down the stairs and sat in the drawing-room, leaving the door open, and after an hour or so she heard stealthy sounds from the room above; drawers were opened carefully and Henrietta, in slipperless feet, padded across the floor. Rose looked at her watch and rang the bell.

'Please take a tray to Miss Henrietta's room,' she told Susan, 'with tea, and sandwiches and, yes, an egg. She had no luncheon. A good, substantial tea, please, Susan.' If the child were anticipating a journey, she must be fed.

A little later she heard Susan knock at Henrietta's door. It was not opened, but the tray was deposited outside with a slight rattle of china, and Susan's voice, mildly reproachful, exhorted Miss Henrietta to eat and drink.

At half-past four the tray was still lying there untouched. This meant that Henrietta was in no hurry, or that she was too indignant to eat: but it might also mean that she had no time. Only half-past four and Charles Batty was not due till five! He might be there already; in his place, she would have been there, but men were painfully exact, and five was the hour she had named. But again, Charles Batty was not an ordinary man. Trusting to that fact, she went to her room and provided herself with money, and, having listened without a qualm at Henrietta's door, she ran out of the house.

190

The church facing The Green sounded the three-quarters and there, on the seat by the old stone, sat Charles, his hands in his pockets, his hat pulled over his eyes in a manner likely to rouse suspicions in the mildest of policemen.

He rose. 'Where's your hat?'

'No time,' she said.

He repeated his lesson. 'We were to walk towards the avenue.'

'Yes, but I daren't. I want to keep in sight of the house. Come with me. Here's money. Don't lose it.'

He held it loosely. 'Some one's been playing "The Merry Peasant" for half an hour,' he said. 'I'll never sit here again.'

'Charles, take care of the money. You may need it. There's ten pounds – all I had – but perhaps it will be enough. I want you to watch our gate, and if Henrietta goes out, please follow her, but don't let her see you.'

'Oh, I say!' he murmured.

'I know. It's hateful, it's abominable, but you must do it.'

'She won't be pleased.'

'You must do it,' Rose repeated.

'She's sure to see me. Eyes like needles.'

'She mustn't. She'll probably go by train. If she goes to London, to this address – I've written it down for you – you may leave her there for the night and let me know at once. If she goes anywhere else, you must go with her. Take care of her. I can't tell you exactly what to do because I don't know what's going to happen. She may meet somebody, and then, Charles, you must go with them both. But bring her home if you can. Don't go to sleep. Don't compose music in your head. Oh, Charles, this is your chance!'

'Is it? I shall miss it. I always do the wrong thing.'

'Not to-night.' She smiled at him eagerly, imperiously, trying to endue him with her own spirit. 'Stay here in the shadow. I don't think you will have long to wait, and if you get your chance, if you have to talk to her, don't scold.'

'Scold! It's she that scolds. She bullies me.'

'Ah, not to-night!' she repeated gaily.

He peered down at her. 'Yes, you are rather like her

in the face, specially when you laugh. Better looking, though,'
he added mournfully.

'Don't tell her that.'

'Mustn't I? Well, I don't suppose I shall think of it again.'

'Remember that for you she is the best and most beautiful
woman in the world. You can tell her that.'

'The best and most beautiful – yes,' he said. 'All right.
But you'll see – I'll lose her. Bound to,' he muttered.

She put her hand on his arm. 'You'll bring her home,'
she said firmly, and she left him standing monumentally,
with his hat awry.

Charles stood obediently in the place assigned to him,
where the shelter of the Malletts' garden wall made his own
bulk less conspicuous and whence he could see the gate.
The night was mild, but a little wind had risen, gently
rocking the branches of the trees which, in the neighbourhood
of the street lamps, cast their shadows monstrously on the
pavements. Their movements gradually resolved themselves
into melody in Charles Batty's mind: the beauty of the reflected and exaggerated twigs and branches was not consciously realized by his eyes, but the swaying, the sudden
ceasing, and the resumption of that delicate agitation became
music in his ears. He, too, swayed slightly on his big feet
and forgot his business, to remember it with a jerk and a
fear that Henrietta had escaped him. Rose had told him he
must not make music in his head. How had she known he
would want to do that? She must have some faculty denied
to him, the same faculty which warned her that Henrietta
was going to do something strange to-night.

He felt in his pocket to assure himself of the money's
safety. He rearranged his hat and determined to concentrate
on watching. The pain which, varying in degrees, always
lived in his bosom, the pain of misunderstanding and being
misunderstood, of doing the wrong thing, of meaning well
and acting ill, became acute. He was bound to make a
mistake; he would lose Henrietta or incense her, though now
he was more earnest to do wisely than he had ever been.
He had told her he was going to make an art of love, but he

knew that art was far from perfected, and she was incapable of appreciating mere endeavour. He was afraid of her, but to-night he was more afraid of failing.

The music tripped in his head but he would not listen to it. He strained his ears for the opening of the Malletts' door, and just as the sound of the clock striking two steady notes for half-past five was fading, as though it were being carried on the light wings of the wind over the big trees, over the green, across the gorge, across the woods to the essential country, he heard a faint thud, a patter of feet and the turning of the handle of the gate. He stepped back lest she should be going to pass him, but she turned the other way, walking quickly, with a small bag in her hand.

'She's going away,' Charles said to himself with perspicacity, and now for the first time he knew what her absence would mean to him. She did not love him, she mocked and despised him, but the Malletts' house had held her, and several times a day he had been able to pass and tell himself she was there. Now, with the sad little bag in her hand, she was not only in personal danger, she threatened his whole life.

He followed, not too close. Her haste did not destroy the beauty of her carriage, her body did not hang over her feet, teaching them the way to go; it was straight, like a young tree. He had never really looked at her before, he had never had a mind empty of everything except the consideration of her, and now he was puzzled by some difference. In his desire to discover what it was, he drew indiscreetly close to her, and though a quick turn of her head reminded him of his duty to see and not to be seen, he had made his discovery. Her clothes were different: they were shabby and, searching for an explanation, he found the right one. She was wearing the clothes in which she had arrived at Nelson Lodge. He remembered. In books it was what fugitives always did: they discarded their rich clothes and they left a note on the pin-cushion. It was her way of shaking the dust from her feet and, with a rush of feeling in which he forgot himself, he experienced a new, protective tenderness for her. He realized that she, too, might be unhappy, and it seemed that it was he who ought to comfort her, he who could do it.

He had to put a drag on his steps as they tried to hurry after her, through the main street of Upper Radstowe, through another darker one where there were fewer people and he had to exercise more care, and so past the big square where tall old houses looked at each other across an enclosure of trees, down to a broad street where tramcars rushed and rattled. She boarded one of these and went inside. Pulling his hat farther over his face in the erroneous belief that he would be the less noticeable, he ascended to the top, to crane his head over the side at every stopping-place lest Henrietta should get off; but there was no sign of her until they reached that strange place in the middle of the city where the harbour ran into the streets and the funnels and masts of ships mingled with the roofs of houses. This was the spot where, round a big triangle of paving, tramcars came and went in every direction, and here everybody must alight.

The streets were brilliant with electricity; electric signs popped magically with many-coloured lights on the front of a music hall where an audience was already gathering for the first performance, on public-houses, on the big red warehouses on the quay. The lighted tramcars with passengers inside looked like magic-lantern slides, and amid all the people using the triangle as a promenade or hurrying here and there on business, the newsboys shouting and the general bustle, Charles did not know whether to be more afraid of losing Henrietta or colliding with her. But now his faculties were alert and he used more discretion than was necessary, for Henrietta, under the influence of that instinct which persuades that not seeing is a precaution against being seen, was scrupulous in avoiding the encounter of any eye.

He followed her to another tramcar which would take her to the station; he followed her when she alighted once more and, seeing her change that bag from one hand to another, as though she found it heavy, he let out a groan so loud and heartfelt that it aroused the pity of a passer-by, but he was really luxuriating in his sorrow for her. It was an immense relief after much sorrowing for himself and it induced a forgetfulness of everything but his determination to help her.

It was easy to keep her in sight while she went up the broad approach to the dull, crowded, badly lighted and dirty station: it was harder to get near enough to hear what ticket she demanded. He did not hear, but again he followed the little, shabby, yet somehow elegant figure, and he took a place in the compartment next to the one she chose. It was the London train, and he found himself hoping she was not going so far; he felt that to see her disappearing into that house of which he had the address in his pocket would be like seeing her disappear for ever. He would lose his chance of helping her, or rather, she would lose her chance of being helped, a slightly different aspect of the affair and the one on which he had set his mind.

He had taken a ticket for the first stop, and when the train slowed down for the station of that neighbouring city, he had his head out of the window. An old gentleman with a noisy cold protested. Could he not wait until the train actually stopped? Charles was afraid he could not be so obliging. He assured the old gentleman that the night was mild. 'And I'm keeping a good deal of the draught out,' he said pleasantly.

He saw a small hand on the door of the next compartment, then the sleeve of a black coat as Henrietta stretched for the handle, and he said to himself, 'She was in mourning for her mother.' He was proud of remembering that; he had a sense of nearness and a slow suspicion that hitherto he had not sufficiently considered her. In their past intercourse he had been trying to stamp his own thoughts on her mind, but now it seemed that something of her, more real than her physical beauty, was being impressed on him. He wanted to know what she was feeling, not in regard to him, but in regard, for instance, to that dead mother, and why she ran away like this, in her old clothes and with the little bag.

She was out of the train: she had descended the steps to the roadway and there she looked about her, hesitating.

Cabmen hailed her but, ignoring them and crossing the tramlines, she began to walk slowly up a dull street where cards in the house windows told of lodgings to be let. If she knocked at one of these doors, what was he to do? But she did not look at the houses: her head was drooping a little, her feet moved reluctantly, she was no longer eager and her bag was heavy again, she had changed it from the right to the left hand, and then, unexpectedly, she quickened her pace. The naturally unobservant Charles divined a cause and, looking for it, he saw with a shock of surprise and horror the tall figure of a man at the end of the street. She was hastening towards him.

Charles stood stock-still. A man! He had not thought of that, he had positively never thought of it! Nor had he guessed at his capacity for jealousy and anger. Then this was why Rose Mallett had sent him on this mission: it was a man's work, and in the confusion of his feelings he still had time to wish he had spent more of his youth in the exercise of his muscles. He braced himself for an encounter, but already Henrietta had swerved aside. This was not the man she was to meet; her expectation had misled her; but the acute Charles surmised that the man she looked for would also be tall and slim.

Tall and slim; he repeated the words so that he should make no mistake, but subconsciously they had roused memories and instead of that little black figure hurrying on in front of him, he saw a young woman clothed in yellow, entering from the frosty night, with brilliant half veiled eyes, and by the side of her was Francis Sales.

Again he stood still, as much in amazement at his own folly as in any other feeling. Francis Sales, the fellow who could dance, who murdered music and little birds! And he had a wife! Charles was not shocked. If Henrietta had wished to elope with a great musician, wived though he might be, Charles could have let her go, subduing his own pangs, not for her own sake but for that of a man more important than himself, but he would not yield the claims of his devotion to Francis Sales. He should not have her.

He walked on quickly, taking no precautions. He had

lost sight of Henrietta and he could not even hear the sound of her steps, yet he had no doubt but he would find her, and she was not far to seek. A turn of the road brought him under the shadow of the cathedral and, in the paved square surrounded by old houses in which it stood, he saw her. Apparently at that moment she also saw him, for with an incredibly swift movement and a furtiveness which wrung his heart, she slipped into the porch and disappeared. He followed. The door was unlocked and she had passed through it, but he lingered there, fancying he could smell the faint sweetness of her presence. Within, the organ was booming softly and in that sound he forgot, for a moment, the necessity for action. The music seemed to be wonderfully complicated with the waft of Henrietta's passage, with his love for her, with all he imagined her to be, but the forgetfulness was only for that moment, and he pushed open the door.

§ 8

The place was dimly lighted. Two candles, like stars, twinkled on the distant altar; a few people sat in the darkness with an extraordinary effect of personal sorrow. This was not where happy people came to offer thanks; it was a refuge for the afflicted, a temporary harbour for the weary. They did not seem to pray; they sat relaxed, wrapped in the antique peace, the warm, musty smell of the building, sitting with the stillness of their desire to preserve this safety which was theirs only for a little while. Their dull clothes mixed with the shadows, the old oak, the worn stone, and the voice of the organ was like the voice of multitudes of sad souls. Very soon the music ceased with a kind of sob and the verger, with his skirts flapping round his feet, came to warn those isolated human creatures that they must face the world again.

They rose obediently, but Henrietta did not move, as though she alone of that company had not learnt the lesson of necessity. But the altar lights were now extinguished, the skirted verger was approaching her, and Charles forestalled him. He murmured, 'Henrietta!'

197

She looked up without surprise. 'What time is it?' she asked.
'Seven o'clock.'

She rose, picking up her bag.

'Let me have that,' he said.

'No, no,' she answered absently, and then, 'Is it really seven?'

'Yes, there's the clock striking now.' The sound of the seven notes whirred and then clanged above their heads. 'We must go,' he said. 'They're locking up.'

The air was cold and damp after the warmth of the church and Henrietta stood, shivering a little and looking round her.

'I'm hungry,' Charles Batty said. 'Will you come and have dinner with me?'

'No,' she replied, 'I shall stay here.'

'How long for?'

'I don't know.' And sharply she turned on him and asked, 'What are you doing here?'

'I come here sometimes. There are concerts.'

'You'll be late, then, if you are going to dine.'

'I know, but I'm hungry. You can't listen to music if you're hungry. Let's have dinner first.'

The square was deserted, the lights in the little shops, where old furniture and lace and jewels were sold, were all put out and the large policeman who had been standing at the corner had moved away.

'I don't want anything to eat,' she said. She dropped the bag and covered her face with both her hands. She was going to cry, but he was not afraid; he was rather glad and, not without pleasure at his own daring, he removed a hand, tucked it under his arm, and said, 'Come along.'

She struggled. 'I can't. I must go to London. If you want to help me you'll find out about the trains. I can go to Mrs. Banks. I can't go back to Radstowe.'

'Henrietta,' he said firmly, 'come and have dinner and we'll talk about it.'

'If you'll promise to help me.'

'There's nothing I want to do so much,' he said. 'We mustn't forget the bag.'

'Somewhere quiet, Charles,' she murmured.

'Somewhere good,' he emended.

She looked down, 'Such old clothes.'

'It doesn't matter what you wear,' he told her. 'You always look different from anybody else.'

'Do I? And I am! I am! I'm much worse, and nobody,' she almost sobbed, 'is so unhappy! Charles, will you wait here for a minute? I must just – just walk round the square.'

'You'll come back?'

She nodded, and he kept the bag as hostage.

The large policeman had strolled back. He saw the tall young man standing over the bag and thought it would be well to keep an eye on him, but Charles did not notice the policeman. His whole attention was for Henrietta's reappearance. She would come back because she had said she would, but if she did not come alone there would be trouble. He did not, however, expect to see Francis Sales: he gathered that Sales had failed her, and he was sorry. He would have beaten him, somehow; he would have conquered for the first time in his life, and now he felt that his task was going to be too easy. He wished he could have sweated and panted in the doing of it; and when Henrietta returned alone, walking with an angry swiftness, he felt a genuine regret.

'Come along, Charles,' she said briskly. 'Let us have dinner.'

He could see the brightness of her eyes, looking past him; her lips had a fixed smile and he wished she would cry again. 'She is crying inside,' he told himself. He moved forward beside her vaguely. The tenderness of his love for her was like a powerful, warm wave, sweeping over him and making him helpless for the time. He could do nothing against it, he had to be carried with it, but suddenly it receded, leaving him high and dry and unromantically in contact with a lamp-post. His hat had fallen off.

'What are you doing?' Henrietta asked irritably.

He rubbed his head. 'Bumped it. I was thinking about you.'

'What were you thinking?' she asked defiantly.

'Oh, well –' he said.

She laughed. 'Charles, you're hopeless.'

'No, I'm not.' He stooped for his hat and picked it up. 'Not,' he repeated strongly. 'Here's the place.' They had turned into a busy street. 'I hope there won't be a band.'

'I hope there will be. I want noises, hideous noises.'

'You're going to get them,' he sighed as he pushed open the swing-door and received in his ears the fierce banging, braying and shrieking of various instruments played in a frenzy by a group of musicians confined, as if for the public safety, in a small gallery at the end of the room. Large and encumbered by the bag, he stood obstructing the waiters in the passage between the tables.

'They're like wild beasts in a cage,' he said in the loud voice of his anger. 'Can you stand it?'

'Oh, yes – yes. Let us sit here, in this corner.' He was ridiculous, she thought, yet to-night, unconscious of any absurdity himself, he had a dignity; he was not so ugly as she had thought; his somewhat protruding eyes had less vacancy, and though his tie was crooked, she was not ashamed of him. Nevertheless, she said as he sat down, 'Charles, I'm going to London to-night. Get a time-table.'

'Soup first,' he said.

'I must go to-night. I can't go back to Radstowe.'

'Did you,' he asked unexpectedly, 'leave a note on your dressing-table?'

'What?' She frowned. 'No, of course not.'

'Oh, well, you can go back. We're going to a concert together. It's quite easy. I told you you were different from everybody else.' And then, remembering Rose's words, he leaned across the table towards her. 'The most beautiful and the best,' he said severely.

'Me?'

'Yes. Here's the soup.'

She drank it, looking at him between the spoonfuls. This was the man who had talked to her by the Monks' Pool. Here was the same detachment he had shown then, and though the act of taking soup was not poetical, though the band blared and the place shone with many lights, she was taken back to that night among the trees, with the water lying darkly at her feet, keeping its own secrets; with the ducks quacking sleepily and unseen, and the water rats diving with a silken splash.

She seemed to be recovering something she had lost because she had disregarded it, something she wanted, not for use but for the sake of possessing and sometimes looking at it.

Sternly she tried not to think of Francis Sales, who had deserted her. She might have known he would desert her. He had looked at Aunt Rose and she had seen him weaken, yet he had promised. He was that kind of man: he could not say no to her face, but he left her in this city, all alone.

Her lips trembled; she steadied them with difficulty. She was determined not to honour him with so much as a memory or a regret, but there came forbidden recollections of the dance, of the terrace, and of her hands in his. She closed her eyes and a tremor, delicious, horrible, ran through her body. She felt the strength of those brown, muscular hands and she was assailed by the odour of wind and tobacco that clung to him. He had never said anything worth remembering, but there had been danger and excitement in his presence. There was neither in the neighbourhood of Charles, yet she could not forget his words.

She opened her eyes. 'What was it you said just now?'

'You're the best and most beautiful woman in the world. Your fish is getting cold.'

She ate it without appetite or distaste. 'But, Charles –'

'I know.'

'What?'

'Everything,' he said.

'How?'

He tapped himself, 'Here.'

'I expect you've got it all wrong.'

'Yesterday, perhaps, but not to-day. To-day I know everything.'

'How does it feel?'

201

'Wonderful,' he replied. They laughed together but, as though with that laughter the door to emotion had been opened, he saw tears start into her eyes. 'No,' he begged, 'there's no need to cry.'

She laughed again. 'I've got to cry some time.'

'When we're going home, then. We're going home in a car.'

'Are we?' she said, pleased as a child. 'But what about London, Charles? I have to go.'

'Not to-night. Here's some chicken.'

'I can't go back.'

'But you haven't left a note.'

'No.'

'Then it's easy. You and I have just been to a concert. You promised me that long ago.'

She uttered no more protests. She ate and drank obediently, glad to be cared for, and when the meal was over she told him gratefully, 'You have been good. You never said another word about the band and it has made even my head ache.'

'And I forgot about it!' He stared at her in amazement. 'I forgot about it! I didn't hear it! Good heavens! But come away quickly before I begin remembering.'

That they might be able to tell the truth, they went to the concert and, standing at the back of the hall stayed there for a little while. Even for Charles, the music was only a covering for his thoughts. Henrietta, strangely gentle, was beside him, but he dwelt less on that than on the greater marvel of the new power he felt within himself. She might laugh at him, she might mock him in the future, but she could not daunt him, and though she might never love him, he had done her service. No one could take that from him. He turned his head and looked down at her, to find her looking up at him, a little puzzled but entirely friendly.

'Oh, Henrietta!' he whispered loudly, transgressing his own law of silence and evoking an indignant hiss from an enthusiastic neighbour. He blushed with shame, then decided that to-night he could not really care, and signing to Henrietta to follow him, he tiptoed from the hall.

'Did you hear? Did you hear?' he asked her. 'I spoke! I – at a concert! I've never done that in my life before. I'll never do it again! But, then, it was the first time you'd ever looked at me like that, Henrietta! And, oh Lord, we've forgotten the bag. I dare not go back for it.'

'We'll leave it, then,' she said indifferently. 'I don't want to see it again.'

'But I like it. It's an old friend. I've watched it –' He checked himself. 'I'll go. Wait here.'

'Why aren't we going home by train?' she asked, when he returned.

'The angry man didn't see me,' he said triumphantly. 'Oh, because – well, you wanted somewhere to cry, didn't you?'

In the closed car she sat, for a time very straight, looking out of the window at the streets and the people, but when they had drawn away from the old city and left its grey stone houses behind and taken to the roads where slowly moving carts were creaking and snatches of talk from slow-tongued country people were heard and lost in the same moment, she sank back. The roads were dark. They were lined by tall, bare trees which seemed to challenge this swift passage and then decide to permit what they could not prevent, and for a mile or so the river gleamed darkly like an unsheathed sword in the night.

'We shall soon be there, shan't we?' she asked, in a small voice.

'Yes, pretty soon.'

'I wish we wouldn't. I wish we could go on like this for ever, to the edge of the world and then drop over and forget.'

He sighed. He could not arrange that for her but he told the man to drive more slowly. Against the dark upholstery of the car, her face was like a young moon, wan and too weary for its work. He slipped his arm under her back and drew her to him. Pulling off her hat, she found a place for her head against his shoulder and he shut his eyes. She breathed regularly and lightly, as though she were asleep, but presently she said, 'Charles, I don't mean anything by this, but you are the only friend I have. You won't think I mean anything, will you?'

He shook his head and it came to rest on hers. He, too, wished they might go on like this for ever, to the world's edge.

★

The car was stopped at a little distance from the house and Henrietta had to rouse herself from the state between waking and sleeping, thought and imagery, in which she had passed the journey. The jarring of the brake shocked her into a recognition of facts and the gentle humming of the engine reminded her that life had to go on as before. The persistent sound, regular, not loud, controlled, was like existence in Nelson Lodge; one wearied of it, yet one would weary more of accidents breaking the healthy beating of the engine: to-night had been one of the accidents and she was terribly tired. No wonder! She had been trying to run away with a man who did not want her, a man who had a lonely, miserable invalid for a wife, the old lover of Aunt Rose. A little blaze of anger flared up at the thought of Rose; nevertheless, she continued her self-accusations. She had been willing to leave her aunts without a word and they had been good to her and one of them was ill, and the very money in her pocket was not her own. She was shocked by her behaviour. She was like her father, who took what belonged to other people and used it badly.

She sat, flaccid, her hands loose on her lap. She felt incapable of movement, but Charles was speaking to her, telling her to get out and run home quickly. She looked at him. She was holding his friendly hand. What would she have done without him? She saw herself in the train, speeding through the lonely darkness; she saw herself knocking at Mrs. Banks's door, felt herself clasped to the doubtful blackness of that bosom, and she shuddered.

'You must go,' Charles said, but he still held her hand.

He had brought her back to cleanliness and comfort, he had saved her from behaviour of gross ingratitude, he had been marvellously kind and wise.

204

'Charles,' she said, 'it's awful.'

'No, it's all right. We've been to a concert.'

'Yes' – her voice sank – 'I've kept that promise. But the whole thing – and Aunt Caroline so ill. She may have died.'

'There hasn't been time,' he said.

'Oh, Charles, it only takes a minute.'

'Well, run home quickly. This bag's a nuisance,' he said, but he looked at it tenderly. How he had dogged that bag! How heavy it had seemed for her! 'Look here, I'll take it home and get it to you to-morrow somehow.'

'I don't want it. I hate it.'

He thought, 'I'll keep it, then,' and aloud he said, 'I'll wrap the things up in a parcel and let you have them. Nothing you don't want me to see, is there?'

'No, nothing.'

'All right. Do get out, dear. No, I shall drive on.'

She lingered on the pavement. She had not said a word of thanks. She jumped on to the step and put her head through the window. 'Thank you, kind Charles,' she said.

'Henrietta,' he began in a loud voice, filling the dark interior with sound, 'Henrietta –'

'What is it?'

'No, no. Nothing.'

'Tell me.'

'No. Not fair,' he said. 'Just weakness. Good night. Be quick.'

She ran along the street and gave the front-door bell a gentle push. To her relief it was the housemaid and not Susan who opened to her. Susan would have looked at her severely, but the housemaid had a welcoming smile, an offer of food if Miss Henrietta had not dined.

Henrietta shook her head. She was going to bed at once. She did not want anything to eat. How was Miss Caroline?

'Not so well to-night, Miss Henrietta. The doctor's been again and there's a night-nurse come.'

Henrietta pressed her hands against her heart. Oh, good Charles, wonderful Charles! She did not know how to be grateful enough. She moved meekly, humbly through the hall and up the stairs. All was terribly, portentously still, but in her bedroom there were no signs of the trouble in the house. The fire was lighted, her evening gown had been laid out on the bed, her silk stockings and slippers were in their usual places. Nobody had suspected, nobody had been alarmed; she had stolen back by a miracle into her place.

Yes, Charles Batty was a miracle, there was no other word for him and, by contrast, the image of Francis Sales appeared mean, contemptible. Why had he failed her? His desertion was a blessing, but it was also a slight and perhaps a tribute to the power of Rose. Yes, that was it. She set her little teeth. He had stared at Aunt Rose as though he could not look at her enough, not with the starved expression she had first intercepted long ago, but with a look of wonder, almost of awe. She was nearly middle-aged, yet she could force that from him. Well, she was welcome to anything he could give her, his offerings were no compliment. Henrietta was done with him; she would not think of him again; she had been foolish, she had been wicked, but she was the richer and the wiser for her experience.

She had always been taught that sin brought suffering, yet here she was, warm and comfortable, in possession of a salutary lesson and with the good Charles for a secure friend. It was odd, unnatural, and this variation in her case gave her a pleasant feeling of being a special person for whom the operation of natural laws could be diverted. By the weakness of Francis Sales and the strength of Aunt Rose whom, nevertheless, she could never forgive, she was saved from much unhappiness, and if her mother knew everything in that heaven to which she had surely gone, she must now be weeping tears of thankfulness. Yet Henrietta's future lay before her rather drearily. She stretched out her arms and legs; she yawned. What was she to do? Being good, as she meant to be, and realizing her sin, as indeed she did, was hardly occupation enough for all her energies.

Her immediate business was to answer a knock at the door. It was Rose who entered. Her natural pallor was overlaid

206

by the whiteness of distress. 'Oh, Henrietta, I am glad you have come in.'

'I've been to a concert with Charles Batty,' Henrietta said quickly.

Rose showed no interest or surprise. 'Caroline is so much worse.' Henrietta felt a pang at her forgetfulness. 'She is very ill. I was afraid you might not be back in time. She has been asking for you.'

'I've been to Wellsborough, to a concert,' Henrietta insisted. 'Is she as bad as that, Aunt Rose? But she'll get better, won't she?'

'Come with me and say good night to her.' Rose took Henrietta's hand. 'How warm you are,' she said, in wonder that anything could be less cold than Caroline soon would be.

Henrietta's fingers tightened round the living hand. 'She's not going to die, is she?'

'Yes, she's dying,' Rose said quietly.

'Oh, but she can't,' Henrietta protested. 'She doesn't want to. She'll hate it so.' It was impossible to imagine Aunt Caroline without her parties, without her clothes, she would find it intolerably dull to be dead. 'Perhaps she will get better.'

Rose said nothing. They crossed the landing and entered the dim room. Caroline lay in the middle of the big bed: with her hair lank and uncurled she was hardly recognizable and strangely ugly. Her body seemed to have dwindled, but her features were strong and harsh, and Henrietta said to herself, 'This is the real Aunt Caroline, not what I thought, not what I thought. I've never seen her before.' She wondered how she had ever dared to joke with her: she had been a funny, vain old woman without much sensibility, immune from much that others suffered, and now she was a mere human creature, breathing with difficulty and in pain.

Henrietta stood by the bed, saying and doing nothing: Rose had slipped away; the nurse was quietly busy at a table and Aunt Sophia was kneeling before a high-backed chair with her elbows on the cushioned seat, her face in her hands. She was praying; it was as bad as that. Her back, the sash-encircled waist, the thick hair, looked like those of a young girl. She was praying. Henrietta looked again at Aunt Caroline's grey face and saw that the eyes had opened, the lips were smiling a little. 'Good child,' she said, with immense difficulty, as though she had been seeking those words for a long time and had at last fitted them to her thought.

Sophia stirred, dropped her hands and looked round: the nurse came forward with a little crackle of starched clothes. 'Say good night to her and go.'

Henrietta leaned over the empty space of bed and kissed Caroline on the temple. 'Good night, dear Aunt Caroline,' she said softly.

There was no answer. The eyes were closed again and the harsh breathing went on cruelly, like waves falling back from a pebbled shore, and Henrietta felt the dampness of death on her lips. No, Aunt Caroline would not get better.

She died in the early morning while Henrietta slept. Susan, entering as usual with Henrietta's tea, did not say a word. She knew her place; it was not for her to give the news to a member of the family; moreover, she blamed Henrietta for Miss Caroline's death. It was the Battys' ball that had killed Miss Caroline, and Susan stuck to her belief that if it had not been for Miss Henrietta, there would not have been a ball.

Sleepily, Henrietta watched Susan draw the blinds, but something in the woman's slow, languid movements startled her into wakefulness. Her dreams dropped back into their place. She had been sleeping warmly, forgetfully, while death hovered over the house, looking for a way in. She sat up in bed. 'Aunt Caroline?'

Susan began to cry, but in spite of her tears and her distress she ejaculated dutifully, 'Miss Henrietta, your dressing-gown, your slippers!' but Henrietta had rushed forth and bounded into Rose's room.

'You might have told me! You might have waked me!'

Rose was writing at her desk. She turned. 'Put on your dressing-gown, Henrietta. You will get cold. I came into your room but you were fast asleep, and in that minute it was all over. The big things happen so quickly.'

Yes, that was true. Quickly one fell in and out of love, ran

208

away from home, returned and slept and waked to find that people had quickly died. The big things happened quickly, but the little ones of every day went on slow feet, as though they were tired of themselves.

'It was somehow a comfort,' Rose went on, 'to know that you were fast asleep, but living. You never moved when I kissed you.'

'Kissed me? What did you do that for?' Henrietta asked in a loud voice. She had been taken unawares by the woman who had wronged her, yet she was touched and pleased.

'I couldn't help it. I was so glad to have you there, and you looked so young. I don't know what we should do without you, poor Sophia and I. Oh, do put on my dressing-gown!'

'Yes, dear, yes, put on the dressing-gown.' It was Sophia who spoke. Her face was very calm; she actually looked younger, as though the greatness of her sorrow had removed all other signs, like a fall of snow hiding the scars of a hillside.

'Oh, Aunt Sophia!' Henrietta went forward and pressed her cheek against the other's.

'Yes, dear, but you must go and dress. Breakfast is ready.'

Henrietta was a little shocked that Aunt Sophia, who was naturally sentimental, should be less emotional on this occasion than Aunt Rose, but she was also awed by this control. She remembered how, when her own mother died, Mrs. Banks had refused to take solid food for a whole day, and the recollection braced her for her cold bath, for fresh linen, for emulation of Aunt Sophia, for everything unlike the slovenly weeping of Mrs. Banks, sitting in the neglected kitchen with a grimy pocket-handkerchief on her lap and the teapot at her elbow; but she knew that the Banksian manner was really natural to her, and the Mallett control, the acceptance, the same eating of breakfast, were a pose, a falseness oddly better than her sincerity.

At table no one referred to Caroline; they were practical and composed and afterwards, when Sophia and Rose were closeted together, making arrangements, writing letters to relatives of whom Henrietta had never heard, interviewing Mr. Batty and a husky personage in black, Henrietta stole upstairs past Caroline's death chamber and into her own room.

She was glad to find the pretty housemaid there, tidying the hearth and dusting the furniture. She wanted to talk to somebody, and the pretty housemaid was sympathetic and discreet. She told Henrietta, inevitably, of deaths in her own family, and Henrietta was interested to hear how the housemaid's grandmother had died, actually while she was saying her prayers.

'And you couldn't have a better end than that, could you, Miss Henrietta?'

'I suppose not,' Henrietta said, 'but it might depend on what you were praying for.'

'Oh, she would be saying the usual things, Miss Henrietta, just daily bread and forgive our trespasses. There was no harm in my grandmother. It was her husband who broke his neck picking apples. His own apples,' she said hastily. 'And now poor Mrs. Sales has gone.'

'Mrs. Sales?'

'Yes, Miss Henrietta, I thought you'd know – last night. Her and Miss Caroline together.' She implied that in this journey they would be company for each other.

Henrietta found nothing to say, but above the shock of pity she felt for the woman she had disliked and the awe induced by the name of death, she was conscious of a load lifted from her mind: she had not been deserted, her charm had not failed; it was the approach of death that had held him back. She put the thought away lest it should lead to others of which she would be ashamed, yet she felt a malicious pleasure, lasting only for a second, at remembering that downstairs sat Aunt Rose calmly full of affairs, Aunt Rose for whom the love of Francis Sales had ceased too soon! And, suppressed but fermenting, was the idea that in these late events, including the failure of her escape, there was the kind hand of fate.

At that very moment Charles Batty chose to call.

'With a parcel, Miss Henrietta, and he would like to see you.'

'I can't see him,' Henrietta said. 'Tell him – tell him about Miss Caroline.' She had already drifted away from Charles. He had been so near last night, so almost dear in the troubled fog of her distress, but this morning she had drifted and between them there was a shining space of water sparkling hardly. But she spared him an instant of gratitude and soft-ness. His part in her life was like that, to a sailor, of some lightship eagerly looked for in the darkness, of strangely diminished consequence in the clear day, still there, safely anchored, but with half its significance gone.

'I can't see him,' she repeated.

She wanted, suddenly, to see Aunt Rose. Voices no longer came from the drawing-room. Mr. Batty, genuinely sad in the loss of an old friend, had gone; the undertaker had tiptoed off to his gloomy lair, and Henrietta went downstairs, but when she saw her aunt she dared not ask her if she knew about Christabel Sales. Rose had a look of invulnerability; perhaps she knew, but it was impossible to ask, and if she knew, it had made no difference. It seemed as though she had gone beyond the reach of feeling: she and Sophia both wore white masks, but Sophia's was only a few hours old and Rose's had been gradually assumed. It was not only Caroline's death which had given her that strange, calm face: the expression had grown slowly, as though something had been a long time dying, yet she hardly had a look of loss. She seemed to be in possession of something, but Henrietta could not understand what it was and she was vaguely afraid.

It was Aunt Sophia who, in spite of her amazing courage, had an air of desolation. And there was no rouge on her cheeks: its absence made Henrietta want to cry. She did cry at intervals throughout that day and the ones that followed. It was terrible without Aunt Caroline and pitiful to see Aunt Sophia keeping up her dignity among black-clothed, black-beaded relatives who seemed to appear out of the ground like snails after rain and who might have been part of the under-taker's permanent stock-in-trade. Henrietta hated the mourn-ful looks of these ancient cousins, the shaking of their black beads, their sibilant whisperings, and in their presence she was dry-eyed and rather rude. Aunt Caroline would have laughed at them and their dowdy clothes that smelt of camphor, but it seemed as though no one would ever laugh again in Nelson Lodge.

And over the river, in the unsubdued country, where death

was only the repayment of a loan, there was another house with lowered blinds and voices hushed. She was irritated by the thought of it, of the consolatory letters Francis would receive, of the emotions he would display, or conceal, but at the same time she was sorry that in death, as in life, Christabel should be lonely. Her large and lively family was far away, even the cat had gone, and there were only the nurse and Francis and the little dog to miss her. In a sense Henrietta missed her too, and that fair region of fields and woods which had been as though blocked by that helpless body now lay open, vast, full of possibilities, inviting exploration; and when Henrietta looked at her Aunt Rose, it was with the jealous eye of a rival adventurer. But that was absurd: there could be no rivalry between them. Henrietta was sure of that and she tried to avoid these speculations.

And meanwhile necessary things were done and Christabel Sales and Caroline Mallett were buried on the same day. The beaded relatives departed, not to reappear until the next death in the family, and Rose and Henrietta, both perhaps thinking of Francis Sales returning to his big empty house, returned with Sophia to a Nelson Lodge oppressive in its desolation. It seemed now that the whole business of life there, the servants, the fires, the delicate meals, had proceeded solely for Caroline's benefit; yet everything continued as before: the machinery went on running smoothly; the dinner-table still reflected in its rich surface the lights of candles, the sheen of silver, the pallor of flowers. Nothing was neglected, everything was beautiful and exact, and Susan had carefully arranged the chairs so that the vacant space should not be emphasized.

The three black-robed women slipped into their seats without a word. The soup was very hot, according to Caroline's instructions, but the cook, inspired more by the desire to give pleasant nutriment than by tact, had chosen to make the creamy variety which was Caroline's favourite and, as each Mallett took up her spoon, she had a vision of Caroline tasting the soup with the thoughtfulness of a connoisseur and proclaiming it perfect to the last grain of salt.

'I can't eat it,' Sophia said faintly. In this almost comic

212

realization of her loss she showed the first sign of weakness. She rose, trembling visibly, and Susan, anxious for the preservation of the decencies, opened the door and closed it on her faltering figure before the first sob shook her body. The others, without exchanging a single glance, proceeded with the meal, eating little, each eager for solitude and each finding it unbearable to picture Sophia up there in the bedroom alone.

'But she doesn't want us,' Rose said.

'She might want me,' Henrietta replied provocatively, and for answer Rose's smile flickered disconcertingly across the candle-light, and her voice, a little worn, said quietly, 'Then go and see.'

The bedroom had a dreadful neatness; it smelt of disinfectant, furniture polish and soap, and Sophia, from the big armchair, said mournfully, 'They might have left it as it was. It feels like lodgings.' And as the very feebleness of her outcry smote her sense and waked echoes of all she left unsaid, her mouth fell shapeless, and she cried, 'She's gone!' in a tone of astonishment and horror.

Henrietta, sitting on a little stool before the fire, listened to the weeping which was too violent for Sophia's strength, and the harsh sound reminded her of Aunt Caroline's difficult breathing. It seemed as though the noise would go on for ever: she counted each separate sob, and when they had gradually lessened and died away the relief was like the ceasing of physical pain.

'Aunt Sophia,' Henrietta said, 'everybody has to die.'

Sophia heard. Tears glistened on her cheeks, her hair was disordered, she looked like a large flaxen doll that had been left out in the rain for a long time. 'But each person only once,' she whispered. 'One doesn't get used to it, and Caroline –' She struggled to sit up. 'Caroline would be ashamed of me for this.'

'She might pretend to be, but she'd like it really.'

'I don't know,' Sophia murmured. 'She had such character. You never believed her, did you, Henrietta, when she made out she had been – had been indiscreet?'

'No, I never believed it.'

'I'm glad of that. It was a fancy of hers. I encouraged her in it, I'm afraid; but it made her happy, it pleased her and it did no harm. I suppose nobody believed her, but she didn't know. I don't think I'll sit here doing nothing, Henrietta. I suppose I ought to go through her papers. She never destroyed a letter. I might begin on them.'

'Oh, do you think you'd better? Don't you like just to sit here and talk to me?'

'No, no, I must not give way. I'm not the only one. There's poor Francis Sales. If he'd married Rose – I always planned that he should marry Rose – and of course, we ought not to think of such things so soon, but the thought has come to me that they may marry after all.'

Henrietta tightened the clasp of the hands on her knee and said, 'Why do you think that?'

'It would be suitable,' Sophia said.

'But she's so old. Haven't you noticed how old she has looked lately?'

'Old? Rose old?' Sophia's manner became almost haughty. 'Rose has nothing to do with age. My only doubt is whether Francis Sales is worthy of her. Dear Caroline used to say she ought to – to marry a king.'

'And she hasn't married anybody,' Henrietta remarked bitingly.

'Nobody,' Sophia said serenely. 'The Malletts don't marry,' she sighed; 'but I hope you will, Henrietta.'

'No,' Henrietta said sharply. 'I shan't. I don't want to. Men are hateful.'

'No, dear child, not all of them. Perhaps none of them. When I was eighteen –' She hesitated. 'I must get on with her papers.' She stood up and moved towards the bureau. 'They're here. We shared the drawers. We shared everything.' She stretched out her hands and they fell heavily, taking the weight of her body with them, against the shining slope of wood.

Henrietta, who had been gazing moodily at the fire, was astonished to hear the thud, to see her Aunt Sophia leaning drunkenly over the desk. Sophia's lips were blue, her eyes were glazed, and Henrietta thought, 'She's dying, too. Shall I let her die?' but at the same moment she leapt up and lowered her aunt into a chair.

'It's my heart,' Sophia said after a few minutes, and Henrietta understood why poor Aunt Sophia always went upstairs so slowly. 'Don't tell anybody. No one knows. I ought not to have cried like that. There's a little bottle –' She told Henrietta to fetch it from a secret place. 'I never let Caroline know. It would have worried her, and, after all, she was the first to go. I'm glad to think I saved her that anxiety. You remember how she teased me about getting tired? Well, it didn't matter and she liked to think she was so young. Wherever she is now, I do hope she isn't feeling angry with herself. She thought illness was so vulgar.'

'But not death,' Henrietta said.

'No, not death,' and Henrietta fancied her aunt lingered lovingly on the word. 'This must be a secret between us.' She lay back exhausted. 'I only had two secrets from Caroline. This about my heart was one. Henrietta, in that little drawer, at the very back, you'll find a photograph wrapped in tissue-paper. Find it for me, dear child. Thank you.' She held it tenderly between her palms. 'This was the other. It's the picture of my lover, Henrietta. Yes, I wanted you to know that some one once loved me very dearly.'

'Oh, Aunt Sophia, we all love you. I love you dearly now.'

'Yes, dear, yes, I know; I'm grateful, but I wanted somebody to know that I had had my romance, and have it still – all these years. But I was loved, Henrietta, till he died, and I was very young then, younger than you are now. Yes, I wanted somebody to know that poor Sophia had a real lover once. He went away to America to make a fortune for me, but he died. I have been wondering, since Caroline went, if she and he have met. If so, perhaps she knows, perhaps she blames me, but I don't think she will laugh – not now. I hope she laughs still, but not at that. And now, Henrietta, we'll put the photograph into the fire.'

'Ah, no, Aunt Sophia, keep it still!'

'Dear child, I may die at any moment, and I have his dear face by heart. I shouldn't like any other eyes to look at it, not

215

even yours. Stir the fire, Henrietta. Now help me up. No, dear, I would rather do it myself.'

She knelt, her faded face lighted by the flames which consumed her greatest treasure, her back still girlish, her slim waist girdled with a black ribbon, her thick knot of hair resting on her neck.

Henrietta went quietly out of the room, but on the landing she wrung her hands together. She felt herself surrounded by death, decay, lost love, sad memories. She was too young for this house. She had a longing to escape into sunshine, gaiety and pleasure. It was Caroline who had laughed and planned, it was she who had made the place a home. Rose was too remote, Sophia was living in the past, and Henrietta felt herself alone. Even her father's portrait looked down at her with eyes too much like her own, and out there, beyond the high-walled garden, the roofs and the river, there was only Francis Sales and he was not a friend. He was, perhaps, a lover; he was a sensation, an accident; but he was not a companion or a refuge.

And the thought of Charles rose up, at that moment, like the thought of a fireside. She wished he would come now and sit with her, asking for nothing, but assuring her of service. That was what he was for, she decided. You could not love Charles, but you could trust him for ever, and the more trust he was given, the more he grew to it. She needed him: she must not lose him. Deep in her heart she supposed she was going to marry Francis Sales, yes, in spite of what Aunt Sophia said, and it was a prospect towards which she tiptoed, holding her breath, not daring to look; but she, like Rose, had no illusions. She was the daughter of her mother's union with her father, and she was prepared for trouble, for the need of Charles. Besides, she liked him: he was companionable even when he scolded. One forgot about him, but he returned; he was there. She went to bed in that comfortable assurance.

§ 9

There could be no more parties for Henrietta that winter, but Mrs. Batty's house was always open to her, and Mrs. Batty, like her son Charles, could be relied upon for welcome and for relaxation. In her presence Henrietta had a pleasant sense of superiority; she was applauded and not criticized and she knew she could give comfort as well as get it. Mrs. Batty liked to talk to her and Henrietta could sink into one of the superlatively cushioned arm-chairs and listen or not as she chose. There she was relieved of the slight but persistent strain she was under in Nelson Lodge, for Sophia and Rose had standards of manner, conduct and speech beyond her own, while Mrs. Batty's, though they existed, were on another plane. Henrietta was sure of herself in that luxurious, overcrowded drawing-room, decorated and scented with the least precious of Mr. Batty's hot-house flowers, and somewhat overheated.

On her first visit after Caroline's death, Mrs. Batty received the bereaved niece with unction. 'Ah, poor dear,' she murmured, and whether her sympathy was for Caroline or Henrietta, perhaps she did not know herself. 'Poor dear! I can't get your aunt out of my head, Henrietta, love. There she was at the party, looking like a queen – well, you know what I mean – and Mr. Batty said she was the belle of the ball. It was just his joke; but Mr. Batty never makes a joke that hasn't something in it. I could see it myself. And then for her to die like that – it seems as if it was our fault. It was a beautiful ball, wasn't it, dear? I do think it was, but it's spoilt for me. I can only be thankful it wasn't her stomach or I should have blamed the supper. As it is, there must have been a draught. It was a cold night.'

'It was a lovely night,' Henrietta said, thinking of the terrace and the dark river and the stars. She could remember it all without shame, for he had not failed her and her personality had not failed. He had not deserted her, and when they met there would be no need for explanations. He would look at her, she would look at him – she had to rouse herself. 'Yes, it was a splendid ball, Mrs. Batty.'

'And what did you think of my dress, dear?' Mrs. Batty asked, and checked herself. 'But we ought not to talk about such things with your dear aunt just dead. You must miss her sadly. Did you – were you with her at the end?'

But this was a region in which Henrietta could not wander with Mrs. Batty. 'Don't let us talk of it,' she said.

Mrs. Batty gurgled a rich sympathy and after a due pause she was glad to resume the topic of the dance. This was her first real opportunity for discussing it; under Mr. Batty's slightly ironical smile and his references to expense, she had controlled herself; among her acquaintances it was necessary to treat the affair as a mere bagatelle; but with Henrietta she could expand unlimitedly. What she thought, what she felt, what she said, what other people said to her, and what her guests were reported to have said to other people, was repeated and enlarged upon to Henrietta who, leaning back, occasionally nodding her head or uttering a sound of encouragement, lived through that night again.

Yes, out on the terrace he had been the real Francis Sales and that man in the hollow looking at Aunt Rose and then turning to Henrietta in uncertainty was the one evoked by that witch on horseback, the modern substitute for a broomstick. Christabel Sales was right: Aunt Rose was a witch with her calm, white face, riding swiftly and fearlessly on her messages of evil. He was never himself in her presence: how could he be? He was under her spell and he must be cleared of it and kept immune. But how? Through these thoughts, which were both exciting and alarming, Henrietta heard Mrs. Batty uttering the name of Charles.

'He seems to have taken a turn for the better, my dear.'

'Has he been ill?' Henrietta asked.

'Ill? No. Bad-tempered, what you might call melancholy. Not lately. Well, since the dance he has been different. Not so irritable at breakfast. I told you once before, love, how I dreaded breakfast, with John late half the time, going out with the dogs, and Mr. Batty behind the paper with his eyebrows up, and Charles looking as if he'd been dug up, like Lazarus, if it isn't wrong to say so, pale and pasty and sorry he was alive – sort of damp, dear. Well, you know what I mean. But as I tell you, he's been more cheerful. That dance must have done him good, or something has. And Mr. Batty tells me he takes more interest in his work. Still,' Mrs. Batty admitted, 'he does catch me up at times.'

'Yes, I know. About music. I know. He's queer. I hate it when he gets angry and shouts, but he's good really, in his heart.'

'Oh, of course he is,' Mrs. Batty murmured, and, looking at the plump hands on her silken lap, she added, 'I wish he'd marry. Now, John, he's engaged; but he didn't need to be. You know what I mean. He was happy enough before, but Charles, if he could marry a nice girl –'

'He won't,' Henrietta said at once, and Mrs. Batty, suddenly alert, asked sharply, 'Why not?'

'Oh, I don't know. Men are so easily deceived.'

'We've got to take care of them,' Mrs. Batty answered firmly.

'I don't see why we should.'

'We can't help it. You wouldn't neglect a baby. Well, then, it's the same thing. They never get out of their short frocks. Even Mr. Batty,' his wife chuckled, 'he's very clever and all that, but he's like all the rest. The very minute you marry, you've got a baby on your hands.'

Henrietta sighed. 'It isn't fair,' she murmured, yet she liked the notion. Francis Sales was a baby. He would have to be managed, to be amused; he would tire of his toys. She knew that, and she saw herself constantly dressing up the old ones and deceiving him into believing they were new.

'I suppose they're worth it,' she half questioned.

'Men?'

'No, babies,' Henrietta answered, meaning the same thing, but Mrs. Batty took her up with fervour. She was reminiscent, and tears came into her eyes; she was prophetic, she was embarrassing and faintly disgusting to Henrietta, and when the door opened to let in Charles, she welcomed him with a pleasure which was really the measure of her relief.

She had not seen him since she had parted from him in the car. He did not return her smile and it struck her that he never smiled. It was a good thing: it would have made him look odder than ever, and somehow he contrived to show his happiness without the display of teeth. His eyes, she decided, bulged most when he was miserable, and now they hardly bulged at all.

'You're back early to-day, dear,' Mrs. Batty said. 'I'll have some fresh tea made.' But Charles, without averting his gaze from Henrietta, said, 'I don't want any tea,' and to Henrietta he said quietly, 'I haven't seen you for weeks.'

To her annoyance, she felt the colour creeping over her cheeks. No doubt he would account for that in his own way, and to disconcert him she added casually, 'It's not long really.'

'It seems long,' he said.

No one but Charles Batty would have said that in the presence of his mother; it was ridiculous, and she looked at him with revengeful criticism. He was plain; he was getting bald; his trousers bagged; his socks were wrinkled like concertinas; his comparative self-assurance was quite unjustified. He had looked at her consistently since he entered the room, and Henrietta was angrily aware that Mrs. Batty was trying to make herself insignificant in her corner of the sofa. Henrietta could hear the careful control of her breathing. She was hoping to make the young people forget she was there. Henrietta frowned warningly at Charles.

'What's the matter?' he asked at once.

'Nothing.' She might have known it was useless to make signs.

'But you frowned.'

'Well, don't you ever get a twinge?' she prevaricated.

'Toothache, dear?' Mrs. Batty clucked her distress. 'I'll get some laudanum. You just rub it on the gum –' She rose. 'I have some in my medicine cupboard. I'll go and get it.' She went out, and across her broad back she seemed to carry the legend, 'This is the consummation of tact.'

Charles stood up and planted himself on the hearthrug and Henrietta wished Mrs. Batty had not gone. 'I'm sorry you've got toothache,' he said.

'I haven't. I didn't say I had. My teeth are perfect.' With a vicious opening of her mouth, she let him see them.

'Then why did you frown?'

'I had to do something to stop your glaring at me.'

220

'Was I glaring? I didn't know. I suppose I can't help looking at you.'

Henrietta appreciated this remark. 'I don't mind so much when we are alone.' From anybody else she would have expected a reminder that she had once allowed more than that, but she was safe with Charles and half annoyed by her safety. Her instinct was to run and dodge, but it was a poor game to play at hide-and-seek with this roughly executed statue of a young man. 'Your mother must have noticed,' she explained.

'Well, why not? She'll have to know.'

'Know what?' she cried indignantly.

'That we're engaged.'

She brightened angrily. After all, he was thinking of that night and she felt a new, exasperated respect for him. 'But I told you – I told you I didn't mean anything when I let you – when we were alone in that car.'

'I wasn't thinking of that,' he said, and she felt a drop. He had no business not to think of it.

'Then what do you mean?' she asked coldly.

'I've been engaged to you,' he said, 'for a long time. I told you. But I've been thinking that it really doesn't work.'

'Of course it doesn't. Anybody would have known that except you, Charles Batty.'

'Yes, but nobody tells me things. I have to find them out.' He sighed. 'It takes time. But now I know.'

'Very well. You're released from the engagement you made all by yourself. I had nothing to do with it.'

'No,' he said mildly, 'but I can't be released, so the only way out of it is for you to be engaged too.' He fumbled in a pocket. 'I've bought a ring.'

She sneered. 'Who told you about that?'

'I remembered it. John got one. It's always done and I think this one is pretty.'

She had a great curiosity to see his choice. She guessed it would be gaudy, like a child's, but she said, 'It has nothing to do with me. I don't want to see it.'

'Do look.'

'Charles, you're hopeless.'

'The man said he would change it if you didn't like it.' Into her hand he put the little box, attractively small, no doubt lined with soft white velvet, and she longed to open it. She had always wanted one of those little boxes and she remembered how often she had gazed at them, holding glittering rings, in the windows of jewellers' shops. She looked up at Charles, her eyes bright, her lips a little parted, so young and helpless in that moment that she drew from him his first cry of passion. 'Henrietta!' His hands trembled.

'It's only,' she faltered, 'because I like looking at pretty things.'

'I know.' He dropped to the sofa beside her. 'It couldn't be anything else.'

She turned to him, her face close to his, and she asked plaintively, 'But why shouldn't it be?' She seemed to blame him; she did blame him. There was something in his presence seductively secure; there was peace: she almost loved him; she loved her power to make him tremble, and if only he could make her tremble too, she would be his. 'But it isn't anything else,' she said below her breath.

'No, it isn't,' he echoed in the loud voice of his trouble. He got up and moved away. 'So just look at the ring and tell me if you like it.'

He heard the box unwrapped and a voice saying, 'I do like it.'

'Then keep it.'

'But I can't.'

'Yes, you can. It's for you. It's pretty, isn't it? And you like pretty things.'

'I could just look at it now and then, couldn't I? But no, it isn't fair.'

'I don't mind about that.'

'I mean fair to me.'

He turned at that. 'I don't understand.'

'A kind of hold,' she explained.

'How could it be? I wasn't trying to tempt you, but we're engaged and you must have a ring.'

She shook her small, clenched fists. 'We're not, we're not! Oh, yes, you can be, if you like; but I didn't mean it would hold me in that way. I meant it would be like a sign – of you. I shouldn't be able to forget you; you would be there in the ring, in the box, in the drawer, like the portrait of Aunt Sophia's –' She stopped herself. 'And I can't burn you.'

'I don't know what you are talking about. I suppose I ought to.'

'No, you oughtn't.' She sprang up, delivered from her weakness. 'This is nonsense. Of course, I can't keep your ring. Take it back, Charles. It's beautiful. I thought it would be all red and blue like a flag, but it's lovely. It makes my mouth water. It's like white fire.'

'It's like you,' he said. 'You're just as bright and just as hard, and if only you were as small, I could put you in my pocket and never let you go.'

She opened her eyes very wide. 'Then why do you let me go?' she asked on an ascending note, and she did not mean to taunt him. It would be so easy for him to keep her, if he knew how. She expected a despairing groan, she half hoped for a violent embrace, but he answered quietly, 'I don't really let you go. It's you I love, not just your hair and your face and the way your nose turns up, and your hands and feet, and your straight neck. I have to let them go, but you don't go. You stay with me all the time: you always will. You're like music, always in my head, but you're more than that. You go deeper: I suppose into my heart. Sometimes I think I'm carrying you in my arms. I can't see you but I can feel you're there, and sometimes I laugh because I think you're laughing.'

She listened, charmed into stillness. Here was an echo of his outpouring in the darkness of that hour by the Monks' Pool, but these words were closer, dearer. She felt for that moment that he did indeed carry her in his arms and that she was glad to be there. He spoke so quietly, he was so certain of his love that she was exalted and abashed. She did not deserve all this, yet he knew she was hard as well as bright, he knew her nose turned up. Perhaps there was nothing he did not know.

He went on simply, without effort. 'And though I'm ugly

and a fool, I can't be hurt whatever you choose to do. What you do isn't you.' He touched himself. 'The you is here. So it doesn't matter about the ring. It doesn't matter about Francis Sales.'

She said on a caught breath and in a whisper, 'What about him?'

He looked at her and made a slight movement with the hands hanging at his sides, a little flicking movement, as though he brushed something away. 'I think perhaps you are going to marry him,' he said deeply.

Her head went up. 'Who told you that?' she demanded.

'Nobody. Nobody tells me anything.'

'Because nobody knows,' she said scornfully. 'I haven't seen him since –' She hesitated. This Charles knew everything, and he said for her, rather wearily, very quietly, 'Since his wife died. No. But you will.'

'Yes,' she said defiantly, 'I expect I shall. I hope I shall.'

A shudder passed through Charles Batty's big frame and the words, 'Don't marry him,' reached her ears like a distant muttering of a storm. 'You would not be happy.'

'What has happiness to do with it?' she asked with an astonishing young bitterness.

'Ah, if you feel like that,' he said, 'if you feel as I do about you, if nothing he does and nothing he says –'

'He says very little,' Henrietta interrupted gloomily, but Charles seemed not to hear.

'If his actions are only like the wind in the trees, fluttering the leaves – yes, I suppose that's love. The tree remains.'

She dropped her face into her hands. 'You're making me miserable,' she cried.

He removed her hands and held them firmly. 'But why?'

'I don't know,' she swayed towards him, but he kept her arms rigid, like a bar between them, 'but I don't want to lose you.'

'You can't,' he assured her.

'And though you think you have me in your heart, the me that doesn't change, you'd like the other one too, wouldn't you? I mean, you'd really like to hold me? Not just the thought of me? Tell me you love me in that way too.'

224

'Yes,' he said, 'I love you in that way too, but I tell you it doesn't matter.' He dropped her hands as though he had no more strength. 'Marry your Francis Sales. You still belong to me.'

'But will you belong to me?' she asked softly. She could not lose him, she wanted to have them both, and Charles, perhaps unwisely, perhaps from the depth of his wisdom, which was truth, answered quietly, 'I belonged to you since the first day I saw you.'

She let out a sigh of inexpressible relief.

§ 10

To Rose, the time between the death of Caroline and the coming of spring was like an invalid's convalescence. She felt a languor as though she had been ill, and a kind of content as though she were temporarily free from cares. She knew that Henrietta and Charles Batty often met, but she did not wish to know how Charles had succeeded in preventing her escape: she did not try to connect Christabel's illness with Henrietta's return; she enjoyed unquestioningly her rich feeling of possession in the presence of the girl, who was much on her dignity, very well behaved, but undeniably aloof. She had not yet forgiven her aunt for that episode in the gipsies' hollow, but it did not matter. Rose could tell herself without any affectation of virtue that she had hoped for no benefit for herself; looking back she saw that even what might be called her sin had been committed chiefly for Francis's sake, only she had not sinned enough.

But for the present she need not think of him. He had gone away, she heard, and she could ride over the bridge without the fear of meeting him and with the feeling that the place was more than ever hers. It was gloriously empty of any claim but its own. To gallop across the fields, to ride more slowly on some height with nothing between her and great massy clouds of unbelievable whiteness, to feel herself relieved of an immense responsibility, was like finding the new world she had longed for. She wished sincerely that Francis would not come back;

225

she wished that, riding one day, she might find Sales Hall blotted out, leaving no sign, no trace, nothing but earth and fresh spikes of green.

Day by day she watched the advance of spring. The larches put out their little tassels, celandines opened their yellow eyes, the smell of the gorse was her youth wafted back to her and she shook her head and said she did not want it. This maturity was better: she had reached the age when she could almost dissociate things from herself and she found them better and more beautiful. She needed this consolation, for it seemed that her personal relationships were to be few and shadowy; conscious in herself of a capacity for crystallizing them enduringly, they yet managed to evade her; it was some fault, some failure in herself, but not knowing the cause she could not cure it and she accepted it with the apparent impassivity which was, perhaps, the origin of the difficulty.

And capable as she was of love, she was incapable of struggling for it. She wanted Henrietta's affection; she wanted to give every happiness to that girl, but she could not be different from herself, she could not bait the trap. And it seemed that Henrietta might be finding happiness without her help, or at least without realizing that it was she who had given Charles his chance. She had rejected her plan of taking Henrietta away: it was better to leave her in the neighbourhood of Charles, for he was not a Francis Sales, and if Henrietta could once see below his queer exterior, she would never see it again except to laugh at it with an understanding beyond the power of irritation; and she was made to have a home, to be busy about small, important things, to play with children and tyrannize over a man in the matter of socks and collars, to be tyrannized over by him in the bigger affairs of life.

And with Henrietta settled, Rose would at last be free to take that journey which, like everything else, had eluded her so far. She would be free but for Sophia who seemed in these days pathetically subdued and frail; but Sophia, Rose decided, could stay with Henrietta for a time, or one of the elderly cousins would be glad to take up a temporary residence in Nelson Lodge.

She was excited by the prospect of her freedom and some-times, as though she were doing something wrong, she secretly carried the big atlas to her bedroom and pored over the maps. There were places with names like poetry and she meant to see them all. She moved already in a world of greater space and fresher air; her body was rejuvenated, her mind recovered from its weariness and when, on an April day, she came across Francis Sales in one of his own fields, it was a sign of her condition that her first thought was of Henrietta and not of herself. He had returned and Henrietta was again in danger, though one of another kind.

She stopped her horse, thinking firmly, Whatever happens, she shall not marry him: he is not good enough. She said: 'Good morning,' in that cool voice which made him think of churches, and he stood, stroking the horse's nose, looking down and making no reply.

'I've been away,' he said at last.

'I know. When did you come back?'

'Last night. I've been to Canada to see her people. I thought they'd like to know about her and she would have liked it, too.'

A small smile threatened Rose's mouth. It seemed rather late to be trying to please Christabel.

'I didn't hope,' he went on quietly, 'to have this luck so soon. I've been wanting to see you, to tell you something. I wanted to get things cleared up.'

'What things?'

He looked up. 'About Henrietta.'

'There's no need for that.'

'Not for you, perhaps, but there is for me. You were quite right that day. I went home and I made up my mind to break my word to her. I'd made it up before Christabel became so ill. I wanted you to know that. I couldn't have left her that night – perhaps you hadn't realized I'd meant to – but anyhow I couldn't have left her, and I wouldn't have done it if I could. You were perfectly right.'

Rose moved a little in her saddle. 'And yet I had no right to be,' she said. 'You and I –'

'Ah,' he said quickly, 'you and I were different. I don't blame myself for that, but with Henrietta it was just devilry, sickness, misery. Don't,' he commanded, 'dare to compare our – our love with that.'

'No,' she said, 'no, I don't think of it at all. It has dropped back where it came from and I don't know where that is. I don't think of it any more, but thank you for telling me about Henrietta. Good-bye.'

She moved on, but his voice followed her. 'I never loved her.'

She stopped but did not turn. 'I know that.'

'Yes, but I wanted to tell you.' He was at the horse's head again. 'I don't think much of the way those people are keeping your bridle. There's rust on the curb chain. Look at it. It's disgraceful! And I'd like to tell you that I tried to make it up to Christabel at the last. Too late – but she was happy. Good-bye. Tell those people they ought to be ashamed of themselves.'

'I suppose we all ought to be,' Rose said wearily.

'Some of us are,' he replied. 'And,' he hesitated, 'you won't stop riding here now I've come back?'

'Of course not. It's the habit of a lifetime.'

'I shan't worry you.'

She laughed frankly. 'I'm not afraid of that.'

She was immune, she told herself, she could not be touched, yet she knew she had been touched already: she was obliged to think of him. For the first time in her knowledge of him he had not grumbled, he was like a repentant child, and she realized that he had suffered an experience unknown to her, a sense of sin, and the fact gave him a certain superiority and interest in her eyes.

She went home but not as she had set forth, for she seemed to hear the jingle of her chains.

At luncheon Henrietta appeared in a new hat and an amiable mood. She was going, she said casually, to a concert with Charles Batty.

'I didn't know there was one,' Rose said. 'Where is it?'

'Oh, not in Radstowe. We're going,' Henrietta said reluctantly, 'to Wellsborough.'

But that name seemed to have no association for Aunt Rose. She said, 'Oh, yes, they have very good concerts there, and I hope Charles will like your hat.'

'I don't suppose he will notice it,' Henrietta murmured. She felt grateful for her aunt's forgetfulness, and she said, with an enthusiasm she had not shown for a long time, 'You look lovely to-day, Aunt Rose, as if something nice had happened.'

Rose laughed and said, 'Nonsense, Henrietta,' in a manner faintly reminiscent of Caroline. And she added quickly, against the invasion of her own thoughts, 'And as for Charles, he notices much more than one would think.'

'Oh, I've found that out,' Henrietta grieved. 'I don't think people ought to notice – well, that one's nose turns up.'

'It depends how it does it. Yours is very satisfactory.'

They sparkled at each other, pleased at the ease of their intercourse and quite unaware that these personalities also were reminiscent of the Caroline and Sophia tradition of compliment.

Sophia, drooping over the table, said vaguely, 'Yes, very satisfactory,' but she hardly knew to what Rose had referred. She lived in her own memories, but she tried to disguise her distraction and it was always safe to agree with Rose: she had good judgment, unfailing taste. 'Rose,' she said more brightly, 'I'd forgotten. Susan tells me that Francis Sales has come home.'

Rose said 'Yes,' and after the slightest pause, she added, 'I saw him this morning.' She did not look at Henrietta. She felt with something like despair that this had occurred at the very moment when they seemed to be re-establishing their friendship, and now Henrietta would be reminded of the unhappy past. She did not look across the table, but, to her astonishment, she heard the girl's voice with trouble, enmity and anger concentrated in its control, saying quickly, 'So that's the nice thing that's happened!'

'Very nice,' Sophia murmured. 'Poor Francis! He must have been glad to see you.'

Rose's eyes glanced over Henrietta's face with a look too proud to be called disdain: she was doubly shocked, first by the

229

girl's effrontery and then by the truth in her words. She had indeed been feeling indefinitely happy and ignoring the cause. She was, even now, not sure of the cause. She did not know whether it was the change in Francis or the jingling of the chains still sounding in her ears, but there had been a lightness in her heart which had nothing to do with the sense of that approaching freedom on which she had been counting.

She turned to Sophia as though Henrietta had not spoken. 'Yes, I think he was glad to see a friend. He has been to Canada to see Christabel's family. No, he didn't say how he was, but I thought he looked rather old.'

'Ah, poor boy,' Sophia said. 'I think, Rose dear, it would be kind to ask him here.'

'Oh, he knows he can come when he likes,' Rose said.

On the other side of the table Henrietta was shaking delicately. She could only have got relief by inarticulate noises and insanely violent movements. She hated Francis Sales, she hated Rose and Sophia and Charles Batty. She would not go to the concert – yes, she would go and make Charles miserable. She was enraged at the folly of her own remark, at Rose's self-possession, and at her possible possession of Francis Sales. She could not unsay what she had said and, having said it, she did not know how to go on living with Aunt Rose; but she was going to Wellsborough again and this time she need not come back: yet she must come back to see Francis Sales. And though there was no one in the world to whom she could express the torment of her mind she could, at least, make Charles unhappy.

Rose and Sophia were chatting pleasantly, and Henrietta pushed back her chair. 'Will you excuse me? I have to catch a train.'

Rose inclined her head: Sophia said, 'Yes, dear, go. Where did you say you were going?'

'To Wellsborough.'

'Ah, yes. Caroline and I – Be careful to get into a ladies' carriage, Henrietta.'

'I'm going with Charles Batty,' she said dully.

'Ah, then, you will be safe.'

Safe! Yes, she was perfectly safe with Charles. He would sit with his hands hanging between his knees and stare. She was sick of him and, if she dared, she would whisper during the music; at any rate, she would shuffle her feet and make a noise with the programme. And to-morrow she would emulate her aunt and waylay Francis Sales. There would be no harm in copying Aunt Rose, a pattern of conduct! She had done it before, she would do it again and they would see which one of them was to be victorious at the last.

She fulfilled her intentions. Charles, who had been flourishing under the kindness of her friendship, was puzzled by her capriciousness, but he did not question her. He was learning to accept mysteries calmly and to work at them in his head. She shuffled her feet and he pretended not to hear: she crackled her programme and he smiled down at her. This was maddening, yet it was a tribute to her power. She could do what she liked and Charles would love her; he was a great possession; she did not know what she would do without him.

As they ate their rich cakes in a famous teashop, Charles talked incessantly about the music, and when at last he paused, she said indifferently, 'I didn't hear a note.'

Mildly he advised her not to wear such tight shoes.

'Tight!' She looked down at them. 'I had them made for me!'

'You seemed to be uncomfortable,' he said.

'I was thinking, thinking, thinking.'

'What about?'

'Things you wouldn't understand, Charles. You're too good.'

'I dare say,' he murmured.

'You've never wanted to murder anyone.'

'Yes, I have.'

'Who?'

'That Sales fellow.'

Her eyelids quivered, but she said boldly, 'Because of me?'

'No, of course not. Making noises at concerts. Shooting birds. I've told you so before.'

'He's been to Canada.'

'I know.'

'But he has come back.'

'Well, I suppose he had to come back some day.'

'And I hate Aunt Rose.'

'What a pity,' Charles said, taking another cake.

'Why a pity?'

'Beautiful woman.'

'Oh, yes, everybody thinks so, till they know her.'

'I know her and I think she's adorable.'

The word was startling from his lips. Charles, too, she exclaimed inwardly. Was Aunt Rose even to come between her and Charles?

'But of course' – he remembered his lesson – 'you're the most beautiful and the best woman in the world.'

'I'm not a woman at all,' she said angrily: 'I'm a fiend.'

'Yes, to-day; but you won't be to-morrow. You'll feel different to-morrow.'

He had, she reflected, a gift of prophecy. 'Yes, I shall,' she said softly, 'I'm stupid. It will be all right to-morrow. I shan't even be angry with Aunt Rose and you've been an angel to me. I shall never forget you.'

He said nothing. He seemed very much interested in his cake.

And because she foresaw that her anger towards Aunt Rose would soon be changed to pity, she apologized to her that night. 'I'm afraid I was rude to you at luncheon.'

'Were you? Oh, not rude, Henrietta. Perhaps rather foolish and indiscreet. You should think before you speak.'

This admonition was not what Henrietta expected, and she said, 'That's just what I was doing. You mean I ought to be quiet when I'm thinking.'

'Well, yes, that would be even better.'

'Then, Aunt Rose, I should never speak at all when I'm with you.'

'You haven't talked to me for a long time.'

She made a gesture like her father's – impatient, hopeless. 'How can I?' she demanded. There was too much between them: the figure of Francis Sales was too solid.

She set out as she had intended the next afternoon. It was

full spring-time now and Radstowe was gay and sweet with flowering trees. The delicate rose of the almond blossom had already faded to a fainting pink and fallen to the ground, and the laburnum was weeping golden tears which would soon drop to the pavements and blacken there; the red and white hawthorns were all out, and Henrietta's daily walks had been punctuated by ecstatic halts when she stood under a canopy of flower and leaf and drenched herself in scent and colour, or peeped over garden fences to see tall tulips springing up out of the grass; but to-day she did not linger.

It seemed a long time since she had crossed the river, yet the only change was in the new green of the trees splashing the side of the gorge. The gulls were still quarrelling for food on the muddy banks, children and perambulators, horses and carts, were passing over the bridge as on her first day in Radstowe, but there was now no Francis Sales on his fine horse. The sun was bright but clouds were being blown by a wind with a sharp breath, and she went quickly lest it should rain before her business was accomplished. She had no fear of not finding Francis Sales: in such things her luck never failed her, and she came upon him even sooner than she had expected in the outermost of his fields.

He stood beside the gate, scrutinizing a flock of sheep and lambs and talking to the shepherd, and he turned at the sound of her footsteps on the road. She smiled sweetly: rather stiffly he raised his hand to his hat and in that moment she recognized that he had no welcome for her. He had changed; he was grave though he was not sullen, and she said to herself with her ready bitterness, 'Ah, he has reformed, now that there's no need. That's what they all do.'

But her smile did not fade. She leaned over the gate in a friendly manner and asked him about the lambs. How old were they? She hoped he would not have them killed: they were too sweet. She had never touched one in her life. Why did they get so ugly afterwards? It was hard to believe those little things with faces like kittens, or like flowers, were the children of their lumpy mothers. 'Do you think I could catch one if I came inside?' she asked.

'Come inside,' he said, 'but the shepherd shall catch one for you.'

She stroked the curly wool, she pulled the apprehensive ears, she uttered absurdities and, glancing up to see if Sales were laughing at her charming folly, she saw that he was examining his flock with the practical interest of a farmer. He was apparently considering some technical point; he had not been listening to her at all. She hated that lamb, she hoped he would kill it and all the rest, and she decided to eat mutton in future with voracity.

'I was going to pick primroses,' she said. 'Are there any in these fields?'

'I don't know. Can you spare me a few minutes? I want to speak to you.'

Her heart, which had been thumping with a sickening slowness, quickened its beats. Perhaps she had been mistaken, perhaps his serious manner was that of a great occasion, and she saw herself returning to Nelson Lodge and treating her Aunt Rose with gentle tact.

'Shall we sit on the gate?' she asked.

'I'd rather walk across the field. I've been wanting to see you – since that night. I owe you an apology.'

She dared not speak for fear of making a mistake, and she waited, walking slowly beside him, her eyes downcast.

'An apology – for the whole thing,' he said.

She looked up. 'What whole thing?'

'The way I behaved with you.'

'Oh, that! I don't see why you should apologize,' she said.

'It wasn't fair. It wasn't even decent.'

'But it was a sort of habit with you, wasn't it?' she said commiseratingly, and had the happiness of seeing his face flush. 'I quite understand. And we were both amused.'

'I wasn't amused,' he said, 'not a bit, and I'm sorry I behaved as I did. You were so young – and so pretty. Well, it's no good making excuses, but I couldn't rest until I'd seen you and – humbled myself.'

'Did Aunt Rose tell you to say this?' she asked.

'Rose? Of course not. Why should she?'

234

'She seems to have an extraordinary power.'

'Yes, she has,' he said simply.

'And have you humbled yourself to her, too?'

'No. With her,' he said slowly, 'there was no need.'

'I see.' She laughed up at him frankly. 'You know, I never took it very seriously. I'm sorry the thought of it has troubled you.'

He went on, ignoring her lightness, and determined to say everything. 'I meant to meet you that night and tell you what I'm telling you now; but Christabel was very ill and I couldn't leave her. I hope' – this was difficult – 'I hope you didn't get into any sort of mess.'

'That night?' She seemed to be thinking back to it. 'That night – no – I went to a concert with Charles Batty.'

'Oh –' He was bewildered. 'Then it was all right?'

'Perfectly, of course.'

'I didn't know,' he muttered. 'And you forgive me?'

She was generous. 'I was just as bad as you. The Malletts are all flirts. Haven't you heard Aunt Caroline say so? We can't help doing silly things, but we never take them seriously. Why, you must have noticed that with Aunt Rose!'

'No,' he said with dignity, 'your Aunt Rose is like nobody else in the world. I think I told you that once. She –' He hesitated and was silent.

'Well, I must be going back,' Henrietta said easily. 'I shan't bother about the primroses. I think it's going to rain. And you won't think about this any more, will you? You know, Aunt Caroline says she nearly eloped several times, and I know my father did it once, with my own mother, probably with other people beside. It's in the blood. I must try to settle down. We did behave rather badly, I suppose, but so much has happened since. That was my first ball and I felt I wanted to do something daring.'

'You were not to blame,' he said; 'but I'm nearly old enough to be your father. I can't forgive myself. I can't forget it.'

'Oh, dear! And I never took it seriously at all. There was a train back to Radstowe at ten o'clock. I looked it up. I was going to get that, but as it happened I went to a concert.

with Charles Batty. You seem to have no idea how to play a game. You have to pretend to yourself it's a matter of life and death; but you haven't to let it be. That would spoil it.'

'I see,' he said. 'I'm afraid I didn't look at it like that. I wish I had, and I'm glad you did. It makes it easier – and harder – for me.'

'We ought,' she said, 'to have laid the rules down first. Yes, we ought to have done that.' She laughed again. 'I shall do that another time. Good-bye.'

'Good-bye. You've been awfully good to me, Henrietta. Thank you.'

'Not a bit,' she cried. 'If I'd known you were bothering about it, I would have reassured you.' She could not withhold a parting shot. 'I would have sent you a message by Aunt Rose.'

She waved a hand and ran back to the road. She did not trouble to ask herself whether or not he believed her. She was shaken by sobs without tears. She did not love him, she had never loved him, but she could not bear the knowledge that he did not love her. It was quite plain; she was not going to deceive herself any more; his manner had been unmistakable and it was Aunt Rose he loved. She had been beaten by Aunt Rose, and even Charles called her adorable. She did not want Francis Sales; he was rather stupid, and as a legitimate lover he would be dull, duller than Charles, who at least knew how to say things; but something coloured and exciting and dramatic had been ravished from her – by Aunt Rose. That was the sting, and she was humiliated, though she would not own it. She had been good enough for an episode, but her charm had not endured.

Her little, rather inhuman teeth ground against each other. But she had been clever, she had carried it off well; she had not given a sign, and she determined to be equally clever with Aunt Rose. Some day she would refer lightly to her folly and laugh at the susceptibility of Francis Sales. It would hurt Aunt Rose to have her faithful lover disparaged! But, ah! if only she and Aunt Rose were friends, what a conspiracy they could enjoy together! They had both suffered, they might both laugh. How they might play into each other's hands with Francis Sales for the bewildered ball! It would be the finest sport in the world; but they were not friends, and it was impossible to imagine Aunt Rose at that game. No, she was alone in the world, and as she felt the first drop of rain on her face she became aware of the aching of her heart.

She stood for a moment on the bridge. A grey mist was being driven up the river, blotting out the gorge and the trees. A gull, shrieking dismally, cleaved the greyness with a white flash. It was cold and Henrietta shivered, and once again she wished she could sit by a fireside with some one who was kind and tender; but to-night there would only be Aunt Sophia and Aunt Rose sitting with her in that drawing-room, where everything was too elegant and too clear, where now no one ever laughed.

§ 11

They sat by the fire as she had foreseen, Sophia pretending to be busy with her embroidery, Rose, in a straight-backed chair, reading a book. Henrietta sat on a low stool with a book open on her knee, but she did not read it. The fire talked to itself, said silly things and chuckled, or murmured sentimentally. That chatter, vaguely insane, and the turning of Rose's pages, the drawing of Sophia's silks through the stuff and the click of her scissors, were the only sounds until, suddenly, Sophia gave a groan and fell back in her chair. Rose, very much startled, glanced at Henrietta and jumped up.

'It's her heart,' Henrietta said with the superiority of her knowledge. 'I'll get her medicine.' She came back with it. 'She was like this when Aunt Caroline died, but I promised not to tell. If she has this she will be better.'

It was Henrietta who poured the liquid into the glass and applied it to Sophia's lips. She was, she felt, the practical person, and it was she, and not Aunt Rose, who had been trusted by Aunt Sophia.

'She told me where she kept the stuff,' Henrietta continued calmly. 'There, that's better.'

237

Sophia recovered with apologies: a little faintness; it was nothing. In a few minutes she would go to bed. They helped her there.

'You ought to have told me, Henrietta,' Rose said on the landing.

'I couldn't. She wished it to be our secret.' It was pleasant to feel that Aunt Rose was out of this affair.

'We must have the doctor and she ought not to be alone to-night.'

'I'll sleep on the sofa in her room.'

'No, Henrietta, you need more sleep than I do.'

'Oh, but I'm young enough to sleep anywhere – on the floor! But let Aunt Sophia choose.'

Henrietta went back to the drawing-room, and the house-maid was sent for the doctor. Shortly afterwards there came a ring at the bell; no doubt it was the doctor, and Henrietta wished she could go upstairs with him, for Aunt Rose, she told herself again, was not a practical person and Henrietta was experienced in illness. She had nursed her mother and she liked looking after people. She knew how to arrange pillows; she was not afraid of sickness. However, she would have to wait until Aunt Sophia sent for her; but it was not the doctor: it was Charles Batty who appeared in the doorway.

'Oh,' Henrietta said, 'what have you come for?'

He put down the hat and stick he had forgotten to leave in the hall. 'I don't know,' he said. 'I had a kind of feeling you might like to see me. It's the first time I've had it,' he added solemnly.

He really had an extraordinary way of knowing things, but she said, 'Well, Aunt Sophia's ill, so I don't think you can stay.'

He looked round for her. 'She's not here. I shan't do any harm, shall I? We can whisper.'

'She wouldn't hear us anyhow. It's my room above this one.'

'Is it?' He gazed at the ceiling with interest. 'Oh, up there!'

'I should have thought you knew by instinct,' she said bitingly.

'No.'

'Come and sit down, Charles, and don't be disagreeable.
I shall have to go to Aunt Sophia soon, but then you will
be able to talk to Aunt Rose. That will do just as well.'

'Not quite,' he said. 'I really came to tell you –'

'You said you came because you thought I wanted you.'

'So I did, but there were several reasons. You said you
were going to be happy to-day, not murderous, do you
remember? And I thought I'd like to see how you looked.
You don't look happy a bit. What's the matter?'

'I've told you Aunt Sophia's ill. And would you be happy
if you had to sit in this prim room with two old women?'

'Two? But your Aunt Caroline is dead.'

'But my Aunt Rose is very much alive.'

He wagged his head. 'I see.'

'But she isn't lively. She sits like this – reading a book, and
Aunt Sophia, poor Aunt Sophia, sews like this, and I sit
on this horrid little stool, like this. That's how we spend the
evening.'

'How would you like to spend it?'

'Oh, I don't know.' She dropped her black head to her
knees. 'It's so lonely.'

'Well,' he began again, 'I really came to tell you that
there's a house to let on The Green: that little one with the
red roof like a cap and windows that squint; a little old house;
but–' he paused– 'it has every modern convenience. Henrietta,
there's a curl at the back of your neck.'

'I know. It's always there.'

'I can't go on about the house unless you sit up.'

'Why?'

'Because of that curl.'

'And I'm not interested in the house.' She did not move.
'Whose is it?'

'It belongs to a client of ours, but that doesn't matter.
The point is that it's to let. I've got an order to view. Look!
– "*Please admit Mr. Charles Batty.*" I went this evening and
we can both go to-morrow. It's really a very cosy little
house. There's a drawing-room opening on the garden at

239

the back, with plenty of room for a grand piano, and the dining-room – I liked the dining-room very much. There was a fire in it.'

'Is that unusual?'

'It looked so cosy, with a red carpet and everything.'

'Is the carpet to let, too?'

'I don't know. I dare say we could buy it. And mind you, Henrietta, the kitchen is on the ground floor. That's unusual, if you like, in an old house. I made sure of that before I went any further.'

'How far are you going?'

'We'll go everywhere to-morrow, even into the coal cellar. To-day I just peeped.'

'I can imagine you. But what do you want a house for, Charles?'

'For you,' he said. 'You say you don't like spending the evenings here – well, let's spend them in the little house. We can't go on being engaged indefinitely.'

'Certainly not,' she said firmly, 'and I should adore a little house of my own. I believe that's just what I want.'

'Then that's settled.'

'But not with you, Charles.'

He said nothing for a time. She was sitting up, her hands clasped on her lap, and as she looked at him she half regretted her last words. This was how they would sit in the little house, by the fire, surrounded by their own possessions, with everything clean and bright and, as he had said, very cosy. She had never had a home.

Suddenly she leaned towards him and put her head on his knee. His hand fell on her hair. 'This doesn't mean anything,' she murmured; 'but I was just thinking. You're tempting me again. First with the ring because it was so pretty, and now with a house.'

'How else am I to get you?' he cried out. 'And you know you were feeling lonely. That's why I came.'

'You thought it was your chance?'

'Yes,' he said. 'I don't know the ordinary things, but I know the others.'

240

'I wonder how,' she said, and he answered with the one word, 'Love,' in a voice so deep and solemn that she laughed.

'Do you know,' she said, 'I have never had a home. I've lived in other people's houses, with their ugly furniture, their horrid sticky curtains –'

'I shall take that house to-morrow.'

'But you can't go on collecting things like this. Houses and rings –'

'The ring's in my pocket now.'

'It must stay there, Charles. I ought not to keep my head on your knee; but it's comfortable and I have no conscience. None.' She sat up, brushing his chin with her hair. 'None!' she said emphatically. 'And here's Aunt Rose coming to fetch me for Aunt Sophia. Mind, I've promised nothing. Besides, you haven't asked me to promise anything.'

'Oh!' He blinked. 'Well, there's no time now. Good evening, Miss Mallett.' He pulled himself out of his chair.

'Good evening, Charles. I'm glad you're here to keep Henrietta company. The doctor has been, Henrietta –'

'Oh, has he? I didn't hear him.'

'Sophia is settled for the night, and I'm going to her now.'

'But she'll want me!' Henrietta cried.

'No, she asked me to stay with her. Good night. Good night, Charles.'

'But did you say I wanted to be with her?'

Rose, smiling but a little pitiful, said gently, 'I gave her the choice and she chose me.'

She disappeared, and Henrietta turned to Charles. 'You see, she gets everything. She gets everything I ever wanted and she doesn't try –' Her hands dropped to her side. 'She just gets it.'

'But what have you wanted?'

She turned away. 'Nothing. It doesn't matter.'

'Is she going to marry Francis Sales?'

'What makes you ask that?' she cried.

'I don't know. I just thought of it.'

'Oh, your thoughts! Why, you suggested the same thing for me! As if I would look at him!'

241

Charles blinked, his sign of agitation, but Henrietta did not see. 'He's good to look at,' Charles muttered. 'He knows how to wear his clothes.'

'That doesn't matter.'

Charles heaved a sigh. 'One never knows what matters.'

'And the Malletts don't marry,' Henrietta said. 'Aunt Caroline and Aunt Sophia and Aunt Rose, and now me. There's something in us that can't be satisfied. It was the same with my father, only it took him the other way.'

'I didn't know he was married more than once. Nobody tells me things.'

'Charles, dear, you're very stupid. He was only married once in a church.'

'Oh, I see.'

'And if I did marry, I should be like him.' She turned to him and put her face close to his. 'Unfaithful,' she pronounced clearly.

'Oh, well, Henrietta, you would still be you.'

She stepped backwards, shocked. 'Charles, wouldn't you mind?'

'Not so much,' he said stolidly, 'as doing without you altogether.'

'And the other day you said you need never do that because' – she tapped his waistcoat – 'because I'm here!'

He showed a face she had never seen before. 'You seem to think I'm not made of flesh and blood!' he cried. 'You're wanton, Henrietta, simply wanton!' And he rushed out of the room.

She heard the front door bang; she saw his hat and stick, lying where he had put them; she smiled at them politely and then, sinking to the floor beside the fender, she let out a little moan of despair and delight. The fire chuckled and chattered and she leaned forward, her face near the bars.

'Stop talking for a minute! I want to tell you something. There's nobody else to tell. Listen! I'm in love with him now.' She nodded her head. 'Yes, with him. I know it's ridiculous; but it's true. Did you hear? You can laugh if you like. I don't care. I'm in love with him. Oh, dear!'

She circled her neck with her hands as though she must clasp something, and it would have been too silly to fondle his ugly hat. And he would remember he had forgotten it; he would come back. She dared not see him. 'I love him,' she cried out, 'too much to want to see him!' She paused, astonished. 'I suppose that's how he feels about me. How wonderful!' She looked round at the furniture, so still and unmoved by the happy bewilderment in which she found herself. The piano was mute; the lamps burned steadily; the chair in which Charles had sat was unconscious of its privilege; even the fire's flames had subsided; and she was intensely, madly, joyously alive.

'It's too much,' she said, 'too much!' And for the first time she was ashamed of her episode with Francis Sales. 'Playing at love,' she whispered.

But Charles would be coming back and, tiptoeing as though he might hear her from the street, she picked up his hat and stick and laid them neatly on the step outside the front door.

She slept with the profundity of her happiness and descended to breakfast in a dream. Only the sight of Rose's tired face reminded her that Aunt Sophia was ill. She had had a bad night, but she was better.

'She's not going to die, too, is she?' Henrietta asked, and she had a sad vision of Aunt Rose living all alone in Nelson Lodge.

'She may live for a long time, but the doctor says she may die at any moment.'

'I don't suppose she wants to live.'

'What makes you think that?'

'Because of Aunt Caroline – and – other people. But if she dies, whatever will you do?'

The question amused Rose. 'Go and see the world at last,' she said. 'Perhaps you will come, too.'

Henrietta laughed and flushed and became serious. 'She mustn't die.'

For, after all, Aunt Sophia was not a true Mallett, according to Aunt Caroline's test; she believed in marriage, she would like to see Henrietta in the little house; one of them would

243

be able to call on the other every day. It was wonderful of Charles to have known she would like that house: she knew it well, with its red cap and its squinting eyes; but, then, he was altogether wonderful.

She supposed he would call for her that afternoon and they would present the order to view together, but he did not come. With her hat and gloves lying ready on the bed, she waited for his knock in vain. He must have been kept by business; he would come later to explain. And then, when still he did not come, she decided that he must be ill. If so, her place was by his side, and she saw herself moving like an angel about his bed; and yet the thought of Charles in bed was comic.

At dinner she ate nothing and when Rose remarked on this, Henrietta murmured that she had a headache; she thought she would go for a walk.

'Then, if you are really going out, will you take a note to Mrs. Batty? She sent some fruit and flowers to Sophia. I suppose Charles told her she was ill.'

Henrietta looked sharply at her aunt: she was suspicious of what seemed like tact, but Rose wore an ordinary expression.

'Is the note ready?' Henrietta asked.

'Yes, I meant to post it, but I'd rather she had it to-night, and there is the basket to return.'

'Very well, I'll take them both, and if I'm a little late, you'll know I have just gone for a walk or something.'

'I shan't worry about you,' Rose said.

Henrietta walked up the yellow drive, trembling a little. She had decided to ask for Mrs. Batty who was always pleased to see her, but when the door was opened her ears were assailed by a blast of triumphant sound. It was Charles, playing the piano; he was not ill, he was not busy, he was merely playing the piano as though there were no Henrietta in the world, and her trembling changed to the stiffness of great anger.

She handed in the basket and the note without a word or a smile for the friendly parlourmaid. She walked home in the awful realization that she had worn Charles out. He

244

had called her wanton; he must have meant it. It was that word which had really made her love him, yet it was also the sign of his exhaustion. Life was tragic: no, it was comic, it was playful. She had had happiness in her hands, and it had slipped through them. She felt sick with disappointment under her rage; but she was not without hope. It stirred in her gently. Charles would come back. But would he? And she suddenly felt a terrible distrust of that love of which he had boasted. It was too complete; he could do without her. He would go on loving, but, she repeated it, she had worn him out, and she could not love like that. She wanted tangible things. But he had said that he, too, was flesh and blood, and that comforted her. He would come back, but she could do nothing to invite him.

This, she said firmly, was the real thing. It had been different with Francis Sales: with him there had been no necessity for pride, but her love for Charles must be wrapped round with reserve and kept holy; and at once, with her unfailing dramatic sense, she saw herself moving quietly through life, tending the sacred flame. And then, irritably, she told herself she could not spend her days doing that: she did not know what to do! She hated him; she would go away; yes, she would go away with Aunt Rose.

In the meantime she wept with a passion of disappointment, humiliation and pain, but on each successive morning, for some weeks, she woke to hope, for here was a new day with many possibilities in its hours; and each evening she dropped on to her bed, disheartened. Nothing happened. Aunt Sophia was better, Rose rode out every day, the little house on The Green stood empty, squinting disconsolately, resignedly surprised at its own loneliness. It was strange that nobody wanted a house like that; it was neglected and so was she: nobody noticed the one or the other.

Every morning Henrietta took Aunt Sophia for a stately walk; every afternoon she went to a tea- or tennis-party, for the summer festivities were beginning once more; and often, as she returned, she would meet Aunt Rose coming back from her ride, always cool in her linen coat, however hot the day. Where did she go? How often did she meet Francis Sales? Why should she be enjoying adventures while Henrietta, at the only age worth having, was desperately fulfilling the tedious round of her engagements? It was absurd, and Aunt Rose would ask serenely, 'Did you have a good game, Henrietta?' as though there was nothing wrong.

Henrietta did not care for games. It was the big sport of life itself she craved for, and she could not get it. All these young men, handsome and healthy in their flannels and ready to be pleasant, she found dull, while the figure of the loose-jointed Charles, his vague gestures, his unseeing eyes screening the activity of his brain, became heroic in their difference. She never saw him; she did not visit Mrs. Batty; she was afraid of falling tearfully on that homely, sympathetic breast, but Mrs. Batty, as usual, issued invitations for a garden-party.

'We shall have to go,' Sophia sighed. 'Such an old and so kind a friend! But without Caroline – for the first time!'

'There is no need for you to go,' Rose said at once. 'Mrs. Batty will understand, and Henrietta and I will represent the family.'

'No, I must not give way. Caroline never gave way.'

There was no excitement in dressing for this party. Without Caroline things lost their zest, and they set out demurely, walking very slowly for Sophia's sake.

It was a hot day and Mrs. Batty, standing at the garden door to greet her guests, was obliged to wipe her face surreptitiously now and then, while the statues in the hall, with their burdens of ferns and lamps, showed their cool limbs beneath their scanty but still decent drapery.

Mrs. Batty took Sophia to a seat under a tree and Henrietta stood for a moment in the blazing sunlight alone. Where was Aunt Rose? Henrietta looked round and had a glimpse of that slim black form moving among the rose-trees with Francis Sales. He had simply carried her off! It was disgraceful, and things seemed to repeat themselves for ever. Aunt Rose, with her look of having lost everything, still succeeded in possessing, while Henrietta was alone. She had no place in the world. John's affianced bride was busy among the guests, like a daughter of the house, a slobbering bulldog at her heels; and Henrietta, isolated on the lawn, was overcome by her own forlornness. It had been very different at the ball. And how queer life was! It was just a succession of days, that was all: little things happened and the days went on; big things happened and seemed to change the world, but nothing was really changed, and a whole life could be spent with a moment's happiness or despair for its only marks.

Henrietta, rather impressed by the depths of her own thoughts, moved through the garden. Where was Charles? She wanted to see him and get their meeting over, but there was not a sign of him and, avoiding the croquet players and that shady corner where elderly ladies were clustered near the band, the same band which had played at the ball, Henrietta found herself in the kitchen garden. She examined the gooseberry bushes and strawberry beds with apparent interest, unwilling to join the guests and still more unwilling to be found alone in this deserted state. It was very hot. The open door of a little shed showed her a dim and cool interior; she peeped in and stepped back with an exclamation. Something had moved in there. It might be a rat or one of John's ferocious terriers, but a voice said quietly, 'It's only me.'

She stepped forward. 'What are you doing in there?'

'Getting cool,' Charles said. 'I thought nobody would find me. Won't you come in? It's rather dirty in here, but it's cool, and you can't hear the band. I've been sitting on the handle of the wheelbarrow, so that's clean, anyhow. I'll wipe it with my handkerchief to make sure.'

'But where are you going to sit?'

'Oh, I don't know.'

'There's room on the other handle.'

Henrietta sat with her knees between the shafts, **and he** sat on the other handle with his back to her.

'We can't stay here long,' she said.

'No,' Charles agreed.

The place smelt musty, but of heaven. It was draped with cobwebs like celestial clouds; it was dark, but gradually the forms of rakes, hoes, spades and a watering-pot cleared themselves from the gloom and Charles's head bloomed above his coat like a great pale flower.

She put out her hand and drew it back again. She found nothing to say. Outside the sun poured down its rays like fire. Henrietta's head drooped under her big hat. She was content to stay here for ever if Charles would stay, too. Her body felt as though it were imponderable, she had no feet, she could not feel the hard handle of the wheelbarrow; she seemed to be floating blissfully, aware of nothing but that floating, yet a threat of laughter began to tickle her. It was absurd to sit like this, like strangers in an omnibus. The laughter rose to her throat and escaped: she floated no longer, but she was no less happy.

'What's the matter?' asked the voice of Charles.

'So funny, sitting like this.'

'What else can we do?'

'You could turn round.'

'There's not room for all our knees.'

She stood up with a little rustle and walked to the door. 'No, it's too hot out there,' she said, and returned to face him. 'Charles,' she said in rather a high voice, 'did you find your hat and stick that night?'

'What? Oh, yes,' and then irrelevantly he added, 'I've just been made a partner.'

'Really?' She was always interested in practical things. 'In Mr. Batty's firm? How splendid! I didn't know you were any good at business.'

'I've been improving, and you don't know anything about me.'

'I do, Charles,' she said earnestly.

'No, nothing. You haven't time to think of anybody but yourself. And now I must go and look after all these people. You'd better come and have an ice.'

There was ice at her heart and she realized now that her past unhappiness had been half false; she had been waiting for him all the time and trusting to his next sight of her to put things right, but she had failed with him, too.

248

In that dim tool-house she had stood before him in her pretty dress, smiling down at him, surely irresistible, and he had resisted. Well, she could resist, too, and she walked calmly by his side, holding her head very high, and when he parted from her with a grave bow, she felt a great, an awed respect for him.

She went to find her Aunt Sophia, who was still sitting under the tree, surrounded by a chattering group. She looked tired, and, signalling for Henrietta to approach, she said, 'I'm afraid this is too much for me, dear child. Can you find Rose and ask her to take me home? But I don't want to spoil your pleasure, Henrietta. There is no need for you to come.'

Henrietta's lip twisted with dramatic bitterness. There was no pleasure left for her. 'I would rather go back with you, Aunt Sophia. Let us go now.'

'No, no. Find Rose.'

There was another buffet in the face. It was Rose who was wanted and Henrietta, walking swiftly, crossed the lawn again, casting quick glances right and left. Rose was nowhere to be seen. Perhaps, for their ways had an odd habit of following the same path, she was in the tool-house with Francis Sales, but as she turned to go there, the voice of Mrs. Batty, husky with exhaustion and heat, said in her ear, 'Is it your Aunt Rose you are looking for, love? I think I saw her go into the house, and I wish I could go myself. It's so hot that I really feel I may have a fit.'

Henrietta went into the cool, shaded drawing-room on light feet, and there, against the window, she saw her Aunt Rose in an attitude startlingly unfamiliar. She was standing with her hands clasped before her, and she gazed down at them lost in thought – or prayer. Her body, so upright and strong, seemed limp and broken, and her face, which was calm, yet had the look of having composed itself after pain.

There was no one else in the room, but Henrietta had the strong impression that someone had lately passed through the door. She was afraid to disturb that moment in which an escaped soul seemed to be fluttering back into its place, but Rose looked up and saw her and Henrietta, advancing softly as though towards a person who was dead, stopped within a foot of her. Then, without thought and obeying an uncontrollable impulse, she stepped forward and laid her cheek against her aunt's. Rose's hands dropped apart and, one arm encircling Henrietta's waist, she held her close, but only for a minute. It was Henrietta who broke away, saying, 'Aunt Sophia sent me to look for you. She doesn't feel well.'

§ 12

Mrs. Batty was cured of giving parties. It was after her ball that Miss Caroline died, and it was after her garden-party that Miss Sophia finally collapsed. The heat, the emotion of her memories and the effort of disguising it had been too much for her. She died the following day and Mrs. Batty felt that the largest and most expensive wreath procurable could not approach the expression of her grief. It was no good talking to Mr. Batty about it; he would only say he had been against the ball and garden-party from the first, but Mrs. Batty found Charles unexpectedly soothing. He was certainly much improved of late, and when she heard that he was to go to Nelson Lodge on business connected with the estate, she burdened him with a number of incoherent messages for Rose.

Perhaps he delivered them; he certainly stayed in the drawing-room for some time, and Henrietta, sitting sorrowfully in her bedroom, could hear his voice rolling on monotonously. Then there was a laugh and Henrietta was indignant. Nobody ought to laugh with Aunt Sophia lying dead, and she did not know how to stay in her room while those two, Aunt Rose and her Charles, talked and laughed together. She thought of pretending not to know he was there and of entering the drawing-room in a careless manner, but she could not allow Aunt Rose to witness Charles's indifference. All she could do was to steal on to the landing and lean over the banisters to watch him depart. She had the painful consolation of seeing the top of his head and of hearing him say, 'The day after to-morrow?'

Rose answered, 'Yes, it's most important.'

Henrietta waited until the front door had closed behind him and then, seeing Rose at the foot of the stairs, she said, 'What's important, Aunt Rose?'

'Oh, are you there, Henrietta? What a pity you didn't come down. That was Charles Batty.'

'I know. What's important?'

'There is a lot of complicated business to get through.'

'You might let me help.'

'I wish you would. When Charles comes again – his father isn't very well – you had better be present.'

'No, not with Charles,' Henrietta said firmly. 'Does he understand wills and things?'

'Perfectly, I think. He's very clever and quite interesting.'

'Oh!' Henrietta said.

'I'm glad he's coming again. And now, Henrietta,' she sighed, 'we must get ready for the cousins.'

The female relatives returned in dingy cabs. They had not yet laid aside their black and beads for Caroline, and, as though they thought Sophia had been unfairly cheated of new mourning, they had adorned themselves with a fresh black ribbon here and there, or a larger brooch of jet, and these additions gave to the older garments a rusty look, a sort of blush.

Across these half-animated heaps of woe and dye, the glances of Rose and Henrietta met in an understanding pleasing to both. This mourning had a professional, almost a rapacious quality, and if these women had no hope of material pickings, they were getting all possible nourishment from emotional ones. Their eyes, very sharp, but veiled by seemly gloom, criticized the slim, upright figures of these young women who could wear black gracefully, sorrow with dignity, and who had, as they insisted, so much the look of sisters.

The air seemed freer for their departure, but the house was very empty, and though Sophia had never made much noise the place was heavy with a final silence.

'I don't know why we're here!' Henrietta cried passionately

251

across the dinner-table when Susan had left the ladies to their dessert.

'Why were we ever here?' Rose asked. 'If one could answer that question –'

They faced each other in their old places. The curved ends of the shining table were vacant, the Chippendale arm-chairs were pushed back against the wall, yet the ghosts of Caroline and Sophia, gaily dressed, with dangling earrings, the sparkle of jewels, the movements of their be-ringed fingers, seemed to be in the room.

'But we shall never forget them,' Henrietta said. 'They were persons. Aunt Rose, do you think you and I will go on as they did, until just one of us is left?'

'We could never be like them.'

'No, they were happy.'

'You will be happy again, Henrietta. We shall get used to this silence.'

'But I don't think either of us is meant to be happy. No, we're not like them. We're tragic. But all the same, we might get really fond of one another, mightn't we?'

'I am fond of you.'

'I don't see how you can be' – Henrietta looked down at the fruit on her plate – 'considering what has happened,' she almost whispered.

Rose made no answer. The steady, pale flames of the candles stood up like golden fingers, the shadows behind the table seemed to listen.

'But how fond are you?' Henrietta asked in a loud voice, and Rose, peeling her apple delicately, said vaguely, 'I don't know how you measure.'

'By what you would do for a person.'

'Ah, well, I think I have stood that test.'

Henrietta leaned over the table, and a candle flame, as though startled by her gesture, gave a leap, and the shadows behind were stirred.

'Yes,' Henrietta said, 'I hated you for a long time, but now I don't. You've been unhappy, too. And you were right about – that man. I didn't love him. How could I?

252

How could I? How could anybody? If you hadn't come that day –'

Rose closed her eyes for a moment and then said wearily, 'It wouldn't have made any difference. I never made any difference. You didn't love him; but he never loved you either, child. You were quite safe.'

Henrietta's face flushed hotly. This might be true, but it was not for Aunt Rose to say it. Once more she leaned across the table and said clearly, 'Then you're still jealous.'

Rose smiled. It seemed impossible to move her. 'No, Henrietta. I left jealousy behind years ago. We won't discuss this any further. It doesn't bear discussion. It's beyond it.'

'I know it's very unpleasant,' Henrietta said politely, 'but if we are to go on living together, we ought to clear things up.'

'We are not going on living together,' Rose said. She left the table and stood before the fire, one hand on the mantelshelf and one foot on the fender. The long, soft lines of her dark dress were merged into the shadows, and the white arm, the white face and neck seemed to be disembodied. Henrietta, struck dumb by that announcement, and feeling the situation wrested from the control of her young hands, stared at the slight figure which had typified beauty for her since she first saw it.

'Then you don't like me,' she faltered.

Rose did not move, but she began to speak. 'Henrietta, I have loved you very dearly, almost as if you were my daughter, but you didn't seem to want my love. I couldn't force it on you, but it has been here: it is still here. I think you have the power of making people love you, yet you do nothing for it except, perhaps, exist. One ought not to ask any more; I don't ask it, but you ought to learn to give. You'll find it's the only thing worth doing. Taking – taking – one becomes atrophied. No, it isn't that I don't care for you, it isn't that. I am going to be married.'

Very carefully, Henrietta put her plate aside, and, supporting her face in her hands, she pressed her elbows into the table; she pressed hard until they hurt. So Aunt Rose was going to be married while Henrietta was deserted. 'Not to Francis Sales?' she whispered.

'Yes, to Francis Sales.'

She had a wild moment of anger, succeeded by horror for Aunt Rose. Was she stupid? Was she insensible? And Henrietta said, 'But you can't, Aunt Rose, you can't.' Her distress and a kind of envy gave her courage. 'He isn't good enough. He played with you and then with me and you said there was some one else.' The figure by the mantelpiece was so still that Henrietta became convinced of the potency of her own words, and she went on: 'You know everything about him and you can't marry him. How can you marry him?'

A sound, like the faint and distant wailing of the wind, came out of the shadows into which Rose had retreated: 'Ah, how?'

'And you're going to leave me – for him!'

'Yes – for him.'

'Aunt Rose, you would be happier with me.'

Again there came that faint sound. 'Perhaps.'

'I'd try to be kinder to you. I don't understand you.'

'No, you don't understand me. Do you understand yourself?' She left her place and put her hands on Henrietta's shoulders. 'Say no more,' she said with unmistakable authority. 'Say no more, neither to me nor to anybody else. This is beyond you. And now come into the drawing-room. Don't cry, Henrietta. I'm not going to be married for some time.'

'I wish I'd known you loved me,' Henrietta sobbed.

'I tried to show you.'

'If I'd known, everything might have been different.'

Rose laughed. 'But we don't want it to be different.'

'You won't be happy,' Henrietta wailed.

'You, at least,' Rose said sternly, 'have done nothing to make me so.'

Henrietta stilled her sobbing. It was quite true. She had taken everything – Aunt Rose's money, Aunt Rose's love, her wonderful forbearance and the love of Charles.

'I don't know what to do,' she cried.

'Come into the drawing-room and we'll talk about it.'

254

But they did not talk. Rose played the piano in the candle-light for a little while before she slipped out of the room. Henrietta sat on the little stool without even the fire to keep her company. She was too dazed to think. She did not understand why Aunt Rose should choose to marry Francis Sales and she gave it up, but loneliness stretched before her like a long, hard road.

If only Charles would come! He always came when he was wanted. A memory reached her weary mind. This was 'the day after to-morrow,' and Aunt Rose expected him. She leapt up and examined herself in the mirror. She was one of those lucky people who can cry and leave no trace; colour had sprung into her cheeks, but it faded quickly. She had waited for him before and he had not come, and she was tired of waiting. She sank into Aunt Caroline's chair and shut her eyes; she almost slept. She was on the verge of dreams when the bell jangled harshly. She did not move. She sat in an agony of fear that this would not be Charles; but the door opened and he entered. Susan pronounced his name, and he stood on the threshold, thinking the room was empty.

A very small voice pierced the stillness. 'Charles, I'm here.'

'I won't come a step farther,' Charles said severely, 'until you tell me if you love me.'

'I thought you'd come to see Aunt Rose.'

'Henrietta –'

'Yes, I love you, I love you,' she said hurriedly. 'I'm nodding my head hard. No, stay where you are, stay where you are. I've been loving you for weeks and you've treated me shamefully. No, no, I've got to be different, I've got to give. You didn't treat me shamefully.'

'No,' he said stolidly, 'I didn't. Here's the ring, and I took that house. I've been renting it ever since I knew we were going to live in it. Here's the ring.' He dropped it into her lap.

She looked down at the stones, hard and bright like herself. 'Aunt Rose will be very much surprised,' she said, and she was too happy to wonder why he laughed.

Standing on the stair, Rose heard that laughter and went on very slowly to her room. She had, at least, done something for Henrietta. She had given Charles his chance, and now she was to go on doing things for Francis Sales. She owed him something: she owed him the romance of her youth, she owed him the care which was all she had left to give him. Things had come to her too late, her eyes were too wide open, yet perhaps it was better so. She had no illusions and she wanted to justify her early faith and Christabel's sufferings and her own. There was nothing else to do. Besides, he needed her, and with him she would not be more unhappy; he would be happier, he said. She had to protect him against himself, yet even there she was frustrated, for he had, in a measure, found himself, and now that she was ready and able to serve him there would be less for her to do. But she had no choice: there was the old debt, there were the old chains, and as she faced the future she was stirred by hope. She could tell herself that something of her dead love had waked to life, yet when she tried to get back the old rapture, she knew it had gone for ever.

She entered her room and did not turn on the light. There seemed to be a strange weight in her body, pressing her down, but, as she looked through her open window at the summer sky deepening to night and letting out the stars, which seemed to be much amused, there was a lightness in her mind and, smiling back at them, she was able to share their appreciation of the joke.

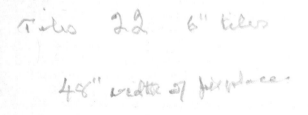

Also of interest

THE LOVE CHILD
by Edith Olivier
New Introduction by Hermione Lee

At thirty-two, her mother dead, Agatha Bodenham finds herself quite alone. She summons back to life the only friend she ever knew, Clarissa, the dream companion of her childhood. At first Clarissa comes by night, and then by day, gathering substance in the warmth of Agatha's obsessive love until it seems that others too can see her. See, but not touch, for Agatha has made her love child for herself. No man may approach this creature of perfect beauty, and if he does, she who summoned her can spirit her away...

Edith Olivier (1879?-1948) was one of the youngest of a clergyman's family of ten children. Despite early ambitions to become an actress, she led a conventional life within twenty miles of her childhood home, the Rectory at Wilton, Wiltshire. But she wrote five highly original novels as well as works of non-fiction, and her 'circle' included Rex Whistler (who illustrated her books), David Cecil, Siegfried Sassoon and Osbert Sitwell. *The Love Child* (1927) was her first novel, acknowledged as a minor masterpiece: a perfectly imagined fable and a moving and perceptive portrayal of unfulfilled maternal love.

"This is wonderful..." — *Cecil Beaton*

"*The Love Child* seems to me to stand in a category of its own creating...the image it leaves is that of a tranquil star" — *Anne Douglas Sedgwick*

"Flawless — the best 'first' book I have ever read...perfect" — *Sir Henry Newbolt*

"A masterpiece of its kind" — *Lord David Cecil*

THE SHUTTER OF SNOW

by Emily Holmes Coleman
New Introduction by Carmen Callil and Mary Siepmann

After the birth of her child Marthe Gail spends two months in an insane asylum with the fixed idea that she is God. Marthe, something between Ophelia, Emily Dickinson and Lucille Ball, transports us into that strange country of terror and ecstasy we call madness. In this twilit country the doctors, nurses, the other inmates and the mad vision of her insane mind are revealed with piercing insight and with immense verbal facility.

Emily Coleman (1899-1974) was born in California and, like Marthe, went mad after the birth of her son in 1924. Witty, eccentric and ebullient, she lived in Paris in the 1920s as one of the *transition* writers, close friend of Peggy Guggenheim and Djuna Barnes (who said Emily would be marvellous company slightly stunned). In the 1930s she lived in London (in the French, the Wheatsheaf, the Fitzroy), where her friends numbered Dylan Thomas, T.S. Eliot, Humphrey Jennings and George Barker. Emily Coleman wrote poetry throughout her life — and this one beautiful, poignant novel (first published in 1930), which though constantly misunderstood, has always had a passionate body of admirers — Edwin Muir, David Gascoyne and Antonia White to name a few.

"A very striking triumph of imagination and technique... The book is not only quite unique; it is also a work of genuine literary inspiration" — *Edwin Muir*

"A work which has stirred me deeply...compelling" — *Harold Nicolson*

"An extraordinary, visionary book, written out of those edges where madness and poetry meet" — *Fay Weldon*